PENGUIN BOOKS
BOMBAY DUCK

Farrukh Dhondy was born in Poona, India, in 1944 and first went to England in 1964. He read English at Cambridge and then taught for several years before giving this up to concentrate on writing. His books for young readers include *East End at Your Feet* and *Come to Mecca* (both winners of the Other Award), *Poona Company* and his short story collection *Trip Trap*. *Bombay Duck* was shortlisted for the 1990 Whitbread Award for the best first novel.

The author has written widely for television and the stage, including two situation comedies for Channel Four: *No Problem* and *Tandoori Nights*, and was a recipient of the Samuel Beckett Award for a series of six plays for BBC TV.

BOMBAY
DUCK

Farrukh Dhondy

PENGUIN BOOKS

Penguin Books India (P) Ltd., 11 Community Centre, Panchsheel Park, New Delhi 110 017, India
Penguin Books Ltd., 27 Wrights Lane, London W8 5TZ, UK
Penguin Putnam Inc., 375 Hudson Street, New York, NY 10014, USA
Penguin Books Australia Ltd., Ringwood, Victoria, Australia
Penguin Books Canada Ltd., 10 Alcorn Avenue, Suite 300, Toronto, Ontario, M4V 3B2, Canada
Penguin Books (NZ) Ltd., Cnr Rosedale and Airborne Roads, Albany, Auckland, New Zealand

First published by Jonathan Cape 1990
First published in India by Penguin Books India 1999

Printed at Chaman Offset Printers, New Delhi

PART
I

Fortune smiles. Is a routine with fortune. No guffaws, no big laughs, just Mona Lisa auditioning and being blood claat quizzical. Backayard, them woulda ask her, 'Whey 'tis yuh smile at girl? Yuh have a date with a Yankee sailor?' Maybe sometime she frown, but she don't wail and bawl and call on her mother and God's mother and the mother of the devil to rescue her. And she ain't no whore neither, because when she bestow herself she don't want payment or bread or slackness – only, eventually, your soul.

In my case, boss, she came in three disguises. First as a school teacher who tell me, 'Gerald Blossom, you have to be joking!' I never hear this expression. I wasn't joking but the English tell me I have to be. Maybe it was a false alarm, a mistaken identity thing. I see fate and think it's fortune.

Then in the darkness of my bedroom, a Buddha, he smiled. A gift from an uncle who came back from Hong Kong. A plastic Buddha which glowed in the dark when yuh plugged it in. And I check it and it smiled and the next day my father's woman, she have a big fight with my dad and she who used to torture me was gone.

And the next time, brother, it maybe wasn't fortune at all, it was fate, coming to the fancy dress ball – my life. She came dressed as a little English man in the uniform that the middle-aged hippy-maan them wear, balding with blue cord trouser. And I knew him on the spot, boss, because you can't be an animal on the ark and not know Noah. Me boss, G. Blossom, alias Ali Abdul Rahman, yours truly, or

3

crucially as we say, being an actor, recognised the man of the moment, the one and only David Stream Esq. etc., a director, *the* director, of Britannic Theatre. I knew him as a sheep knows his shepherd as a squaddie knows Winston when him pass on the beach at Dunkirk.

For months, maybe years before, fortune didn't smile on me at all. Like a bitch she passed me by and now and then sniffed at my ankle and pissed on my leg. I had had no luck, in other words, Jah (if you don't mind me call you so while we still sniffing each other). Then Bawdy come to me. This is a friend, small time director of a lickle group called Blade Star Theatre. How would I like the lead role in *Tony and Cleo*, a modern adaptation by the Pakistani writer Jamil Jamal, a reggae musical no less, with a small budget and a drum and bass machine 'pon the tape and me to sing the few tracks to the audiences of London and Edinburgh?

'Cool,' I say. Beggars and choosers and ting – and at the time I have nothing against Jamil Jamal, except I know he is a loudmouth who prides himself on put-downs (he said to an actor once, 'You call my script shit? Well you're the arsehole it refuses to pass through, you're fired'). Such was the calibre of his line in humour and so we played it and a man came to check it and buy us up for the Edinburgh Festival, fringe of fringes. Nothing happened for days. It was a job. Then Edinburgh, I'll tell you about it in a minute, yielded up the smile of fortune in the person of the man himself.

While I slept in bed as a child, the naughty uncle from Hong Kong (whom I had heard from Dad had married three separate women in that feisty place, three women who never know about each other) bestow this gift of the Buddha which glowed, reminding me of adultery, of my step-mum, of my real mum, of the girls I couldn't have at the age of ten, creatures great and small . . .

An actor finds a director. I mean, boss, that all of us are actors (check Shakespeare in *Merchant of Venice*) and maybe once in our life we find the spirit whose guidance and encouragement are so fucking charismatic that a man is willing to put himself at his disposal like and allow an intelligence outside to dictate what must be. That sound heavy.

So I tell you how I found my director. He appeared as I knew he would. At a performance of my play. I recognised him from telly, from posters, from everything that makes a man famous. But how! 'Probably', as the lager advert say, 'the most famous stage director in the world.' The Stream himself and he come not for the joys of Jam the Pakistani's stupid lickle play, but to check me.

He had a girl younger than himself in the next seat. I didn't know her at the time. I could see he didn't like the play, because he stayed sober for a bit and dead pan but then he smiled and the knife of that smile went into my heart. Still I knew, it was fortune and, yes rasta, I bristled like a peacock on stage. At points in the performance I was sharing the joke we had between us through a glance.

It's funny, you know. An auditorium is always dark and the actor sees only a oneness of highlights on hair and the teeth glistening, but occasionally a face is illuminated by a halo, a special spotlight picking out radiance in the quality of attention the party in the audience has for the play, for an actor, for me! I was right. He spoke to me after. In the foyer, not the dressing rooms, you know. He waited till all that was over. He says straight away, 'We are dying, Egypt, dying.' Now that's one of the lines from the original that Jam has left in this jazz version. I don't know what the fuck it actually means. I've fought with that line, and maybe David witnessed the battle on stage, so we both laughed and that first laugh became the cement of fate. And still today it comes back to me, like even if I'm saying it, it's outside myself in a Mickey Mouse voice, 'The earth compels. We are dying, Egypt, dying and loving every fucking moment of it.'

But that ain't even from the play, that's just how it comes to me now that the whole dream is over.

The play had nothing to do with Egypt at all. It's just an adaptation of *Antony and Cleopatra*, change from Rome and Egypt to the yuppie and stockbroker culture and sleaze and drugs and street-wiseness of London and New York. Yuh sight it? Wild. The songs, truly speaking, were indifferent, no big thing, you know, not no Nobel prize lyrics, more the kind of thing that French and German and Swede peoples who buy the record will think is 'hard', in a ghetto stylee.

The story? It don't mean much, but if you want to know, I play a British bad man, sent by my boss to deal with a mystery character in Jamaica who send or don't send the drugs that the gang's running. I have to sort the thing out. Well, back in the big apple, I'm taking a bite and findin that the big man is not only a woman called Cleo, but that my boss is playing some bullshit games with me, sending me out to deal on a kinda love score. You know the rest of it. Love and open hostility and death and reggae. Cheeky stuff. No respec for the bard.

Maybe I had my criticisms. What's this kid Jam, randy little Pak, know about Jah culture and gangs and drugs. I mean to say, rasta, the closest him get to drugs is Alka Seltzer after three ciders. The boy saaft. But then work is work and the man was dealing the Edinburgh card, so I pick it up.

I liked it. Paris of the north, a place of noisy coach parties and guys in quilts, kilts, puking on the cobblestone streets. A city where at least half the night is for sleep because nothing ah go on.

You come out of the train with your hold-all and go up a slope and you're in the town centre, the main shopping street. Magic. Like a town in a western, where the railroad goes to the dust-driven heart. There's a dip and a garden with bagpipes playing in the valley and then a castle right inside the city, looking over it. Stone everywhere, boss, stone shop, stone pub, stone statue, stone like dirt.

Makes you feel 'yes, I reach a real historical place here, full of beauty and splendour,' because the castle and the great walls and the bridges hang over a valley, which divides the town in two and you think 'maan, there have to be a river going through that gorge, a noisy, foaming, rocky river tamed at the banks by hardy Scots over the years' – and you look and there's only a fucking railway line. Big deal, small disappointment, we are dying, Scotland, dying. Man dere! Man survive!

On the first night five persons turn up to see *Tony and Cleo*. Three of these was birds Bawdy (his name was actually B. Audley, but description had caught up with him) pick up on his rambles round the bars and the Assembly Club. On the third day there was maybe ten. The audience was outnumbered by us but Bawdy said it would get better. Jam came up on the third day from London. He asked everyone, but everyone pretended they hadn't counted the actual numbers in the audience. I said hundred per cent improvement.

One day out of the two weeks we got fifty or sixty souls. I think most of them was German tourists who said 'ja, ja' when they applauded and stamped their feet when the reggae came on. We done two weeks of that. I was getting pissed off and so were the rest of the cast. We'd go around during the day and try and drum up support. Hanging around Edinburgh is OK but you meet all sorts and everybody's selling, the buyers aren't really there and then the trade-off starts. 'You see mine, I'll see yours.' And everyone looks frantically through the *Scotsman* for reviews and if you get a bad one

6

you go to the Assembly Rooms and some prat will come up and sympathise because he's got a bummer too and then you tell each other how biased and provincial the Scottish critics are, that's why they couldn't make it to London because what kind of guy wants to work for a Scots thing anyway. And then the guy stops and wonders whom he talking to and he looks at me and maybe thinks, 'What's this guy doing talking about Scots minorities, that's a bit racist.' I can see it in their eyes, boss.

Then this gang comes to Bawdy and ask us to do a gig. The big pull? Tele-boxy-visualisation-ary! The break. The guy says, 'What's interesting about this Edinburgh is that there are seven black groups on the fringe and it's international. We thought we'd have a forum on that and the channel want to cover it as a debate'.

Six other black shows in town. One dance group. Two comediennes, one who does a kind of mediocre rap, stereoptyes mostly. Then Bev, she's been on TV, does Margaret Thatcher and Roy Hattersley and Neil Kinnock. Bloody good with voices. Not much timing, some decent songs, but into the woman thing. Then the Yanks have a play about the massacre of the red man. Weird story about a black rebellion of slaves who believe they are the souls of the red man come back for revenge on the conquerors. Solid technique. Five of them make it seem like there's twenty people talking at the same time. The group has been written up big by the *Guardian*. They didn't sell much tickets in the States, but they were in the struggle – up front. Then the Zimbabwe play and a couple I'd never seen.

Circulating around Edinburgh is a real trip. You hang around the shows, the bars, and other actors mostly. Apart from Bawdy, I'm moving with this guy Gabriel in our band. I ask him to come to the debate and give some support but the son-of-a-bitch don't want to leave his mattress. He only gets up for performances. Boy, he got lucky with some white girl who he found in an opera, Jesus help me, with an opera voice and everything. Offstage she was like onstage, never give up. It's not something you can ignore. I mean if you have a relationship.

Say you walking the street or going in a pub, and, OK, she's opera, so people understand she has size – I mean you can't go with a Russian lady javelin and putt-shot and not expect size. Same for opera. Problem is both javelin and opera is no big thing, most people don't check feh it and don't know who is a star and who is not. As far they concern, you stuck with a fat lady, or, depending on taste, you have the benefit of one, and them might think you some kind of pervert. So you have feh make excuses. You gotta go round saying, like dropping the information: your girl is in opera or in the Russian javelin and putt-shot team. It becomes a nuisance.

In London Jam tell me Edinburgh full of girls, 'wall to wall pussy' or some such crude expression is how he put it.

*   *   *

If the devil like shit he hangs round the latrine. That was an old saying my father give me. How the old sayings come true. There, in the flesh, hype made meat and blood, was David Stream, like an apparition flitting about in the worst theatrical dives of Edinburgh. And thus, to turn a phrase, rasta, did I spot the man! Ecce, OK, homo!

Shorter than I imagined and at the age when the belly competes with everything else for prominence. The gossip had gone about the bar in the Assembly. The man is looking for a black, a genuine negro, an actor of semantic and syntactic and interpretative arts and everything that these guys want. I swear I never thought of it. I know he was there – the great, the most fantastic, the serious and crucial Mr On-stream, Mr Big-D. The greatest director on earth. After Allah.

In the bar, the world's derelict hip-talking actors would gather and spin stories about his legendary techniques of 'casting'. The smart money came out with mention of his New York production of Chekhov. Check this:

Stream's Chekhov at once confirms the Europeanness of Russia and denies the common tradition. This is raw stuff. Here's a Russia, a bourgeoisism unravaged by the angst of the late nineteenth-century, it is a Russian passion they play, as peculiar to the play as Cossack dances are to Tchaikovsky . . .

So it goes. Now the same paper on my . . . well, our play:

The play attempts to fight stereotypes, but falls into the trap of reinforcing them. The modern day lieutenant of the mostly absent Godot-like Caesar, called Tony, of course, is played by Ali Abdul. This Tony, though endowed with the menace of the street, seems strangely vulnerable. Not exactly the sort of street-wise dope dealer who would strike terror into the stout hearts of Brixton. Abdul struggles against the role, his discomfort emerging in the violence

8

with which he wields even the comic lines. The play preaches to a small audience of the mainly converted, and even they yawned.

Perhaps the comparison to *West Side Story* was never far from their minds. The lyrics plonk along as does some of the more meaning-laden dialogue of the playwright who can't resist throwing in a few lines of the original to wake his audience up with a Shakespearian twist of phrase totally missing from the banality of the rest of the piece.

Nice one. You know, I was in a state of agreement with that review but Bawdy nearly bawl. For years the white boy thinks that running the Black Star Theatre gives him the right to pick up black chicks and actresses and go around pretending he's street-wise and house-foolish.

Generalissimo, this debate forum pack out. I'm pushed to the speakers' table, with five other guys there. I know them because in Edinburgh, after a few weeks playing there and sleeping on the floor of various flats and drinking at the same parties, the same people come.

On my left the American, George. On his left the Zimbabwean, Tawanda. The Yank is playing in the dance thing. A kind of light skinned guy, with slight pock marks and heavy black talk. Then the Zimbabwe guy, whom I met in the bar of the Assembly a few times. Shy, even after a few drinks. Decent brothers, you know. They don't think of asking anyone for anything. They are playing to full houses in an Athol Fugard play about the writer's life. Sweet piece.

What happens is this young white guy, crazy, returns to this kind of general store somewhere in the outback which his mother runs. There's two black servants there who looked after him since he was a child. This guy talks to them like friends and it gets pretty lyrical with the servant saying how they used to fly kites together – get the message? – and then some tension starts with the white guy and his mum comes on the phone and its a reminder of where they really are, South Africa, apartheid, all that. He gets uptight with his mum and you can see the Oedipus thing clearly. Brilliant acting from this young white Zimbabwean guy. She never comes on stage but you can hear her crunching away, eating his balls by phone. The blacks watch his humiliation and he turns the challenge against his dad and mum on to them. The black servant tries to tell him something and the kid turns it into an assault on the servant's racial dignity. Then surprise, yeah, he spits in the man's face. The time I saw it the audience gasped.

9

The blacks are paralysed. Can't retaliate, trapped like flies in the jelly of history and a real human thing they got with this white kid who's a monster and yet they love him and that. I liked it, you know. But the Americans freaked out.

Bawdy told me there was going to be trouble, but push me on the stage and say it'll have to be me cause he's white and the playwright, Jam, would be chairing the session. Really the mother just want to sit down anonymous and check the runnings and contribute when he knows which side the crowd is on so he don't lose his street-cred.

I was thinking what sort of speech I'd make, and had some notes on how I became an actor and that and what I thought of our Tony loves Cleo piece. I never got a chance. The TV was there and they lit the place heavy and started on the audience. Jam sat us down on the platform and the audience went upwards from the front of the floor like a science lecture hall.

Tawanda gets up and talks about the Front Line States and how he became an actor. He's standing up, easy like lemon squeezy, on my right. George, the Yank, is on the other side of him. Tawanda gets to the point of how South Africa is producing tremendous cultural resistance and whites and blacks are working together and how all black actors must start in a theatre of suspicion. Then George gets up, stands up lazy and draws himself to a height and goes close up to Tawanda who doesn't stop his flow and he spits in his face: American black spits in the face of Zimbabwe black. In front of TV cameras in Britain. The audience goes 'oooh', or maybe it's more 'unhhh'! No one says nothing. Just Jam, Jamil Jamal (maybe his parents didn't call him that at all, he dream the crazy name up himself to fuck with people's heads), who thinks he's nicely in charge and before his eyes one of his speakers get insult. Big gob. I watch Tawanda. Handsome. Cool still. The gob starts dripping down his face in a white beehive of bubbles. He just moves his right hand to his hip and his muscles tense up. His cheek muscles stand out and his neck muscles tighten up. Then the hush is broken. The crowd starts to yell and Jam is standing up trying to pull George down by the shoulder and offering his hanky to Tawanda. George shakes off Jam like he was a monkey on him back. He's looking at Tawanda waiting for a reaction. Then he kicks his chair back and bawls, 'OK, come on, man. I spat in your face, motherfucker. I'm here. Defend what you do, nigger!' Again a stunned noise. George holds his hand up. The other Zimbabweans appear from the side and from the audience and the Yanks are there too behind George.

I never seen an actor so alert, George steps behind his own chair. 'I'm pushing him because I hate to see a brother of mine stand up night after night and take that shit. He takes it from a white man every day, twice at matinées. You wanna talk black theatre, you wanna talk of prostitution?' The crowd don't know which way to roar. Tawanda stands there, the spit dribbling down his face. No hanky. Like a statue. Once an actor always an actor. The fucker just stands there. The compassion of the United Nations shines down on him. Mr Zimbabwe, doing it for South Africa.

Captain, in case you don't know, Athol Fugard is a South African white man. I heard the same George the night before and it was not that he didn't like him being white or a playwright, it was he didn't like everybody going to see that play on Broadway when his play off Broadway had two cents for the budget and the local garbage dump for the set. That's bullshit too, because in New York you have to be stupid if you can't get some form of aid or promotion. Nobody dies in America.

If I get sentimental, boy, I'll tell you about my moron cousin from Jamaica who lives in Harlem and isn't worth a jug of spit and hustles off other Caribbean folks by selling them land in Hicksville with promises of prosperity and heavy printed colour brochures attached.

'Hold your horse, there,' I say and stand up. 'I liked the play. Athol Fugard, it's real. The guy's an actor like you and me and if the script say spit in the face and wipe it off then you wipe it off. The man has self control, he is free but he exercises his self control because he's a player and I know what you're saying, bra, but you done a dirty thing . . .'

Gob. The man gobs in my face. I see it coming, a white shower, even though I know his mouth is dry with funky challenge. So I pick up my fist and hit him. That's what you call a platform. Black spitting at each other, the Yankee boy playing some philosophy, the African man steady as an idol, crying but no tears, crying for the world, and I, the nice British black boy, playing off punches. He never hit me back. God save the Queen, these American man believe what they talking about. Bullshit mainly, but they'll take a punch and they'll spit in two men's faces in front of an audience to make a point. That's what them arseholes are about, all Americans – making some point with their arguments or with their lives, their style, their sexuality – they get born again black or born again woman or Jewish or Spanish or something, born again mafia even – did you see the film? Ace, boss, Brando like shoved a boxer gum shield right up him cheeks.

Jam is frantically trying to call Bawdy and the rest to help divide the Yankees and the Zimbabweans.

These Yanks, boy, cool as cucumbers and not half as green! George, spitting all over the place now, starts playing Martin Luther King: 'Brother, you're both my brothers and I'm motherfucking shamed to have to come to Edinburgh to tell you what's going down.

'This brother has a white man spitting in his black face every show of the day. And you can tell me till the cows come home and get milked the next day, but I ain't listening, cause something's wrong when the game takes us that far from reality. That's a role I say no to, that's super-exploitative-neo-colonialistic-white dominational trash.'

Some cheers. Tawanda stands unmoving in his Dashiki top and jeans.

'You want to talk about black theatre, let's start from where a white man spits in a black man's face and you can buy tickets to see that,' says George.

'You are a prize American arsehole. I seen your show. You dance and you wear little blue sash round your waist and you want to look like a girl and sing some soul songs. And you're not even black, like me, or him . . . rasta (I begin to revert to a general Jamaicanised Caribbean under pressure) you just shaping, and spit and ting – bwoy is dead you wan' dead!'

Oh God, the words tumble out, unscripted and Bawdy is on the stage and says we ought to end the proceedings and old Jam is trying to tell the TV crew that they got real live drama and did they want it to continue. That's Jam all the way. He's chairing this meeting but he begins to enjoy the fight. You can see it on his dirty little face. And then George takes out his handkerchief and tries a no-hard-feelings gesture with it on Tawanda. He holds it out. Boy, I seen some fake acting in my time. There's this telly report last month of an American preacher who screwed some woman, some kinky scene, rubber bootie and ting; he get caught. He's one of these guys who makes cash on telly, yelling at the faithful to send their dollars. Well, when he gets caught in scandal he thinks about it for a few days and then decides, 'What the hell, if I can sell them bullshit, why not sell them the bull.' He comes on the nine o'clock news and pulls out the same American large hanky and holds it out to camera, like the theatrical idiot shaking a spear and he puts it to his cheek. 'Here's the hanky, brothers and sisters. Here's the hanky, brothers and sisters. Here's the tear. I'm crying for I have sinned.'

That's what old Georgie Porgy was doing with his hanky, holding it out for the audience. And it made me see red. Fuck acting. You don't do that, man, whatever opinion you want to put across. Check me, I earn my living from standing up and playing rough and Tawanda works for something he believes in. He must do. He let the white guy, who is definitely a friend of his from some revolutionary theatre in Zimbabwe, spit because that very spitting does the white man down. At least that's what a theatre audience would think. If you take a football audience, they would probably think the guy who spits is the hero, the guy who take it is a sucker. So.

When I hit him again I felt it connect, knuckle with jaw and consciousness. He fell heavily forward, down. Then all hell broke loose because the crowd began to disperse, pushing towards the doors and shouting. The Zimbabwe troupe came and took their guy and a couple of reporters got me and Bawdy. We talked to them, first on the steps and then in the bar over triple white rum and water which they paid for.

It was in the papers next day, even in some London mags. I was a hero. You don't normally get heroes in debates, but there I was. So it was that Mr D himself, whom I'd noticed, as maybe John the Baptist noticed a carpenter's apprentice hovering by the stream, through this little play, came to see mine.

He says, 'I'm getting together a team, I'd like to talk to you.'

I knew this was the biggest lasso that ever caught my arse. A bones feeling. Yes Mr D. The Break, it had come. Hallelujah. Mr D and little ole me. Shall we have a drink, Mr D? So you don't drink, Mr D, but you will have a tomato juice or a designer water. He said no and he wanted I should see him after the run of my play, before I left Edinburgh.

Funny thing was Mr D had seen a different meeting. He says it was brave of me and he admired my courage and the American was an arsehole and he saw me do my second strike but he left the hall when the woman with the anti-apartheid slogans started shouting to free Nelson Mandela and began hurling chairs and attacking white liberals. 'She was white herself,' Mr D observes.

I didn't sleep too good that night because Bawdy said we got to wrap up the show, and when the man said see me the next day I didn't have a place to stay and I thought I'd hit the jackpot, but maybe the jackpot would wait so I called him and he said OK see me in London, so I dossed down on a chick's floor, not even in her bed because that night I didn't know where she was, a white chick, an actress and she had this show in which she wore a black bow and dressed up like a man with three other chicks and they played the clarinet and did some funny stuff. All the time I was sleeping in her sleeping bag I could smell her and all her visitors, the blokes who'd been through the scene and I was reciting to myself. Tell you some lines: Because I shall not turn again, because I shall not turn, because

It's something like that. A lickle T. S. Eliot and it kept going round in my head and I was thinking it was about me in this sleeping bag. And the next one:

> The sunlight on the garden
> Hardens and grows cold,
> We cannot cage the minute
> Within its nets of gold,
> When all is told
> We cannot beg for pardon.

Like it.

Was I conscious of what I was doing when I slugged him in the face? Sure I was conscious . . . several guys came to grab us, but he, George, he was cowering down on the floor because I knocked his fucking gold tooth out and he began to scream for his tooth and before I got lost in the excitement of it I sight it gleaming on the floor next to the chairperson's table so I picked it up and pocketed it and I had it when I got home that night. It was in my trouser pocket, real American gold.

Just one last performance, Bawdy said that evening, but the whole thing was reported in the papers and that's when the audience started coming. I was written up as the guy who bust up the meeting with punches and then people came to see our show and, sure, I bristled.

I carried the gold tooth with me back to London. I took the night train back alone and slept from Edinburgh to London and when I got out the other end at Euston in the morning my wallet was gone. I'd been mugged. I could have gone home but without any money and no chance of getting any more till Bawdy reached London and gave me an advance I thought best to go and see Maureen who is a girl who has a baby for me. I don't live with her because she threw me out. Don't get me wrong, she's sort of independent and a kind of feminist . . . she's white . . . and I didn't abandon her, I was quite happy living with her and bringing the kid up but she kicked me out because she didn't like my habits and I told her I didn't like the paunch she was

14

getting and bags under the eyes and any rude thing which was true and then she said to go. Now and then I go back there because I want to see my daughter who's called Martha and not Blossom because being independent her mum gave her her own surname.

She's not a freak or nothing Maureen, she's fairly straight but got these ideas, reads a lot, makes Martha read and doesn't tolerate me. OK so she's got her own thing but I don't think she liked me being successful at all. She used to like me when I started acting and we used to do bum plays in bum theatres and it was a struggle and nil bread all the way and I'd lie back with her in bed and we'd smoke some ganja and then screw all night. Later she didn't want to screw. She wanted the ganja but then she'd turn over and go to sleep or just have the ganja in one room and say when she was ready to go to bed in the next room and the baby was waking up and crying and when I tried to get the baby it would cry more so we got used to her sleeping with the baby in the bed and I sleeping on the floor.

When I started getting newspaper cuttings and calls from my agent and the minutes of the theatre group I was involved in coming through the post . . . well, she didn't like blacks being organised and famous and I told her and she said it was just that I belched and farted in bed and was a real pig and I could fool the people in the audiences I was getting through to but I couldn't fool her at all because she'd been to university and her dad was not a rich guy contrary to all appearances. He was really working class and smoked a pipe and was brought up without tuppence to rub together (ole English habit). Anyway she's been through school being the brightest little girl in her class. That was the deal.

She didn't mind me turning up and I said 'I got mugged' and she thought that was funny because black guys don't get mugged but it was early in the morning and she made me some wicked tea and when I suggested other things she just said she had to go to work. She even bothered to sneer. She'd read about the row I had in Edinburgh because it was in the *Guardian* and in the *Independent*.

In the old days I would have asked her whether she agreed with my point of view or did she agree with George. I could predict her answer. She'd side with George and come some heavy black militancy as justification: 'Just like you. You'd allow someone to spit in your face for stagecraft. That's the sort of Uncle Tom that this television work has turned you into. And yes, George is right. You can't do anything to amuse middle-class idiots and put them through their theatrical learning curve. There are house niggers in South Africa too.' That's not something I imagine from the past, that what she says. Then she gets on to what I'm doing – 'a flippin' Tony and Cleo panto'. She talks about 'the community'. Whenever she talks about them, they're always on her frigging side. I don't say it, because it just gets worse, but I know what there is of 'the community' and they'd hustle anybody and they ain't on no one's side.

That's why it's a joke which is why I began to laugh and she just said in that case I could take some responsibility and carry the girl to school, and dress her up and do her hair. I said cool and she just flounced out.

Martha was washing and she knew how to dress herself. She's six years old. I did her hair. Just combed it through with an afro comb and got her in her coat and walked her to school.

Her classroom is in a mobile and I take her in sometimes so I know the scene. She has a nice teacher, a half-caste girl always full of 'good morning'. Once she even said she saw me on telly because I had this part in a play. She never alluded to it again, even though I dreamt that I was meeting this teacher girl and she was treating me like a big star.

I know what must have happened. I must have had a fight with Maureen during that screening or the day after and she must have gone and made some shameless reports to the kid's teacher. Maureen's like that. She doesn't mind who she blabs her personal affairs to, so long as she can put me in the wrong with some young teacher or some other woman. She uses all that woman-together thing, the feeling how bad men are, especially black men.

So the teacher said, 'You have given Martha her dinner money?'

I say, 'What dinner money?'

A twinge of shame and panic, because it just struck me I had no cash. I didn't know whether to say I'd forgot it at home but I knew Martha wouldn't want to hear any of that when all the other kids were sitting round the class and their parents were collecting the cards to pay at the dinner money trolley, so I just searched for her card and walked out of the classroom. Then I thought best to be straight up so I called the teacher from the door again and asked her to step this way.

She said, 'What?'

'Just come out a minute.'

She must have seen something in my manner so she never came out.

She said, 'I haven't got a minute as you can see. Johnny, it's a very sweet cat but can you please take it back to your mum if she's still here.'

Martha looked at me with big eyes.

I went to the dinner trolley. I can remember bloody school dinners and the kids who used to have free dinners with white and red cards and the kids who had green cards and it was a shame and I promised myself whatever happened never to let any kid of mine suffer dinner money humiliation. No suh! My dad dragged me from Jamaica when I was a kid and dumped me in a school with fisticuffs from the off. I complained to him a few times and he would only say how I was spared a beating in Jamaican schools rasta (how them ah seh: 'Know your culture, know your history'), God help us all. And the devil refurbish the larder.

I tell you what I did at the dinner trolley where there was this white woman about fifty years old collecting the dinner money. Mums and dads were going up to her in the corridor, leaving their cards and I didn't even have forty-five pence. I was digging in my pocket out of embarrassment because I thought my last hope was to explain that I'd pay the next day but there was two black women paying their children's money and they were standing gossiping to this white teacher or helper or whatever she was.

I said, 'I'm Martha's dad' and she just held her hand out for the card and the money. I thought last minute salvation, maybe the black women had heard of me in some play or seen me on the telly and then I could borrow some money, but they just looked me up and down. My clothes were crumpled from sleeping on the train and maybe my hair wasn't combed out. One of them was taking in every crease of my trousers and every crinkle of my hair.

So I looked back at her up and down and you know what the woman says?

'Eh, don't fuck me with your eyes, black boy.'

In an infant school! Blood and fire. Give us the teachings of his majesty, me no want no devil philosophy. I said, 'You what?' and the sentence just continued in my mouth.

'Listen, here's a gold tooth. I forgot my wallet in my suit.'

I put the tooth down and turned a hard corner on my soft shoe and walked off.

The headmistress sent a note to Maureen saying that Martha's dad had left a gold tooth instead of dinner money and that caused a lot of arguments that night so I moved out again.

*   *   *

Gerald, my dad wasn't thinking. Gerald Blossom, Gerry! One easy leap to boot polish. I called myself Ali Abdul Rahman. My daughter should now be called Martha Rahman. That too caused a fucking argument because I told the woman (it's a next word came to my mind) that a father's daughter should be called by his name and she say, 'Your name is Blossom and it's typical of your parents not to have thought of it when they called you Gerry.'

I don't strike women. Not my style. But irey and vexed I was.

'She could be called Martha Ali or Martha Rahman, then they wouldn't wonder why a black girl was called by a slave name in this day and age.'

'All that finished with the 'sixties.' She was laughing at me. 'You're twenty years too late, you oaf. If you wanted to be a black Muslim you should have thought of it earlier.'

I tell you she didn't like Martha being called no black kid.

In fact it wasn't no black Muslim kick I was on at all. Some guys, actor friends, they'd turned Buddhist and called me once and I went with them to a house in Harlesden where they all took off their shoes and wore white dressing gowns and chanted in front of some brass monuments and flowers and all this shit.

This friend Digger takes me down to the place and says just to behave myself and check it. As I walk in they ask if I'm wearing any unguents. I said don't know what unguents means so how could I be wearing any. And she could see I had trousers and a jacket.

It's a little twenty-two-year-old girl and she says, 'I mean after-shave or deodorant or even strong soap.'

First time a girl asked me in a sort of bouncer context what I had on my body.

'Can't afford it,' I said.

She says, 'The Lama has asthma and he can't stand people in the same room with powerful scents.'

Then she says, 'Can I just sniff you.'

I looked at Digger and he nodded so I says yes she could. Two of them they sniffed me like dogs from hair oil to toe jam.

They let me through to the front room and then a guy asks me if I have any cold or flu or anything and I said no and he says any stomach trouble? Now apart from the curry I'd eaten the previous night at Ullah's because Maureen wouldn't open the door when I got back from the club, I didn't know of no stomach disorders so I said no. But I twigged what he meant. In the middle of the chant they didn't want any sniffing and sneezing and farting and that.

I took my place on the prayer mat with I tell you sixty others in this small room and when after half hour my stomach started to rumble and I couldn't hold it I just continued chanting and shifted a little piece and hoped Digger hadn't noticed. But then another buddhist or two started looking at Digger and he started looking at me and I knew it was time to withdraw from the chant because . . . well they say a fox smells his own hole first.

I went back to Ullah that night and ate a prawn korma and tarka dal with naan and I'd had six pints in the bar at the Riverside where I was just doing this thing holding props for a couple of black guys who were doing a sort of drama karate demo and needed me for a few lines.

There were only three or four people in the restaurant, the guy who managed the till and Ullah.

He was happy to give me the food. And happy to see me. He says, 'Polish, how is performance.'

'I don't like you calling me Polish, just rest the Polish, call me something nice.'

He brings me a lager and by the time the other customers have gone he sends the other waiters up to share their bunks upstairs, like the sailors in *Billy Budd* or something. Then he brings out a bottle of cheap whisky and he wants to talk theatre with me. Ullah is an educated man in his own way. We talk a lot. In college in Bangladesh he read all of Bernard Shaw's plays. Some in English, some in translation into whatever they speak in Bangladesh. He can actually recite pieces from *Major Barbara*.

It was he who suggested 'Ali' and then he says 'Rasul'.

I asked him what it meant and he said 'slave'.

'That's what I'm trying to get away from.'

So he ketch hold of my hand and asks me about my birthday. And what time of the morning or night or afternoon I was born. He knows shit. And he says he sees two 'a's and one 'r' in my name and urges me to try 'Rasul'.

'Can't have that, sport,' I say, but he's still holding my hand and it's incredible, how he knows Maureen just from the lines on my hand without ever having met her.

'You have white wife,' he says.

'Ullah, you're a clairvoyant,' I say.

'And that was long time so now you running around with flossy.'

'I don't know any Flossy, wrong first time.'

'You know plenty, I seen you.' He's looking at me steady.

'You mean floosie?'

'Yes, you love them?'

'Think I'm daft?' We both laugh.

He's a sport and by now I buy the name trick and say go through it so he gives me more names till we hit upon Ali Abdul Rahman. Nice one. No more Polish, no more Gerry Blossom. Goodbye, goodbye Gerry Blossom.

Ullah says, 'You want to be a good Muslim. The food is on the house today.' I had money but I put my arms around him because these guys are generous. So I said, 'No, I don't know how to be a good Muslim, I jus want to change my name and if the stars are right, well then, the name is fine with me.'

'But Muslims, you know, have to go through certain things.'

He was staring hard at me. Now I never see a man look like that except the moment before he wants to kiss a woman and doesn't know how to ask and doesn't have the guts to grab.

'Ullah, take it easy. Don't dig nothing, right.'

'Ali Abdul Rahman, I am digging nothing,' he says. 'God will not recognise the name.'

Then I got his meaning. 'That's easy,' I say. 'Don't bother your little head. When I was a child in Jah, they had to do something to me. The damn thing swole up and they had to cut something off, so I suppose it's in line with the dealings.'

'Properly cut?'

'Don't know.' I don't know what came over me. No, I do know what came over me. The same thing that comes over you on stage when you are improvising because you want to help your co-actor along and he or she's swallowed a line or gone off riding a tangent and you're still both in the mood of the piece. That's what came upon me. Stage cooperation.

'Have a look,' I said, 'tell me if it's a deal.' And I opened my flies and stood up and let it hang out. God, he was breathing hard and I knew what Ullah was into. He just held me by the waist and he was trembling, shivering like a guy wanting to deliver the kiss and go forth and not knowing whether he was making a fool of himself.

'That'll be all, Ullah,' I said and I put it away, 'thanks for the meal.'

20

I was sober, he was frantic. And then I noticed that he had turned half the lights of the restaurant out and locked the door.

'Rahman means full of mercy and love,' he said and his voice was choking.

'Have a drink and open the bloody door. That was bloody good prawn korma, but yesterday's dhansak got me thrown out of a Buddhist meeting.'

'Your hand shows all things, I have only read a few pages, Ali Abdul Rahman.'

'The library has called for the book back. You don't want to hold my hand, Ullah, you want to do filth with the rest of my things, but you can't.'

'No, sir, you are mistaken,' says Ullah, 'just I will hold your hand and read some more.'

I looked at my hand. 'I don't want to put temptation your way, Ullah, we should really stop meeting like this.' So I laughed and he laughed too and we broke into heavy laughter and I got the key from his pocket and let myself out. I kept the name.

On the programme they called me Ali Abdul.

*   *   *

Plenty ways to skin a cat, really, arse or lip first or knife in the belly. So with a story, or maybe its like there's only two ways to skin a banana. Top and bottom and I'll start from the bottom.

My beautiful Jesus! It's not even a year since all this happen. Since the meeting in Edinburgh. Since Stream pick me up and straight away project me into the care, I can't say loving exactly, but decent, you know, of Sara Fraser Stuart. That is a name her father dreamed up because Scottish don't call themselves all this double name, just ole MacDonald and Haig and Glenfiddich and stuff. Sara had her Stream year too. When I saw them in the audience in Edinburgh I didn't know who she was. Maybe I'd read her stuff in the papers. Can't remember.

Only my own lickle side of it I can tell you from memory. The rest is from Sara's papers, her diary, her clippings of the stuff she wrote about what the papers now call 'The Stream Affair'.

Fact is that Jamil Jamal has been asked to check out the story. To write his book about the whole scene. He calls me.

'So, Ali, what are you doing now, not acting?'

'Jam,' I say, 'I'm in business. Just don't come anywhere near me.'

I play as if I don't want to talk to no one, to erase the whole thing from my consciousness and memory.

'I understand, it must be hurtful for you,' he says. But still he doesn't tell me he wants to write a book. He just wants to talk to me. 'After all, I feel very very lost and hurt myself.'

I don't reply. I let a silence lapse. What's he implying, the son-of-a-bitch? He's hurt as badly as me? He wants to pull me into a trap and he's baiting it with this curiosity angle.

Then he says, 'I have a problem.'

'Don't we all, me ole son.'

'You lived for a while in Sara's house, didn't you?'

'Sure. During the production.'

'Do you still have the key?'

'Well, even if I have Jam, me ole tart, I couldn't give it you now, could I? That would be kinda dishonest. Why don't you go there, there's a geezer called Jerksy or something living there, you know, one of Sara's mates. He has a key, he lives there.'

'No, well, I can't call him. There's a reason.'

'Asian guy, I didn't know you was shy of Asians. Or get a note from Sara.'

'You know that Sara's lost somewhere on the sub-continent, man, don't mess me about.'

'Mess you about, Jam? The great playwright and chronicler of the Stream Affair, would I a humble negro actor mess you about?'

'OK, I get it,' says Jamil Jamal. 'And fuck you too.'

Which is a relief rasta because the next day I go and pick up the stuff myself. Which is what I'm giving you. At least the Sara stuff. The geezer in the flat he don't say much. I know where Sara has kept the clippings and she won't mind me putting it down as it was.

Boy, I find looking through these things that I didn't know half of what was going down.

New Citizen, Saturday Supplement, 3 September
STREAM'S WAY

I didn't know him from bloody Adam. I just happened to be sitting next to him in the audience in Edinburgh when he made one of the most momentous cultural decisions of the century. OK, I protest too much. Of course, gentle reader, normal column-fan, your imperial normal yuppie cultural ruffianship, Sara is playing naïve.

Faux naïve, if you comp! FACT: I paid a hefty bribe to buy the seat next to his because I'd watched a black debate to which he'd been at the Assembly Rooms where this London actor Ali Abdul slung a Mohammed at the leader of the Negro Theatre of Harlem and lived to tell the tale and overheard him saying 'great' and muttering things about theatre as lone old men will and I had resolved to follow Mr Stream around.

It took some neat but modest mind-reading to figure out that he'd want to see Ali Abdul in Jamil Jamal's transfer of *Tony and Cleo* from the Riverside in London to the Assembly Rooms in Edinburgh. At the height of the action the hero says he's dying Egypt dying and he makes it sound like he's talking to a map, so I remark 'Yukk!' and Mr Stream smiles and so I get an interview.

If you've heard otherwise, ducky, a gentle rebuke from aunty Sara – screw you, mister.

David Stream doesn't try to hide his baldness with a slick of hair combed in the right direction. When the temples start gaining territory against a man's hair-line, like some plan of battle drawn in a general's mind, time is on the ascendant and he thinks of losing the battle. So my first question was does death panic him. Not at all, he knows what I mean. That's the reason he still wears a tweed jacket and maybe even a black polo-neck jumper underneath. Would I please refer to it in the article as 'vintage clothing'?

He makes the coffee handing me the mug, holding it with both hands, preciously. Original Warhol on wall. Then spectacles from a case. The man has style. As he puts them on he says he first began to notice the creep of old age, not age because that happens all the time, but real old age when his short sight began to get complicated by long sight and he couldn't read the A to Z so thank God he got, should he say, tight on budgets, (put it that way rather than say the British arts establishment is Philistine) and drove him to America where there isn't an A to Z? Was Warhol a friend? Only a smile, very fetching too, remind me to start a book called *In Quest of the Comforts of Older Men* with David Stream.

'Your height?'

'Five feet and eight and quarter inches, though I don't look it now because . . .' Taps his stomach.

Why is he a vegetarian? I thought he didn't believe in modern fads.

There were vegetarians in India nine thousand years ago,

23

probably. (What kind of Eurocentric spoilt brat was I?) Great, so the answer? Nothing to do with sympathy for animals. He believed in killing for art. He's never said that before. Nothing against fur coats (I wasn't wearing one, folks) because someone has killed and fashioned the extract of that killing. Like rump steak? Did I know that in Turkey they cut off bits of live cow and then stitched the skin up again. You didn't have to kill to eat steak. Where the hell am I? Trapped in a trivial pursuit in Hammersmith?

Give me another example. Killing for art? Oh yes, the gentleman with the tiger's head, the moose's head, the director is like a taxidermist, new stuffing in old skins.

I'm glad I came.

The money for the last production in New York was by subscription from rich Americans. Yes, he's had British money, French money, roubles, baubles, noodles, the lot. Robbed every nation for art.

Money?

Did I really want to get on to that? It comes it goes.

He says he's been through faces like a clairvoyant goes through tarot cards. Something you pick up as director. But talking to an Indian actress in Paris the other month he realised that he was using a young director's mentality to do an old director's work.

Did I know Auden?

'Looking at his face was looking at the ultimate palmist's gift horse.'

'Eh??'

'Lines. You got the feeling that God placed him here with a map of another planet on his face to give us the assurance that we were not alone.'

'Did you say that to Auden?'

'Let's get on to the text,' he says.

'Great, India's answer to *Gone With The Wind*.'

'Considerably older. I was looking for a story . . . As a very young person in the war I was in Cairo and I was put in charge of Egyptian students playing *Antony and Cleopatra*. It was their choice but they had not the least inkling that this was a play which partially dealt with Egypt. They *were* Egypt, but Shakespeare was not. It was their way of being part of an international community, the Second World War, something that had exploded in Europe and overflowed in its terror towards older worlds. I smirked through

24

the rehearsals and sent out self-parodying cards to the rest of the British community in Cairo when the play was ready to be seen. The players, of course, not being British, didn't understand the parody. The rest of the club understood the joke. But time has wiped the smirk off my face.'

He was serious. Charming.

'Yes, I was looking for a metaphor for what I felt was new in internationality. If flight and TV by satellite have brought the world together, where is the refinement of that, the reflection of that in drama? Is drama rooted in severely national cultures?'

He looked for the biggest story of love and life that would incorporate the quest for the ideal man.

'Isn't there something just about it? I knew when making fun of the Arabs during the war that the play would haunt me, that I had done wrong. I had assassinated in my heart another's innocence and this was the great theme of *Antony and Cleo* and the guilt stayed with me. So it was with some poetic alarm that I heard that this fellow Ali was in a black version of the play just when I was enquiring about where in Edinburgh he may be located, what he was doing, what he was in.

'Maybe that's why I chose him. I've looked at fifty actors for the part, but the dignity I took from the Arabs I restored to Ali when looking at him playing Tony. The adaptation is rubbish.'

He had already found the play.

And it wasn't *The Iliad* and it wasn't a combination of *Romeo* and *Lear* and it couldn't be an adaptation of *Karenina*, it had to be something more fundamental, something more of a deposit in the human consciousness than a pointed work. So he came to India. No doubt Clive and Curzon and Dicky Mountbatten, God bless him, had something to do with it, and Vasco da Gama, but basically it was there and the Indians hadn't bothered to sell it but there was the *Ramayana*.

'In a sense I was amazed that it remained for me to do it, that it was still there, untouched by Western hands. They do it all the time but they've become so addicted to the rubbish we've peddled there, that the teenagers of India think cannabis is an American habit they picked up from the hippies.'

Such modesty, such bald courage, but mendacity too. I asked him to explain this business about not giving interviews.

'The only way to give them. But frankly I am appalled at the

25

standard of dramatic criticism and what passes for arts journalism in this country.

'Years ago I resolved never to attack what would seem to me only fashion, only surface tremor, be it in theatre or pop or painting or journalism, for heaven's sake. But it doesn't work: your determinations rebel, you become the old fogey you used to despise.' Then compliments for yours truly: 'My agent, Pam, says you've earned the right to write as you will. Of course, she's afraid your newspaper barons will buy out the theatres.'

I said I didn't want the tired old argument about the theatres and sponsorship and what successive governments had done to the arts. There was always hope and where there was hope there would be money if we market the hope.

'Hope,' he says. 'A poet friend of mine called it a butterfly's wing. Do you like that? I find myself selling snobbery, or I did, till I stumbled on the *Ramayana*. If one has the name, the stature, some bastard from the City whose idea of art ends at Gilbert and Sullivan and the *Messiah* at Christmas is mightily flattered to put a personal name to a venture and tens of thousands of pounds, dollars, roubles soon I suppose . . .'

Rupees?

'Yes, those too. Indian business houses are falling over each other to sponsor the tour of India. That'll come later. I went around seven hundred villages looking at country representations of the *Ramayana* stories. The beliefs that surround them, the – can't avoid the cliché – organic connection of the drama and the story to the ritual and the messages the audience craves. That's still India. Once you fly out to Heathrow or Charles de Gaulle, you realise what a frail deposit of the past you have witnessed, a thin layer, shapeless, a small discovered footprint in a vast expanse of sand. The deposit must be saved, but not transferred to a museum, though that too will happen. There is no harm in taking it over lock, stock and barrel, and making it one's own.

'We've been doing it for years, from Africa, from the Greeks, making them part of our protoplasm. I want recognition. I want them to feel internationally that the play is the thing and the play is my way, David Stream's way of learning something.'

David Stream's way.

Sara Fraser Stuart

She would strike you as a hi-tech girl if you talk to her the time I first met her. You know, the kind who carry a Filofax if not a personal organiser thing and have a fetish for designer pens and ting and ting. But the diary is written in a black covered notebook, the kind one used in school way back in some generation, with red triangular patches of vellum or something on the corners and hard blue ruled lines.

As I'm driving my car a guy comes to me, just as I'm getting in from the flat in Gunnersbury where I now live.

Says he's asking after Sara. Yes, I say, I know her. None of his business. He says he's an official, but he don't say what sort of official and he flashes a kinda card at me. I don't even look at the card. Are you supposed to recognise police cards when you see them for a second?

'She's in India, isn't she?'

'King, I know nothing about her. I ain't denying I used to run with her but that's done, see, and I hear she's in India but take me to a court of law and boy I couldn't hold no Bible with sincerity and swear on it. I'm superstitious.'

'You don't know where in India?'

'Boss, lost touch.'

'No letters, phone calls – she just dropped out?'

'Man, you said it. Dropped is the word.'

The man left me alone. I never tell him nothing and it's one thing I wouldn't even say for the purpose of this account.

If I've been in touch with her and she with me, well, that doesn't touch on this scene I'm recalling here. Maybe she sees life differently now. It's before Jamil Jamal start to tell any lies in print that I'm getting the eye-witnesses assembled here, your honour feh testify. So here goes. From her diary, monsieur:

Aug 6th

Flat's high ceilinged and cold. Two rooms. Bought and sent views of Edinburgh from a young Scotsman selling his personal prints outside the George. Which is also the name of the hunk from the deep deep south – and this particular Mary-Lou loves you a bunch. He's not that black, and plays in a fast-moving black show which takes the piss out of even legitimate stars like Miss D. Ross, the ex-Supreme. George does a drag scene as satire.

I catch George after the performance. He plays what he thinks is cool. Actually naffo, qualmzzzzz! Mustn't let the brandy interfere with the work. Filed a story for Robin.

Says he loves me, but he says it with his eyes wide open watching mine as he's on top of me and banging away and then he slips out this 'I love you, honey', just to see if it'll make me melt. He's surprised the ultimate confession has no effect on me whatsoever.

Aug 17th

I tell George 'no scenes'. The Fugard is supreme. *Master Harold and the Boys* revived by a Zimbabwean troupe. I want to interview the whole troupe and it takes days for them to get it together, there's always someone kidnapping one or other of their stars. So I settle for their leading light, Tawanda. George doesn't want him coming round to the flat. I tell him I spent six years in Kenya. Makes him even more furious and he looks edibly cute when he bites his bottom lip and frowns. Like he's for murder.

Aug 24th

David Stream is in town so I'll chase him shamelessly. George calls me for a meal at an Indian restaurant and turns up two hours late. Says he lost his way in Edinburgh, honey, and thinks he can scowl and settle down to eat. I've waited two hours but I'm not sighing with relief. I waited, not for the meal but for the satisfaction of telling him to stuff it because I know what game he's playing. Went in a cab to Tawanda's. He's staying in the flat of a director who works in London. Something is certainly going on, I make him sweat but he's too shy to say. Instead he says he's debating on a platform about blacks.

Aug 29th

I couldn't believe my eyes. George spat in Tawanda's face and the dude from Brixton, Bawdy's man, threw a rocky fist at his jaw and knocked him out.

George came that night to the flat with his mouth bleeding. Apparently some teeth had been knocked out. I was so furious I had brought Tawanda home to try and cancel the insult. When George banged at the door I tried to pretend we weren't there but he shouted.

'OK, I know he's there. I came to say I'm sorry.' Then we let him in. Big baby. He had one drink scowling at the both of us, Tawanda watching him like a dog a cat. George wasn't shifting. Neither was Tawanda. At one point I said, 'You boys want to fight it out?' It was three in the morning.

George left, polite and angry. I just played the reggae tapes.

The bloody papers fell for George's nonsense. They wrote that the fight was over divergent ideologies. If I file the story even I can't be honest. Sara, you have made a trade of false honesty and you have given it a trademark. They fought over me, over territory. Flattery? Territory?

The girl write well, you know. I looked for the article she coulda writ on the punch-up but she never went into that. At the time I never woulda sussed that this girl with a faint Scottish kind of echo in the mouth and very sharp featured, what we used to call 'devil-daughter' looks, had gone with either of them. She look when I first meet her like she was heavily into Stream himself. I mean why play with monkeys when the organ grinder got the collection hat?

And what's funny is that now, from a distance, she reminds me from her diary of these things, but nowhere does she say she was doing the ole humpy with my new guru, the man who change my life and maybe hers. Here I am still thirsty for a confession from her diaries. Nothing on him, in that way.

Some of the diary is about her dad. Personal things, you know, like her dad living with this little girl, less old than Sara herself, and kick her mum out. So Mum lives up in Derbyshire and Dad lives in town with his little woman who Sara say, diarywise, is a 'contemptible pleb'. Which sound snobbish but Sara ain't like that at all. She's as generous as a harvest. Shameless thing for me to say, being as I am black myself, but there's something kinky if the girl goes with George and then Tawanda and make them fight. Nowhere did she show me that. Till I look in the diary I didn't know. Man, you live and learn. But they musta known, George spitting at Tawanda because he took his girl away, shifting restless, from American black to Zimbabwe scholar, knowing one would be jealous of the other, knowing the black knight would fight for and make some two forward-one sideways moves over the heads of everybody else. Boy, I thought I was in the thick of an ideological dispute, not some pussy fight. Fuck it! I'll tell you about SFS later. Stream now.

Stream say he like the way I handled the thing in the Assembly Rooms in Edinburgh. Then he says did I notice the girl sitting next to him. Matter of fact I had, boss, but prick censorship is not my game, I ain't checking which thing he's moving with, so I say no I never notice her I was intent on what I was doing on stage. Well he say he don't know her but he turned to her and say I'm hired, he want me, just like that to a stranger. And he say she turns out to be a big press reporter on one of the new weekend supplement magazines, a columnist with clout and bitchiness and style and she's gonna write about us all. Cool.

Then he wants to go over the spitting business again. Would I do it on stage, allow a guy et cetera.

Tricky question. I thought about it. If he's for blacks, well, he may fit in with the Yank's point of view, dignity being more important than drama and thing. But then he's a director and earns his living by drama, not by dignity of nobody.

'Whatever the script say for me to do. After all, the stage is not the street.'

'Would you do anything for drama?'

'Actors should, short of snuff movies,' I said.

'They aren't *actors* in snuff movies,' he says like he's real insulted, like he really digs something from that, 'they are never told. *Actors* are directed.'

It was a serious audition. I go for his cool style. Knows what he's doing. Some white directors are so fucking keen to tell you they know how black people feel and all this. Anxious to let you know that in their hearts the rubble has been moved, the right-on flame doth burn.

Maureen said about the myth of me making better love than the next man. Not to hurt me or some scene, just in one of her real intellectual discussion moods in which she used to say anything goes, one can discuss anything, all can be talked about though not everything can be talked through. OK, the reason she went for me was because I was more in touch with myself than the white guys she met. That's not the kind of talk you hear without laugh, but she'd just say it, bland, straight. She said she liked the fact I didn't get snarled up on words, even though she's a bit of a semantic warrior herself.

I met him second time and he's settled on the subjects between us. He opened with what I wouldn't or would do for the sake of drama, how I saw performance and all this. I can bullshit with the rest of them, but I see performance as the stuff which pays the bills. I didn't say so. I told him this play I made up about the snuff movies: 'A guy wants to get into the movies badly and can't make it, so he decides to kill himself and he tells his flatmate. In Islington. The flatmate is an actor and dissuades the guy from killing himself. He says hang on a few days. The flatmate spends a few days writing a play in which a guy shoots himself in the end and tells his friend that he doesn't have to bother about no Equity ticket, he'll turn him into an actor overnight.

'They'll borrow money and put the play on at a West End theatre which they'll buy. Then he can shoot himself on the first night and it'll be a sensation. The play won't close it'll go on forever. The world press will report the first snuff theatre and tourists will flock. The guy says he'll do it, only for the sake of his flatmate's success. The injuries he's sustained in life leave him only death as an option. He gets into rehearsals, they convince a finance man from the City to back it and get the money. The guy fucks up. He begins to like the rehearsals. Acting out his own life makes the idea of death go away, even though he repeats it in every line of the play. Then he can't kill himself. He likes acting too much. He ruins his flatmate and the City gent. Doesn't do it. Shouts for the ketchup on the final night in the final scene. OK?'

David Stream didn't even smile, boss, he just tells me I'm hired, can I come to rehearsal rooms next day and get the script on which we shall work together. He put his hand on my shoulder as he showed me to the door.

He remembered the story though, because he went and told the same story to Sara. I don't now how she got on the scene, but he asked me to repeat the story for her and she crosses her legs in her tight skirt and listens. Whenever I check reporters, I start showing off. Cool, I'm an actor, but still I feel self-conscious when an aunty on a visit turns her instamatic on me.

'You've just been given the biggest part in the world, Mr Rahman, don't tell me you're stage-shy,' she says.

'Stage is all right,' I said. 'It's you. You know Stirling Moss, he said once in interview he finds it difficult to drive down Hyde Park Corner. It's like that.'

No impression. She was busy, you know, writing stuff. David told me that she was packing it in and doing things for 'our' production.

There's copies of letters, typed, inserted in the diary. Some to the man Robin, editor of some page or section or some deal in the *New Citizen*, the flash new newspaper.

*

Yesterday, even as I discover these letters from Sara, I call Robin. Me and my business partner want to place a message in the classified ads.

Simple message which I dream up myself: 'Urban Turban, New Indian Cuisine . . .' Just a message to someone we know. His advertisement man refuses the ad. I get back to Robin and tell him I'm a friend of Sara Fraser Stuart. I don't give him the name but tell him I tried to place an ad and it was refused for mysterious reasons.

He says he'll get the file. He calls me back.

'They are not mysterious reasons,' he says. 'You didn't tell me your name, caller, but the police have asked us to be on the lookout for advertisements for Indian restaurants and check if they are genuine. No such restaurant as you wish to advertise exists.'

'So what? I'm paying the money for the ad.'

'There's a law against that sort of thing in this country, caller.'

'What country, mate. Don't give me that "this country" shit. I'm fucking British.'

'That may be, sir, but we can refuse your ad if we think your product is not as advertised. And you say you are a friend of Sara's? What's your name?'

'Never mind my name, Robin, I've got letters from you to her and back, see?'

'If blackmail is what you're after you're barking up the wrong tree.'

I didn't want it so bad. We just had to get the message across. I'd find a real restaurant that wanted a free ad and place it in the flipping *Guardian* if this lil punk was playing hard feh ketch. 'Barking up his mango tree', my black arse! I just made growling sounds and said 'Woof! Woof!' and call off.

Sara messed him about herself, poor guy.

Dear Robin,

Here's the Stream piece. It's not in the restrained style. He's big and the ideas began to flow from notes. I went in more sarky than I came out.

Nothing phoney about him at all.

He's not riding on the reputation of some good and some indifferent productions, he's moving with the times as no one we know is, not here. Quite unlike your Czech adventurers with sixties drama ideas and bizarre design who want to bounce their

32

way from London to New York. Anyway. He's doing auditions and I'm going to report them. Make way. Three pieces in all.

Sara.
Lots of love. xx.

Sara,

Balls to Stream and his casting couch. It's a day late but get the bloody interview with Mia Dupleix. The *Guardian* has already been there. If we don't run it, I can see you leading the fucking brigade of feminists and black doom watchers into my office to complain that we don't give due care and attention to black females. I skimmed the book, and you've read it, no doubt, with stifling perspicacity. By 9am or anytime at night.

Love to you too,
Robin

I check the Mia Dupleix piece in the paper. At the time, like, I thought she was serious even though the article rebound on her arse. From the colour supplement: A bit of a black expert, and a consultant on Channel 4 kinda pop programmes about reggae and soul and crap, you know, telly trying to keep abreast or on the tit, more like.

KNOCKING THE HUSTLE

Mia Dupleix carries the languor of New Orleans with her. She says it was a lazy town. Compares it to Atlanta where everybody, but everybody, is black. The complaint mechanism breaks down.

'I'd love to take an English liberal back to Atlanta with me, meet Andy Young, drink just the right amount of Dewars and a little white wine. And we'd tell them what exactly Civil Rights did. I remember marching, right up there with Andy and Jesse and, God bless him, Martin, and what it's done is given over the whole structure to blacks, chief of police, mayor and dog-catcher and it hasn't made that much of a difference.' And 'that much' is Georgian for 'nothing'.

She's relaxed and doesn't smile. She lets me speak. I rattle on for six minutes about what I'd found in the novel and the eyes say nothing. It's not a poker game, it's just the black watching the white reporter. My constant fear when interviewing blacks. I gaze at the eyes as one does at a fruit machine. Trumps. Three Aces or

33

whatever the vogue is. The import of my question is why this story?

Her first book was feministic – lesbians, trashing Freud as a white explainer, the deep south and a wealth of stories. This one turns to the relationship between a black male singer and his father. Why?

She's wearing a skirt and a blouse that exposes her midriff, as Indian women expose theirs in a saree. The central heating is pretty good at the Mayfair but her hands go to the midriff, the teeniest sign of her discomfiture too. My instinct is to pounce on it. Say, 'Lady you're as jittery with the British newspaper scene as I am with the black New York literary one, n'est ce pas?'

But the instinct passes. I've thrown the bait. Yes, it's what she wants to talk about.

'I loved Jimmy,' she says and words to that effect which don't merit quote marks and I didn't have a tape-recorder. She means James Baldwin. 'He was the only living daylight who could have written that story. So I thought I owed it to him and I took it on.'

He told her about it (while he was alive, the accusations of necromancy seem false).

'I'd just read Jimmy's essay on Richard Wright. Have you read it?'

I admit I haven't.

'Jimmy says something fine and instrumental there. He meets a black writer in Paris in the days when there were only two of them and they circle each other at the grand cocktail party that is the white literary establishment, Hemingway and Gertrude Stein and all that shit. Like buzzards round a carcass, wondering what the carcass got in it, what it tastes like. Two blacks, Jimmy calls them 'negroes', each one wondering whether the other's for real, whether he has any real talent or he's just invited because he's kissing ass.

'You see, one black can knock another's hustle, tell the family secrets. So you didn't find in those days two black gentlemen in the same literary circle. It was like you got your negro and I got mine and never the twain did meet because when they met, the test of authenticity, of knocking the hustle, began. Tell me ain't it like that in Britain.'

I said it was a bit like that, but blacks stretched to all colours here – we had an Asian population too, different guests, same cocktail party.

So why the novel? Wasn't it based on Marvin Gaye? 'Was that a forbidden question?'

'No, that's obvious. It was Jimmy's book, but I wrote it. See, we don't fight that way no more. There are a lot of us now and we get cast on the circuit. Here I am sitting on my own roller-coaster talking to you, England, France, it's published simultaneously in seven countries, and millions of people know the man who sang 'I Heard It Through the Grapevine' and 'Sexual Healing'. Marvin – I never met him, by the way, or his pa – became a guru of sex and mood and he was getting into all that bullshit about T. S. Eliot dictating his songs from beyond the grave and all that but he was using the medium of blues, they call it soul, to do the thing, bring the emotions about and he was using stuff. That's the story. Black boy gets cast on a storm. I understand those black boys, the ones who want to sing and the ones who want to quote T. S. Eliot, and they're different, not the same man, except they coalesced in Marvin. And that gets somebody riled and his pa shoots him.

'I took a plane to Paris that night on a promotion tour – French edition, 48,000 copies sold in advance – and met Jimmy and we talked. OK, he ghosted the book, no offence intended.'

The novel doesn't explain why a father should shoot his famous son. Mia Dupleix recreates the action with all the restraint of a drum majorette. Inevitably there's a white girl in the story, the bone of contention. I asked Mia. Sensation, or was it true?

'Fiction,' she says, slyly, 'not fucktion! But you can't stroll on Robinson's island without kicking a coconut.'

Yeah, she's real.

Sara Fraser Stuart

Sara,
    The accompanying writ explains itself. Get into a taxi and get here. Take your phone off the answer mode.

Robin

Robin,
    Didn't I invent a good word? – free to you – 'fucktion'.

Love
Sara F.S.

Apology

On March 20th we ran the report of an interview with Mia Dupleix by Sara Fraser Stuart. We herewith acknowledge that the interview as it appeared in our columns was entirely fictitious and that in fact no interview ever took place between Miss Dupleix and Sara Fraser Stuart. We unreservedly apologise and withdraw any allegation contained in that piece, in token of which we have agreed with Ms Dupleix's lawyers on a sum to be paid to charity. We publish a genuine interview conducted by our new arts feature writer Kate Somerset with Ms Dupleix on p. 23. A review of Mia Dupleix's novel *The Wound* appears on p. 26.

Sara,
    Why?

R———

Robin, dearest,
        We hereby unreservedly . . .
Do you want the truth?
Seven reasons:
   1) Since you got the Cit job you haven't pulled off a single org with me. You who were once called Priapus at University.
   2) So many frauds about and I feel Ms Dupleix is one big one.
   3) Our readers are bullshitters.
   4) Mischief.
   5) Ms Dupleix's (white) literary agent kept putting me off saying she was asleep.
   6) I really want to talk to Baldwin but he's dead and to Marvin Gaye, but he's dead and exploited in death.
   7) It's all true anyway.
Believe what you will, I await your call, invitation to a beheading, anything but this deathly silence! Eeeeeeeaaaaaaaah!

Sarushka

PS   Can't I write again after a decent interval?

Sara,
    Decent interval? Sure. I suggest ninety-nine years.

Robin

Robin, baby, baby,
        This is not to say fuck you, but another little

weekly, even more important than diddums, wants little Sassa to come to tea and play. I was even offered a party bag to take home after the inevitable musical beds and pass the gossip parcel. Is Roby-Doby redbreast very hurt now? Shall Sara come back and share her tweeties with him?

Kissy kissy xx.

Sassa

Dear Ms Fraser Stuart,

Sara is NOT, repeat NOT, to try and speak to Robin. She is bad company.

Robin's good fairy

Robbo,

If it's goodbye, then parting is such sweet sorrow and surely you're not so locked into the third floor's bullying that you can't meet me for a drink. *A bas les* fucking lawyers and newspaper proprietors. Did you read Peter's piece on the limits of fabrication in the *Spectator*?

S.F.S.

Sara,

No drink. I think what you did was contemptible and a betrayal of trust. Of all people! You could have said you wanted to write a thought piece on the novel or, for God's sake, on bloody Dupleix – I hate her – but no . . . what is it about this Stream? A fatal fascination perhaps. Rumour has it you've accepted a job with him as amanuensis. True?

As for Peter's piece in the *Spectator*, you did perhaps notice that it wasn't a defence of fabrication. Every other commentator in the field took you apart. I must say I don't read the National Front's publication. Perhaps you did better there.

I don't care for whom you write. I suppose I'll read the column.

Love, but don't come near me.

Robin

I remember when the whole Mia Dupleix thing come out. This woman Mia, a fat American black woman, turn up on telly and put one set of cuss on our Sara. It was only me and Sara and David watched it, but the woman called Sara everything she could without causing a major incident between Scotland and the United States. David laugh, boy. He laugh because he want to be the real representative of the Third World, not all this angry shit from Baldwin and Mia Dupleix.

'You're right,' he say to Sara, 'the woman poses.'

See, at the time I think Sara is a feisty white chick. I had some loyalty and the scandal became big news. Sara lie on a black writer there. Immediately I watch as David appoints her to write the history of our production and keep notes and tell the truth and so on. Boy, I hold my head! Here's a woman who lie and cheat, and now she's chosen for her truthfulness? She can tell the truth? Columbus did discover America after all?

Time passes, Jah. I love Sara. Sister, good luck, righteous sister. Check the diary. Sharp like a pirate cutlass.

Oct 10th

Spilt milk in my little diary has always been worth a tear. Sara darling, you have found the seriousness they, the Saturday rags, the editors in their sad suites denied you. A curse on Fleet Street. They didn't actually ask me to write and Robin would have known of any offers. A curse on the intimacy of Fleet Street!

David's first assignment for me, as amanuensis is to attend a dinner party at some Asian politico's home to which Ali, the man he's already chosen, has enticed him. One meets again Jamil Jamal, the playwright with some girl friend who is all shaven sides and shorts (in publishing, a woman of little sense). Ali comes with his wife Maureen who looks very uncomfortable in this set and tells me she's only here because Ali thought it would be a disaster if Mr Stream thought that he was a conventional actor and didn't have a steady relationship (this over the game pie which Mrs Politico has contrived).

Mrs Politico, offended by any intimation that her hub isn't centre point itself, tall and erect and troublesome; Ms Jam of the moment believing, and what's more saying, that Mr Jam, the Asian playwright, is better than George Bernard Shaw (she got the first name right, though she was just the sort who'd call him John Bernard etc). David smiles at everything. He is amazed that he's there, but something about doing the Indian project in London has softened him. Or so it seems from a few days acquaintance. David politely asks Jamil Jamal for Asian casting tips.

38

'I enjoyed *Tony and Cleo* so much,' he says. By which Jam knows he hated every second of it.

Jam will no doubt write his meeting with D. Stream up in some magazine and say how scatching D. Stream was of the real creations of Pakistanis, viz. Jam Inc. supported by chorus of Ms temp-Jam. (Maureen confesses in the loo of the game pie house that white women who have this particular hypnotised adoration for their black/brown spouses – spice??? – are molto contemptible. So fawning, so sick. Do I protest too much, am I becoming a groupie to an Indian idea? I deny it to the last syllable!)

*   *   *

We casting seriously now, but I never see nothing like it. OK I'm hired, and then there's Sara buzzin about all day on the phone and sometimes going off by aeroplane, man, and coming back a day later with someone. Japanese, Chinese, Red Indians, Eskimos, all sorts, boy. Like David want to make a kinda human Noah's Ark.

Tell you the truth I get bored because the auditions I have to sit in on, it's just David and he asks them to tell stories. The Japanese can hardly speak English. I drink a lot of Special Brew. It gets so I can't sit on the raas claat bench without one. It's like three corners down to the nearest offy but I bring in supplies. Soon David notice and he get vexed. He knocks a can out of my hand.

I get vexed. I never been treated so on a production. Just waiting. David hasn't even set himself no deadline and can't say when it is we are going to slide into rehearsal. Slackness. But some good stories.

David get hold of Claude the frenchy and tells me to take him away and listen to the stories he tells and then correct the accent. Not the English, just the accent.

'I tell you ze sto-wy of ze man K.'

So it go on.

'Ze sto-wy of ze man K is quite good. You zee zere waz zis man whom Claude knew who has gone to the Himalayas and zat was why Claude applied to come with David on ze great quest of ze *Ramayana*.

'Zis guy is ze expert in Soviet Union politics in France and wites for ze, how you call it, ze papers, ze soshyalees papers. Is strenj how all zem midel-Europe characters are called K. Like Kafka, a Kafka story. But now yes, he departs for ze Himalayas and become a Buddhist monk. Zere was a reason. He lived in France since the war zo he was

39

from Poland and he brought up his daughter to be twenty-two years old. Byoooteefool geirl. She catch cancer and is dying. He write about it in the papers. Everybody reads zis thing, knows his sorrow. Zen one day in hospital she asks him to tell her ze truth. She has seen something in his eyes. The lie it remains like, how you say in ze bible? – a bote? – a mote? Yes, he says he understands what she wants. He will go for a walk and come back. So must he commit suicide when he goes for zis walk because what he has to tell her is bad. He comes back to the hospital and very how you say it? – disturbed. His secret is he has no right to be alive. He and his uncle and aunt and everyone collaborated with the Nazis. Zey were Jewish and his uncle was an official of the community and the synagogue. The Nazis tortured him and ze whole family gave away secrets, other people's hiding pless. Ze money from ze commune, everyting zey gave. When the war was to finish the Russians came and zey knew that zis family was collaborators so zey took them away and kept zem separately for kvestioning. And ze boy begin to sing, like zey say in gangster movies. Zey will set him free if he condemns the uncle as a collaborator. So when he confesses and accuses his uncle zen ze bastards bring zem face to face. Here is proof, your own nephew has confessed. Good sto-wy, eh?'

But boy, it made me think we are going to India with a load of goons.

'Oh ze gel? Well, she died a few days later having found out zis useless truth.'

We don't start rehearsal yet. The cast ain't complete. We have plenty people, all doing language work. Stories, boy, I get so sick of stories.

Every day I try and ketch David to ask him when we moving into performance etc. But he's never on him own.

I watching, boss, like a corbo on the beach, a buzzard circulatin for the dead in a desert of communication (take that! Jazzbo!) thirsting for a word from the man.

Then after rehearsal he call me suddenly for a drink. I say to David over a drink – he don't drink but he hands out the best. I say, why you give this play to people who, well, can't, you know, pronounce the things? Friends of mine ring up and say why not get David to get some British actors in, after all it's a union matter also. I don't mean no disrespect to Japanese Nō plays, but surely this is a yes play. I'm getting to grips with it. David doesn't want to know anything. Is like he genuinely doesn't think, after all his experience with actors, of the accent angle. Is like I tell him the sky is blue or something, a 'so what?' situation.

Sara hangs around the outfit. She fit and tense like a fiddle.

'Why don't you mek me a star, Sara. Do an interview and write it in the *New Citizen* like your Mia Dupleix thing.'

She laugh but she say I should tell her anyway. Tell her what? Well, how I started in this trade.

I tell her I walked off a bus. I was bus conductor. I got a job on the transport because no one else would have me and my father's friend, who struck first and gave advice later, took me one day to the garage and said linc the boy up. I was conducting this bus, which means not only collecting fares and keeping a cheery face on the day, it means riding shot-gun in badlands of London. Hampstead and Clerkenwell, Camden and Putney, Highgate, Primrose and Ludgate . . . a sort of bus-conductor's lament by T.S. But this day I was on Oxford Street, which is crowded as hell and some guy calls me a nigger. I'm not standing for that so I said to the whole bus this bus ain't moving till the rider here apologises. He wants a twenty pence ticket and he don't want to pay for it and he turns it into a constitutional race question. I call upon the whole bus. I pull three bells so the driver would know to come in case of trouble and I didn't want to proceed to Shepherds Bush at all. The guy say he's not paying and he's not apologising and so I tell the driver the bus ain't going nowhere and some other passengers begin squabbling with him and I'm fed up, he's calling me a nigger all the time so I throw my ticket case and belt down and my jacket and I walk off. Next day I go down the depot for my shift and supervisor says, 'You left a bus in the middle of Oxford Street yesterday, thereby immobilising the service and the route and half of London's traffic.'

I say, 'Yeah, the guy call me nigger.'

'That's bad but, you are black, aren't you?'

'Sure.'

'You ought to adjust the punishment to the offence. You should have turned him off the bus.'

'He was the size of a gorilla.'

'You should have called for assistance.'

'Listen, man, I been calling for assistance for the past three hundred years. Nobody come.' I was allowed to carry on with my shift.

'So how does that explain why you became an actor?'

'Well, it wasn't so much the pull of the stage, it was the push of the bus.'

*

Of course Sara never print that story. I check very close in the cuttings, every cutting, and she wouldn't leave no report she had done to posterity and chance, she would collect it, but it warn't there.

The last person to join the case was the girl herself – Anjali. Import straight from Paris in grand Stream stylee. She was working boss on a film for Hollywood, dig it, and couldn't get no release and Mr Stream had messed us all about with accent work and shit because the great actress was delayed.

The feelings weren't so hot for the girl in the camp, if you ketch my meaning. Stream didn't want to tell our agents that we were on half pay because the star hadn't joined and when she was on full pay everybody would ketch equal bread.

Mus one say any more. Anjali plays Sita. Opposite me, man. And when I'm introduced, no wages and conditions come in my head, boss. David select her from two million actresses and you know, man, he done right.

In Ullah's restaurant there's one song on the tape:

Tell me how the moon does come out in the daytime.
Watch how she shifts the end of her saree from her face!

OK that don't sound too hard, in fact it sound saaft in English, but with the sounds it's really hard.

But actions speak louder than looks, boss, and the first thing old Anj does is speak to David about S. Patel.

Now S. is a sparky lickle actor. I work with him on several TV things and he's cool and friendly, you know; sitting in a rooming house in some town on TV location, he'd pull a spliff with a man. None of this religious Asian nonsense. And I always respec a man who comes on time even if he's been boogeying in the clubs, because I tell you S. likes a bit of woman. He don't care which woman, like he's conducting research into their parts. Shameless. He goes to clubs, smokes ganja, like any black boy, takes out three girls at the same time. He was in some big time BBC soap, man, and the producers them victimise my boy. He get thrown out because they asked him to do heavy breathing down the phone and the boy say he refuse.

He have a nice lickle line for the papers: 'Until I came to this series I used to go and cheer for the cowboys, now the way they treat me I realise we are the Indians.'

Every low grade and high grade newspaper printed this line and S. Patel became famous as the man who got slung out of stardom for his principles. (Actually he stole the line from James Baldwin, but no one ketch him out.)

I fell for it too, boss, until I met this director and he said S. Patel had twenty-three takes at heavy breathing. He didn't sound like a sex maniac, he sound like he copped some heavy asthma. So they wrote him out of the series. His agent even phone up and say he'll take breathing lessons and do it right if they'll hold on to him.

No deal. There you go, you see? He's a natural sexual pervert, but can't pull it off on camera.

Anjali tells David, 'The Gujerati accent is so strong, you won't be able to do anything about it. He says ko-fee instead of coffee and he calls it "pope" music.'

I can't suss at first why she wants to put him down. Later I catch on. Is a class thing with Asians, like mongoose and snake – they have to go for each other.

David laughs and S. Patel becomes a spear bearer. Power. She is close to Indian accents and don't say nothing about the Japanese and the French and the Koreans and God knows who we have working on this production. But she homes in on S.

Now S. tells me that that's because she is connected, boss. She is the daughter of somebody very big in India. Sort of girl who latches on to guys like David Stream and suck the blood of guys with way back backayard, home-game accents, victimises the low born. Nice one, S. Patel.

I could see she was what he says she was. But she was beautiful. Smart.

I wanted her for her brains, body, the lot. She was it.

The day she come was the day rehearsal begin in earnest. As soon as David want me to start on the big game my mind was another snakes and ladders.

Ali, Ali, I tried to say to myself, where did it all go wrong, boss? Desperation reach me, boy. Something rotten as them cockney say, something chronic and lasting.

And it start nagging at my heel, snapping like a discontented hungry dog. Or maybe, just to pull style, like a toothache, it wouldn't go, even when I slept and all I could think was, bwoy Ali, you have it bad, you need a dentist.

The whole scene with me is I can only talk to *women* about women. Maybe it's jus competition – I guess because you don't want to tell your best friend even that you want it something chronic, because man thinks, this boy is a pussy freak and to start protest that it's love you want and not reggae in the jeggae, well, it sound saaft.

I didn't know at the time Sara thought anything of the girl Anjali at all. I thought, yeah, cool, they work in the thing together, maybe Sara is a bit jealous that David love Anjali a bit and take her advice and thing, and Sara just takes notes and ain't really in the runnings, but I never realise till now, till I pick up the diaries that Sara all through was taking no hostages, man. She have the kinda mind that feeds off judgement. Check it:

Sept 20th

The new girl is what Toad of Toad Hall would call 'all the rage'. David has known her in some *demi-monde* of theatre in Paris. It's not the tooth of envy that's sharp, it's her vocal chords. The truth about her is modest, though she doesn't think so herself. She has been with the most respected feminist theatre of Paris, with another one of these directors who never gives interviews but is always in the papers and on the arts shows on the box. If she was a Deutscher she would be called Frau Dulent.

The episode of S. Patel is over, without pain to all concerned except yours truly up whose nostril it was forced. Anjali breezes in to David in mid-rehearsal. She's the only one who can stop the clock. She has an aristocratic assumption. I am told her father is a corrupt Indian politician and a businessman. He used to run protection rackets amongst the peasantry, or maybe that was her grandfather. But one of them was a judge in some far flung territory of the Indian empire, elevated by the Brits and given a manor to which the rest were born – born subject, that is. So what's new. Bolingbroke was a bandit according to le bard.

She complains to David that she can't hack it. Patel was to go through Sanskrit translations with her but she 'can't understand his English'. Mind you he speaks perfect English. The poor boy was brought up in Kenya and blundered into acting through the enthusiasm of some BBC gang that was looking for an Indian boy and a sixth form drama teacher pushed him forward and gave him ideas above his station. He was, by family trad and lore, supposed to be married and join his uncles in the great culture of confection-

44

ery and sub-postofficing, but he got a taste for being on BBC screens and at first nobody noticed that he had a heavy Kenyan Asian Gujerati accent.

And here, as the schoolbell said to the old form, class will out. Nationality is nothing and the order of the house is to ignore it and behave with no attention to even suspected bigotry. But then class is beyond bigotry. With Anjali, the Indian caste system, I presume, dressed in *bon chic*, pronounces over gulfs of time and space.

David's house rule, imposed in subtle ways by the maestro, is to ignore nationalities and their mention. Anjali looks at people with an assessing contempt. She's used to having servants though I'm as sure as Lord Curzon was of the white persons' burden that S. Patel's ilk were not amongst them. From what Ali tells me, S. has wealthy connections in India, could buy out Anjali's aristocratic lot six times over. I watch carefully one dinner time.

David throws us together for eat-and-be-dramatically-pretentious seminars. Anj holds forth on the racism of the French and how it compares in brutality with the British version which is more subtle – they shoot Arabs in France and the police are never held accountable. All this stuff she sold to the French press when she was doing journalism between bouts of classical dance and acting.

You name it, she's done it, fish in pond style, one Indian fish, large Parisian pond. Everyone knows Anjali. She goes from translator's conference to cultural adviser's forum. Miss Big Deal herself. No penetration into the French bourgeoisie. (God, two weeks away and I'm a-changing muh prose style, takin on the shenanigans of Ms Mia Dupleix. What's the difference between the bourgeois and the bourgeoisie. One sounds more entrenched, with a whole 'ie'.) Clothes – Indian for evenings, jeans and smart shirts for the set. Long black hair, which she wears loose constantly, and slim, sort of non-child-bearing hips. Yes, very beautiful. Yes, I'm post-feminist jealous, just for my own record. But the disdain of the lips, even though the eyes laugh and try to assure you what a good sport she is – the message of the lips is: 'S. Patels of the world, know thy place and come to me only when I'm playing multi-cultural and have to hide the almost South African crassness of my assumptions.' The mystery is she likes Ali.

As chronicler I already begin to interfere. A young man, very clever he was, explained to me once that it was called Heisenberg's uncertainty principle, this propensity of the observer to displace the observed. But I can't stop myself. No such thing as objectivity etc.

I don't dislike A, but early days yet.

Some may judge me foolish to throw up the nine to five on the Street of Shame and take up with David, but truth to tell there was the calculation that a book may come from the bowels of the experience.

De F rang again to say he'd like to publish my essays if I could write them up as adventures in the arts journo trade and gossip. But replied I that I was off to Inja's sunny clime with Streamo and a full account of Gunga Din would be rendered. Smashing idea, he says, just the book, he thinks but doesn't say, that a bitch like you should do. But prospects of this stuff being leavened into a book aside, a closeness to Streamo and the great great idea of international culture, whatever one stuffs that pancake with, was too much to resist. And one doesn't retire from being a hackette. All of life is a long c.v. Silly Sara, I did not reckon with Anj. She comes. The red rose cries she is here she is here, and the white rose weeps she is late, the larkspur listens, I hear, I hear and the Lily whispers I wait. Daddy used to say some such thing in the days when he was hot to trot with his toy girl. Mamma said Tennyson was for the feeble-minded and bits of Tennyson were nothing more than Mills and Boon and she couldn't understand a man conceiving such passions, especially Daddy. She is coming my life my fate. There has fallen a splendid tear from the passion flower at the gate. I thought 'gate' spoilt it but I couldn't say that to Mamma. She discovered it in a note to Daddy's Pinocchio, the little lying girl with a long nose.

I never thought I'd be learning no principles of yoga, boss. David want to teach me real breathing and real archery and two guys, masters, gurus, come and do the thing. Jah only know where him get this money from. It come.

Maureen got a man. I go back there and Martha tell me, 'Daddy, Mummy has a boyfriend.'

I never cut up nothing or say nothing or dig nothing at all. When the time right to spring, I jump. 'Martha tell me you have a man.'

'What man? I see plenty of men.'

'Me know that, but what about this one who lives in my house here. Eats my food.'

'Listen, Boot Polish,' she say. 'You paid me twenty pounds for

Martha and that was four weeks ago. I buy about sixty pounds worth of groceries every week and it goes. Don't ask me where it goes . . .'

'Sainsbury champagne, I seen it,' I said, 'and then a few quid for ganja.'

'Not your money.'

She gets rage. She gets up and go to the kitchen and pull out a chopper. I'm not scared of Maureen. She can't and never will do me nothing. She gets it and says OK, I'll get your daughter's share, you can take it away. She opens the fridge and cuts every tomato in a piece and chips off a shaving from each potato and from the pack of butter and begins to saw into the salt carton and cuts it in two and then as I watch she takes the tomato ketchup out of the cupboard and pours a bit into an empty jar and then some Fairy Liquid and then some cooking oil and then a spoonful from each can of spices and says, 'You can take your share, take your lousy twenty pounds worth and go fuck yourself with it. Martha doesn't need it and neither do I and don't come asking who any man is here.' Just as she don't hit me I don't hit her, but I want to make her feel ashamed of her temper so I chuck the whole lot into a plastic bag, bits of potato, the jar with the mush, everything she's destroyed. Then I ask her for the chopper.

'What for?'

'I'm going to make my own assessment of percentages here, I want to take the record player twenty per cent and the washing machine and the doorstep. I'm going to chop them all up.'

Then she says let's be sensible and she puts the chopper up.

'I can have what relationships I want.' She's calmed down.

'You know where you learnt it from?' I ask.

'Learnt nothing.'

'Something. This get violent first and talk sweet later,' I says. 'You learnt it from me. So let's stop the games. Now what?'

'Now you kiss Martha goodnight and fuck off.'

So I did. The sunlight on the garden hardens and grows cold. Boss, when all is told we cannot beg for pardon.

We see pages of the script but not the whole thing. Sara catch sight of the whole thing and David now wants us to find out, construct the play in our head as we pick up this discipline and move to the next.

Now David have some trouble explaining these names to us. He says in scholarship, Raam isn't Ram, it's been written by English book writers as Rama. And the Laxmana, but that's just a way of dealing

47

with the Sanskrit, actually the masses in India, they say Ram and Laxman, so when we reading books about it (actors read books? make me laugh, boss) we just drop the 'a' in our minds and read Raam.

So I say, 'Well, "Sita" is then "Sit".'

Anjali begins to laugh and puts her hand in front of her mouth. She does that because David is watching and she wants to play little girl in front of him, like a teacher and pupil in the class thing. I seen her laugh otherwise, a big laugh with all the teeth even, but if you look close, little gaps in the front ones to add to the charm.

So David say, 'No, it's Sita. You've got to leave that one alone. That's a real "a".'

'But Ravana, that's not another one.'

'No, quite right, that's Ravan.'

She corrects him, tosses her tongue for the final 'n'.

He gets it. Makes us all say it, opening his mouth and indicating how the tongue moves.

Rehearsals get heavy. Stream moves us like a pharaoh building his raas claat tomb. Now me know what them Israelite felt like, the sufferers. Not like Irish maan who build up Britain nowadays – quick dash from the Guinness between breeze blocks. No sir, the Israelites were under the lash. Stream is a master of slavery. Sara gives us the info. We rehearse for five weeks more, till the beginning of November. Then a two-week run in an open space that David want to take us to in his own sweet time, somewhere in London, sure, just to run the play in. Then we launch in India. When we done twelve weeks in them places, we rest and wait for the climate be cool in the US of A and maybe Canada and maybe any other place with English or where they would have the great Stream production.

OK, nice one, I go along with all them prospects and I gossip with the rest about their families and why they have feh go and make this arrangement and that. I have no arrangement. I sleeping on people's floors anyway – Bawdy, the Black Star Theatre director and my ole generalissimo, or Bev, the actress who played Cleo. No intimate thing. I had a lickle thing with her once, but not while this rehearsal was on. Anjali live in some remote place where she come and go by taxi. And all the time Sara is checking us. I can't improve on what she say.

If Jam, in the book him wan write say different, well, remember it ain't me making no protest. This is a true thing, written maybe one day by Sara. She didn't see everything, but bwoy, she see enough:

'All art is allegory', pronounces the maestro. These are the mysteries of working for David. I choose not to apply his apothegms to trivial occurrences like those on stage. I'm much more interested in life and she seems to be being lived to the full around here.

Instancing Ali. He gives off the steam of macho, devil may care and a false intensity and concentration when he's listening to David as he is eight hours a day now. He lets it slip. Some black people have that ability of supreme confidence and then just a touch which unconsciously proclaims they don't feel all that secure or that superior at all.

It clicked, I can't have been far wrong. I saw him in the bar after rehearsals. The place is haunted. Anjali turns up and goes straight to Ali who offers her a drink. He's in a black T-shirt and still sweating from rehearsals and wipes it away with a big white handkerchief and then carefully puts the handkerchief into his jeans pocket. Now he's got a blazer on top, checked. So who breezes in, not to be far from the ethnic action, but Mr Jamil Jamal, pimp of the simple idea, playwright and playboy of the Western world. He surveys the scene. Walks up to Anjali and says, 'You must be Anjali,' and she turns and is flattered. He's wearing a black hat, pushed back and a waistcoat and trousers turning half-way up his calves.

Ali doesn't appreciate the interruption.

'It's stopped raining outside.'

The playwright doesn't think this is funny and Ali's eyes trace the carefully careless turn-ups and long socks pulled down to the ankle.

'I'll have to ask David's permission,' Anjali says because he's said that some friends of his in the press would love to do an interview with her. She says 'excuse me' to Ali, leaves the drink he's bought her on the bar and goes off with JJ. The said playwright seats her at a table and comes to the bar. Ali watches him buying a lager and a gin and lime. He doesn't say she's already got a gin and lime and would she like it brought over.

I go up to the bar and drink the gin and lime without a word to Ali.

'You're a decent girl, Sara,' he says. 'It's hurting.'

I don't recall saying no 'hurting' but I can't say that something in my face didn't say it for me.

*

The worst thing an actor can do, boss, is to quit the stage. To walk off, to acknowledge defeat and say to all the world, 'You won't die if you don't see me.' That's the sin, boss. Forgetting lines, drying up, corpsing, it's all part of a career if not the best thing for it.

But if I don't have a line, in real life, it gives me bad feelings.

The first time I got to talk to Anjali, I mean talk to her like not about how wonderful David's discipline was and how spectacular to be given the opportunity and how marvellous the production's going to be and all this, I mean the first time it was personal, she says she speaks seven languages, four Indian and three non-Indian. Heavy. I just speak one, I say.

Then we move to where she born and how she came into the production and everything and she asks me the same and listens too damn carefully with her head cocked to one side and her eyebrows trying to be so attentive they nearly get 'x'ed. She's saying how she shared David's philosophy and how it had changed since he wrote his book even. I say to myself, Ali, she wan cruise on her smartness, jus blow some wind in her sail.

'The internationalist flavour of it, it'll just blow their minds, you know, it's never been done in bloody theatre, Eastern or Western. It's just so right. David says he got the idea in America because the one culture the US doesn't have represented is the Indian. There are Europeans, Africans, Japanese, Latins, Christians, Jews, Muslims, the whole melting pot with one great culture missing, the Masala.'

'What's that? Remember, only one language, and that six out of ten.'

She laughs. 'Spices, stuff you put in curries.'

'I love chicken tindaloo, man. Hotter the better. Killer tindaloo like Ullah makes.'

'You don't eat in these so-called Indian restaurants, do you?'

'Sure. We're finishing rehearsals and it come to seven o'clock and David's telling me to feel the loss as I recreate the emotion of exile, and I'm thinking "only two hours to go before that tindaloo".'

'There's no such thing, of course.'

Suddenly I was speaking to the headmistress. King, had I said the wrong thing.

'Just eat it because I'm hungry, real hungry, ma'am, and the Injuns done saved my life.'

She don't smile. She's wondering whether I was serious or not about not hanging on every word of Mahatma Stream.

50

There was a joke once which all the black actors knew – 'you seen the Asian cloakroom attendant? Nice guy, Mahatma Coat.' I wanted to tell her that joke but I knew it wouldn't go down too well.

Last night I got to thinking about it. I always thought Asian guys were soft. Sharp at some things, but soft when it came to chatting up or impressing a woman or anything. No style. Nice guys, but wear anything, nylon shirts and flares. Then just as I was finishing drama school they started get smart. Two gangs. One copied the white kids and one copied the black kids.

See, them Asian guys had to construct themselves from scratch. Zilch. Zero. No reggae, skank, no black power, just plenty rules – eat this, eat that, can't go here, can't marry this, can't fuck that – tradition and some get push into heavy education. Anjali fell for it. Boy, as true as the fact that I'm burning. The steam is coming out my head, but then I'm like a modern kettle, it switches itself off as soon as the steam starts to spout.

Maureen come and dump Martha on me. Says she'll give me the keys to her flat. Her flat! And I got to live there and take Martha to and from school and look after her for seven days because she's leaving the country. No explanation. Just the keys and says Martha will finish at quarter to four.

David lines up a guru for that afternoon. I am going to dance. I am going to wear leotards and learn the elements of Indian dance. This guru is coming all the way from Slough, so I can't mess about. And it's only me, we're getting individual sessions. I can't leave it.

Damn fool. I tell S. Patel, my last hope. He's not dancing having got sidelined. So I describe Martha to him, tell him how to get to the school and beg him to do it and bring her back here and give her a MacDonalds on the way if she's hungry and I'd pay him back at the end of the week. S. Patel is a man sent by God to mankind, he says 'no problem' and pushes.

One big relief. S. Patel comes back after three hours. No Martha. I'm balancing on a foot and the guru has a table and David's sitting on the bench with Sara. S. Patel interrupts. Nobody interrupts when David is watching anything, man, that's like loosing a fire extinguisher on the burning bush in front of Moses. Straight to me, 'They are not releasing her, Ali. They don't know who I am.'

'What seems to be the problem?' David asks.

'I have to go, my daughter, I'm sorry David.'

'The problem?'

'He asked me to fetch his daughter from school but I went to classroom and got her and told her who I was and her daddy sent me, but she says she doesn't go with strange men. So I called the teacher, and the whole lot turned up, two came with sticks and they called the headmistress who said I couldn't take her if she didn't know me and they'd phone her mum and they'd phone her dad and all sort of thing. So I come back. The ones with the stick were ready to beat me, guy. They might have called the police. I showed them my driving licence but it didn't convince them.'

'God, I'm sorry.'

'Well, I don't think you can go, Ali. We have rehearsals till eight. But I see the problem. The young one will be restored to you. Sara will sort it out.'

'They won't know her either.'

'How long have you lived in Britain?' David asks.

'See, if she goes, maybe you should take this ear-ring, Martha, my daughter, knows it.' That's what came into my head and I unscrewed the diamond stud in my left ear. Sara took it and smiled.

Well, OK, if they didn't surrender the girl, then she'd have to wait a few more hours, I could phone up the headmistress or something.

Later Anjali, who's watching the dancing and listening says, 'Ali, it was so cute, your little token of existence. Just like the story.'

'It's a real diamond,' I say. 'No messing, none of your European glass stuff.'

She let me buy her six gins the next day when I'd found a baby sitter for Martha.

David was right. Them never question Sara. Now suppose it was some kind of skank and S. Patel and Sara were in some kidnapping ring together. It's happened before. Just because she has a middle-class accent and is white and maybe one or two of the teachers carrying sticks knew her name from the papers, well, they let my daughter go with her. What kinda school is that, trusting strangers to take your children away. If I had time I'd go and shit the place down.

Living with Martha is no problem. God bless Maureen. To get into this technique, I needed the discipline of getting up at the same time each day and making a breakfast for Martha and reaching her to school before rehearsals. The only problem is I asked my cousin, a girl doing her studies to come and stay there seven days and deal with Martha in the evenings. This cousin studying drama at 'A' Level so she knows the score about David Stream and how I'm in the play and need the rehearsals and all this.

Of course I can't take any women back there, but then the only woman I want to take back anywhere, she's never going to come one way or the other.

To make it worse, Martha lets slip that her mum has gone to Africa with her boy friend who sells spare parts. Martha don't know what spare parts, but I've lived long enough, man. I want to ask Martha whether the guy is white or black but then I feel embarrassed. It's my own daughter.

Then she releases the info voluntarily. 'Daddy, his name is not really Slim, that's just what I call him. It's something else and even Mummy can't say all of it.'

So he's a Pakistani geezer.

'And he's got three cars.'

So he's a rich Pakistani geezer.

Maureen boy, gun-running in Africa. Got to laugh.

Akiro has marvellous concentration. I have to control every face muscle to match his exaggerations. Boy, the man short, like a real Bonzai actor, but him well rough, powerful. You look at his lips and he could contort them to make you think he's eating meat or that he's Valentino kissing a girl whom he don't really want.

Life in signs is what this play is about. Indian dance is sweet, man. The guru teach me to make waves with my fingers and when I begin to move them he says, 'No, no, no, no, no, no – not this spaghetti classical, your mind should control your movement, not your instinct. You are dancing when you *think* of the dance.'

Now there's more than thirty people on the production. The music is being written. The walls are thin and the musicians are banging away. They are going to be on stage.

Never met a thief like David, bwoy. He steal and confess he stole and then carry on enjoying the fruits of his theft. Lines, verses, music, movements, ideas. The man is a magpie.

'The difference between theatre and magic is that in magic the audience wants to catch the magician out, to find out how its done. With theatre they are begging to be conned. The magic of theatre is to get the audience in that state of mind.'

Cool.

Some days, my cousin can't deal with Martha so I take her with me to the workshops and like the baby brought to Solomon she get divided in half – not really, just her time. Sara and Anjali share her.

Anjali give her Indian beads. Martha says she want to be like Anjali. Even when Maureen returns she must come and play, Anjali insist.

'I can't pick her up. This fatherhood business is heavy. Slaving for a crust and having to mother the pickney meself.'

'We can get Sara to pick her up,' Anjali says.

'We can ask her,' I say. I love that 'we'. It ain occur to her that she's not entitled to ask Sara for nothing. The regality performs.

'You don't live with Martha's mother?'

'We split long time,' I say. 'She's got a next man. Indian, actually. Nice guy, stinking rich. International arms dealer.'

The desired effect is *a*) she knows I'm single, and *b*) it intrigues her arse to hear that I kinda get along with the boyfriend-in-law and that he's not some pretentious son-of-a-bitch who talks adventure and writes it – he *is* fucking adventure. Desired effect a flop.

'There are some dreadful regimes in Africa which turn against their own people. I hope he's not selling missiles and rockets and guns to police forces.'

'Probably is. Man who can deal with Maureen have to be immoral and bad.'

'That's so sick. About your former wife.'

'What wife? But you're right. I need healing.'

By now I don't care what I say to her. We're rehearsing six hours a day together and even though it's stylised, we're playing off against each other and I've got to know her and she must know me, even though none of us are the same kind of actor. David says there's something the same about actors the world over, 'I am seen, therefore I am.' He's taking the piss but I don't check what it is he means.

Then David says he's interrupting rehearsals for a crash course in Indian culture and thing. He wants to show us films. Sara has had to fix it. Not normal films but the Indian cinema stuff. Bullshit. Just to get the exaggerated gestures and tones and singing and thing that the Indian public are used to.

David's explanations even, man, heavy. The guy knows his shit.

From Sara diary, same thing about films, only she see it different:

Oct 30th

After four days of Indian films my head is spinning. Even David

54

can't have suspended judgement so far. It's mind-numbing kitsch, but it doesn't raise a smile from him and the translations, the subtitles are worse than 'the peasants are revolting' species of naffitude.

Their faces, my, my. I can see that Anjali hates this stuff but has the canniness to know that if she sits through them with David Stream, he'll let fall a few gems, perspectives, which she can then use in the drawing rooms of Delhi. She's grown up not despising Hindi films, but knowing they were good for the servants.

When David's blurb comes, it's, as always, good: 'It's kitsch, but it has a purpose in the psyche of the millions that watch it. The stories are all religious. Good triumphs over evil. There is a natural order to things. Sons and daughters love their father and do them respect. There's friendship and fifty-seven varieties of love. The hero is inevitably a simpleton, a peasant who carries the talisman of the natural order with him. He meets the hucksters, the traditional villains, the money-lender, the confidence trickster, the rich man corrupted by modern consumerism. He is pitted against them and he loses and then they cliffhanger his triumph over the forces of darkness in miraculous ways.

'You know where else we've seen something similar?' David looks around the faces. He may be a brilliant director but he's a transparent actor. His half-bald head gleams under the bulb of the preview theatre.

'In Shakespeare! Sixteenth-century Britain was also a society in transition from the peasantry to the rigours of the city, the corruption of it. Not all the plays, some of them. Lear, Othello, caught in the web of sophisticated malice, the primitive black adventurer and an enlightened man and great soldier. Only, Shakespeare realises that Othello has to die. Your Hindi movie doesn't yet. We've set out to do an epic that tells the story of Ram and Laxman and Sita and the forces of heaven and hell which are unleashed on the earth, only it's a heaven and hell we have to regain touch with. Is that enough for the day?'

The adoration on Anj's face. A magus to our podgy balding Jesus.

I've got that almost verbatim. We walk out of the preview theatre and Anjali sidles up to me. 'I'd never thought of these junk films that way. He really is the best director I've worked with.'

She hasn't worked with too many. But yes he is. Maybe it's different for her. She has said a thousand times that she grew up with the story of the *Ramayana* and she sees new things in it every day. I see it for the first time.

In one scene there is a charmed circle in which the two brothers leave Sita to protect her from the demon king Ravan. Enter Ravan. He has enticed her from the magic circle and he does it by taking on the guise of a mendicant and begs her, for pity, to give him water and she, eye to duty, to dharma, steps out and is abducted.

We each have our interpretation of the scene. David leaves us with the Indian film interpretation, the good and evil plot.

I feel there's more to it than that. I get the peculiar feeling that David is not thinking of an Indian audience at all. His little lecture on Hindi picture shows is the sort of self-convincing fraud that I begin to suspect him of being. (Mirror, mirror on the wall, you've started to tell the gnawing nagging truth after all!) Maybe that's unfair, maybe theatre is simplicities. No one would accuse Shakespeare or even Shaw of subtlety of thought – large canvas, good, bits of evil mixed in, the rich are bad the poor are virtuous, maximum points if you can do it the other way round . . . viz. make the poor not so good and the rich not so bad, get the critics drooling . . .

He's thinking out his own political principles: there's a girl, she's abducted, that makes her property. Bad! It's a man who's doing it – Boo! Another man saves her – Good! But then he's a man – not so good. She should have got away through her own endeavours – Hurray! Not fisticuffs, because that's emulating Rambo – Bad! Not diplomacy because that's playing a game invented by the likes of Machiavelli – Disgraceful. Something else, some form of escape that captures the romantic imagination. Can't think of it and neither can David and neither can Anjali, so we're stuck with the story as it is in the real *Ramayana* – Shame!

I go to see friends on my off day and some of them don't know shit about theatre and they don't care shit about Indian culture and some of them rude racist too. Then I feel fuck the *Ramayana* and fuck David Stream and fuck the method of doing things and running a bloody ten hour play in cuts and breaks with long intervals so the audience walk about and don't catch gangrene. One of the posse them ask me down in the Grove, 'Is this some Oscar scene you on.'

'No, it's not a film, it's a play.'

The guy don't know what a play is.

'You mean, I turn the telly on and you won't be there.'

'Right, Scoby, how you get so clever.'

And the rest of them, even down the little card playing den with rum feh drink and a piece of the prairie to smoke and talk flowing, they know what a play is and how acquainted I am with David Stream, they show some respect. One guy there goes with rich Americans from the Hilton when the agency calls him, he even knows Sara because he used to read her in the posh newspapers, because these rent dudes got to read the hot columns of the poshies to keep up with the news and make some conversation, drop names. (Escort business have a lot of reading in it, boss.) He says 'knock knock' and when you say 'who's there' he takes great pride in the expression 'Wilde!!!'

There is no play within a play. Man, I don't have to tell you the story of the fucking *Ramayana*. But check this, this is something I read in a book by some famous Indian author who has lent his time to write again about the *Ramayana*. I'm getting drawn into it.

> When Rama, Lakshmana, and Sita reached the Godavari river's bank, they were enchanted with their surroundings. Rama felt a great tenderness for his wife, who looked particularly lovely adorned with the ornaments given by . . .

This is the kind of garbage I have to read before we start rehearsing a scene. And then when David gets us to do the script it ain't nothing to do with the reading except that he wants me to feel this 'great tenderness' for Anjali which I'm not about to be faking boss.

This kid I know what starred in the *Tony and Cleo* play with me as Charmagne, she sends me a long protest letter to sign saying, 'Blossom darling, you the man now. David Stream. My, my. Well, we started this petition to go to the Arts Council about Caribbean cultural plays, because they refuse Norman a grant and they turned Donna down yesterday, and, man, it's becoming a refusal epidemic. We have to have a meeting to see what can be done. There's plenty of support. But maybe you busy, eh? With Hasian cultural ting. Love and prosperity. Daisy.'

Caribbean cultural plays. What the fuck is that? Cricket, Calypso, Reggae, slavery, KFC (Kentucky Fried Chicken)? Give us a break.

*　　*　　*

The thing coming together like a jigsaw and only D.S. have all the pieces. We now make up the whole cast, extras and all, and on a whim David makes us change positions, keep everyone on the hop like.

Today you the lead maybe and next day you get your role slashed and move into some twenty-line job.

One day after rehearsal:

'Ali, my dear, I'd like to try Siegfried in some stretching exercises and want you to flex your muscles from new angles.'

For just one day he asked Sieg to learn my lines, go through the paces. Political games to keep your arse in line.

See this bastard Jam, I hear from other black actors that for the whole time we was in India he went around saying, 'Ali only got the part because Stream is a closet queen and fancy black prick. He fucked up my *Tony and Cleo* with his miserable acting and now he's going to fuck up Stream. Serve the old pederast right.'

What can I say? Best I give you Sara:

Nov 7th

Siegfried is a German mime artist. He jumped the wall.

He's bald and he's strong and he's exactly the same stature as David except he doesn't have a paunch and if you imagine a lion tamer without a chair, and without the moustache and a little less muscular, and wearing a shirt and trousers, that's him. The stance would tame lions. Or me. Stick your chair leg in my face anytime, geddit??? He's hired to play Ravan. But David seems to be doing something strange. He asks him over two days to learn the part of Ram. Ali says nothing, just licks his lips like a whipped dog. His eyes shine revenge. I question David later. It's a political ploy. Our insurers have refused to insure Ali for travel abroad. Something to do with his wife and possibly with a previous connection with drug smuggling. The insurers have picked up something about Ali that David, I suppose rightly, doesn't want to know and the insurance company won't disclose in any case. There might as well be someone in the cast ready. It would change the play totally.

Yes maan, the boy Siegfried, a demon to play a demon.

Look like a water-melon. He have seven children to support inna Berling town. I ask him, 'Wha happen them don't have TV in Berlin?'

But to come serious, he's a good brother to have on stage. He wears a mask of several heads and David choreographs him to fly. My God, it looks like he's flying when he crosses his legs half sitting, half standing and the mist covers his calves and knees and from the thigh up he's floating in blue and red smoke and the stage is lit so that the light catches only his head, boss, and diffuses down to his body and he begins to fling frisbees at the audience. Some primitive Sanskrit weapon. The last thing Sieg played in was a film by a nasty young German director who died of drink and drugs. Sieg showed us the video cassette. He was a balding skinhead, playing working-class German bully boy very unconvincingly, because Sieg is twenty years older than any of them kinda bully boys what I've met, right on the streets of Hamburg and Munich when I was doing theatre tours for Black Star.

He never say nothing about his trial day when I sat around without lines. You take lines from an actor is like tearing the meat from the jaws of a lion – maybe jackal, but John Crow have to eat too.

The play, we're stuck with the play. It's about finding the perfect man. Baby, I and I here get the feeling as David lectures about this with passion that he's trying to be IT, you know, the perfect man himself. He gets a passion in the voice when he talks about Ram, as though him playing the fucking thing himself and he holds his hands before his chest and shakes them expressively as he speaks. The picture is funny, but if you shut your eyes, the expression, the way he control lines, is perfect.

But that's what the play is about.

* * *

Maureen man get arrested. She gets Martha to phone me at rehearsals and I come out and take the phone in the foyer. Then she comes on. I tell her I don't want to know her troubles. But she's shedding tears. She's scared for herself. They beat him up in the police station and none of his money could protect him.

'Something must have changed in the political climate,' I say.

'Don't be such a wise guy, it's typical of you, Gerry, you don't give a shit unless it's to do with you. They are racist, the police.'

'The guy is running illegal guns, maybe selling to IRA, anybody, and they are racist? And call me Ali, nuh maan.'

'Right, Ali. But I don't know what's happened to you. This bloody David Stream thing has bought you off. It's British Imperialism, they can sell arms to anyone, you wouldn't know and what's more you wouldn't care. But someone who's dealing with regimes they don't approve of . . .'

'Look, hang on, Maureen. Some of the regimes they don't approve of are fascist. They're shooting down innocent people. Isn't he selling to Savimbi in Angola?'

'I don't know who he's selling to, but I never thought I'd hear you defend the British police and MI5 and all this.'

'I never defend no police I just said your fucking boy friend is selling to whoever he can and he don't give a shit about politics and what's more the British state have a little more concern about politics than Mr Pak who is selling to all comers and you sleep with the fucker.'

'I'm sorry,' she says and she's on the phone and there's a silence. And I can see her. God, Maureen, where did it all go wrong, why am I shouting at you about another man?

I know the message of the silence. It's that she's fucked up or I've fucked up, but please will I help. She fucks up, she comes to me!

OK.

'You have a solicitor?'

'I don't know if that'll do any good. He's guilty as hell.'

She says it with a kind of pride, she loves him being guilty of this shit. Martha is my daughter and now I have confirmation that Maureen is a monster. She wants her kicks off guys who break the system.

Maureen, I love you. But I lust for the woman Anjali.

I say I'll come after rehearsal. I leave the phone in the foyer and carry my halo on to rehearsal stage.

Nov 22nd

I don't really miss writing columns for Robin.

David doesn't want to read what I take notes on. He says he'll see it when he's old and falling apart. I must write what I like and I mustn't miss a trick, but then tricks can only be constructed from one person's point of view. Touché. So he says only God can be objective, the Hindu God and one must aspire to have an eye in the heavens. Quod erat Demonstrandum. Can't argue with him, but he's wrong in the subtle and yet blundering way that men are always wrong. Long live sisterhood. Sara, really!

The guy is kept in a jail in Southampton and so Maureen removes herself and Martha down there. It's school holidays, otherwise I'd have kicked up a fuss about her education and so on. I have the keys from the last time so I move back to the flat and Maureen, expecting me, boss, has left a note by the phone with her phone number and saying to keep the place clean.

I read in the papers that they allow prisoners pending trial some visits from women for conjugal rights. Should that be spelt 'rites'? Anyway, conjugal, whatever it costs and it costs me some sleep. But she's guilty and she's declared it by going down for conjugals in Southampton with a fucking Paki jailbird and gun-runner and son-of-a-bitch who's probably selling missiles to South Africa or something and has broken some sanction deal. The words want to tumble out of me when I visit her after rehearsals that night.

Martha's in bed. Or at least she's on the floor next to the bed, she always falls out and Maureen wants me to pick her up. A little domestic scene. I misread it, I think her red eyes and her very very soft approach is a come on, but when I try and put my hand on her wrist as she pours me a drink (boy, this house lousy with Chivas Regal and all them sort of whisky the Asian rich drink) she gently moves it. I got it. She needs the assistance, she don't need the love. She wants to go with him. And me, it's cool, I tell myself, I want to go with Anjali, but Anjali ain coming nowhere near me.

Nov 24th

David calls me in, secretive. I am, I suppose, running the production's press effort. There's some problem with Ali's insurance. Apparently, Ali's former wife, or 'woman' as he'd say, is tied up in some arms business the police are investigating. Ali is not as yet suspect but seems to keep in touch with the 'wife' and with the circle that is under surveillance. The insurers did a police check and some friendly public network spilt some uncertain sort of beans on poor Ali. I can't myself see Ali getting involved in anything of that nature.

David tells the press that there's money problems, government problems, fire risk to the theatre. The whole world of British arts is riddled with bureaucracy. He is going to have trouble with his opening night, but he doesn't intend to postpone it. It's going to open on the 1st of December.

The theatre is on to the fact that our star is uninsurable, or at least suspect. The theatre asks David to replace him. David tells them to take a swift and peremptory jump in the lake.

He wants to speak to Ali. They talk. The result of the conversation is that Ali comes out quite bewildered. I am then summoned. The Führer bunker is working full-time. Rehearsals commence without the master.

'I believe Ali has another name? He has worked as Gerald Blossom before in the theatre, hasn't he? Well, from today the cast are to be told to call him Gerry. Recall all the programmes and have them print the new cast list excluding Ali Abdul and including Gerald Blossom as Ram. You can't of course let out an official release but you can write something in the gossip columns about Ali being dismissed from the Ramayan rehearsals for a drink problem and a new actor Gerald Blossom taking his place. I've squared it with Ali.'

'You'll never get away with it,' I say. But I have the curious feeling that he will.

Shit. The man tell me a lie. Of course I find out the truth later. But the maestro bring us through months of rehearsal with all this bullshit about trust and mutual respect and then he go and lie to me. I didn't get it that day. He said it was a drink problem I have with the Brew. All this moving names and shifting face and being kept in wraps. The bastard call me and say it's your drink problem, you drink too much Special Brew and the insurance company thinks you might die of a heart attack. He don't tell me it's anything to do with the Maureen scene and foreign relations.

Sara come to me and say, 'Ali, David says you trust him completely, and apart from the drink, there's one more thing. We'd prefer it if you move in with me, into my flat. It's closer to the theatre and I can take care of your washing and cleaning and looking after your daughter when it's necessary. David wants you to concentrate.'

I say I can't there's a dog to think about, but she says, well, as soon as I can then. As long as I'm careful about speaking to the press. At the time it didn't puzzle me too much. I just think, boy, these theatre people paranoid.

Anyway I promise to pack up the booze. Even Sara keep it from me that they think I was in with Maureen man at the time, selling guns and them talking mega-bucks over my head about my death by fire – blood seed and destruction!!!

OK, so, first night. Everybody tense like a tuned guitar. She wears a green saree and comes out to meet the waiting millions, my Sita, my

Anjali. Oh yeah, the performance was heavy, man, heavy. But Aki, the Japanese guy, he bring me a snort, a little fixer in the changing rooms.

We are supposed to move on courage and here we were, at least two of us moving on coke.

Scene? You never seen nothing like it in your life. Boss, I'm in all the press. They are writing David up and taking pictures of me, and I'm in the *Observer* and the *Sunday Times* and any magazine you want to name except *Piano Tuner's Weekly*, and it's probably they didn't have the space this week.

She looked stunning and I look in her eyes and I see them perusing the crowd looking, I knew, oh hint, oh heart, oh troubled heart, for Jam the playwright and joy to me hosannah in the fucking highest, this dog of a Jam is almost handcuffed to his little white girl from some publishing business who has brought the boy's genius to public light in hard cover and is no way going to miss the first night of the David Stream extravaganza without tagging along, as woman, when everyone know he has a wife, and just hoping that people will think there's a legitimate question mark over ownership of the feller.

He looked hunted. I just stood with my back to the bar and check Anjali seeking him out. I couldn't hear them, but it was like watching one of them movies about high power bugging devices. Suddenly its noisy and then it goes dead silent and you watch the gestures and you have to make out what they're saying. Yes, this is so-and-so and she's my publisher, well, not really, she's nearly my wife but I hate to tell you that, but then you don't care and this is Anjali and I've sort of flirted with her and she's the star today and I'd love to be with today's star. Oh God. I know the dialogue, but I stand at the bar, burning, burning. So I go up and say, 'Hi, Jam. And you are, no doubt, Mrs Jam.'

'No,' she says, 'I'm not.'

'Sorry, mistake. But I'm sure it's you he's talked about. Aren't you in a bookbinding thing?'

'Publishing,' the girl says.

Anjali start to giggle. Jam knows what I'm after and he takes his woman thence. But Anjali feels sad.

We were standing in the middle of the floor, dodging the white wine guzzlers and sherry drinkers and beer swillers who hadn't even come to see the play, just come to the bar. I gave her her drink.

'I've got to know you so well,' I say.

'It's fantastic. I never in my dreams thought it would get all this attention.'

'We're dealing with a genius!'

We just done the first half. The same crowd would be coming back for the second half, five hours the next day. Some fellers swim the channel. Some climb Everest.

Siegfried comes up to us. He's been wearing a mask all the time so no one in the press recognises him, they think he's a German tourist. Ravana, the god of all wrath, the embodiment of everything the flesh would be if it was not governed by the spirit, stands before us and confesses he has lived through every moment behind that mask. Sieg, the mother-fucker, breathes the play.

Anjali doesn't. She's thinking of the playfellow and his wife.

'Did you intend something serious with him?' I ask, just like that.

'Ali, I'm hungry, take me to dinner. Let's get out of here.'

The sunlight on the garden, boss, I'll take a woman on the rebound any time.

She says she'll sleep in my house, yes, but she won't sleep with me. Is that OK? It is in the nature of Ali Abdul, slave to Allah, chattel of the twentieth-century trans-oceanic cultural trader, David Stream, to be ever hopeful. So when we finish a Chinese meal I get a taxi back and we look for the overproof of white rum that I have hidden. For the life of me I can't remember where. I start stalking about, looking to search it out, playing hide and seek with a bottle; and cool as hell, she takes a ganja out of her handbag and starts to undo a cigarette. I suggest we turn the lights down and rest our brains for the next day's performance, the finale, the continuation, the great scenes, the reconciliation. She wants to drain the tobacco by rubbing it between her hands and then put the ganja back in the cigarette paper with the filter and all. I tell her why you don't roll it in a Rizla. Stupid and backward.

I sing it:

When I was a youth I used to burn kali weed in a Rizla
I used to rub it in a Rizla
Now I am a man I jussa burn kali weed a in a chalawa
I just rub it in a chalawa.

She says it's an Indo-Caribbean song because did I know 'ganja' was an Indian word? I did. Then chalawa, what's that? A chillum? Right first time.

64

So don't get sentimental, Ali Abdul Boot Polish, but with the waft of a song, here with a stick of hash beneath the bough, a flask of rum, a reggae song and thou beside me after a performance in which we mash up the critics – man it bring back to me the smoke of Caribbean hills, the sunset over the Savannah . . . and my heart is glad.

We smoke her little cigarette. I put on the soul music, even Marvin Gaye pleading for sexual healing. Anjali like to shake her hips to Marvin Gaye.

When I get that feeling, boy, I want sex-u-al hea-ling.

And then I make my move with a close dance but she still wants to sleep alone and she goes, breaks loose of my clinch and walks into Martha's room with Marvin singing his balls off and starts to say the posters and all that Maureen put up in Martha's room are cute. And then she looks at Martha's books, all Little Red Riding Hood and some elephant stories and then she goes and sits on Martha's bed and says she'll sleep there and looks at me with doe eyes. I haven't the heart, boss. I say OK. I am a decent guy, don't want to argue this toss.

'You sleep in your saree or shall I give you Maureen's nightie?'

'I sleep in my . . . we used to call it birthday suit.'

It drives me wild, boss, but we're working the next day and she's playing and I don't want to play because I'm the gasman and I read the meter and I know the damage to the heart and mind and ego.

She don't want coffee, she don't want another smoke, she don't want nothing. I want to see her change, but she's careful about that too. She knows I'm goin to come back with some dumb question about whether she wants an alarm in the morning and she wraps a sheet around her.

I surrender in the flesh. I don't sleep easy, boss, I don't sleep at all. I toss in the master bed. Toss, that's the word. Gerry, Boot Polish, gone are the certainties of Ali Abdul, take thy love to bed and nurse it thyself. For shame. You cannot make your move. She has inspired in you shame, and for that be grateful.

All hell break loose the next morning.
Headlines:

STREAM IS A LIAR

'RAMAYANA' OPENS TO GUN-RUNNING SCANDAL

In a form it mek me feel good, See, Stream underestimate my arse. At least one critic there knew that Ali was the same guy as Gerald Blossom. Some black theatre gossip must have reach him and someone tell him, Gerry Boot Polish change him name.

So he follow the trail and tell the management and the theatre guys them call David and David say he don't know what they're talking about and while I am off with Anjali, oblivious to all and everything, Sara and David sorting out this shit. David think he can get away with it because he has sculpted my career, and now he get kick out of the theatre. I went to the corner to Mr Patel to get the papers for the reviews. Sure there were reviews, but the *New Citizen*, the *Guardian*, *The Times* and the *Telegraph* all ran the story about insurance and ting.

I took it back to Anjali. We called Sara. She said keep cool, she was sending a cab round for all the cast to meet with David.

Dec 1st

The meeting. He assembles all the players and the stage hands, and the management of the theatre, who've talked it over with him, strongly disagree, protest ruination etc., are allowed as observers.

The speech:

'You had to know before I went to the press.'

He stands with his hands in his cord trouser pockets, his belly out and a turtle head hooked into the spotlight, a hand going up now and then to shield his eyes from what he pretends is an unwelcome but necessary focus. The players sit in the second row of the auditorium and I sit on the first.

'Some good reviews today, but if I look at it with the background of my hopes and fears for the production, for you, for what we are together trying to do, it's a bloody slap in the face.

'I asked Gerald to revert to his earlier name because I thought that what an actor does in his private life is his own business. I was tactically wrong. I didn't think the management would find out so soon. We have to contend with the publicity concerning Gerald's private life. I hope that those of you who are close friends of Gerald will tell the others in some quiet moment that Gerald has nothing to do with the gentleman on whose trail the police seem to be, some ring of weapons merchants. Our own dear Gerald remains so. The management, who are here and listening, have given me an ultimatum. Get rid of Gerald Blossom, alias Ali Abdul, or cancel the booking. I have chosen the latter course.'

(Loud applause from the cast and musicians)

'I must say I understand the management's point of view. An international investigation into weapons dealing is pending. There will be no bail for any of the accused when they are caught. Also the sponsoring bodies of the theatre, three local councils, have heard of the rumours and the suspicions now and will not continue to fund the production and the premises if we have as one of our central performers someone found guilty of arms supply to South Africa, to the nasty forces of Renamo in Mozambique and, to the South African backed rebels in Angola and other places. I understand their anxieties but I've talked everything frankly over with Gerald and I can say he knows nothing of it. He doesn't even know where Angola is!'

(General laughter.)

'Now the good news.

'As I've always maintained, one of my concerns has been to get away from the confines of the theatre and when I read the *Guardian* review, it confirmed it. It came like a flash. We have to have an outdoor location. I called this meeting to admit a small error. I've kept you in the last few months away from the air and the sky. That's where the *Ramayana* was born. I've talked to the lawyers about the contracts and they're getting on to your agents. First things first.'

(Laughter.)

'Let's do it this way. There are two coaches outside and they'll take us to the site of our new opening. Incidentally, everything else remains the same. The tour is on.

'We are going outdoors and I need five days to dress the site. Your first question – 'in the cold?' It won't be cold. Technology is about to create a miracle, not huge burning fires, but a new method of machine which heats large open areas. Ask me how? You may as well ask if I can read Hebrew (I do, by the way).

(Laughter.)

'Miracles and British Gas.'

He speaks with the passion of a general rallying his troops after a rout. He takes responsibility, his syllables begging for their loyalty. It's infectious. It's a mission, it isn't simply a supreme act of theatrical ego.

I watch Ali and Anjali, who presses Ali's hand.

The press follow us to the site. There are seven articles about it in the next day's papers.

Robin rings on the production's field telephone.

'Can you give us an exclusive, Sara?' As though nothing ever happened. Just the hint of a beg and grovel in the voice.

'As the production's press representative, I shall speak to any journalist you choose to send.'

'Right,' says Robin and the 'fuck you baby' doesn't even register time on British Telecom.

So have the management of the theatre been set up, deliberately tricked, ruined, fucked over? I don't think David quite planned it, but points win to D. Stream.

Anjali sits rapt. She flies to the bus like a woman going to her own suttee. Ali walks behind her. The Muslim husband in reverse. Through all the talk, the logic is financial. The sponsors, who have already guaranteed the rest of the run, will share box-office with the production in more generous terms than the theatre who have fixed contracts. Base motives, David?? Naah! Must have got it wrong.

And I, S.F.S., am a creature of the cities, a sponge for petrol fumes, a bunker for viruses, a reader of daily newspapers, a buyer of trendy wines, a frequenter of the shops round one's flat that sell Parma ham and Dolcelatte and non-English foods, but a frequenter too of Wimbledon when the right man asks and of Henley when the family friends choose to invite as they always do, and a sharer with Daddy of the box at Ascot, a wearer of black bows in long brown-blonde tresses, a creature though who can be excited by a move to the wilderness where the bulbul haunts the eaves or whatever happens in the wretched Ramayana. And also, S.F.S., you have understood cultural movements these last thirty years, you have friends who make Britain what it is today though you've decided that D. Stream and his humble cast above all make it what you would like it to be and the rest are serving well-trodden time with Ascot and Henley, though you have no inverted snobbery about it and are not, God save the mark, a revolutionary or a radical of any stooping sort or Bolshy to boot, you have found the precise niche for which you would wish, not adventuring but serving with a defined salary, a press-officer, that's comfortable. A 'chronicler' is less well defined, so the crisis, engineered for whatever reasons by Streamers, have given us something concrete to do.

68

But why do these people pay twenty-five pounds a time to go? I, S.F.S., know enough intellectual snobs who wouldn't understand a word of the proceedings, but would pay ten times that sum to have seen a D. Stream Inc. production. But surely all of them are not like that? Is there a percentage of Britain really looking for salvation?

'It's so obvious, so bloody obvious. He should have done it a long time ago.' Anjali is *for*, boss.

I'm dead against. The place is out in the wild and no pub and no cigarette shop and nothing for three miles round. Same money, though. So why should I care? The reporters try and come near me but Sara is there. The last thing I want is to be slung off and there's just a lickle hint that that's what the maestro would do if I fuck about. So who's fucking? Right? David is playing smart man. Bossy, I knew he was the boss of bosses in the direction business, but I didn't know he was a hustler of such dimension. He pulled it hard on the press, low on jaw and full of religious fervour. 'The establishment this and that, a mission to ignore, a conspiracy to keep theatrical culture within the pyramid that bad reviewing and commercial criticism had built as a monument to its own mummification.' Nice one, David. Heavy shit! Sock it to their boomber claat.

Dec 6th

The money for India may dry up if a scandal emerges. David has tapped several sources. Something has always told me that real genius is not good at accounts, insurance, that sort of thing, you know Einstein not making sure his household goods were insured. David's good at it.

On the second night of the play, she says S. Patel made a pass at her. She says it to David. She's a professional, she won't stand for a two-bit idiot fantasising about her. She's convinced that S. Patel is secretly and revoltingly letting his imagination run. Davey buys it. He pacifies Anj. Does Sara know the little reason behind that move, that reluctance to bring the eye-rapist to justice?

Maybe something to do with the fact that S. Patel has an uncle with loadsamoney. A financier who makes hot water machines in India and has 'diversified', as S. Patel says, into computer techno-logy. Rajiv Gandhi loves him and has given him some boss power to pull together all the guys that leave India for wages in the US and call them back and develop a decent technology for India on the basis of number crunching machines.

The boy knows what he's talking about. S. Patel says people come from all over the world to see him because whatever money the Indian market has to pass on in the computer field, this cat has it, controls it.

The great director, the great Indian mythology show. Anjali tells me they don't reckon their money in millions but in hundreds of thousands and ten millions and they call them lakhs and crores. The man, 'uncleji' as S. Patel calls him, is delivering unto the coffers of D. Stream some heavy load to take the scene around India, no questions asked and the man himself, R. Gandhi, has to say yes if Patel senior, the whiz kid, says nod nod wink wink.

I take Anjali to the East End. A meal in Brick Lane because she wants to see the famous café with nudes on the wall painted, as she say, in 'Indian baroque'. It's just dirty pictures and bad art to me, boss. Seen better on Bayswater railings. But she wants a lickle taste, a sample of the common Hasian and I know of no commoner Hasian than what lives in the fucking East End.

So I take her and it's Sunday so we walk past Petticoat Lane and check the Indian traders who flog leather stuff and then the white stalls with fish and ting and she wants to stop and the guy is putting on the cockney for her, rhyming slang and shit. He probably learns it off *EastEnders*, the cunt, but she's impressed and we buy some prawns and she gets sentimental.

The guy takes us in the back room. He's checking Anjali and probably thinking to himself, what's this Indian girl doing with a blackhead. Fuck him.

I tell Anjali I think I fancy duck and she say that's cool.

'How come they selling it so cheap, man?'

'It's your patch, you should know.'

So when the guy comes I say I'll have this Bombay Duck and the man say, 'How many?'

'Just one, captain, how many you think I want?'

Anjali starts to laugh and she asks for this and that in Urdu or whatever and the guy smiles but he goes and gets it.

He comes back with this thing which looks like the penis of an opened up mummy I saw in a museum once.

'Your Bombay Duck,' and he plops it on the table.

'I said duck, man, not shrivelled in-soles.'

The thing was stinking. Anjali was looking amused with her tongue literally in her cheek.

'We Indians call that duck. Bombay duck.'

'Smell like salt fish gone bad.'

'That's what it is. Try it.'

Bwoy, I was too polite to say what it taste like. A fish called duck, cool, well, you live and learn, boss.

Nice. We're dribbling over a bad brandy because we have to fetch the booze ourselves here, they don't sell it but you can bring it in, and she tells me, 'You know, Ali, I never knew what cockles and mussels were. In India, I mean, when I was in college and moving with a very fast set. I learnt about that in Paris.'

'Good thing to pick up in Paris, all I pick up was two girl and some bad French reggae.'

'We used to sing', she say, 'in Dublin's fair city where the girls are so pretty . . . "Molly Malone".'

'I sing that too, but in school we had a bad version.'

'You don't understand. I was an Indian child, who didn't know where Dublin was or whether it was a place or a coin. And I remember my parents and their friends, Indians, all singing "Molly Malone" heartily and not one of them knew what a cockle or a mussel was.'

'Shouldn't eat that filth,' I say.

'That's not the point of the story, Ali. It's that Dublin's fair city was a really really sad song for me. I sympathised with Molly Malone when millions of people were dropping like flies all around us.'

'My parents sang "God Save the King" in the Caribbean.'

'"Molly Malone" was worse. It was subversive. It was the best kind of propaganda because it wasn't intended as such, it just ate like a bloody worm into my sympathies until all the romance of fifteen and before wrapped itself around the unknown life form of cockles and mussels.'

'You're crazy, you know. If you have that kinda thoughts you must introduce me to your dealer.'

'I thought you knew him. Name of David Stream.'

'Heavy.'

'Not so heavy. You know why I joined the troupe? I think David is doing the exact reverse for the *Ramayana*. It stunned me when I first heard of it. The real Eastern myth, the whole soul of Hinduism and everything comes West. It's not some kind of complaint cultural thing, something done by a cultural promotion agency, like some artificial non-political message of peace play. It's what Indians really believe, the sort of belief they give their lives for, fanatically, and through David it becomes mainstream, a direction in European theatre.'

The trick I was missing was I had nothing to offer her. A woman who has just been struck by a philosophy, and it's not yours, well, you don't have much chance until the philosophy wears off and she begins to have doubts and sees the little bit of fraud that there is in everything, then you can play your hand.

She never picked up on any bait either. I'd talk to her about other plays I'd been in, about actors' careers and life and style in London and how Birmingham was an interesting city, a bit of race relations, a little shot at feeling out if she was anti-apartheid or anti-racist or anything, but she wasn't nothing. She was just a David Streamer for the moment. And the agony of it is the moment has just begun. We're booked for the next six months.

There's no books I can lend her or topics I can afford to continue. Maureen say I can't love women who don't fall at my feet. She wrong. I love who I like, yeah, it's only that I can't get a woman like Anjali interested in anything I got to sell. And if you can't sell you have to buy. That means you got to listen. Now she's got books to lend you and the topic to go into, you know – our work – David, the fucking *Ramayana.*

I said, 'Blood claat!'

'As good a response as any,' she says.

'Not you, Anjali, I forgot the fucking dog.'

'What dog?'

'There's a dog. I forgot to buy the food, the dog cans. I haven't been back home for forty-eight hours and the guy must be starving.'

'You have a dog and you treat it like that?'

'No, no, nah, it's not my dog. It's been leant to me.'

She'd never got into the topic of what Maureen was doing and ting and this wasn't the time to start. It was the bloody jailbird's dog. His friend came and dumped it on me saying is this Maureen's house? I gotta keep the dog while she's looking after the man and visiting and keeping my daughter from her righteous education and taking her probably to jail visits to see some gun-running bastard in detention. And this hound turns up on my doorstep. So I told the friend to go his way, you know, with the dog. But he was nasty and just left without the dog and slam the door behind me, leaving the leash in my hand and the dog settling down on the carpet to chew up a little Santa Claus doll which I bought for Martha. It chewed it into cotton wool and shreds before I could look around. I never see a Santa Claus destroyed so fast.

I whack the dog one and it was no good he whimpered and sat down and stuck his tongue out and tried to lick his way to forgiveness. You know that way there: grovelling with a lolling tongue, neck stretched right down along the carpet. But forgiveness wasn't in me. I was well vexed.

Stuck with the hound and I didn't even know a name for him, so I tried Bonzo and all them kinda stereotype names but he wasn't interested. Then I thought maybe if I live a coupla weeks with this dog I'll get some clues as to his master's character. And anyway, I couldn't chuck him out.

'What kind of dog is it?' Anjali asked.

'Same as usual, four legs and all this.'

'A mongrel?'

'That's rude. On our estate we used to call them "Bombay Terriers".'

She was concerned. I was a brute. The dog would starve. He would die. I had to get back home straight away.

'Feed him what?'

'There must be something here,' she say and walk to the man who counting he money because the place shut down.

Anjali sweet talks the man. They go in the kitchen and she comes back with a plastic bag full.

'They unloaded the leftovers. At least he won't die of hunger. Now go.'

'This is what they sell to the pig farms. You don't know this dog. He'll never eat that.'

She steer me to the door.

'Get going, I always believe in teaching old dogs new tricks. That's why I talk to you.'

She give me a kiss for goodnight, on my lips. She was feeling maternal towards the dog and I was daddy. She was wrong, the dog never ate a scrap. When I get back, it's just slumped in a corner and opening an eyelid to see me and then jumping up all over me. They lick their torturers.

He was never thinking this guy don't come back to feed me. He probably just thought, no food and when the God comes back I'll get some. No blame. That makes me like the dog so I spread out some

73

sausages and that from the fridge which he eats raw. Then I reach for my stash full of good feeling towards the dog and the bastard has eaten my dope. All of it. I keep a lump by my bed in a plastic bag which he's shredded up to get at the stash. No wonder he didn't complain about the food. You win some, you lose a lot. I couldn't kick him, he wouldn't understand. I just wished I knew his name.

*   *   *

Dec 7th

The arena, cleverly done for the play. Six by two is twelve performances of one half of the epic each.

The docklands of London are being developed and the ruin stands like burnt fingers thrust up from the earth in complete isolation from anywhere else. The last three or four hundred yards are just dirt track.

When he gathers the actors to speak to them, he talks like Mahatma Gandhi, gentle, firm, persuasive. When he's talking to me or planning the next big move he thinks he's Napoleon. He surveys territory like a man about to conquer and his eyebrows shade over his rather froggish eyes.

So it shall be written, so it shall be done. S. Patel taught me that. As a young man in India, he said he went to see *The Ten Commandments* (with Charlton Heston?) twenty-seven times. He spent his entire term's college fees on *The Ten Commandments*. Thou shalt go to the cinema. From the film he brought away the abiding irony of his phrase – so it shall be written, so it shall be done.

The Moghul emperors had a man to feed them, to hold the spoon and bring it to their mouths. He stood to the left of the throne and was known as the 'Chamcha', the spoon. David craves chamchas but doesn't want them seen as such. I am not such a one.

I wonder if any other city apart from London would have tolerated David Stream's ploys. New York or any other place – well, there's only two – wouldn't stand it. But here's the maverick guru. Cancel the tickets that have been booked for the month, we'll do twelve days in the wilderness. He tells the press he'll be running it, two performances deep. Nothing about the blow and burn machines. Yet he tells the cast about nothing else but the heating machines. I get it. Finally he is playing God. He is going to change

74

the weather of Britain, nay, the climate, and do it around a theatrical event. He relies on the cast leaking the heating idea to the press. They do and there's nothing but heating talk in the press. 'Stream to heat the world' sort of editorial in the *Stage*.
Even *The Times*, *Guardian*, *Independent* pick it up.

I can't even remember a sequence of events as it go down. The docklands, the Paris tour etc. but Sara have it day by day.

Dec 8th

David pulls a stroke. Being Monday its cast rest, no performance. He tells me to tell the cast he's cancelled the Paris trip till after the world tour.

'The translations are not ready.'

Thereby hangs a tale. She comes over from Paris, the translator. She has been working with David for more than two years. She is in her late fifties or maybe even older. Full of French pretension. She doesn't realise that you don't tie scarves round your head anymore but she doesn't seem to care. The wrinkles, the long fingers. I imagine them through the evenings after rehearsals, after performance times, back in his flat arguing it back and forth, the meaning of the universe, whether the line can go down in history when she has gesticulated it. I must confess I disliked her from the moment we were introduced: 'This is Sara, our chronicler and Annie, my old friend.'

I'm of course supposed to know who Annie is. To extend, as with all D. Stream's friends, my respect and wonder. But I bitch. I do know who she is, the communist of the fifties, the director and playwright, the *feminence grise* of Paris.

'I've known her for forty years. I didn't know she'd turn out to be a racist.'

That's strong for David, but the row was awful. They disagree about philosophy. I ask, 'Are you going to release the disagreement to the press? They'll ask why we aren't going to Paris?'

'I can't say it, I've known her too long, it would be a betrayal. The bloody French don't understand internationalism.'

'Isn't that a little less than internationalist a statement?'

'Don't be timid,' he says, not taking the situation seriously even now. 'Always characterise people by their nationalities, just don't use that to define their rights and abilities.'

I don't understand, I leave him. I piece together the story from Anjali.

Before we start rehearsing, Anjali has, in consultation with David, employed a young Indian poet who lives in Paris to do an alternative translation into French. Annie has never been told this. When the philosophical disagreement (I'd love to know how it went but that's a gap in the chronicle which David refuses to fill) arose she was summoned. Trump card.

'Anjali here has a friend who has been telexing a very different translation from ours, darling. Just pure enthusiasm for the project.'

Annie wants to know who and when.

'He's only a young Indian poet, but he's brilliant.'

David says to me later that you can take away a Frenchwoman's money, mug her in the streets, drag her name through the yellow press but if you want to give her offence say that somebody else is brilliant. Since the Revolution the French have lived with the idea that individual brilliance is the essence of life and progress.

Annie throws a little bit of a fit.

To Anjali: 'He may be a genius, but he's David's kind of genius. They understand each other, yes? They know English, eh, Indians know English like they know their mother's milk and they don't remember the taste but they grow by it.' Wonderful line, and Anjali thinks so too, but David fastens on it as the point of dismissal. He can't have Annie saying that about another translator. So what if the poet is Indian?

Annie: 'Paris is full of fiddlers with, what's the word, terminology who call themselves poets. Translation and poetry are different. One is simply a gift to impress yourself upon the world, the next is a gift to give only that which you take.'

David: 'Translation has to be faithful and beautiful. A pity that some can't manage both.'

Annie (to Anjali): 'You see, this man whom I love, a dirty chauvinist through and through.'

Anjali says she pronounces 'through and through' very 'sweetly'.

David works himself up to say that her remarks against the Indian poet are racist.

She packs her bags and leaves, I take her to Heathrow.

Annie: 'I really love David and we have worked together and we will again. He doesn't see his folly, eh?'

76

I say I've never known a man who is so conscious of his own folly. After all, what is it but folly to bring a play which is a prayer book in India to Britain and have all the races of the world play in it to European audiences for ten long hours, but he invents excuses and then is convinced by them. She has stepped on his territory.

David doesn't like the Indian poet's translation either. He proclaims it to be rubbish.

Me: 'So Annie was right.'

David: 'Annie has been consistently wrong for the years I've known her. Last year she thought the Algerians in Paris were going to overthrow the French state if they made an alliance with the prostitutes they used.'

Me: 'Isn't that a slightly false paraphrase? I talked to her. She loves the production and the script.'

David: 'She loves the script too much. It's just a piece of theatre. It's not propaganda, you've got to think about that more carefully or it doesn't work. She was steering me into French sentimentality about the moon and the sun and the gods and I don't know what's happening to her but that's not our business.'

Yes, the business, he's good at it.

Anjali is disappointed that her poet was not taken on and can't hang on the coat-tails of the great Stream, but she's philosophical.

'He's worked at it for the last seven years or more. Of course he feels it's his baby and he doesn't want anybody else muscling in. It's a bloody good translation and I'll find him a French publisher for it.'

'And fuck David?'

'I have no such ambitions,' she says and looks me straight in the face.

'I was being very metaphorical,' I say.

'Metaphor has saved a lot of situations, hasn't it?' she says. She's still thinking how to tell her Indian poet that what she fixed is a dodo.

*　　　*　　　*

Here beginneth, boss, the story of a guy called Binky and a next one called Tilak and the Asian activist girl, Sonya. And if it sound like a fairy tale to you, bwoy, remember that fairy only have tail like fish have fingers. And now me res the ragamuffin stylee and go inna the fairy tale stylee . . .

Once upon a time there was this actress called Anjali and the stars shone out of her eyes and she was everything I wanted and since there was a day's break in our proceedings we had the evening spare. But there was a wicked director named David who insisted we worked at rehearsals every day of the week until Anjali took this publicity brochure from the Barbican to him and said, 'Look, master, more Indian culture, good for the soul. Let's go.'

Anjali was going to the opening of *Sanskriti* and joy of joys she asked yours truly to learn from it. After all we were the principal characters in Asian culture in Britain, me a West Indian and she an upper-class Indian who lived in Paris. And Sara said she'd love to go along and Siegfried, the man who played demons, and so we went of an evening to the opening.

In this very city there were evil influences at work to undermine the very purpose and existence of the exhibition. It was a good exhibition and it was in a big fortress with lots of car parks and roads in tunnels and the greatest arts Britain could afford. It was the veritable belly of the beast with its concrete structure and maps on the walls to tell you where you were and give you instructions on which button to press how many times in the lift to get to the floors and half floors and all this jazz, just like going to a new capital, all done to make Britons feel that travelling in space was equivalent to travelling in time. You were ahead of anything else you'd seen. Also it reconciled one to death. If this was the map of the future, the future generations could keep it. One wasn't missing much!

We park the car two streets down, Sara's Japanese number, not wanting to pay fifty pounds or whatever it was for parking.

And Anjali had hinted to the great black hero Ali that she would love to discuss the decision that the great white director had taken to axe the French production. From which small acorn, the mighty oak of hope grew in Ali's beating breast.

And Sara would understand as he had the key and she really wanted to promote him with Anjali, or at least that was his understanding because Sara, despite a certain air of upper-middle-class cynicism which comes from being in the papers and all, was really soft on multiculturalism and next to black bedding down with whites like herself she was in favour of them bedding down with Asians like Anjali. Besides it would stop Anjali giving herself such airs in Sara's eyes, I would think. Sisterhood, yes, but other things go on too.

I was sleeping on Sara's floor now, not only because of the scandal,

78

but because the man had been release from jail with insufficient evidence and lots of bail, so Maureen and Martha were back in the flat and I never went to see them because I didn't want to trip over no kalashnikovs the guy might be selling to the next South African Boer. I just phoned up Maureen and wanted to cuss her out but instead I asked the health of Martha and on being reassured that my offspring was in the pink, hummed and before hawing, even fucking asked her how she was, and before I knew what I was saying even how the gun-running old Pak was, and then got angry with myself and put down the phone.

We have to wade through a blood claat crowd of protest-merchants, Jah, maybe thirty people, mostly young Asians and a couple of blacks and lots of whites. They hold up cards, like slogans:

THIS IS A RACIST EXHIBITION.

THE MASSES OF INDIA ARE NOT ANIMALS TO BE PUT IN A ZOO.

Rastafari, save I! This here exhibition as Anjali had told us was a delight of all the acts you could see with beggars and street performers and village dancers and everything that was spontaneous culture in India.

The demonstrators were giving out leaflets and going up to the people who were going into the Barbican to tell them not to go. Anjali pretended they didn't exist, man, she just glide past them as though they were trying to sell her charms and she had long since abandoned superstition. Sara and Sieg followed and Sieg said, 'No, danke! Thank you very much, no, no, nein, no leaflets. Thank you.'

Bless him. A black guy shouts, 'Yow Ali, star of stars.'

I stop.

'You don't want to go in there, man.'

'You seen the show?'

'Naah, I don't see racist shows. They put the poor on display for the viewership of the bourgeoisie.'

He indicated the crowds going in. Didn't look too much like bourgeoisie to me, just one bald guy with his children and a couple of art students.

By which time of course Sara and Anjali and Sieg had disappeared.

'I'm an actor, Jah, I need to go and see. You know I'm doing the *Ramayana*.'

'Yeah, everybody know that, Ali man. I know you from time you hang about with Scoby and them, but since you became famous I haven't heard of you. Tcha, these people are herded like cattle, animals into cages and brung here and flung on the public.'

'You know all about India?'

'The Asian . . . friends, they are in the forefront of this struggle. It's symbolic because most Indians are working class in this country, just like these performers, and they'll feel for them.'

I looked at the pamphlet. It said, 'Printed by the Centre For Indian Progressive Organisations' – the CFIPO, boss.

'I tell you what, I'll see it in the evening and picket tomorrow.'

A young Asian 'friend' comes up to us and asks if I'm going in.

'Don't bother speak to him, he's lost all touch with the roots since he became a big actor and got on the telly.'

'I saw you in the *Guardian*,' she says. 'You're in that Stream so-called *Ramayana*.'

'I was just telling your man here. I'll see it today and picket with you tomorrow. I got nothing to do. You should see it too. People would believe you better if you check it out and then hate it.'

She laughs. 'Hate is a bit strong. I know what I hate. I don't have to see that.'

'They don't capture them performers, do they?' I say. 'Bring them to Britain in chain and ting?'

'I have nothing against the performers. But your *Ramayana*, David Stream, this cynical parading of people – it's just an extension of tourism.'

'Tourism man, shit,' the black guy says.

'I don't think you understand what David's trying to do.'

'David, who the fuck is David? Some trendy white director thinks he can capture Indian culture?'

I turn to the black boy, 'Brother, you can't go to Zion with a colonised mind.'

Then I turn and walk. He shouts, 'Yow, you brainwashed, man, know your culture.'

The Asian activist girl has light brown hair, very almond eyes and a fair skin, not white but light. Must be a half-caste sister.

The black guy I know. He's Scoby's friend though I never meet him and he deals in grievance.

The place is packed. I find it by the map and find there's ten other entrances, so the demonstrators can't win at all. I catch Sara and Anjali and Sieg. They're waiting for the man of the exhibition himself to come and see Anjali because she's sent one girl from the barriers to announce her arrival.

He comes and they hug and kiss. 'Binky!'

'Shush, Anjali, Vinayak here, please.'

'Vinayak? You bloody fraud, I'm not going to change your name because of any British audience!'

'All right, but introduce me to your friends as – Vinayak, hi, glad you could come.' He repeats our names as we tell him, 'Sara, Ali, yes, you play Ram and Sieg, Hanuman, no, Ravan, sorry, my God the best of mythology all gathered under this Barbican roof. It's a nightmare, yar, they have unions and things, so sticky. I'll never bother with this place, your bloody Britain, again. They are so bloody nasty and the management take their side. They wanted money to put the flats up and they didn't know how to unpack or handle the hessian. You see I've coated it with special things, yar, and they were crumbling the whole deal. British workmen, honestly, I'm a socialist and all, but these fellows really, biscuit is not the word for what they take!'

'Take a deep breath, we know you work hard, now show us what you've brought of old Bharat,' says Anjali.

Marvellous, king, really something else. If these are the Indian streets, give me the dust of their pathways forever, because the scene is boss! First act we see is the wrestlers, greased and massive, not like Sumo buffalo, but like Sumo deer, throwing each other fast but with the grace and deliberation of slow motion.

Then a guy with an infant daughter, balancing her on a pole and spinning her on a wheel and the kind of thing which made several people in the audience, you know the kinda British who would come to this, make mutter about whether it was legal in Britain. And his wife walking on a rope between two bamboo tripods, her saree tucked into her crotch, and juggling old light bulbs.

The guy with the balancing kid, his eyes are checking the crowd. I clap. Anjali squeezes my arm – she likes me appreciating it loudly.

'Normally his eyes would be asking for money and he hasn't lost the habit. Of course he's on Binky's wages here, he's not going to pass the dirty handkerchief round.'

Each act is in a little enclosure, decorated like the walls of an Indian village hut. All the colours and mud-plaster and whole scene. A kinda substitute for the streets, because really all this stuff, the harmonium player, the girl with the cymbals and a kind of wailing voice and wild hair with jingles on her ankles – all this thing would carry on in the Indian street. I check Binky. He's all the time looking at the door to see if important guests have arrived. He calls for a guy who works for him.

'I'll leave you with Tilak here and the puppeteers and we'll meet after and go for a meal. Please, be my guests. There are some others coming. Ciao!'

Hair long, real camp Indian-style clothes with tight pyjamas, a raw silk kurta cut close at the waist and his embroidered bag flowing over his shoulders under the shawl which he deliberately tosses as he speaks. Anjali says he's big in the cultural establishment and if we want a good India tour we'd better be nice to him.

The puppeteers are wrapping up as we reach their stall, four in the troupe and Anjali leans over the cloth barrier to talk to them as the buzzer goes and the blue uniform Barbican chaps come and announce to people on all levels that it's closing time and we should be heading towards the exits.

The place is done up in little stages on the various levels, like an Indian village in the foothills of the Himalayas, the huts hanging like flashy washing on a line in the valley.

The guy Tilak is a kinda manager, fixer, in charge of all of the performers. He talks English and Anjali introduces us as from *Ramayana* and as Binky's friends.

'They're tired,' Tilak says.

'Please,' Anjali says, 'I'm Sita, this is Ram.' She's playing little girl.

He is not impressed. He looks smashed out, tired, but, just as Anjali has calculated, the puppeteers sit up.

'Ram? Sitaji? You?'

'Yes, us,' Anjali smiles. 'We're playing the *Ramayana*, right here in London.'

'We've heard,' says one puppeteer, the youngest.

They exchange a few words. They want to show us a Ram-Sita sequence with their puppets.

'They are dedicated. First day in London and they want to play extra for you,' says Tilak.

It's a Punch and Judy *Ramayana* and the lines don't sound at all poetic through the kazoo the guy uses for the speeches.

By the time the performance is over, the general public have gone and Binky is bustling people about and finally comes to us. 'Thank God we got through the first day. Miracle.'

'It's fabulous, Binky,' Anjali says.

'Very interesting. I suppose the press have been in?' Sara says.

'Everyone. Even the *Sun* came nosing around for stories about stubborn wogs – me – but I read David's thing about France. Sorry your tour is cancelled, yar. Was the translation really that undo-able?'

'It wasn't awful, it just didn't satisfy David and he's a perfectionist,' Anjali says. 'He didn't think it was faithful.'

'My God,' says Binky, 'which of us is faithful nowadays? What does David care about faithful when he's probably bastardised the whole thing anyway and who cares? You should have translated it, Anj. You know French and David so well and you're such a good politician.' He turns to us. 'I keep telling Rajiv she should be ambassador to Paris, my dear. But he doesn't want my suggestions. I told him he has to be a bit like Castro and that got into the newspapers, if you please, just little old me talking nonsense.'

I see him check who laughs at his joke, the man is taking it all in as he prattles and then he turn to Tilak and say to get the people into the bus and make sure the driver know where him going. An open gesture. Binky's the boss. Like Anjali, a man of Indian class; Tilak is the stooge, skills, but no polish – maybe S. Patel again.

'Really like loaves and fishes I tell you, we've booked an Indian restaurant but my people are quite mind blown, first day out of India, straight to work on the set and this fantastic opening. Pierre and Annabelle and all are coming to dinner too. You must come.'

We go to an Indian place off Warren Street there. The performers are taken by Tilak in a London Transport bus, specially hired for the occasion and carry their bundles and parcels with them.

When we get there the tables have been joined up in the restaurant and Binky and guests are already there. He indicates to Tilak that the gang of performers are to go downstairs to the basement. Binky is entertaining his ten guests, including us, upstairs – a couple of clothes designers, a High Commission man and his wife and a couple more Indian women in sarees and a white guy who runs some theatre whom I've seen around.

I take off downstairs to piss and see the performers at the other end of the corridor crowded into a room, seated on the floor in rows with paper plates, the food laid out in huge saucepans and in a pile of chapattis on a mat in the corner. So that's how they feed the extras in them Raj extravaganzas. Not your Ullah meal with the chicken madras. They call to me, the puppeteers.

'Ramji, come in, eat with us!'

Tilak is sitting next to the door. I look again. This girl in saree is no performer, but I seen her somewhere before. She's sitting next to him eating from a paper plate with her fingers. It's the raas claat Asian activist girl outside the Barbican what was demonstrating against the show.

'Hang on, I thought you was against this lot.'

'I was invited,' she smiles.

'So what you give me all that lecture outside the show for? You a double agent or something?'

'You know each other?' Tilak asks.

'We met politically. I stopped him outside,' she says. 'Hi, I'm Sonya.' She puts a handful of rice clumsily into her mouth. Tilak tells her she mustn't mess the lower digits of her fingers while eating. It's an art. I go back up and drink the wine. Anjali is going back to Binky's to catch up on old times. Sara takes me home.

Dec 11th

Tilak wants to see a performance. He doesn't accept my invitation to come to rehearsals as he feels David might object.

I am at the exhibition on my own the next day and see Binky but he doesn't recognise me. Tilak comes up to me. He's happy to see me back. He has nothing much to do, he says, the performers are now looking after themselves. It's an absurd idea, having him as a nanny for them.

I ask if he sympathises with the demonstrators outside, the zoo aspect, the herding, the curiosity, turning poverty into a spectacle . . .

He doesn't agree. He gestures with a large open palm towards the performers. 'They're not innocent. They know rates of exchange for dollars, pounds, rupees, better than you or me, black market rates and everything.'

I go a third time. Tilak sits at a table sipping orange juice in the small café of the exhibition. I join him. He is harassed. Too much to do? No, Binky's gone off and left him to deal with the fall-out. The previous night the puppeteers went off with some white women who'd invited them home and didn't get back till noon. Binky wanted to phone up the police from the YMCA to which they were supposed to return, but Tilak dissuaded him. Then in the morning the rest of them, the magic man and the fellow with the balancing act had gone and bought themselves all manner of electronic gadgets – ghetto blasters, tape-recorders and the like. They had got the rest of the performers to pool their money and had defied Binky who insisted he wasn't going to help them get this stuff through customs.

'Is that the problem? Doesn't sound too serious.'

'Not the goods. These girls they went off with. One of them said the others behaved badly and tried evil things with these women.'

'Sounds interesting.'

Tilak doesn't know what I mean by interesting so he breaks into a huge smile. Am I thinking evil things about Tilak?

Ali snores. He's actually jealous of Maureen's new man.

It weighs on his mind because he has constructed some elaborate theory blaming America for all gun-running anyway.

He is performing superbly and he knows it. The crits from the dailies have all been plus.

Man, could you forget a feller called 'Ellythorn'? Is like Englebert Humperdinck, innit? Invented to catch the attention. Or put it a next way, wouldn't you remember a black guy called Doomsday Jones and a girl called Trial, you kidding?

Like a serpent he struck. I didn't keep the review, it didn't bother me too much, but Sara file it.

New Citizen, Saturday Supplement, 11 Dec

. . . and claims of Mr Stream these last thirty-five years. I remember, as probably few obliged to comment today would, his production of *Coriolanus* in 1954. Mr Stream was young, as was this reviewer, and both of us recall that the production came to a sticky end.

Mr Stream must still believe it was 'before its time'. It made some play with fads that had surfaced in the post-war continental confusion when nothing was certain except revivals of drawing room comedy, when none of the Pinters and Beckets had risen with obfuscative determination to confound us. In that production, Mr Stream manipulated the Shakespearian text. He contrived to make us believe, I think, that the wrong side had won the war because we British were not sufficiently democratic.

This is what he said to press, at the time at any rate. As for the play itself, it had an actress playing Volumnia speaking in a cod Russian accent and Coriolanus himself in the accents of what Mr Stream then took to be a new Tory class, denizens of the 'garden cities and suburbs'. It was clear that Mr Stream had a message for post-war Britain.

There followed many conventional successes for the guru. He presented enjoyable versions of Brecht and Pirandello to the British public but really came into his own when there emerged what are known in the footnotes as the 'angry young men'.

It was with this vogue that Mr Stream came to general notice rather than sporadic notoriety. Suddenly class and pedigree were in question. The son of a labourer might, through social climbing, get into the knickers of the Colonel's daughter. The Colonel would of course be displeased and the putative and rejected son-in-law would preach a sermon to the Colonel's daughter blaming her for the privation suffered by his ancestors and, presumably, for the school meals he endured as a grammar school *ingénue*.

The movement thronged the citadel and Mr Stream was in the midst of the throng, not as one of its sole and leading lights, but as the man with the smarmy knowing smile. He alone knew that all this was leading inexorably to the sixties, to his production at the Round House where exasperating American actors did little more than hold candles and chant and walk naked amongst the ticket holders. The 'little more' was reciting lines from Keats, Wordsworth and Tennyson as though they were to be scorned. And on whom was Mr Stream playing that elaborate joke?

Mr Stream didn't pause to enquire. The Arts Council and the more gullible American funders were falling over.

Of his *Ramayana*, it will be said it was greater in the hype than in the flesh.

The cast has been assembled with great fanfare from all corners of the globe. The accomplishment of the actors is not in question, save for the slightly macho performance of a young actor who plays Ram, one Gerald Blossom, who can't make up his mind whether he's in an Indian epic or a reggae band.

Some members of the cast should certainly have had more extensive English pronunciation rehearsals. Their rendition reminded one of the TV comedies in which Albert Ross is a character in Coleridge.

The work itself is a muddle with individual stories breaking away from the main current and making their own puddles. Unfortunately, the ten-hour dramathon is not a suitable vehicle for the tales which every Hindu imbibes at mother's breast or father's knee. The rivulets seem to join each other or overflow their meanings until Mr Stream (sic) leaves us battling with meanings in a swamp.

Mr Stream's *Ramayana* is not so much a harbinger of a new season but the last dark cloud of the sixties which produced nothing but a mish mash of agitprop, wishful thinking, 'yah-boo' debunking of authority without wit to press its points home and plain proselytising which is in essence anti-dramatic.

Lest I be thought grudging, I must commend the pageantry and the colour of the production, the technical expertise which gives us some hologramatic scenery of stunning effectiveness. The acting of the one Indian in the production, Miss Anjali Patnaik as Sita, is controlled and professional. She brings to the false poetry of Mr Stream's scripts a certain class.

Ellythorn Griffiths

And in the same page of the review, Sara's note:

Dec 11th

Being an *enfant terrible* wears off. I miss the lunches, salads mostly but just occasionally the afternoon steak, a secret love affair with the heaviest claret, taxi back to the flat, phone-call to Robin, start writing at eleven at night and finish the column by three.

Robin gives this toad a chance to spit his venom? Robin, Robin, did I really injure you so?

Dearest Sara,

You may have read Elly's piece. Shall we have that drink after all?

Robin
xx.

It has been like meditation, boss, where the mind gets fixated on a zero. Nothing. I pass my days asleep and am only available to myself after four each afternoon when Sara wakes me with a cup of tea and I have a smoke and am ready to get going by six.

It's the fourth day of performance and Sara is at my elbow. I'm on a mattress in her front room. You wanna know how Ram speaks? I rise to wakefulness, emerging from fragrant layer upon layer of sleep, and feel that beyond Sara stands a greater power, a more malicious one, one that will make demands on my soul . . . It's Ullah. He has discovered me with the help of S. Patel. I must go with him, he says.

I've never seen Ullah dressed so. He's wearing a pinstriped suit and his moustache is shaved so neat that it looks like it smell of aftershave. You could almost see the ghost of a carnation in his lapel so I ask him if it's his wedding, sixth time round. And he say he's in deep trouble and I am his only trusted brother, his soul mate and even his co-religionist.

Trouble, boss. I never even knew Ullah had a family and a son and all this but he keeps them hidden and some newspaper, some local rag, has exposed his son with a photograph and everything.

The story is quite simple. The boy is waiting outside. They have to go to an enquiry that afternoon at the school. I rub the sleep from my eyes.

'I can't get involved in that, me old son. I'm on a twenty-four-hour play, Ullah. I'm eating and breathing lines and sequences.'

He don't know where to turn. Sara offers him a coffee and he takes it with trembling hands. Sits on the sofa and pulls the cutting out of his pocket.

'They make trouble for me, Ali sahib, you are the only brother who can give help, come and speak for me and sort them out. The governors.'

That sounds heavy.

'What fucking governors?'

'i-skool guvnur,' is how he says it. He shows me the newspaper:

IS THIS YOUNG MAN REALLY TWELVE YEARS OLD?

There's a picture of a guy with a growth of beard a few weeks old who looks like he's eighteen or something, but I'm not much good at ages, especially of Asians and white people.

'So who's this?'

'Read it, Ali.'

The article says the boy Hussain got into a dispute with one of his classmates in the playground and beat the shit out of him, a white boy, and the mother of the white boy came to the school playground and Hussain duffed her up too so she's complained to the newspaper and the headmaster and the local education authority and all hell broke loose because a fellow comes down from the education authority and says, 'this boy is obviously not twelve or thirteen,' or whatever Ullah has claimed for his son on his passport and he looks more like nineteen or twenty even though he's short and then the Home Office comes in on the act; they send a passport inspector down to Ullah and ask him to prove that his son is really his son and the school is going to determine whether the boy can stay in secondary education as defined by the Education Act 1944.

The woman tells the paper, 'This boy should be conducting the buses. Look at him, he's got a beard.'

'This fellow has a beard,' I say to Ullah. 'Is he your son?'

'All our family get early hair,' Ullah says.

'Look, boss, you'll have feh count me out, no bakshish, can't do. David Stream, who is next to Allah only in importance will throw me out on my neck. I'm not allowed to think of anything like this, bearded boys, talking dogs, while I'm doing this run.'

Now while Ullah is there the bell rings and Sara lets Anj in. She's gonna make us breakfast and she's walked in with a necklace of delicatessen sausages round her neck in a piss take of the garlands she has to wear on stage. The sausages are hefty and go round twice. She carries the free-range eggs and french bread and stuff.

Ullah can't take his eyes off them sausages.

'Morning folks,' is Anjali, and Ullah is, 'You eating pork sausage, Mr Ali?'

'No man, that's Anjali, she's gonna eat the lot. Hindu person, it's all right.'

'After all she is Indian woman. Miss, you go with this sausage necklace in the public?'

'My God, I'd thought I'd come to make you breakfast, not to a meeting of the medieval affairs collective of Brixton.'

'My friend Ullah,' I say.

And Anj gives him a look which if she was a dog would have been a stream of cold piss.

'He doesn't seem to approve of the food or the costume.'

'No, no. No breakfast, miss, I just come to save my boy.'

'What's wrong with your boy?' Anj asks from the door of the kitchen.

'He's young, missus, with facial hair.'

Anj says, 'Good grief! Not exactly my sort of breakfast conversation.'

A. goes in kitchen. S. feels compassion for U. She says,

'Ullah, what needs doing?'

She says she'll go and speak for him, what does he want saying.

'There are plenty of our boys with little beard in their school.'

Sara says Ullah ought to bring the boy in. He's been waiting outside. When the boy come in I see he don't have much of a beard at all. He is short with googly eyes and has clipped his chin clean with a machine. He looks easily twenty years old to me.

89

'Can they test him?' Ullah asks.

'I don't know whether there's any reliable test for age, but is it possible you made a mistake on his passport about his age?'

Ullah looks a bit shamed. 'It is possible,' he says. 'They were teasing the boy, calling him Paki-bashing and all things, and I always tell him fight back, the blood of Hussain is in your body, show them muslim spirit.'

'That's probably not very helpful,' Sara says. 'Listen, Ullah, can't you ask them to wait for five or six days, do the medical tests next week and we'll get hold of a lawyer for you?'

'I don't mind if he is work on bus or get job, but he come only three months back and he don't speak too much English.'

Ullah is proud of his boy. He sweats and takes out a brown handkerchief to mop his eyebrows.

'Sara will go with you, I gotta brush my teeth,' I say.

Sara don't say goodbye to Anj who's still doing her fry-up. She don't much care for this Ullah scene or Sara.

'What's eating her? She's turned into the Bay of Bengal love league?'

Dec 12th

I catch the coach at Covent Garden with the other performers. It's packed. David says nothing before performances but he sits backstage for half an hour as we prepare in the caravans he has set up for the actors and costumes and props. Silent. The reviews don't affect him. All through the performance I am thinking of Ullah and his bearded boy.

Jamil Jamal has given the play a bad bad bad review and especially Anjali. He calls her (nice, wicked little phrase, the son-of-a-bitch) 'a young Sita playing an old Mother Teresa. The Calcutta slums and concern for them ooze out of the performance Stream has induced in Ms Anjali Patnaik. Sita goes from goddess to social worker. Perhaps Mr Stream believes he is the baptist of the era which does replace the one with the other.'

That's the only thing Sara diary say about Jam's thing in her old paper. Anjali is poisoned by it and it make me mad to see her boy.

She is mortally injured by the hyena who wait this long.

Silver lining of a little tiny chance for me.

I tell her that I don't need to sleep, I could get off the coach with her and go to her place. Sure, she says and she holds my hand in the coach.

'He's just a little show-off boy. Man is man and boy is boy and, tcha, Anjali don't bother with him. Some stupid groupie white people build up the boy. I played in one or two of his tings. You know, but then the liberals start encourage him to write shit about Indians and Asians and the boy begin prosper with soft porn and ting. You can't turn round but he springs some lesbian or incest or something on you. Don't feel no way about him,' I say.

'You know why I bother with him. I thought I could trust him.' Man, she has changed from her saree-and ting into her dressing gown and she gives me a coffee and some scotch in it.

'I invited him to a performance and we'd discussed what David is doing endlessly, and this is what he goes and writes!'

She gives me the piece of print and she's underlined several sentences:

David Stream fits firmly into the stereotypes of Indian culture that have become the fashion since the British took to looking back nostalgically at the Raj. When I was a kid growing up in London I used to go and cheer for the cowboys until Britain compelled me, culturally and spiritually to realise that I was on the other side, I was an Indian.

Plenty stuff like that.

'It's cliché after cliché, I heard that cowboy and Indian thing way back when I was listening to Stokely Carmichael in 1968 or something. I don't think your little boy was born then, or if he was he was masturbating in short trousers with his loving English mother and proud Paki father.'

'Read it all. He's pretty vicious.'

'What you done this guy?' I ask.

'He's a bastard,' she says, 'I asked him what he wants out of life and he's just not serious. He said he likes being a playwright because he can get to screw the actresses. It was all social workers and teachers before and now he can "pull", as he calls it, actresses.'

'Including you?'

I was looking at her as though to say she should be ashamed of peddling this shit.

She says, 'When two people meet and inwardly have attained union there is no need to seek the sanction of the society or the elders . . .'

She was quoting her part where she looks into my eyes and the

91

spotlight from behind her is straight in my face and my shadow stretches over the audience.

'No, not including me. I think he meant a different sort of actress.'

'There ain't no different sort. And I'm not asking out of academic interest, doing research in the sex life of Pakistani playwrights.'

She smile, 'Good.' And she give me a kiss on the mouth but when I go to put my arms about her to accept wholeheartedly, she push my arms away with her elbows and just kiss me standing on tip-toe, mouth to mouth her eyes closed.

My brain start singing like a synthesiser when we go to find David at the hotel. We get in a minicab. The ras claat minicab son-a-bitching blackman asks me if I am the man who ran out of his cab a week ago without pay him the money. I just kiss my teeth and tell him to behave himself. The guy say I look just like the bloke who mugged him for a ten pound fare. Anjali laughs and holds my hand.

'See this ghetto here? The famous Brixton? You know we don't produce no teachers or lawyers or bank managers at all, just minicab drivers. You know why? Because people who live here want to go anywhere else all the time.'

In the foyer an old white woman comes up to us.

'That was David Stream, wasn't it? I saw your marvellous performances. Is he in there?' She points to the entrance to the bar.

'Yes, we're having a conference.'

'So you should, dear,' the old woman says but she won't let us pass.

'I was in India,' she says.

Anjali smiles politely and looks beyond the old lady to see if she can see any of the crew.

'I was with the Girl Guide movement. May I just speak to you. I don't mean to take up your time, but I tried to tell Mr Stream, but he was in ever such a hurry.'

'We've got a meeting,' Anjali says and we hurry off.

The woman live and direc from an Agatha Christie movie with long hair in a black bow and slightly crazy.

David herd us all into the small room behind the bar and says we're doing sixteen performances in India.

There'll be six performances in Delhi, at the same pace, two parts twice and then a day off. Then six in Bombay, probably by the seaside, so he's going to reblock it for the sand and the beach because he's found a location where we can have two sides of sea as the edges of

'Xerxes.'

'Oh hi!'

He's certain I've seen him.

I go close up to him.

'Raincoat brigade?'

He smiles nervously.

I grab the end of the raincoat where the two books have gone and before he can protest or step back, I lift the hem of his garment, like a wife removing fluff from hubbie's trousers. I pull the two books out. His eyes open wide. There's so much of a crowd in the shop that no one notices.

'Do you know Naipaul on India?'

'Yes,' he says, lame, as though I've hit him with a cricket bat in his ribs. I take the books, pick the two Naipaul's I want off the shelves leaving Xerxes stunned and hand the lot over the counter. I join the queue where one pays for books with Xerxes alongside me.

'Look, I'll pay for those.'

'Be my guest,' I say.

As we walk out together I turn to him.

'For someone so smart that's a really stupid thing to do. They have electronic alarms going off if you take the books out of the store.'

'Haven't done this for a long time.' He is embarrassed.

'I thought your trade was babies, not books.'

Now I take the books out of the packet and hand them to him.

Two books on babycare, on bringing up infants.

'What are they for?'

'Just interested. I'm sort of broke at present.'

'Silly stunt to pull.'

'Great, you saved my life, I can't even buy you a drink.'

I bought him one.

He said he was working on something for the BBC but was between homes and jobs and sob story all over.

I told him I was soon off with the production to India.

'It's like that bookshop, crowded, they've got everything, but nothing's where it should be.'

'Find out for myself,' I said.

Robin has been sceptical and scathing about my trip. He's jealous. He says I don't know anything about the place, I'm wandering in like the heroine of *A Passage To India*. I reply that one doesn't have to go to India to know about it, it's like Darwin's theory, everyone knows what it is even though very few have read *On the Origin of Species* – the idea of India is almost bigger than the experience of it. He says that's bullshit, I don't even know any Indians.

Now I do, I know XX, funny shoplifting Indian.

We drink till closing time and then he walks me down Oxford Street and gets in a cab with me.

He leaves the cab at Ladbroke Grove. I wait while he disappears with twenty pounds I give him to fetch some drugs from a council estate.

Ali is asleep when we get in so we tiptoe past him. Xerxes is the kind of guy you can talk into the night with. Then it strikes me I don't want to sleep with him, but I'll do it. It's uninteresting in itself. It's funny how thin he is with bony hips like a pun on the hollows in his cheeks. I don't want to wake Ali who'll leave for David's sessions early in the morning, so I ask him to creep about.

A useless precaution. Ali wakes up in the middle of the night, just as we've decided to get to bed and, knocking once, barges in. He takes in the fact of Xerxes and looks away from him.

'Sara, disaster, bwoy, Maureen and the girl can't do the thing.'

'What do you mean? Not at all?'

He shakes his head. Shit. Ali was going to get his ex-wife to look after the flat and feed the cats once a day but he tells me she's moving away, out of London and will be coming and going from the city. She has to earn a living, he says, and her boy friend has worked out some deal. He had to tell me so I could think of something else.

I do think of something else the next morning as Xerxes puts on his socks. Maybe he could keep an eye on the place while we are in India. He says he'll phone. Sure, he hasn't got a place to live and he needs a quiet place to write. Besides the cat licks his face as he sleeps.

Dec 27th

Anjali brings Ali to Binky's party. David doesn't know they'll be there. It's in Hampstead in one of the roads that leads off the Heath in a huge mansion where Binky is staying for the duration of his designer tour. David is one of the guests of honour and the other is the Indian Deputy High Commissioner.

I can see that Anjali keeps her eyes on the door. She is expecting someone.

The party splits into men and women. The women are dressed in elaborate sarees, the Indians and two or three of the Englishwomen, old India-followers all, are dressed as they ought to be to meet a Deputy High Commissioner.

Binky comes up with an Englishman in pinstripes. Yes, a junior Home Office minister is introduced. I am just about beginning to smile at him, and we are summing each other up, wondering, as Ali would say, what each others' hustle is, when there is a mild flutter signalling a shift in the room's attention. The Pakistani playwright, Jam, walks in, wearing for once not his hat and waistcoat, but a baggy suit made of raw silk. Binky has of course gone up to greet him. He himself is dressed in ultimate camp Indian style, with his coloured shawl about his shoulders which he pushes back as he greets his guests much as an Englishman from the *Brideshead Revisited* era would push back the long golden locks which fall into his eyes.

Jam's entry has disturbed the composition of the room.

The Deputy High Commissioner's wife is introduced to me.

'And who is that person in the pinstripe three-piece suit?' she asks me, female confidentiality to the fore.

'That's some Home Office minister,' I say. 'I believe he's very important, in charge of immigrants and the police.'

The irony escapes her.

'Police? You can introduce me,' she says, and walks over to him flourishing the end of her radiant peacock-blue saree.

Mrs Deputy needs no introductions, she's taken a bit of him before I can follow holding my glass of wine.

There are servants in white jackets, Indians, handing out the champagne and wine and whisky. Binky assures people that it's Chivas Regal, he never drinks anything else.

I am looking at the playwright. Anjali is conspicuously trying to ignore him and has taken Ali into a circle of Indian women who are asking him about the joys of playing Ram.

'But something must be able to be done,' Mrs Deputy High Commission is saying at my elbow to Mr Pinstripe in charge of the police.

The junior minister looks amused but slightly taken aback.

'It's very difficult if they haven't broken the law. Besides where would we find them? They must have disappeared into Manchester or Bradford or God knows where, working in some Indian restaurant. When their diplomatic visa expires we shall get on their tails.' He smiles.

'And meanwhile what do you suggest I do for servants? I know it's not really a police problem, but surely you must keep some tabs on people who come here on diplomatic passports?'

The servants she brought from India have run away.

'Scotland Yard won't treat them as missing persons,' the minister says, with the air of a good constituency MP who has encountered the problem before but can't do much about it.

'If this was New Delhi and a British diplomat or American had complained that their servants had gone absent without leave, we'd get them back for you like a shot,' Mrs Deputy High Commission says.

'What a civilised place,' says the junior minister from the Home Office.

Ali delights the Indian ladies with a recitation in Sanskrit.

David is deep in conversation all evening with the Deputy High Commissioner and Binky. Binky goes into the adjoining room which is a Hampstead 'library', all false oak panelling and leather-bound Walter Scotts, and fetches a book for him. David leafs through the book. We eat Tandoori chicken and kebabs and pilau rice and the most exquisite vegetarian kofta I've tasted. Binky claims he cooked it himself. He took time off from the exhibition. Tilak of course is not invited here.

Oscar and Scobie check me *chez* gun-run, in other words Maureen House. We got three days to catch up with life and back on the *Ramayana* bandwagon. I welcome the break, except for the fact that Anjali and I will not check each other visage as Shakespeare might have say. She to Windermere has gone. She say 'friends', I suspect Jam the Pak playwright. She has audacity. Give her that. Sir, it is given! Who are we to withhold such dessert.

To throw bloodhound off track she invents the red herring of trust.

'Will you see me off at the station?'

I am willing to do and dying to know where she goes. To Windermere, 'Wordsworth territory, just to get away from it all'.

'Wordsworth? Listen, "The sunlight on the garden hardens and grows cold" . . .'

'Does it? That's not Wordsworth, is it?'

'All I know of Wordsworth is *The Charge of the Light Brigade*, half a league and into the flippin valley to get bad cut-arse. Boy.'

'It was Tennyson.'

'Win some, lose some. Name one man who could quote hundred per cent.'

'Give up.'

'David Stream?'

She laughs. I carry her bag, a dark blue real canvas job and when we get to the station I say I'm going for a leak and she says leave the bag.

'Not while you browse through the W. H. Smiths, too many muggers.'

I take it with me and I don't know what the attendant thinks but I open the raas claat bag and rummage in it. Nighties, T-shirts, black jeans, bloody tops with Next labels, compact for make-up, a magazine call *India Today*. God forgive me, I know what I'm looking for. There's that little circular plastic case and my hands, trembling, prise it open. Mirror and powder. Another secret-powder. I am ashamed of myself. Still, I can't stop. The piss-house attendant is getting vaguely curious because I dig like a dog teased with a scent of bitch-heat.

I am innocent, I do it, comes the cry down the corridor of the ages, for love, for jealousy, for the burning feeling that she is only a quarter mine, her heart belongs elsewhere and she is willing to endow her body with her heart. Stop. There's no disc here. Jah forgive I, I zip up the canvas bag and take a leak, my heart still thumping, and walk out into the shaded sunshine of the railway station.

Without guilt I hand over the bag. It was my right to look and I have found zilch. I now think nothing. A lie. I think has she switched to the pill? Is she that smart? Is the pill case the little plastic thing distorting the back pocket of her trousers? Can I see its trace. Worse, will the bastard come out to India? She catches her train.

Why do I love thee, let me count the whys.

I find it impossible to examine my heart. When I start a conversation like that with myself, I get bored. I can't say why, beyond a sexual thing. I imagine her at various angles, with and without clothes on. But I don't know the shape of her body, the subtle nuance of bone structure, of the colour of her skin, something, the size of her bum, the way it falls. Her nipples. Brown on brown. I want to see that. That's only one of the whys. I don't know about her mind. You know, when I was first going with Maureen, I could count off why I loved her on the fingers of one hand. And then I'd go on to my other hand and, if I was recounting the romance to her, I'd move to my toes.

There were so many reasons.

Sometimes I fall for a girl, eh, just like that, a girl in the bar at a theatre where I'm working. I see her in my sleep. If she drives a beige Metro, every time I pass a beige Metro on the streets my heart skips a beat. My sleep is infested and my dreams held hostage by the beauty of it, by the beige Metro, by the thought that fate is cruel, that her wonders are reserved for the younger, the subtler, the richer, the more successful, for that prince who is not tainted by being a lousy actor and my heart is held in suspended animation and the day's under eclipse and sun's blotted out if she frowns. And after the production, after I drop in once or twice to the bar just to see her I get to thinking what the hell did I see in that woman anyway? That kinda love wears off. Then there's sociological reasons.

They are good reasons for love and I see it all around me. People love people because they represent some missing thing in their world. The white rich longs for the black poor, like a yin going for a yang, the *nouveau* goes for the class, the classy go for the energetic.

Such thoughts, such reasons for loving, which ultimately become the reason for living, hang about like dim actors who have forgotten their lines in the wings of my imagination! Take it away, Ali!

That's playing on my mind when I go down the Lion for a drink with Scobie and a nest boy, Oscar.

'Production going all right? Can't turn round but my boy is on the radio. Big star now, Ali. Known to the underworld as Boot Polish. So wha happen, Boot?'

'I dere,' I say.

We get to drinking the sixth pint and talking about the dolphins. There's this article by a scientist in America, or some interview with the feller and Oscar and Scobie have bothered to read it and they find that I, by supreme coincidence, or the love of Allah who ordains our literary foraging, I have looked at it too because Sara show me it. The guy says he's done plenty experiments with dolphins and they are racist, because dolphins of one colour don't mess with dolphins of the next colour. So then he applies the name 'racism' to that and bingo, everyone's thinking you can't get away from it. When in Dolphinia, do as the dolphins do.

'But, king, we don't live in Dolphinia,' Scobie say.

'The guy is right,' Oscar says.

'Then how come you fuck girls of all colours?'

'Because my sex instinct, boy, is stronger than my dolphin instinct. That's me. That's the way I am. Born with a good sex drive. But these racist boys there, National Front and all this arse. Their dolphin instinct, it stronger than their sex, can't overcome and conquer it. This, the American scientist feller got something. But, Ali, boy, Scobie don't agree because you know what Scobie go and do?'

'What?'

'I'll tell you if you want to know, it's no big thing,' Scobie protests. But Oscar have him on the run. He's doubling up and holding his gut.

'Oooo. This boy Scobie go and register in a Southall agency. I tell you he's something else. He hear it on the Asian pirate radio. There's an agency for Asian girls who don't want to marry Asian men. They want to go further afield. Plenty white men join up because they don't want white women. So Scobie signs up by post. They don't know he's black. The boy goes on his first date with a bunch of flowers. She slam the door in his face in Ealing and you could hear it in Brixton. Scobie left standing there on the doorstep. The saree-clad angel waiting for her knight in shining armour opens the door. Guess who's coming to dinner? Oooo. Scobie, boy, she thought he was the minicab man.'

We are both laughing now and Scobie stands and looks around the pub, half amused himself.

'There stands Scobie, his flowers turning to dust, and turning to ashes his dreams of the conquest of Asia.'

'Why do these white guys want Asian women?'

'Because white girls too bad for them. Run around, demand their rights and keep them on their toes. Want this, do that, be a man and grow bigger than the next one or richer than the last one. It's shit. So they reckon they can send for some Filipino girl or some Asian bride.'

'They're making a mistake with these,' I say. 'If an Asian girl breaks loose enough to join the agency and dodge Asian men, then she's not going to take any shit either. So the agency can't work.'

'See what I mean?' Oscar says. 'A dead loss from the start and you're bound to find Scobie investing in that. Like the time some fool tell him to join his business selling life insurance for pets. "The English will buy it." Tchahh. So much dogs died on him, they got bankrupt in three weeks. Prince, you shoulda done some market research on the death rate amongst gerbils and budgies.'

'I hear you got an Indian girl there, Ali bwoy,' Scobie says.

'His wife run off with a Paki man so he thought he'd catch his own lickle Asian thing,' Oscar says.

'If you weren't my friend I'd belt you. I know some heavy kung fu now and I'd put your jaw in such a big sling, you'd look like one of them babies who are carried by storks.'

'This play get you sensitive, boy. Or you really in love or something. So she taking you to India?'

'She is. You must have a good astrologer. Or maybe you even read the papers. You been going to evening classes?'

Oscar means well, he means well. My heart burns.

*　　　*　　　*

I choose from among the letters now. Some don't make no sense, some of the things Sara does I don't even suspect. Some people just write to her in a code, like some CIA business. Them kids like to play James Bond. I didn't check it then, because I saw all the letters, diaries, papers in the study, but that wasn't what I was bothered with, I was at the time snooping around her toiletries, picking up a spots cream tube or a herb thing for the skin. I found a couple strange things, cocoa butter, I thought only black guys used that for chapped lips and black girls used it for skin shine and that.

A card turns up?

Safe-as-'ouses,

Quand du bist nether et how's-that! Like a Bridge Over Troubled Waters (sic).

And what will the Redbreast do then?

I don't suppose he want to disguise the fact that it's Robin, but what the fuck it means is another man's guess, because I don't want waste my time, but a next letter, (same pile, probably same day) is something new:

Dear Sara,

Tilak talks to you but he won't say what's really on his mind so I have to do the dirty work. He's very proud and you know that. He's told you all about himself and the commune and the seeds he's buying and all the help he's giving all the people in his village.

But he can't ask you the question (not that question, silly!). We'd like to know if you would introduce his work and his talent and perhaps him and me to Robin Minster, your boy friend I believe (now don't ask me how I know, girls will talk) and former editor who's been appointed on to some big wheel committee of parliament on the ethnic arts.

116

As you know, and Tilak has learnt this very fast, black people suffer all kinds of institutional racism and no funding exists for the arts because of all the cuts, especially in the ethnic scene, if you know what I mean. I know as well as you that a lot of crooks get funding too by calling themselves black. We call them coconuts – because they are white inside and brown outside. Tilak has some great ideas about how consciousness can be raised through art. He said he's mentioned it to you but I've forced him to write a paper on it and maybe Robin should see it. Basically of course, and I want to admit it to start with, we hope we can get some funding and start the things that need doing badly.

I am sorry to burden you with this, but you strike me as someone who cares. And who respects Tilak as much as we all do.

Yours very sincerely,

In sisterhood

Sonya (You know the one. Banner in hand, slogan in mouth)

PS   Tilak found this letter and we've just had three hours worth of flaming row about sending begging letters, but I won and he sends his love.

Sara confide in me: 'Sonya's a funny girl, I know her dad. He knows David and he wants the account of the whole production when it's done and David knows Sara and Sara knows Tilak and Tilak wants to know Robin who lay in the house that Jack built.'

'So then write the book about me.'

'Ali, the world will know so much about you, they won't need a book from me.'

She so nice.

'Write about police giving black youth a bad time in a police van or something. Them Hampstead people who buy books live on that shit.'

She say, 'Ali, you know, the only thing you're cynical about is black people. About everything else, you're an optimist, a man of generosity and with flourish. Tch, Tch.'

She wrote about the music changes David was doing with us.

Dec 23rd

The chorus of forest creatures is a sound effect the cast have been taught. David's taken it into his head that he was wrong about the

117

chorus, it ought to be an inarticulate chanting as taught by the musical crew, it ought to have an overt message. He wants, he tells me, to use every millimetre of his canvas. The chorus is taught a new message. It is, I believe, Binky's doing. He has been discussing Sikhism with David and David has been out and about in the London University School of Oriental and African Studies, looking for a Sikh professor. He finds one in the faculty of physics. 'A man,' David tells me, fascinated, 'who has devoted the last thirteen years to studying matter that passes through other matter. Only, this matter doesn't exist, if you see what he means. You can measure its spinning velocity, but you can't touch it or have anything else touch it.'

But that wasn't his business with the professor. He now has a series of verses translated and some not translated, from the Guru Granth Sahib, the Sikh scriptures, written into the chorus.

'For the Sikh widows, a gesture,' he says. He twinkles.

Dec 30th

Sonya sends me Tilak's memorandum on the ethnic arts. It's not the kind of thing I can send to Robin. Basically because it's illiterate. Robin, I think, would be easily put off by the ungrammatical and slightly pompous nature of its claims. We'd get no further.

Item:

'The Asian civilisation is a vast and wonderful arch beneath which humanity can take shelter. There is temporary aberration, but Rome was not built in one evening and we have here only the twilight of the western concept of material progress and material culture. Beneath that archway of Asian culture can be found means of survival which the peasants in numberless villages in India have preserved the best.

'Examine the persons who come to your fair country from our land. Who are they? Some are fake peoples from a middle class which is more vicious than the South African whites. They flog their servants and they have laid waste to the culture and potential, economic and philosophical of India. Yet most of them, and we are talking here about the common Asian citizen, be they Muslim or Hindu or Sikh or any other thing from the minorities, are from the peasantry and are now in two generations or more out of touch with their roots.

'Yet you cannot transplant a tree without getting some change in the character of the leaves. What soil has it fallen on? This soil of Britain is hostile to black people. At least West Indians can speak the language but many of our people cannot. They need much more the tying down to their roots which only arts and culture and the way of life that they have left behind can give them.

'We propose a small academy, on the scale of the village, to be financed partly by the hard work of those who participate also. We are thinking here of the way that art grows in India, organically from the society in which it is born for thousands of years. The peasant has no suspicion of machines. Only the way they are used. In our model village in Rajasthan, the peasants all earn their living by work on the soil and on animals and take their culture as part of that life without wanting full-time money from it. In the west art has got divorced from work. Both spectators and producers of art are alienated as Brecht said . . .'

Dec 31st

'Mirror, mirror on the wall
Was woman guilty before the fall?'
Robin buys a small piece. He instructs the diarist to use it.

Step-motherist running dogs: 'The cast of the *Ramayana* has had an imported guru lecturing them at the behest of supremo David Stream. The sleek Indian *nouveau*-guru came up with a formulation worthy of notice by the readers of the diary, worthy phoneticians and lexicographers all. The concept of step-motherism, as in fairy stories, is part of multicultural Britain – every Hindu child reads this disguised bias in the *Ramayana*. Now will there be violent protests against Mr Stream's production by those of the chattering and letter-writing classes who have second marriages and, in the manner of the civilisations of Islington and Hampstead, have a very apologetically forward view of step-motherhood? Will the *Ramayana* offend this growing minority of organised women? Step-mothers of the world unite, you are younger and prettier than Cinderella or Snow White think!'

David didn't see the piece or didn't comment on it. As his press secretary, I didn't clip it out for his particular attention. Deceiving him has an edge, a thrill about it.

Jan 4th

'OK, what does he want?' asks Robin as soon as I meet him at his club. I haven't taken my coat off.

'Do you really think we should be seen here together? Maybe the gossip columnist of our dear paper has some stringers right here, at the next table, leaning on the bar. "Editor meets ex- hackette who still owes the paper fifty thousand pounds in fines."'

'I chose the venue. What's your friend's submission?'

I give him a piece of paper on which I've tried to summarise what I think are Tilak's arguments.

Robin takes half a minute to peruse the piece of paper.

'Sounds a good man. Amazing the number of friends you make, when you're grand panjandrum on this kind of committee. Every reggae artist in Brixton is ringing me up and asking me out for a meal.'

'He is actually a remarkable man.'

I tell Robin the story of Binky and Tilak. Binky does the front of the house, the concept, the design, the public relations. Tilak does the managing of plastic bags holding yoghurt cartons at the YMCA.

'Isn't it time we changed the cultural leadership of the ethnic arts?'

'All arts?'

I think about it.

'I don't suppose so. David, for instance, is a Western artist and has earned his place. Despite your bitch of an Ellythorn writing his poison pen open letter in your, shall I say "my", space.'

'The committee is taking evidence, Sara and all sorts of interesting bods turn up. But this fellow has something new to say, by all means send him along. I'll send the invite via you. Does he have a work permit?'

'He's here on a visa but that's secondary. I've been covering theatre for you and others for long enough to recognise something authentic when I see it.'

Robin looks at me as though he wants to ask me if I only see and hear it. I reply with a look I've practised, God help me. Yes, Robin, I haven't fucked him. You cheapskate.

He takes the point. He orders the wine. His cuff button is missing. 'There's not much time. The committee is "consulting the community" till Thursday and then we shut shop.'

'He'll be there tomorrow. And to answer your unspoken question, he'll bring along his girl friend.'

The wine is satisfactory. I have acquired a taste for salt lassi.

*

Next letter from the girl Sonya in Sara collection.

Dear Sara,

Thanks a zillion. Kiss kiss and grovel. Your Robin and my Tilak are in love and Tilak went to dinner with two of the MPs on the committee. You know that *Sanskriti* has packed up and the lads have gone home. It was a hell of a job seeing them all off. One idiot had bought a fridge and thought he could smuggle it on to the aircraft as hand-baggage. Economy class too.

Binky has gone to Geneva. And Tilak had to get back to the Houses of Parliament for the interview, to give evidence etc. and I had to deal with all their bloody excess baggage. The man with the baby and the bamboo was the worst. He just couldn't understand why they wouldn't load his bloody fridge on with the rest of his baggage as it belonged to him. He said he'd hold it on his seat and sit on the floor if necessary. Finally he had to be separated from his thing by persuasion and a little bit of force and the threat that if Binky heard about it, he'd have him castrated in Delhi. They may have said it as a joke but Tilak swears it's what would happen.

Actually baby-bamboo man was playing a very subtle trick, Tilak thinks. They know all about freight costing money, but they also found out that Binky has arranged with Air India to take all their baggage and charge the entire freight bill to the Cultural Ministry because they had all the props and stuff to take back.

I had to arrange for it to go by sea in the end.

The black MP was very impressed with Tilak. I think when they get going the committee will see that funding bodies pay attention to us. What it is to have influential friends. Tilak says he didn't know it worked like this in England too, but I assured him it did. I just bloody hope you get this letter, but I've made a photocopy and am sending it to the Oberoi in Delhi because I hear that's where you and David and the bigwigs are staying.

Tilak sends a million salaams.

If my travelling scholarship comes through, maybe I'll be in India too before the tour is over. Very very good luck with your wretched *Ramayana* and Tilak sends his oodles of love and kisses and his thumbprint next to mine.

Yours forever. We love you Sara,
Sonya and Tilak

Last night and I'm sleeping. Anjali returns tomorrow from Windermere. I tell her she must help me pack because I don't know how hot it'll be and she tells me if I have some favourite trousers which really fit me well or make my vanity swell, like some big brand name or somethin, I should take them to India and have them duplicated.

Maureen phones me two in the moring. 'You've got to come. There's no one but you. Martha is in danger, just come.'

I drag on my trousers and I go. Her voice sounds desperate, curt. She's not one to raise false alarms and she doesn't even say nothing as introduction.

I run, slam the door behind me. The streets are deserted and a slow drizzle earlier has made it wet and brought out that smell of dust to which I'm addicted. The only place alive is Big Momma's Mini-Cabs with its blue light that should be whirling, but has been smashed. I catch a lazy orange Cortina with a lazy black driver. My heart thumps like a Sly and Robbie sessions track. Maureen has left the door slightly open for me.

She looks green, boy, shivering. Thank God and all this.

She starts crying as soon as she see me. I go in. The hall light is off and the front room light is on. She motions me to be quiet, hush.

Martha is sitting in the front room with her face against a pillow to stifle her crying.

'He's gone wild. He's got a gun and he's drunk, but I can't pull the gun away from him, he might wake up. I don't know what's got into him.' Then she stops. 'And . . . and . . . my God . . . he shot the dog, Gerry. His own dog. It's lying there in Martha's bedroom. I can't go in there . . .'

This ain't no joke. One dead dog in one bedroom, one drunk gun-runner with a pistol in the next. But the sight of Martha, I didn't want to ask no questions.

'Get me a broom handle,' I say.

I motion her into the bedroom. The boy has collapsed on the floor and he's still clutching a little revolver.

I motion Maureen to my left and take up my position over him.

I smack the gun out of his hand with a swipe of the broom handle and it scuttles across the floor to where Maureen is and she picks it up and the guy awakes.

'Next one to your head, John,' I say.

He's grabbed his wrist. I must have bust it. He screams as the pain and realisation come on and he lurches forward and falls again.

'Hit him on the head if he wakes up, I'm calling reinforcements.'

I give her the broom handle. I go in the front room and phone up S. Patel to come straight away and bring Ullah with him, wake his arse up, it's an emergency.

They come. I find the dead dog in the next room. It's brains blown out. Maureen is crying in the front room. Mess of her life or mess of her house, I don't ask. We wrap the dog in an old blanket. Ullah sits guard over Mr Gun-run-pissed. He opens his eyes and don't know what's happening to him.

Maureen says he's turned the dog neurotic, the pressure of being under arrest and pending trial was getting to the man and it got to the dog too. The dog tried all kind of funny tricks. It started masturbating at every opportunity. Climb on anything. And Mr Gun-run-paralytic didn't like that and he started spanking him and bringing him under control and a battle of wills began. He drank a whole bottle of Chivas Regal and some other famous whisky that was left over, then he started training the dog not to masturbate. So the dog took a piece of his thigh off. So the guy got wild and brought out a gun which Maureen didn't even know he had and he confronted the dog and the dog, his lifelong friend and amigo and kemo sabbay, gave him the sign of the bared teeth so he punched the dog and the dog bit him again and he got furious and shot the dog in the head and Martha saw the dog dying.

We wrapped Mr Gun-sling-dog-shooter in another blanket and dragged the dog and the man into the back of Ullah's van.

I said goodbye to Maureen. I had taken a bucket and cleaned up a bit of the mess but the carpet would never be the same again.

'Do you want him dead or alive?' I asked Maureen.

'He'll be all right tomorrow. I swear. I don't know what's got into him.'

'I thought you were against macho guys.'

'I am. He uses a real pistol, not his prick.' She said it automatically and immediately she clutched my arm.

'Gerry, I'm sorry, I didn't mean that. I'm sorry, I don't know what I'm saying, you've been really so so sweet, a darling. I'd never have asked anyone else on earth, I couldn't and not just because you're Martha's father. I rang you because there's no one else I can ring.'

'Sure, you know you walk all over me when you can.'

'Please don't hurt me. You don't know how grateful I am. Or maybe you do know, you bastard, and you'll take advantage . . .'

'No I won't. I'm off to India tomorrow, Maureen.'

'What are you going to do with him? Take him to your place?'
'I don't have "a place", remember?' I say.
'Don't take him to the police.'
'We'll put him in Ullah's bed and let him wake up with a sore bum and a broken wrist and feel the pain. Then he'll know not to terrorise little girls and beautiful women.'
She said, 'You can come back home if you like, before you leave. I mean tonight.'
Maureen, Maureen!

*　　　*　　　*

Jan 11th

Heathrow. A sense of ceremony about this departure. David is garlanded by various ethnic organisations such as the Anglo-British Friendship Association. He doesn't quite know who they are, or the Sanskrit Study Circle or the Bharat Bhavan of Loughborough, but he accepts the garlands and the congratulations and is copiously photographed with the worthies of the associations standing beside him. He has to smile though he is unprepared for any of it. He is wearing jeans and a safari shirt, ready for Delhi and carries his cotton jacket over his arm. A lot of dignified actors attacked by the paparazzi, Sieg and Akiro especially, hanging about, both wearing shades, standing in a queue of baggage and all the Air India staff getting autographs before the event. Ali comes late. He's spent the night out somewhere and had a hassle getting into my flat. Not to get his luggage, because I've left him a note saying I've taken it to the airport, but to pick up a book of poems which he's left in the front room by his bed. S. Patel is there to see us off.

Anjali, bright green slacks and smart travel luggage, a shawl for alighting in Delhi, looks very seasoned. She stands above the necessity for travel, she is truly international. Planes are only a temporary nuisance, not an occasion. Sita, Sita, queen of the jungle, queen in exile, returns to India.

The flight is uneventful. The cast sing songs, a Japanese ditty, all those vertical notes and then the musicians, the tablawalla and Sunil the sitarist, start Lennon–McCartney as we are crossing Syria and the pilot tells us to look out of the window and see the petrol fires burning like sore eyes in giant earth. I see nothing. The entire cast

124

sings the Lennon–McCartney songs. The sitar cries like a Jimi Hendrix guitar in Sunil's hands.

'Don't make it bad. Take a sad song and make it better.'

David reads newspapers and smiles. He didn't want to be in charge of the marines, but some of the cast are drinking and there is a tension beneath the uneasy truce of internationals here. I have never heard Ali say that anyone from the cast, apart from Anjali, has ever alluded to or shown any interest in his being a black in Britain. Maybe a Japanese from Tokyo thinks being Japanese in Tokyo is unique enough. Yes, they've marvelled at each other's dramatic technique. That too is fucking pretence. Akiro knows about Nō, but then I've read books which explain it and Sieg talks about Brechtian theatre but any drama student from a reasonable polytechnic knows that stuff, though actors carry on the pretence that humanity has heard it for the first time. Maybe its part of the discipline of their profession, making the lines new every night. Anjali says nothing. She smiles and sits next to David and discusses newspaper articles no doubt. Ali walks up and down the aisle till the hostess tells him to stop it. He's sitting next to me.

'Scobie come from Trinidad las year. He's moving with this steelbandsman called Fantasy, one ugly brother if ever you want to see him. Nose like vulture beak, lips like an American hamburger advert,' he says when the reading lights are on and the plane is in darkness. 'Scobie was returning and Fantasy was turning up to play in the Notting Hill Carnival, first time out. Boy, Sara, they was dying to have certified fun.' Ali is cute when he gets going.

'They start roll a spliff, turn on the Sony Walkman full blaas, and she come up and say, "Put that thing out," and then they playing a tape and gallerying in the gangway and drinking champagne. She can't handle it, the air hostess, black girl on WIAA. Scobie start cheekin her. "I'll smoke what I want, girl, just look out of the window, do you see Trinidad? Do you see England? Is pure blue sea and Atlantic Ocean. You don't believe in democracy and rule of law?" The gel don't understand. "Is not much people to pass law here, too much water." They start laugh at her and Scobie gets up, shaking his arse and dancing in the aisles.

'"Champagne, get some champagne, sister, and join the ravers."

'The hostess doesn't want to join the ravers.

'"I am sorry, sir, but you are subject to the law of the originating country of the aircraft."

'Scobie tell her, "Yeah? Where the Trinidad policeman? You turn police?" Poor girl couldn't take it. She went and call the captain. He come out of his cabin and when they see him approach they panic the rest of the passenger and shout, "Captain abandon the steering wheel, we moving on automatic pilot to raas claat." The captain walk in full regalia up to Scobie and Fants and they dancing and grooving in the back. Suddenly Scobie shout, "Victor, man, you driving planes now? Last time I saw you you was running a taxi between Port of Spain and San Fernando." He knew the guy. They'd been in school together and Scobie was really pleased to see him. "Eh, remember the time you copy my homework and the maths teacher said you copy Scobie and licked down your arse, bit lathi in little batti, not for copying but for foolishness. The teacher say, dig this, "Turning the lame blind is a bad miracle."

'The captain retreat, boy, he say, "Yes, Scobie, how are you and glad to have you gentlemen on board," and all this. Him gone back to he cockpit and tell the hostess to give the boys a couple of champagne on the house.'

Ali tells his story and watches Anjali. She is dozing after a few glasses of wine. David drinks orange juice. The best joke he can muster is that Air India doesn't serve lassi. The cast sitting around him laugh politely.

That's the story I was supposed to have tell her on the plane as it is in her diary, but I swear something has knocked the memory out of my head. There was no such story and I don't remember it. But the guys, Fantasy and Scobie and that, maybe I mentioned them differently to her and she's put them into this scene but I don't remember saying or even hearing myself nothing like this.

Check the rest of the diary, it's getting close:

Jan 12th

They say people, people, people, the throng, India, the mob given national status, the ant hill searching for statehood, the font of philosophies, the overwhelming case for birth control, the place where square inches of land are overwhelmed by the pressure on them . . . the magnificent cliché. No such thing. Delhi airport, Paalam, is deserted. A few porters, a great many policemen and some passengers, but no throng. A raw edge on everything. You look at the buildings and they don't pretend to be architecture, they are just steel and glass, fixed together as best it could be done. Garlands again, a reception committee of a few souls. There are coaches laid on by the hotel. The run from the airport is empty. Vast open spaces, and this is a city? Then the houses, mile on mile of detached houses in cement. No stone, it's all new.

The name plates of the owners are inscribed or painted in ground glass with a bulb behind them cemented into a box on the gate posts. Very little traffic till we hit the nebulous centre of town. The musicians are sitting next to me. They haven't been home for months. They look more eagerly out of the coach window than the foreigners. That word is banned. David tells us before we start that we are not to use that vile word. No 'foreigners', the planet belongs to us. Etc.

The second day, a woman reporter wants to write me up. We're at the Oberoi and David has set us loose. He's fixing lighting and contracts and government stuff and he's dining with ministers and Rajiv Gandhi's closest, closest associates (a buzz word, one constantly hears of the firm contact, the 'right hand-ness' of the man you have just spoken to, the closeness to power and prestige of the man you thought merited nothing. So-and-so, who can be introduced the next day, is at only one remove from the throne. So-and-so, whose phone number can be obtained even now, only he's gone to Agra or Bihar or Madras and is only expected back by the third plane on the morrow, is very very close.)

She wants an interview. I tell her about the production and little ole me. This person has done some research. She's from the hot daily. She comes across in her kurta and churidar pyjamas as really, truly, no bullshit, on the side of the universal female. We talk for six hours, first by the poolside then in my room on the sixth floor, then in the bar, then in the drive and I walk her to her car in the moonlight and go back up the driveway to join the rest. She's a sister. Her headline is not very sisterly:

FROM MEDIA BITCH TO GURU PITCH — SARA FRASER STEWART, 'CHRONICLER' OF DAVID STREAM'S RAMAYANA TELLS HOW SHE GOT INVOLVED

Burn me with a joss stick. She got the spelling of Stuart wrong. A fairly accurate representation of what I'd said to her, but not what I meant at all. David looks at it when he visits. He's not at the hotel. He's at Binky's mansion. He's on the phone to the production people all the time. Ali is amused at my having been set up for the first big interview. There have been puffs in the papers about the cast of Ramayana having landed.

EARTHLINGS BRING ATHLETES FOOT EPIDEMIC TO MARS. BEWARE THE HUMANS BEARING SOCKS.

(It's not funny. I was actually asked on my first day in the foyer of the hotel if I had any Marks and Spencers socks or stockings or anything like that to sell).

We go to Connaught Place, the real centre. Ali takes a look round at the neat streets, the Lutyens set-out, the scale of building which on the approach to the heart of Delhi is grandiose.

'British intended feh stay here, boss! Them is serious buildings there. They didn't plan on movin at all.'

It is apparent, just breathing the night air of Delhi, what he means. I've travelled to the Caribbean islands, to Barbados, Jamaica one or two smaller places, and they've got a building or two, but there's no doubt why someone named this place the jewel in the crown. The *ding an sich*.

Marvellous massage. Goes on the bill. The aura of an American sauna club. The imitation Coca-Cola is called 'Thums Up' (sic).

We haven't seen Anjali. Third day she moves in. She's had a chat with David. She's a star. She can't live with friends while she is doing the tour. She has to live with the cast. The outside world of India overwhelms her.

'We have to keep tunnel vision. That's what acting is about. I'm going to live here and swim in the pool with you and be rich and decadent and bourgeois and work damned hard at the play when we get going.'

We have only three days rehearsal.

Paradise, boss. First day I go out and buy shirts on their main street called Jan Path for one pound each, cotton stuff that sells in the Oxford Street shops for thirty pounds. Joke. As you walk down they know what you want.

One thing, they don't hold doors for you and wait and hang about and be polite because you're a black man like some English do. I didn't notice it till I hit this here town. Indians are polite, but they not patronising your race. They don't look at a black face and go 'stand back make a demo'. They pass and they smile and they love you maybe. I don't think half them know Jamaica from arsehole. Maybe they heard of the West Indian cricket team. In fact they most certainly heard of the West Indian cricket team because people shout Viv Richards at me once or twice across café floors. Too many people held doors for me in merry England. I hate it.

David says three days rehearsal with the lights and for the musicians and we see the theatre. Outdoors, huge arena. They used it for some Asian games. A taxi man tells me Daley Thomson came. I don't know why Daley came, but this guy seemed to know and he's seen Muhammed Ali too. I don't mind.

Anjali takes me to a tandoori place. No chicken and chips here. If she wasn't anywhere on earth I would enjoy India more. I can't tell if she's deliberately tormenting me. I can't bend the pride and ask, man. She's living at her friend's and after dinner she takes me. These people dressed in sarees and suits and they pass the nuts around. It could be Hampstead except it's hot here and the place is not cocooned and carpeted, though there are sumptuous Persian rugs. The room we sit in opens on to the veranda and the trees beyond. It seems wrong to be sitting here sipping Bacardi and talking shit.

Man. One of them even says they better have music because it's after dinner. He puts it on. CD.

These people don't boogey. They put on a record and someone begins to twist. Anjali is embarrassed when one son-a-bitching woman in a saree asks if I know break dancing. Second day she says we should go to see the Son et Lumière at the Red Fort. After rehearsals we take the bus to the hotel and she's sticking with me as though her life depended on it.

Folding metal chairs. Everything freaks me. Everything. This is the place, mein Herr, the place. India, richest, poorest, they got guys without legs, just stump, talking to you from like a head and shoulders stuck on a cart and asking whether you from the USA. I'll repeat that for the benefit of those at the back: he's got no legs, just one arm and he asks me whether I'm from the USA and he makes a filthy kissing sound with his palm against his mouth and asks if I want to change dollars.

Anjali says there are only two reactions to beggars: Christianity and Hinduism. Christianity gives because it feels bad. Hinduism gives because that's the way things are.

The Son et Lumière is spoken by voices which are familiar to me, at least two of them, from the London stage. The English accents are pronounced but of course they are Indian actors from England, some RADA training, a piece at the National, a stint with the Royal

Shakespeare, a part in *Jewel in the Crown*, and we home. Commenting now on the Red Fort and how it changed hands through many cultures, the Hindus and the Muslims and all this kinda ting. Weird to hear the voices of actors I've worked with coming over the lawns of the fort, its red pavilions silhouetted against the opal sky of Delhi. After the performance we ain suppose to linger. Darkness has fallen and the attendants are coming to see that the audience is gone, but Anjali doesn't obey no rules in India. This is her place. She takes my hand and walks me to the walls of the fort. Our ground is higher than the ground across the wall, it's like we on the first floor and right down below the lights of huts as though villages have grown up in the shadow of protection. They call it a building but it's just a pavilion, roof and platform and only one wall backing it. It's where the Moghul emperors kept audience with any guy who had any hassle and wanted to put a petition. Like a court and the dole-hole combined.

It ain cold. I'm just in a T-shirt and jeans and she's in a saree. We are alone and I say Delhi is good, and she says she frets about the performance. We kiss. The attendant fellow sees us and he rattles some chairs for shame. And says we better go. The guy at the gate smirks at her.

We catch a cab and go back to her friend's place. Her family live in Bombay so she's with these smarmy bastards who are still awake when we get there and steer us to a kinda drawing room and it's clear I'm a guest and whatever Anjali wants I can't stay there and have to go back to the hotel. The guy, her friend, says, 'You realise we got the biggest story in Delhi under this roof, Ram and Sita together. Why don't you hold hands? I'll take a snap.'

He fetches a heavy camera. Anj has had a few brandies and some devil gets into her and she sits on my lap and he snaps us. Mrs House don't like it. The servants come in and gather at the door while the master is snapping and Mrs is embarrassed. Miss Anjali sitting on dark persons's lap. No good.

The master says he'll drive me to the hotel and Anjali says she feels like walking and she'll get me a cab from one of the corners. We walk.

'You see what they're like?'

'Well, I'm cool. I'll see you tomorrow. Why don't you come to the hotel?'

We kiss again. Something's changed. The air of India.

Next day she wants to move into the hotel.

DEATH TOLL OF SEVEN IN NOVEL RIOTS IN PUNE

Seven people were shot dead and twenty-three suffered bullet injuries when the police opened fire on a hostile mob in Sadashiv Peth in Pune today.

Eighteen police were also facing injuries from brickbats thrown by demonstrators when a protest called against Star Publishing House went ahead as scheduled.

The protestors' leader Mr D. D. Dixit said the demonstrators were objecting to the marathi version of an English novel entitled *The Elephant Man*.

The protest began some time in the afternoon and a crowd of twenty thousand people gathered outside the house of Mr P. Parnjype, the publications director, and demanded an apology for what the leaders of the demonstration claimed were anti-Hindu sentiments.

The translator of the book Mr Shinde and the publisher, who were accused in a literary meeting earlier this week of associating the Elephant God Ganesh with a physically handicapped person, were present in the building.

On police advice they emerged at 5.30pm to mollify the crowd and placed their turbans at their feet in a show of apology. The demonstrators in the fore of the crowd demanded that the translator put his head on the ground and bow to the demonstration. Mr Shinde replied to this demand by removing his belt from his trousers and assaulting the members of the demonstration nearest to him. Violence then followed and several buildings were set alight by the demonstrators before the police fired volleys into the air and then into the demonstration.

We are performing the next night for the first time and there are reporters like dirt, boss, photographers wall to wall, all moving between the bar and the massage parlour, the swimming pool and the hotel lobbies in total consternation with David coming up and down and calling us together in Sara's room and everyone crowding in and drinking lime with water and sugar, which is good for you instead of the tap water.

Then last day the curfew falls. Sara gathers us in the hotel lobby by phone and by putting out a call on the tannoy. We are not to go out for the next day. Curfew. David says Delhi is now shut to us because we have to understand that before such a performance we should stay closeted by ourselves. Sara says she's sent the cars home. I join her in the bar. She don't look too happy. When she call us that evening she say the electricity cuts in the capital mean that we have been delayed by two days. The opening is cancelled for two days and our second performance will now open the play. Not to fret. She and David have arranged for us to just stay in the hotel. The reporters have been banned from seeing us because David says so.

Then a funny thing go on. The hotel goons come and take away our televisions. I'm in Anjali's room and they say all the tellys are to go for repair. The phone rings and Sara calls us together in the durbar room. There's fifty of us with the Indian musicians and all. Sara says, 'Sorry David can't be here. I am not much good as a director, but he wants me to tell you that India awaits the first performance and we should all meditate and relax and come to it afresh. You may have noticed that he has requested the hotel management to stop you watching TV . . .'

At that point David walks in.

David: 'Sorry, Sara, can I take over please? My dear friends, something very serious has come up. The performances are of course sold out. I have been having talks with the government and with the TV stations and we are set to go. However, I must tell you that there are some people who object to the play. I don't want that to weigh on anyone's mind. We must prove our play on stage, we have no other weapon. There is a controversy in the press and on television about the play, but then if you remember Ellythorn's criticism that's nothing new. The philistines everywhere will make their challenge. I'd prefer it if you left that side of things to me and I'd beg you not to enter into the questions of criticism that are posed. Actors should prepare. We've been together many months now and this is the final test. Of course no one is denying you India. Between Delhi and Bombay we shall have five days of free travel and holiday. Then we meet again in that most enchanting of cities by the sea . . .'

I went to Anjali's room after. I knew she'd moved into the hotel because of a row her friends had had over me.

The night before the performance we make love.

The Lord smile down on me and send an angel to love. She has some dope on her. Isolation. We've been talking for a day and a night. Sara comes and has a drink in Anjali's room and goes. She's checking what we're doing and is nervous to see what the rest are up to. She says she's not sure she likes India. Anjali doesn't laugh.

'Why doesn't David ask me? I've got contacts, I know how the place works . . .'

She puts the question to Sara.

'I don't think he wants to burden you with anything but the greatest performance of your life on this tour. You've got enough on your plate.'

'We rehearse so tight, I feel like Muhammed Ali, man, and I feel like another vodka. Shall I phone for it?'

Sara goes. Anjali brushes out her long black hair. OK, I waited, she's ready. She is silent while we make love. She acts as though she's not completely solemn about what she's doing. She takes her clothes off nonchalant and says let's go to bed and when I take my clothes off she averts her eyes and lies under the quilt.

I get in with her and like a boy I'm shivering with anticipation. She gets hold of me with a sweaty hand and crudely pulls it to and fro. No arts of the Kama Sutra here. The girl is like a nervous bird and I was so greedy to look at every inch of her, the colour of her skin, the exact shape of her back, her legs, whether the tiny wisps of black hair behind her ear were repeated elsewhere on what promised to be a smooth body. But faced with it my greed disappears. I look into her eyes. She shuts them and when she looks at me it is to kiss and then she drowns her lips in mine. She wants to lose herself somewhere in the kiss so she doesn't admit what we doing.

Her nipples are small and brown and the hair in her crotch is thick and her cunt is tiny, a fish's mouth. She lets out a little cry and closes her eyes when I enter her and she puts both hands on my hips and shoves me out.

'It hurts.'

'I'll go easy, I promise.'

She kisses me again, as though the kiss legitimises what is to her a stolen moment in fear, in isolation, in the Indian air. The curtains of the seventh floor open to the air outside. She wants to turn the light off and let me penetrate her from behind. But she doesn't know even that game. I have to coax her on to her knees to get the angle right and then I'm flowing, I can't hold it no more and I'm gone and she's almost relieved and profoundly disappointed at the same time.

'Don't say sorry, just kiss me.'

'I wasn't going to say sorry,' I say.

In the dark, lying quiet for twenty minutes she curls like a prawn against me.

'Ali, I don't know much about you and I don't know if I love you.'
'You don't have to love me at all, I don't expect it. Let's do one thing at a time. For now, the play. But I tell you something, I do love you.'
The bullshit flows. But I do love her.

Next time round there's no fever in my bone and as the dawn comes up it stops hurting her and she gasps long and loud as she maybe used to do for some French boy friend.

She wants me to wear my clothes and go back to my room because she don't want the servants to bring coffee to us in bed together. But if I have a shower she says I can come back and we can share coffee.

Jan 17th

Delhi before the sun comes up from the top-floor window of the lounge of the hotel: a grove of trees with bare open spaces and minarets and domes, discoloured by time, ancient, the city flat with birds hovering low in the sky and a dancing shimmering heat making mist in the distance.

The big six is what David calls them. They've put up the money for the production and they send a fleet of cars, Ambassadors and Fiats all with chauffeurs to take the whole contingent to the stadium. We pass police cordons on the way. Little sentry boxes with two or three policemen lethargically hanging about, a string bed next to the sentry box for their relaxation. I take the last car with Sunil and Anjali. We have to be there three hours before the performance and David is relying on me for timekeeping. The fleet of cars has been available since seven in the morning and only getting the gang out and on parade is a nuisance.

Anjali's nerves have taken a strange turn. She seems very far away, lost in thought. Not at all like a first night.

From *Satya*, The Daily of National Pride and Rebirth

Mr Rajiv Gandhi's zest for selling the country to the foreigners knows no bounds, economic, political or cultural. The latest offering to amuse the rich of Delhi is a travesty of a play insultingly called 'The Ramayana' which is the product and brainchild of one Mr David Stream, a failed producer of Hollywood movies. He has

134

been instigated by the Gandhi government to bring provocation in the name of the twenty-first century into our very city. In this production of our most sacred text, the *Ramayana*, Ram, the incarnation of God, is played by a negro actor called Ali Abdul Rahman. This man is a black Muslim. He is from West Indies near America and the infectious disease of Islamic fundamentalism has spread to the poor of that country just as it spread in India when the untouchables of the Hindu dharma were transferred to Mohomed-dan belief by zealots backed up by the Mughal soldiers, cruel taxes and oppression.

The black Muslims are more fanatical than those devotees of Islam in Iran and Pakistan because they are latest converts. In English they have a saying that the new person converted to Christianity is even more zealous than the pope! He is a five star Muslim, this Ali Abdul Rahman, and he mocks our gods by performing Chinese tricks and fighting like a trained animal against the forces of evil in the play rather than dissolving them as in the original story with the power of the Hindu dharma which is invested in the God Rama. Does God need to fight with swords and sustain injuries as though he was Bruce Lee from the Chinese cinema?? The Muslims of America and the West Indies swear allegiance to Islam because they are not accepted by their own countries and are converting to this religion in the name of domination of the other people in their country. Their biggest leader who was called Elijah Muhammed said all other people of other religions were devils and had to be killed. This typical message of violence is given to Mr Ali Abdul Rahman to play in his role of Rama. In this transparent guise which will not fool the people of Delhi except for the few 'pedigree' people who revel in foreign imports of theory, religion and slavish patriotism towards foreign countries, notably the United States and communism.

To add deep injury to this insult, the role of Laxman is played by a Chinese man. Every day the patriotic people of the Punjab are being killed by terrorists in the name of Khalistan. The terrorists are getting arms and succour from Pakistan and the proved fact is that manufacture of the rifles they use is the Chinese A 26 Kalashnikov. This is a conjunction of foreign powers trying to destroy our home-land and our nation and our culture by the bomb and the bullet and by means of ideas which our rulers are willing to pay for in the taxes they collect from the blood of honest Indian citizens.

Mr David Stream is featured in some newspapers that toe the government line as being a genius. What kind of genius has mixed up verses from the Koran and the Guru Granth Sahib with the holiest of Hindu holy books? Is it mischief and total disregard or deliberate insult? Those who want to break up our country are given their religious plantation right inside the heart of our holy of holy legends and stories on which every patriotic family brings up its newborn generations.

The policy of *Satya* is to preach the truth. We ask in fairness, how would the Muslims react if we were to inject into their mosques the verses of the *Ramayana* inside the Koran for their mullahs to recite? How would the Sikh react if right inside the heart of the Golden temple we took the statues of Durga or Krishna and declared it a space for Hindu worship? The minorities have no courage to do that mayhem here and the government in their name is bringing foreigners to do this dirty work against Hinduism and the Dharma.

Satya demands from Rajiv Gandhi that he withdraw his foreign cultural troops, that Mr David Stream goes back to Hollywood. That Mr Ali Abdul Rahman goes back and reports to the Muslim leadership for world domination that India has a Hindu majority which will not be fooled and that Indians are watch-dogs with keen teeth of their own culture and religion.

As for those traitors who are Indian passport holders who play the music and Miss Anjali Patnaik, daughter of the infamous politician and industrialist, they must answer to their own consciences, for aiding and abetting foreign powers on our soil.

The curfew is bad, boss. India here at my feet and I can't march out to see it. Anjali wears jeans and that in the hotel room and coming and going from the swimming pool and the restaurants, but on the evening of our first night she takes three hours to dress and wears the most ravishing peacock blue and gold saree. Her friends come to fetch her. She has no way renounced her crowd.

'I suppose I'll have to go with them, you understand. When we tour Jamaica, I'll let you go with the boys.'

This she says while brushing her hair in front of the mirror and getting her lipstick on. She's going to change when she gets to the theatre, sack cloth and plenty ashes, but she's in a serious mood to impress.

There are TV crews coming. From the BBC, the Yanks, Germans, all sorts.

We go down the car park after Sara assembles us in the foyer. There are three production managers, two new Indian guys, one with a lousy fake American accent like some of the guys down the Grove who spend two weeks in New York and come back sporting a lickle speech impediment.

We decide who is going in which car. You know, on this production, I've never seen the stars play big and the rest play small. OK, I'm one of the stars, the big star, but with massive cunning David has blocked all that shit. We eat together and we don't make no big thing of Anjali or me or Sieg or Akiro or anyone. The musicians get in the same car and everything is everything. Even on the posters my name appears with the rest, at the top, but no big print or nothing. I've never played in the West End. Well, one or two things I did for a black theatre season and that, and there were posters and everything, but it was like a mock West End scene because it was paid for by grants which help blacks and there was no real West End tourist crowd and people queuing up to pay twenty-five pounds for seven-pound tickets and the actors coming by the stage door. It was playing at being in the West End. And then see how it happens to me – David Stream, bigger than anything the West End wants to know, destined to go down in history and no neon lights with my name. Cool, I don't dig nothing. David has fucking brainwashed me.

But I mustn't think them kinda things. I am Ram, a God, a spirit which teaches the Indian nation how to live, the ideal of the perfect man, the valiant, the strong, the brave, the humorous, the whole in body – you know heroes don't catch chicken pox and get hernia and VD and athlete's foot.

Delhi has plenty trees and wide roads like runways and big houses set off from the road with walls and then the imperial drive with the President's house at one end and a gate leading nowhere in the middle, just a gate with a soldier who is guarding a lamp. I pass that with Anjali as she explains the city to me. Now we pass a flyover, cement, which tells me this is not no joke city, and police everywhere again.

At the stadium there is a cordon of police and the cavalcade of cars passes through. David receives us personally and sees us to the preparation rooms at the far end under the stands. There's a lot of people today just hanging about. Indian workmen and guys in bush shirts just walking wherever David goes, some twenty guys tailing

137

him whom he can't shake off, like a general staff following a general before a battle.

Night falls fast and the stadium is packed. It's like they come to see a football match or something. The performance is great. Except in the stadium you can hear the insect life of Delhi like a buzz on the radio. The musicians go wild. I am hot, boss, and when you're hot you got no need for warm up. Anjali is sombre and perfect on stage. Her eyes, though, they look at me different. A new Sita, one who has seen into my soul and is shy of what she sees. Indian, she looks so Indian here, surrounded by her people. They clap. At every speech and fight sequence and the end of every scene this audience goes wild.

When we finish there's the dawn coming up early and a thousand photographers and press brigade. The police stand between us and them and we come out of the dressing rooms like athletes. We are ushered by Sara and David to the cars. They are in the stadium and they take us away. David handles the reporters. That evening there's a big party at the hotel.

Sara says she knows we should sleep now as David has planned a big scene at seven in the Durbar room and we had better get there because all the glitterati of Delhi will be in attendance.

Binky gives us a copy of a letter he has written. I've still got it.

For the Personal Attention of the Prime Minister

Dear Rajivji,

       The show is really great. David Stream has made a sparse but spectacular thing of the *Ramayana*. At times it is Ram Leela, at times a simple village recitation in modern verse. I went to see it in London. Perhaps we could sponsor it as an export to the Soviet Union, certainly to Poland and GDR and Czechoslovakia. I asked Stream and he is not averse to the idea if we'll put up some money or bilateral agreements.

I am jealous because it's spectacular and every designer in London and New York is ooing and ahhing about the rolls of colour, literally, the Oriya, Kerali and Rajasthani fabrics he has used specially dyed and designed, a real dream boat production. And he learnt it all at the knee of the Indian people.

Of course his friends are dissidents so called in these countries but he doesn't mind official sponsorship as long as the cast can be treated as visiting cultural troupers and not be surrounded by goons from their secret service.

My special plea is only that this *Ramayana* be seen by you, because it does stand up to examination and secular honesty. Stream is the biggest thing intellectually and creatively this side of Teheran and really, Rajivji, even the detractors and critics have had to admit that without this Indian epic he would have been floundering around with more Hedda Gablers and smaller things like feministic messages. You and Sonya and a cross section of the cabinet and the cultural Camelot of New Delhi must be seen at the first performance.

I am back in Delhi in three days but I rushed this to you as you requested.

I am sending all the cuttings of *Sanskriti* to you and hundreds of copies to the cultural ministry and will be talking to the New York people this afternoon. Thank God my people have behaved themselves, with a few minor hitches. The man Tilak is a real find. Maybe one day he should be ambassador to Outer Mongolia or some place. With respect and affection.

Jai Hind,
Binky

Them hold this party on the lawns of the hotel. We ain allowed out by Sara, she's the chief and she guards the gates. There are polis like dirt in the drive. Anjali and I walk about the lawns and I start a little chat with the coppers. Anjali, at first reluctantly, does the interpretation scene. The copper wants me to take a picture of him with my camera. He says he'll pose with me. We chat for ten minutes. I pick up seventeen facts about him by going through impatient Anjali.

She's bored with it, but appreciates the fact, the man is talking to a next man through her. This is how she talk: 'He joined the force in the village. He has had three years training and four years in the force. He controls eight guys. He has four children. Yes, he believes in birth control but it's more for the rich than the poor. Yes, he counts himself as "the poor". Sure, he loves movies. Amitabh Bachchan is his favourite actor, but when he thinks about it, there were better actors in the old days such as Balraj Sahni. He learnt to drive in the police force, part of the reason he joined. No, he's not never shot anyone though he's been in a few strikes and riots. In the barracks just to the south of the city. Once a year he returns to his village, I must go with him next time. Yes, if his superior officer catches him chatting he's for the stick. He'll risk it. He'll stand at attention and I can stand next to him and

Anjali will snap us together. He will remember this moment forever. He will show his grandchildren the snap and when he comes to England he will show it to the first person on the street who will be impressed by his friendship with the great actor.' What was my name?

I tell him my father call me Gerald.

'Jayral, a very good name,' he says. It's the first time I impress a copper. Anjali wants to get away from him and walk back down towards the end of the garden.

Kojin is there. He passes the time reading books on the lawn in a cotton shirt and shorts.

Some servant bwoy are putting up a Shamiana for the party. Them have servants for everything here. David stroll in and out of the hotel. He have meetings all day with guys from the ministry and guys from the Indian telly and all sorts. Binky is around and he waves every time he passes. He stops to talk to Anjali.

With him is a harassed-looking American called Dr Steinmann who wears a beige cotton suit and specs. The kind of man who likes to be good to blacks in Africa, India, wherever he find them. Hair getting thin. Cheeks eaten up by worry and age. He follows Binky with a sheaf of papers in his hand. Binky brings him over to us and introduces his arse.

It seems Dr Steinmann is under threat from the polis. OK, good bwoy! The man is to be deported.

'Not very serious,' him say. 'Every three months they threaten to deport us.'

What does Dr Steinmann do to deserve being treated like a ping-pong ball? He runs the Street Clinic Movement. And what's that? Oh yes, Anjali knows about it. In Bombay and Calcutta mainly.

'Sure, amongst the poor. They've got rid of the beggars and tidal population from New Delhi.'

But he's become a begger himself. Every time the state polis bust up his scene, dispensaries and all this, with strong arm tactics, smash his medicine and confiscate his arse out of existence, he has to come to Delhi and find someone like Binky who will intervene and start to beg like a trained dog. I check Binky. He wants this guy, white man to be his client, begging.

'Binky's much too busy with David Stream and your production today, but I've got to get him to do it, cause they're poised to send two of my doctors back to the States and Scotland. Like tomorrow.' The bwoy is a sad case.

He shakes his head. Anjali promises to have a word with Binky. The man, she tells me, does good work, taking in the derelicts and treating them, a kind of low-key Mother Teresa – she deals with the dying, he with those a little less dying, those who'll die later.

The party is spectacular, heavily crucial. We are presented as the cast to ten or twelve dignitaries from the Indian side. Never seen so much coppers in my life, boss, not even in the Carnival riots in Notting Hill. Pure khaki wall to wall.

At eleven o'clock David come round and whisper to each person ear.

'Curfew, I'm afraid, Ali,' he says. 'An early night and a triumphant performance tomorrow. I have to stay on and see our guests off.' He don't look too happy, knitted brow, the bottom lip grows thicker with concern. Delhi is cool, but David sweating like a beer bottle. Sara follows and Binky has taken some sort of charge as he sees that the players are hustled back to their hotel rooms.

I knock at Anjali's door having given Sara the slip. Anjali lets me in with a finger on her lips. I raid her room fridge. I want another whisky. Which idiot told me that India is overflowing with weed? Not a fucking smoke in sight. No one knows what I'm talking about in the hotel. A locked world.

There's a knock at the door and Anjali motions me to stay where I am, sitting on the sofa. She answers it. There are two guys there with garlands in their hands. I can't see them at first but I can hear Indian accents. Compliments.

'We have come to pay respects, Miss Anjali Patnaik. We are looking for Mr Ali too and he came up here with you so we want to give our greatest thanks to both.'

Anjali says, 'I don't know where Ali is and I don't know who you are and I don't receive visitors . . .'

'We don't want any reception, Miss Anjali, we are journalists and you have brought great honour on our country . . .'

Then I hear Anjali shout, 'Don't!'

I jump from my blood claat whisky, bounding like a cat on a corrugated iron roof in Jamaica. I get up and go to the door behind Anjali. These two Indian maan are struggling to put a huge garland of flowers round her neck and she is trying to back off and shut the door on them. One of them has got his knee in the door.

'Oi, if she don't want no garland, no garland, get it?' I say.

The two guys, one short the other very tall, smile. They step back.

'Mr Ali, we mean nothing but honour for you, we came to give you these.' He stretches the garland out to me.

I don't know what to make of it but Binky comes down the corridor of the hotel.

Binky must be some kinda big noise here because the guys see him and begin to back off.

'I told you not to pester the cast. Just fuck off, leave the hotel or I'll call the police.'

Binky looks flustered and he puts his hand on the tall one's shoulder.

'Yes, Binky sahab, drowning man clutches to straws.'

They go. Binky shoves his way past Anjali after seeing that the duo is safely in the lift.

'Who are they guys?'

'Don't worry your little head. They are bastards. Journalists, of sorts. I know what they're after and they got it.'

'Got what?'

'Look, you two in the same bloody room, that's what.'

'Come on, man, I don't believe this!'

'You don't know what's going on down there, Ali, let's finish your drink. I'll have one too and then get an early night as David suggested. There are all sorts of bods floating about.'

'What did he mean by drowning men and all this?'

'In politics you make enemies,' Binky says. He gets himself a mini champagne from the fridge, examines the label and opens it. He gets a glass from the bathroom.

'Binky, why don't you mind your own business? How come you've got in on this thing?'

'Orders from right on top. Please do as I say. I'm bloody shocked at you, Anjali, yar. Ali is probably puzzled but you know the score here. Even the girls who clean the rooms . . .'

'The score don't sound worth knowing,' I say.

'As we say, "ay shutup yar"; to bed with you and that's an order, Ali. After this run in Delhi I've got a place outside Bombay, come and be my guest, just you two and Kojin and Sieg and whoever you want to bring from the cast, I leave it up to you. But for now, even David won't quite know what hit him. Not to worry yourself though. I thought it was the best I've seen it last night and the party was a success. They came, the faction that was wavering.'

'You are turning us into your politics?' Anjali says.

'You are politics, darling,' Binky says. 'The high command of the Party put a whip out. Seven of the opposition within our own party turned up and talked to David. He's magnificent, charming and totally confident. It's the bloody backwards, your British equivalent of country squire politicians, the old guard. But Rajiv will be pleased, I've got to see him tonight.'

'How wonderful for you.' She is still annoyed at the intrusion.

'No need for that, darling. And so to bed?'

Binky hangs around till I put my glass down and say goodnight to Anjali. She don't want to give me no kiss.

Sara comes in with my breakfast tray in my own room.

'Gerry, drink your tea and eat your eggs. Your boy-friend-in-law is in the news. David says you should know. Same old thing it's blown up again.'

I wipe the sleep from my eyes and put on a towel. Sara's seen me naked before. What is she talking about?

'One newspaper has picked up on the fact that Salim Anwar Khan, you know who, Maureen's boy friend, has been found guilty of dealing in arms.'

'So what's new and what the fuck has this got to do with David?'

'Same story as your insurance. Some Brit police unit has probably leaked this nonsense to someone. The newspapers here are making a connection between him, the Khalistanis to whom he was about to sell armaments, not just Chinese Kalashnikovs, but big time stuff through African governments, rocket launchers, anti-tank missiles, stuff like that, to your Maureen and hence to Maureen's "husband", one Ali Abdul, currently playing an Indian incarnation of God in New Delhi. Get it?'

Gob-smacked. 'I thought we'd been through all that.'

'Well, it's back.'

'The British papers apparently said you used to look after his vicious dogs. Maureen seems such a nice woman, what's she follow this bastard round the country for? Or is that tactless?'

'How the hell do I know? She just took the girl down because Mr Gun-run was in jail in Southampton or some place. What's his name?'

'Well, he wasn't.'

'OK, so he wasn't.'

'I know you had nothing to do with it, but David asked me to make sure.'

143

'So you made sure.'

'Sure, now eat some breakfast. Will you be all right for tonight?'

'I'm an actor. I don't know about nothing else. I don't even know about how you play politics in this place here with all them religions and Ayatollahs and what-not them got here. I'm here to do a play and I'll do it and then I'll go back to London and get into a black comedy series and I'll make the punters laugh.'

I dial London, Maureen's place. No reply.

'Just calm down.'

'I am calmed down. I'm going to go over the whole play with Anjali this morning and afternoon and act my arse off this evening. And take it easy, like the routine this afternoon, get three hours' kip before opening times and I never heard David or you say once that you're paying overtime. If I had a Swiss bank account it would die of starvation.'

I was pissed off with Sara.

'Those chaps who came and knocked at Anjali's door. They got Kojin last night. They walked into his room and were waiting with a knife. Luckily he's good at some martial thing and saw them off. He still thinks they were muggers. For money. He doesn't quite understand intellectual mugging.'

'Them must be crazy, Kojin is an ole cockney with a chink eye, that's all.'

'Do you know his elder brother was the Maoist bagman in London in the 'sixties?'

'Big deal.'

'Precisely. But they look at him and see Mao Tse Tung. Yesterday the police in Punjab captured a cache of Chinese arms from a terrorist arsenal and the news today is that the arms come via Afghanistan and Lahore into India.'

'Then David's right,' I say.

'How do you mean?'

'OK, let me go into the spiel: that's what this production is about, Sara, we teach people to see the trans-cultural, the human beneath the skin, the conflagration of nationalities, the global nature of bullshit and terror.' I do this bit in David's voice.

'Don't get cynical. You sound like a bad New York preview. But you're right. Look at Binky, or your Anjali, are they really Indian? I don't feel any red white and blue in my veins . . .'

*

144

Sara calls us out two hours early that evening. The cars are assembled and we're going to get to the stadium two hours before schedule.

A hundred years before we get to the stadium there's a road-block. I'm in the car with Sara. The front car. There are coppers who want the driver to get out. Sara steps out. She reason some heavy reason with the Indian copper them.

'Call your superior officer. I don't want to speak to you.'

'Madam, nobody is allowed to go here before seven o'clock. This is orders from the Superintendent.'

'I don't care about your orders. We are the stars of the production. We decided to come early. You'll just have to change your rules.'

The walkie-talkies get active. Couple of jeeps pull up and government stylee maan step out. They explain that they are vetting all cars. Later on there'll be free traffic. Sara draws herself up to full memsahib height.

'This is a British production and the High Commissioner will want to know why you are obstructing us,' she says.

The officials debate the issue amongst themselves and wave the cavalcade of cars on. David is waiting for us. He wants to calm us into performance mood.

Anjali and I walk out into the open stadium. At twilight in India the birds gather in the trees and make a helluva racket, boss. Sparrows, crows, I'm bad at bird spotting.

The Indian twilight makes me sad. Reminds me of death, of lost opportunities, makes me want to get inside a well-lit room with friends. Anjali kicks stones with a lazy foot as we walk. There's two and a half hours to kill. I didn't like the look of those policemen. They weren't menacing, they were scared and Sara was pulling British on them. She have to.

David appears in the changing room.

'It's a packed house, Ali. Just concentrate, dear boy.'

The axle of King Dasratha's chariot breaks and his young wife Kaikeyi substitutes her finger for the axle and saves his life. Ram is sent into exile. The sky is pitch black when we begin to perform and the jets fly overhead as the first stage lights come on. David has arranged the effect of slow floodlight till the full illusion of day is realised.

By the time we get through the second part of the third phase, most of the audience has gone. From behind the screens we can see the empty seats and David is in the dressing rooms. Unusual, because the man's never there. Just one frowning message on his face. 'Keep going, great, tremendous.'

No doubt has ever entered that mind, only thoughts about how to dispel contrary thoughts. I love the man. I am nobody, Gerry Blossom, Boot Polish, Ali Abdul. The sunlight in the arena comes up with the end of the performance and its rays fall on the last row of seats. Only seventeen people remain as this dawn drags with it fatigue as never before after a performance and the lights of the stage adjust to allow the mellow morning. It's like swimming length after length, you get lost in the stroke and in your exhaustion. Ram is restored to his kingdom and his kingdom is silence and the sound of thirty-four hands clapping.

No one says anything as we take our make-up off. Sara comes in and says there's been a hitch in the transport.

'No cars?'

'No cars!'

'They withdraw?'

'I don't know. We're trying to fix something. Just be dressed and David and I will see you at the back door of the stands in fifteen minutes. Everyone quick, it's pretty vital.'

There are taxis outside and David hustle the cast to pack into them. The musicians go first. They are Indian. He is bunching the foreigners together. He wants Anjali to go with the musicians.

'No way,' she says and he shrugs.

She holds my hand. There's trouble. I can hear the sound of a mob and some shouts, constant, coming through in the morning light and then some sounds like large balloons popping. Anjali points to smoke rising, maybe four hundred yards away.

'There's nothing to explain. There's just trouble in the city and we've got to get back to the hotel, urgently. We've been assured full protection.'

Tilak appears next to Sara. Don't know where he came from but, he tells her, he's brought five more taxis by a back route. They'll be here soon. I say 'hi' to him and he smiles and nods.

I climb into a black and yellow Ambassador with Anjali and Kojin and Sieg and Tilak says something to the driver. There's twelve more and Sara and David to get away. The driver answers Tilak in Hindi and we move off and Sara shouts she'll see us back at the hotel.

The polis hold them hand up and stop us at the first checkpoint about a mile down the road. I don't know this road. The driver is driving madly and turning on two wheels. He screeches to a stop. The police turn us back. I can hear the mobs and the firing louder now. The driver says he has to take us back, there's no going on. Anjali speaks to him in Hindi.

I don't understand Hindi, but I swear to you, boss, I understood every word of what was going on from that moment on. She tells him he is a coward and she'll pay him ten times the amount if he steers through a way she knows. He is telling her that it isn't a riot, that it's us they're after. She don't want to panic us and leans forward and talks to him soothingly like one would to a scalded cat.

It's us they're after. My heart fucking sinks – is like we turn fugitive now. The driver turns down a side avenue. Tree-lined Delhi and not a soul in sight for six hundred yards. Then we come to a roundabout and we take the broad avenue to the right. There's another group of police trucks and a herd of police coming running towards them. They're getting into the trucks.

We pass them and no one stops us. Anjali is urging the driver to reconsider and still take the route she thinks she knows. He shakes his head. He steps on the gas. Bwoy, I'm looking at Kojin's face, hunted, and Anjali, leaning forward grips my arm with both her hands. I must have blinked or looked away. There's a clump of police in blue uniforms this time, one with blood on his face by the side of the road. One of them motions us to stop and to turn round as we pass.

Anjali's shouting at the driver now. The guy just speeds on. No sign of any mobs till we get to a roundabout and then a phalanx of people, shouting, waving sticks and bars and throwing stones. The driver stops and appears to be fighting the gear stick to get it into reverse. Then he throws it like a man who subdue a giant. I can't swear to it. I shall never be able to swear to it in a court of law, but I fancy that I see him in that instant smile, as his face turns to get a line of sight through the back window. Why has this guy a faint smile?

He moves slowly back, backwards into a mob. Boss, where did this thing come from? The car is completely surround. The windows are up and a few stones crash through the windscreen in front and one from the window in the back.

'Get down!' I shout. We're crouching and cowering in the bottom of the car. Sieg shouts in German. The people strike at the body of the car. The driver ducks with his hands protecting the top of his head and shouts something in Urdu and tries to open the door next to him. Kojin clutches his face where a shard of glass has hit him.

The doors are levered open. In an instant the hands, a million hands of the mob grab us, rasta, God forgive me. I never been drag like that before. I grab on to Anjali as the two of us are pulled out of the cab and into a parting in the crowd. She lands on top of me and hands grab her to separate us. Hands! Where do these fucking hands come from? And one thing I remember, clear as a soda, I'm thinking the palms of the hands aren't brown or black or white, just the colour of flesh. That's hands! I clutch on to her, shout to her to hold on to her and all I can hear is her scream, words, unknown to me.

Then it's like slow motion; it takes maybe ten seconds. I feel the hands actually prising us apart, not being able to, standing us together upright and then hands pulling me to the ground and her away.

There are feet and legs all round me, a jungle and the shouts and sticks, and a clear sight of Indian leather sandals with hobnails as they come down on my head. It's crystal clear, boss, no mystery of language or translation. We have insulted their gods. The rage breaks loose. I never get to look into anyone's eyes but I can swear that if I looked into one of their eyes it is affront and civilisational insult I would see there. You think I'm kidding, boss? The big words? That's what I saw! The black man has dared to play Ram. The hussy has dared to portray Sita, the gun-runners, the destroyers of countries, the alien Chinese, the German, we have sacked their Dharma we have ventured into the heart of their country to steal its heart. To eat the entrails of their religion and make what is mysterious into a message. Not their message. When all is told we cannot beg for pardon.

*   *   *

I lie in Binky's house in another town. The servants look after me and the nurse comes three times a day. The doctors were here all the time just after the operation. But the thing itself, boss, is gone, my memory of those days is nil. David sit by my bedside day after day. The fuckers slit my throat, literally. I can write but I can't speak. It'll be OK in a few months. When I'm strong enough Binky will fly me back to London.

They killed her. Or as the newspapers put it, she was murdered in the riot, by no one in particular. I knew and know nothing about her. Nothing, nothing, nothing.

Her mother, a dignified lady in a saree with a white streak in her hair, comes with her stepfather just to sit in my presence. The lady is struck down but elegantly dressed in a black saree with a white embroidered border. Binky stands by and tells them I can't speak. I try. I write down things on a pad.

'I tried to save her. They pulled us apart, but I saw an iron rod come from across my face at her.'

I think before I write it. Do human beings want these details or would they rather obliterate such a mess. I decide they want the details. I am right.

The stepfather reads it and nods. He passes the pad to Mummy and Mummy can't read it. The tears fill her eyes, she cannot see. Binky takes the pad, which she just holds listlessly, away. The servants bring tea.

Sara is here every day with Tilak and his girl. They just sit around. No one has anything to say. Tilak is dressed like a peasant in large leather slippers and a thick cotton kurta and pyjama. Now and then he tells Sara how uncomfortable he feels in Binky's house. I don't know the house. I only know this room and the bathroom and the veranda outside my door from which I can see a walled garden and sometimes pedestrians, one or two, and a rickshaw and a car passing. The knife went through my windpipe. Through my heart and mind.

For her mummy I wrote down that we were friends but I never really understood her. Maybe it was because of me. I don't give a shit.

One day when Sara and Tilak are sitting by my bed I write a note: 'Tilak, where did you get that taxi? Did he get the taxi driver:'

The thought has crossed Tilak's mind too, but not Sara's.

He replies, curiously enough writing his reply down instead of saying it: 'In the street from Old Delhi, near Dilli Gate, Sara sent me out.' I read it and nod. God, I'm a shit. How could I ask them kinda question. Just lying here and your mind wanders. Tilak, the taxi driver, expressions, an exchanged glance. Actors are trained to catch it to talk in twenty different ways. But all the world's no fucking stage. Thing happen because it just happen. There's chance and acting can't rely on chance or accident, every expression has to mean something, every stage direction, who fetches whom from where, has to be work out. Tilak is a good man. He didn't deliberately get no fundamentalist taxi. He knows it's what I'm thinking. But we never say nothing.

When the parents are here second time, Maureen phones and Binky gives me the phone and Maureen asks questions. She doesn't know I can't talk. She goes on and on, not caring for a response and how she'd read it in the papers and thank God I was alive and David had given some interviews when he got back to London. No, he wasn't going to revive the *Ramayana*. I hand the phone to Binky who explains to Maureen that I can't talk but he's sure I've appreciated every word she said and I am well and would be fine. Mummy and stepfather sit silent while I listen to my woman in London.

I read Binky's books; a biography of Mountbatten, a thing about Calcutta and on his shelves, this is why I mention it, there's a book of 'thirties verse and the poem, a dude called McNiece.

The sunlight on the garden . . .

I sit on the veranda and watch the sunlight harden as it can only do in India. But it don't go cold and nothing is told, and there's nobody from whom to ask for pardon.

PART
2

We fed the heart on fantasies
The heart's grown brutal from the fare

W. B. Yeats

Dear Sara,

You may have heard, maybe from Sonya or her parents or from the newspapers, that they caught up with me (at last) and I'm waiting for an extradition hearing.

Your flat's OK. I gave the keys to Leslie De F, Sonya's dad, and he got Ali to move back in, so the cats will be fed.

Leslie's been incredibly kind and came to see me straight away. I had four phone calls (rumour has it the police allow most people one, and most Asians and blacks none, but such was my charm). It paid off. He came to see me and got me a solicitor, an Indian girl, name of Mira, who doesn't think she can get me off the charge, but adopts a sort of amused, slightly distant attitude.

Of course you remember the night you asked me about myself and I said I stole babies as a profession, but not for money and you laughed. But it's true.

The police arrested eighteen people the night they came for me. They thought I was the missing link in their chain. Some Filipinos, some South Americans and three or four Indians or Pakistanis. They don't believe that I have nothing to do with the baby smuggling international ring, I only did it for kicks. To them of course it's bullshit. Like telling feminists that you're only an amateur rapist. Doesn't help.

Leslie says he wants the story behind the headlines. He knows me as Sonya's teacher, not as a dealer in the international traffic in babies. While I've been here, two newspapers have approached me for the whole story. By my whole story they mean two pages of 'confession'.

It's funny, Leslie didn't take me seriously as a writer. I could see in his eyes that he thought I was ponderous.

He made noises about being interested in my religious ramblings about Zoroastrianism. But he really got interested when I got arrested and the story broke all over the *Sun* and the *Star*:

ASIANS IN BABY SMUGGLING RING ARRESTED

and

I BOUGHT HER BUT I LOVE HER — TAKE–AWAY MUM'S STORY

I am putting my whole story down, a sort of biography, for Leslie. Writing it down helps me know what I think about myself. I hope this gets to you at the ashram. Anyway, the flat's safe and the cats are fed. Relax.

Love
Xerxes

Nirmala Bhavan
Ootacamund
Nilgiri Hills
Tamilnadu

Sept 22nd

My dear XX,

For God's sake, is it serious? If they extradite you to India what sort of trial will you get here?

It's so sweet of you to think of the flat but I'm more concerned about you. I remember our conversation that first night very very clearly and a phrase keeps coming back to me. When I asked you what you were most afraid of you said 'falling into the hands of the ignorant'. Your letter (I've read it for between-the-line messages now ten times) is cheerful enough.

Look, Xerxes, you may not hear from me for some time as I'm travelling around India, but write to the same address. Most people come and go from the ashram and use it as a base. Meanwhile I've

written to Robin (the features editor of the *Citizen*) who is a very good friend and he'll get in touch to see what you need. I feel helpless and very curious. What's a nice boy like you . . . I tell you what: I don't know when I shall get back to Blighty, but send me the let-it-all-hang-out confessions of a child-snatcher as told in the piece for our Leslie.
Take care.

Sara FS

Hardmondsworth Det. Centre
Oct 5th

Dear Sara,

     Your Robin did contact me and offered to be of use. They let a lot of people in to see me as I'm still on remand and not convicted of anything.

He says the trials will be fascinating, but everything is subjudice and nothing can be written. He's suspicious. There's been some strange things, demonstrations by National Front types outside Brixton where the other baby smugglers are held – and they got joined by some women's groups who attack the trade in women and children.

The book isn't going to be a book – it's fragments, pieces, stories – what was it Blake said (I think it was *Proverbs of Hell*)? 'Truth can never be told so as to be understood, and not believ'd.'

I'm sending you the first few pages. Believe me, I think of you as I get it all down. My audience.

A month at least before the hearing comes up.

Love
Xerxes

THE BOOK OF XERXES XAVAXA, HOAX
XTRAORDINAIRE

Ex-tradition. Not within our tradition!
  X-communicate!
XX (me). X my heart and hope to XXX. (Censored through shame). They will go through due process and send me back to stand trial.

There was a fellow a few months ago, was deported to Sri Lanka. He holed himself up in a church and grew a beard and became a cause célèbre in the Midlands. The immigration service were after him because he'd overstayed his visa as a student. He'd done all sorts of things to stay in Britain – married a white girl. Several groups of student lefties, whose stomachs turn at the thought of anyone being forcibly sent away from Great Britain, gathered round him and chanted 'fascists' at the police as they took him away from the church wrapped in a blanket. He said at his hearing that he'd be killed once he got to Sri Lanka. Yesterday I read an article about him. He's living with his mum somewhere in Colombo. No one, apart from his mum, knows or cares that he's there. I suppose the best stance when imprisoned is to beg for sympathy or to raise a lot of bleeding heart support by playing tough and blaming it all on the system.

> The walls are plain and deathly grey
> They never see the light of day
> I wish that I was miles away
> I wish that I was miles away.
>
> (apoplectics to Robert Frost)

Actually it's not like a jail at all, more like army barracks.

How the hell did I land up here, me a 'decent family' boy from a garrison town in India – one who should have been content to get a B.Sc. and work in a formica factory. I was smart. I realised I was smart when I knew that I didn't believe what others believed. I sought evidence. Dad said there was a God. I agreed. But in my own company I denied him several times. They said cows were holy. To me they were only animals who shat in the street. Astrology – people believed – to me it was wishful. Ceremonial – waste of time, degradation. Prayer – vomit. America – lies, emptyheadedness, Coca-Cola, *Time* magazine, junk food, death. USSR – good idea, we could do it better here (India) providing I was in charge. India – Out!

Maybe I'll come back to Poona, my home town, but let me start at the point at which this scepticism turned into the urge to leave.

I couldn't see myself as a research chemist, no sir. Every boy who loves his ayah and sees his parents steadily ignoring beggars who stretch out maimed limbs for alms, has the seeds of socialism sown under his/her skin. I passed my exams and applied to Lumumba University in the USSR for a course of studies. They were keen on Indians. They wrote back in official English saying I'd have to study Russian for two years before starting any course.

I'll go somewhere where they speak the language, I thought, America or Britain and when Cambridge accepted me to read Oriental languages, to Mecca I came.

My tutor said I'd go far. I could see him wishing. It was the age of America and Americanness, when ethnicity – Jewishness, blackness, etc – mattered to everybody. If you didn't have that as a badge to wear in all those competing cultures, well then, you found something else for which 'they' victimised you. It started with wanting to be part of a victim group and moved on to asserting that together you were tough.

Good years, but they kick you out so fast from university. Your time's up, the last term's over, you've danced at the May ball now get the hell out with your bags.

I got the hell out to London. To Earls Court. A room. No money. A few unfashionable clothes. Had to find a job. I answered an ad on an Earls Court tobacconist's notice board promising fabulous wealth to those who applied. An Indian guy answered the door. The game was to sell his invention in which he had ultimate faith. He had bought hundreds of ladies' umbrellas and thousands of battery-operated torches and fitted them up with a gismo which caused the torch to come on when the umbrella was unfurled, thus allowing you to use it at night and see where you were going on rainy nights in the dark. I left my watch as a deposit and actually sold seven to shops the same day. Beginner's luck. The following day shopkeepers took me for a chancer, or a man demented.

There were others selling. I met them. No one sold. The proprietor, when I went to give him his illuminative umbrellas and get my money back, was gone. With my grandfather's Rolex watch.

I stood outside Earls Court tube and sold one umbrella to a couple when it started raining.

I hadn't eaten for twenty-four hours and went into the snacketeria for a doughnut. Two blacks came and sat opposite me. They didn't have money for coffee, they decided, so the guy pulled out a wad of paper and tried to sell it to me. Sure, it was poetry, doggerel–'Babylon is bad/ain't it sad' sort of stuff. They insisted I buy it and I was embarrassed knowing they needed the sixty pence, so I bought it and left. Coffee to the creative.

Nothing to do the next day, I read this junk poetry lying on my bed and my eye moved to the address. A project. For ethnic minority writers. I went.

It was in Brixton, an address which I even now tremble at disclosing, because 'the brothers and sisters' behaved as though we were terrorists. All we were doing was writing poetry and attending interminable meetings.

One day after a 'political collective' meeting at the workshop, I got home to find a funeral in progress at the building. I enquired who was dead and was told that it was the Sri Lankan guy in the basement. I knew him, he had passed me in the hall and we had exchanged a few words. I'd been to his room for coffee–no milk, no sugar, the cheap sort of instant which stinks of chicory. He slept in a bed he'd constructed from crates. He'd died in his sleep. Now they were carrying him out in the crate bed. Did they intend to bury him in it? A Mr Dexter and Mr Khan turned up the next day and the landlord asked me to keep the key to the Sri Lankan's room and let them in. They were going to take his stuff away. They knew him vaguely. They were both from the BBC and he occasionally worked for them when he wasn't drunk, they said. He translated Indian languages. I said I did too and they offered me his job, providing I could be there that afternoon.

Translating is pimping for the inter-cultural voyeur. It was my job, the occasional crumb thrown by Dexter and Mr Khan at the World Service. The wrestle with languages by day, radical politics (meaning 'history' meetings and some posturing and a lot of conviction) by night.

The day came when, delivering scripts to Bush House, Mr Khan stops me in the corridors.

'Aren't you a Parsee, Xavaxa?'

'I was born a Parsee.'

'Then why do you spell your name in this funny way? I thought you were a West Indian fellow or something.'

'I have worked with West Indians.'

'We are doing a series on religions, world religions. How about you researching the Zoroastrians, the whole Parsee religious ceremonies, philosophy, etc, etc.'

That's where the ticket to Bombay came from and that's when I met Tilak first.

He was groping for me in the dark. I was asleep on the twentieth floor of a Bombay high rise in the flat of a dear friend. The front overlooks the south of the island and in the day time you get the most magnificent view of the placid reach of water that is Bombay harbour, and of the palm trees and the thatched shanties standing next to new skyscrapers. The shanties look wholesome and picturesque and the new buildings are blackened by the corrosion of the sea air.

The curtains that divide the front room with its tiled floor from the balcony were drawn to let me sleep. My friend was asleep in his bedroom. His wife was away for a day or two in their country house in the hills to the east of Bombay. I was not aware that anyone had a key to the flat and at first, before sleep took me hostage, I could hear the occasional rumble of the lift and its trellised metal doors banging. Bombay, for the rest, is quiet. I vaguely heard the rattle of a key in the large wooden door and an attempt to tip toe into the dark. Then a man's hand fumbled with my waist.

'Brother?'

'Who's that?' I sat up. I slept with my head towards the curtain and by the light of the sky that came through I could see a large man kneeling by me.

'Have no fear, brother, Firdaus has gone to sleep, yes? I am another pilgrim.'

159

If he was an intruder, he was a calm one. He'd got past the night watchman.

'Tilak, he must have told you.'

'He didn't.'

'But you are Mr X?'

'Yes, I am.'

'Pleased to meet you, very pleased, I too am a searcher.'

It was then I vaguely remembered that Firdaus had said something about a lunatic who had attached himself to the flat and occasionally came to sleep.

'I'll just lie down here beside you and in the morning we can talk over cup of tea.'

'Why don't you sleep on the settee.'

'If you object', he smiled, 'I will sit all night on the balcony. Sleep is not important for me.'

'Don't do that,' I said. 'If you want the floor, it's all yours, I'll go on the settee.'

'How long you've lived in England?'

'Long time.' I was going to say something to the effect of long enough not to sleep with strange men but I was too groggy to start an argument in the dark.

'You sleep, and forgive me, brother.'

He went to the balcony and opened his cloth bag which was full of papers and files and took something out and began to peruse it in the dim light. I couldn't sleep with him doing that.

'Would you like some rum?' I asked and went to the kitchen where the dregs of a bottle still stood in the fridge. I fetched two glasses.

'I can drink it. My preference is for well water, but where I come from, the water is scarce and rum is more a done thing, except we don't call it rum. What my people call it is Mohvra, made of flowers.'

His grin was like a moon in the dark. I sat cross-legged and drank the rum. Around his eyes were crows' feet, marks of life and benevolence. He looked like a wise Red Indian from a corny western.

He said he knew I was a writer because he was a writer too.

'Really I'm a kind of religious scholar,' I said. 'I'm trying to get some writing done, but not imaginative, just factual.'

'Yes, Firdaus told me. You are looking for the Parsees. Did you find some?'

I liked his irreverential tone.

'And you are a project hatcher, aren't you? Land and environment and all this bullshit?'

He smiled. '"Bullshit" is only an abuse in the West. Here it is a God-given blessing. So much you can do with shit of bulls.'

In the two hours it took to drain a second bottle of rum, we were friends. He read me a story he had written. He insisted. He opened the ledger-like book in which he wrote and asked me if I understood Hindi. I said I'd stop him at the sentences I didn't understand. He said asking to sleep next to me reminded him of the story he'd written.

It was all about himself and how he had to ask his wife if he could sleep next to her after a hard day's work on the soil. He was bored with his wife and the only thing that could rouse him to sexual activity was thinking about the fertility of the land he had worked on all day and all year, the idea of seeds growing, of the plough breaking and turning over the soil. Of the soil accepting aggression and the abuse which gave rise to its fertility, of the pain of the soil in its round of growth. Poetic stuff.

'It's a bit like D. H. Lawrence,' I said.

'Who is D. H. Lawrence?'

'A writer. Something in your phrases and the mood of your story reminds me of him.'

He licked his lips to moisten them as he read.

'I'd like to meet him. I thought Englishmen had forgotten such things.'

'You can read his books but you can't meet him. He's dead.'

It was bizarre but that's how I remember it.

We slept till Firdaus woke us up with cups of tea and an assurance from Tilak that the rum hadn't given him a hangover. The sun was hard and hot behind the curtains. The monsoon was over but Bombay is never cool and always moist.

Tilak is a magnificent man. Tall and with the haircut you get by the side of the road, short on top and shaved all round the back and sides. He disappeared for a few days again.

Firdaus said he was slightly mysterious. Everyone he had introduced Tilak to treated him as something of a bore because he was always touting his photographs of village life and his wretched model village development around. He had written ten ledgers full of stories and chronicles of the land but he wouldn't show them to Hindi publishers because he didn't want to be 'touched by the corruption of the commercial world'.

161

I asked if he was slightly fraudulent – an educated man disguised as an innocent.

'Don't think so,' Firdaus said. 'But he does carry the self-educated village school-boy image a bit far. Bombay is bored with it.'

We went to the Parsee fire temple near Princess Street. 'Just to get the old juices flowing,' as Firdaus put it. I with my tape-recorder courtesy of the Beeb. The priest asked me to leave it outside and looked at it covetously.

Firdaus was mildly amused that I had taken up with Tilak.

I wasn't to know then that Tilak was to be the great white whale in Sonya's voyage. Or maybe no, she was just buying, window shopping in the High Street of culture – and we were selling, me and my orientalisms, Tilak and his patter about a poor but rich nation. So it is with Tilak the story begins, that night and the next in Bombay.

We talk again through that night and wake up late to greet the day. Allow me to tell it as my memory, five years later, tells me it happened.

This day Firdaus is on shift. He and Naomi are both doctors. Firdaus comes back but not to sleep, he says he wants to watch. The day is to be short lived, the darkness will fall again soon. I haven't kept up with the newspapers and Tilak and I are both caught unawares. Bombay is to witness a total eclipse of the sun. For a few minutes.

We must wander out.

'Dey Daan Chootay Gheraan.' The cry goes up. Give to charity (plate outstretched) and the eclipse will release the world.

The crowds of Bombay take refuge within doors, under roofs, behind walls. No cars, no taxis, just clumps of people hurrying to the beach like funeral processions walking at a bizarre rhythmic pace. Like a movie speeded up.

There is a clangour in the city, the sound of temple bells, a racket, a barbarian clashing and a wailing sound of congregations praying for deliverance.

This is the city in which millions of businessmen think of ways to dodge tax. They import left-footed shoes one month, buying the consignment at government auction after having them declared useless, only to buy the consignment of right-footed ones in Calcutta a month later. A city where the neon signs boast pseudo-American jokes. The dark falls over the business men and the neon signs and people wash themselves on the beaches to free the world of the oppression of God's anger.

Here and there on the buildings we see scientific-minded fathers with their children looking at the progressing eclipse through glass darkened with smoke. Fear and curiosity and still, after Galileo and Newton and Einstein and the boast of a thousand scriptures of Hinduism that preceded Galileo and the boast of the Muslims to have discovered astronomy, the boast that the Zoroastrians invented the universe and God and all eclipses and systems and the atomic theory and what's more Heisenberg's Uncertainty Principle, after all these vain boasts the city falls silent, struck dumb and trembling by a natural movement of the planetary orbs. Tilak and I walk on in the silence. It is as though a plague of the mind has struck, or something more glorious, a really general strike. The temples are thronged and the fire-temples and the mosques and the beaches for those who prefer ritual by water. No vendors. Beggars with snakes on plates, sucking milk who ask for charity for the upkeep of the revolting reptile. With the relentless forward roll of a crowd of locusts comes the darkness and there is purple in the sky. The eclipse. Pitch dark for a moment which seems then like an eternity. How fast the planets move. If I look I shall be blinded. The fringe of darkness blinds. I say this to Tilak. We are walking by a low wall and I hear a wail, a thin cry. It persists. I remark to Tilak that someone's crying.

He says something like, they always do. The crying continues. The wall reaches my waist and the crying stops and starts just under its shadow. Except in the dark there is no shadow. So this is what cosmic darkness is like in which stars shine but shed no light. When the darkness passes we both look over the wall. A baby. The baby of sociological real life drama, which follows the pattern set for it by Moses in the bullrushes – the princess finds it, it gets left on a doorstep . . . only this time I'm the princess.

As you drive to north Bombay you pass a place named after a temple called Prabha Devi. There on the main road is a shop with a hammock hung outside it. The hammock is for rejected babies who may be left there by distraught mothers who, in the argot of the West, 'can't cope'.

I cope. I take up the baby. At first I don't know how to carry it. Tilak grabs it firmly, gently, easily with great experience and hushes it up. I find myself looking over my shoulder for a policeman, for an avenging angel for a mother claiming her baby back with sharp nails and the face of a bereaved witch. Nothing.

Tilak is philosophical about it. We should wait there, he says and we do. We walk a distance to where the rocks lead to the sea and keep our eyes on the spot where the baby has been found. No one comes past. After two hours of vigil we take the baby home. Naomi cleans it.

I am at first afraid to open the bundle. When we kept squirrels as pets in school and let them run about our shirts, there would occasionally be someone who had captured or bred a pregnant squirrel and the babies, like little pieces of meat, would be born, hairless and pink and wriggling. We called these babies 'skinballchies' and fed them with wisps of milk-soaked cotton wool. My baby is a bit of a skinballchy. Naomi and Tilak instinctively understand my fascination for the discovered baby. It's a girl. I dare not call it anything. Naomi calls it 'gheraan', eclipse. Firdaus will know what to do with it. The hospital, he said, registers these babies with the police, there are homes, there is a formula for adoption.

I forget about Bombay and my tape-recorder. I have enough interviews anyway – the priests, patriarchs, matriarchs, businessmen, factory-workers, theologians, shysters, the lot. The baby takes up most of my time. I go out and buy stuff for it. Even if it is to be given away to the police, we'll fatten it up first, get her the sterilising sets, clothes, bedding, everything she needs. She cries when I pick her up, only Tilak and Naomi are expert with her and it makes me more determined to be so. I clean her little purplish-red-tanned arse; her tiny fingers that make you wonder about evolutionary theory, clutch loosely, momentarily; her bald head with its faint down of black hair nods. I'm told she doesn't smile, it's the grimace of pain that wind in the stomach brings. How do they know? I keep comparing the colour of my skin to hers.

Firdaus talks of adoption. I announce, matter of factly, that I am going to take her with me.

'I found her.'

I feel it's lame as I say it, but nevertheless true.

Firdaus laughs. Naomi knows I'm serious. Tilak adopts a philosophical stance, babies grow up everywhere in the world, they don't belong to any one person, rhubarb, rhubarb.

I know a couple of fixers. It takes a few days, but for a small sum she is entered into my passport as my daughter. Absurd.

She enters my passport as Fara. Daughter. I must confess the word makes me paranoid. A cold-sweat dread overtakes me – me, an orphan, brought up by my grandfather. 'Daughter' – a knot of blood, which is thicker than water.

Suppose someone should trace her or the neighbours complain or the police come. I have to get out of Bombay. I lie to Firdaus and Naomi.

They knew I lived somewhere in Earls Court and that the Beeb was paying for my trip and for the interviews with Zoros. I told them about the translations, about the death of Wigasekaram, the Sri Lankan in the crate.

Of course I had spoken to them of politics of the drift of London, and of my break with the black writing group and their shenanigans (more of that later). The lie I told was that I had a woman waiting for me, a girl friend with whom I lived. Firdaus knew I was lying but he also knew why I was lying. He knew me well. Naomi knew I was lying too, so it was not a good lie, but she squeezed my arm when I mentioned this invented girl friend again as though to say I needn't prove to her that I could provide.

The day I decided to leave Bombay I went to the fire temple.

We put on our black velvet caps, bought sticks of sandalwood. I was wearing a sudra and kusti, our investiture vest and string, and we washed our faces and stood before the eternal fire in silence and reverence. We watched as the emaciated and buxom Parsees came to worship. I took Fara who didn't protest. A few women came up and examined her when I put her down on the bench. Unusual for them to see daddy with such a young baby.

Then we went to a taverna and drank cashew nut liquor and walked into the evening of Bombay.

Naomi and Tilak come to see us off. At Sahar airport, Bombay, there are no problems. The hostesses are very solicitous. Is it still such an unusual sight? They look at you and wonder what happened to Mummy and you look back with half an offer of acquiring a new one, just for the sake of the child of course, the deep tragedy of the mummy never escaping your lips.

Despite the game, Fara was absorbing. At Heathrow there was a moment of panic, twenty minutes of it more like. They asked me to wait in the immigration office. A man came in and interviewed me. He looked at my passport several times. Then he nodded me through to the baggage claim and professed himself satisfied. He explained, very many immigrants try it on, they bring in children not their own. At the time there was no DNA fingerprinting test, it all devolved on the trust of the officer, the accent of the interviewee. Yes, BBC World Service, I said, I was a free-lance.

Fara in a sling, my bag in one hand, I rode home on the tube.

The Zoroastrians had suddenly taken a back seat – not on the tube but in my scheme of things. I am not born again, just edging towards self-conception. I want to know if there is any mileage in Zoroastrianism, though I don't believe in anything. Not anything that goes beyond the evidence of my senses, books, talk, faces, most things short of ghosts and automatic faith.

I think of Tilak. Like Fara he was my discovery.

He is generous with his money. We walk around Bombay and when we take a bus or a taxi or a train he pays the fares. He buys the tea in cafés and I buy the bottles we take back to Firdaus's flat. In the evenings we talk about books.

On Marine Drive we walk hand in hand, like lovers. What's wrong with me? Other men do it in India. It does not betoken homosexuality, or maybe just the mildest kind. Tilak doesn't understand my withdrawing my hand when we come across somebody I know. I have some notoriety in this city. Of the most peripheral sort.

Best of all he takes me seriously as a writer. All I have published that he has seen is this one long poem in a magazine which publishes nudes and crude sexual joke-pages, as well as some amazingly serious articles. I don't belong to Bombay, I tell Tilak. I come from further inland, from Poona, or Pune as the Maharshtrians who have inherited this earth choose to call it. But Bombay was built on Parsee endeavour.

When I was a kid I lived with my grandfather and he had one bookshelf. It had twenty books maybe, and along with the works of Kahlil Gibran and the prayer books in Gujerati and the paperback on Napoleon there was a hard-covered blue tome called *Parsee Lustre on Indian Soil*. Vanity publishing. On each page there was the picture of a personage – touted, for instance, as a 'Sandalwood Merchant and Philanthropist. Prominent member of the Deolali Seva Mandal. He loved children and had seventeen of his own. He died in 1922 mourned by his lovely wife Avan and his seventeen children who survive him.' Such was the life and the claim to historical notoriety of Shapurji Maneckji Oontwalla (which surname means 'camelman'. How did the family come to rest and give up their nomadic ways to sell sandalwood and turn philanthropic? What philanthropy did they do? Distribute umbrellas to the poor and soaked? The book didn't say).

It was a thick book. Many such had paid to parade their insignificance.

The word Deolali! My ancestors came from there or owned some land there. And there too was the largest mental hospital, asylum for the deranged of the British in India, especially the Indian army of the Raj. The Tommies referred to madness as the 'Doolally Tap', with a touch to the forehead and a twisting motion of the forefinger to betoken a loose screw. That was Deolali. And as for 'Tap', no doubt it was the Western Indian word for heat which induced the madness, pronounced 'taap', to rhyme with 'harp'.

I didn't tell Naomi and Firdaus that I had changed the spelling of my name to Xavaxa. That too through embarrassment, stupidity, cowardice.

When I first started going to the group meetings in Brixton, the writers' circle, there were six black men and women in the room. We were asked to read out stuff for consideration by Roby X, the editor of the forthcoming publication of the group, paid for by some arts grant they had hustled. They passed a register round and asked us to sign our initials, not our full names, as 'we have to maintain security', said Roby. He signed himself RX. I was the only Indian in the room, two others signed themselves KX and WX. I signed my initials XX. They knew me as Xerxes and I thought doubling up would do.

Roby looked at the paper and after our meeting he asked what my second name was. 'Shavaksa,' I said and he asked me if he could use the piece I had read. The next meeting he paid for it by cheque. The cheque was made to Xerxes Xavaxa. It looked good. 'That's not how you spell it,' I said.

'You want to teach him how to spell?' said a man called Fat Boy, a rasta with enormous jowls and huge hands, who fancied himself as a dub poet. He curled his bottom lip down. I said I'd accept the cheque, after all the spelling didn't matter.

'I changed my name to X after Malcolm, I don't want no slave name,' said Fat Boy.

I was going to say that I thought he was always addressed as Fat Boy, but thought better of it.

And so it came to pass. I began signing myself XX. More X appeal, as Fat Boy said when I got to know him better. He was very gentle.

The magazine folded after two issues. But for two glorious issues I was a published person.

Roby ran away with the funds and the girl who was supposed to be the managing director of the Black Pen Club declared that she was a lesbian and would have nothing to do with poems like the one Fat Boy had written or with the story that I had bribed Roby to publish.

Having a baby cuts one off from the rest of humankind. Fara demands my time, my attention. The money runs out. I can't go to social security, I'd have to take her with me, they may ask about her, they may take her away. The guy next door has heard the crying. He comes in with the original remark that I am back. He looks curiously at the baby so I bar the door and pretend that there really isn't any crying coming from my room.

For Mr Dexter and Mr Khan, I write a brief introduction (which they reject).

'Zoroastrianism is the oldest religion in the world and the first monotheistic civilisation that we know of. The quarter of a million Zoroastrians who remain are, as it were, cast on an island of their own making. They are the Parsees of India. This small, valiant, tightly knit race of racist settlers, peasants, industrialists, workers, fire worshippers, bigots who throw their dead to the vultures on the towers of silence, who do not admit to their community any converts, who bring their children up to believe in their messianic place in history, are in danger of losing this very place in history through, quite simply, becoming extinct, disappearing into the melting pot as Parsees intermarry with non-Parsees and go their way.

'Often they are compared to Jews. "The Parsees are the Jews of India". One thing wrong with that. There are Jews in India, all sorts . . .'

ZOROASTRIAN CHALK CIRCLE

Now the story begins. I looked after Fara for precisely fourteen days. I saw no one. I bought a second-hand pram from a shop down the sleazy end of West Ken and I wheeled her out, three times a day, rain or shine because my room couldn't have been good for her and the fresh air stopped her howling.

But the money ran out. Really ran out. The landlord called three times for the rent I hadn't paid while I extended my stay in India. I checked with the Beeb. Nothing.

I called Dexter, I called Khan. No reply. I wheeled the pushchair and Fara to the Aldwych and tried to get to see them. Khan came down. He was embarrassed. He said I'd done too much work in India. They didn't think Zoroastrianism merited a whole programme, but they'd pay me for the extracts they used, of course. We were sitting in the high ceilinged hall of Bush House and Fara set up a wail as never before. I stuffed her comforter back in her mouth.

Khan was not curious about the baby till that moment.

'Where did you get this baby, Xavaxa?' he asked peering in a superior manner into the pram.

'I didn't know you were married,' he added.

I thought of saying I was doing a friend a favour, but that wouldn't do because perhaps the next time we met Fara would still be with me.

I said I'd go and call him later. He said they might get me a book review in a month or two.

I starved for a couple of days and then thought this was absurd, I'd get to the point where there'd be no money for baby food or for nappies. Not that I bought the expensive brand names, the drug superstores seemed to store piles of nappies with their plastic bags damaged or torn open which they sold for less than half price. Only sometimes poor Fara didn't get the smallest size and had to swim about in large ones with tapes that didn't stick well enough.

I wheeled her to the DHSS. I tried to see the officer I normally saw but they made me wait three hours and then shunted me off to see a hard-faced black man who told me that my entitlement to benefit had expired and if I wanted to claim for the baby I had to fill in forms and show them a birth certificate and twenty other things. I left the DHSS office with a feeling of desperation, a bloody great hole in my tummy.

I talked to Fara. 'Sunk, baby. We should have stayed in India.'

At the time the only friends whom I could ask for anything were Jam and Cress. Jam was a struggling young playwright and he'd struggled right into the clutches or arms of Cress.

She worked as an actress for a while but she didn't need to work at anything as her daddy and mummy, divorced and sold up though they were, were stinking rich.

Marrying Cress was Jam's way of getting instantly rich.

Good move because it gave him time to write. When Jam was poor he had borrowed money from me, even though I had precious little. He was the kind of person who didn't remember owing money. A tenner taken was a tenner gone. I could at least borrow it back now if I couldn't call in old debts. I called them and told them I had a baby. They both came. Cress loved Fara. I told them the story of where she had come from. They'd brought me a bottle of wine. Without shame I asked Jam for a loan. He was expecting it and said no. Cressida gave me a hundred pound cheque and apologised for Jam being broke. OK, so they kept me alive. Ten days after that I had a telegram from Poona. My grandfather, my mother's dad who had brought me up, had died. He was ninety-five. He had built a small empire by starting to sell kerosene and moving on to owning petrol pumps in the city. I owed him a sentimental journey. My uncle sent the telegram, knowing that I'd want to know, even though I hadn't seen any of them on my journey to Bombay just a few weeks before. He had left a will, not exactly in my favour but 'to be divided between all Xerxes's children at their age of majority'. My son-of-a-bitch uncle wanted to discuss the trusteeship with me. He knew I had no children and he was getting some smart lawyer to contest the clauses of the will so he could get his hands on some cash and property.

Dilemma. I couldn't turn up in Poona with Fara and claim her as my daughter. My uncle would whip out his lawyers, as Gurkhas in danger whip out the kookris. They would know she wasn't my daughter, forged passports are my uncle's stock in trade. He believes all documents are suspect.

I was my grandad's eldest daughter's son. My uncle was his youngest child and only son, though grandad had always treated me as his own since my parents died, my mother in a car accident and my father a week later, 'of heartache', they said. Suicide probably. He had told me the story of how my mother died. They were going on from one party to a house in Bombay for another party, or a drink or something. My mother was sitting next to the driver a male friend. When a child ran across the street he braked suddenly. He apologised for the shock but my mum said nothing. Her neck had been jerked back in what they call a 'whiplash' effect and she was dead on arrival. The friend had to confront my father and tell him that his wife was not alive.

My father died a week later of a 'heart attack'. They said he hadn't eaten or slept since her funeral. Of all this, at the time, I knew nothing. Later, I got the feeling that Dad hadn't died in this natural way.

There was something he had discovered, some story of unfaithfulness too awful for him to contemplate.

Now the telegram said that I had to go in person to collect papers that my grandad had left for me. No one else was to see them and his instructions to his lawyer were that I should be recalled from the ends of the earth to receive the documents within a week from the day he died. If I didn't collect them, they were to be handed to my uncle.

I asked Cress if I could phone India from their house and called the lawyer. No, he couldn't disclose the contents of the will over the phone, but yes, I stood to gain if I went. Perhaps it was the answer. I could pay my small debts, start again in London, find a way to keep Fara and earn a living and write the books that the great British reading public would appreciate.

Yes, I would go. The 'documents', whatever they were, didn't worry me. What did my grandad want to tell me? Letters from my mum to another man? Some secret about my origin? Did I care who I was, I asked myself, or did I know. I decided I knew.

Fara? Cress would look after her. She had been married to Jam for two years and she'd tried to have a baby but something called endometryosis was eating up her insides and preventing her conceiving. Yes, she'd be delighted to keep the baby while I was gone.

I handed Fara over. Cressida lent me more money for the return ticket which I bought from a bucket shop cut-price walla in Soho.

Naomi had left for America. Firdaus was working hard. Tilak had gone back to his village. I spent a few hours in Bombay and took the train to Poona. A light rain was falling. The funeral was actually in progress when I arrived. I touched the foot of the body symbolically as the crowds lined up to pay their respects, the women inside the house, the men outside. My uncles, my aunts, my cousins, the clan.

His flesh looked soapy and clean. He was laid in a shroud and the Dasturs muttered and sang over the body. The dog was brought in to smell death and confirm that the spark was gone, the spirit fled. Then they carried him seven miles to the end of the town and we walked behind in pairs clutching a white handkerchief between us. I walked with my uncle, I was the orphan of the family and my grandfather had paid for my school, for college, for the journey to England. They put him on the towers of silence and the vultures must have cleaned him out. It is forbidden for the lay-person to see it happening.

I stayed four days. There was some money I could have immediately and my uncle made out a cheque. They made jokes about my getting married and getting to work straight away on making sons and heirs.

The family solicitor saw me the next day in the presence of my uncle, and handed me the wax-sealed envelope. It was large and contained three foolscap writing pads, each an inch thick.

I thought I wouldn't open it till I got back to London. Tell you the truth, even if there was some dark and deep revelation, I didn't really want to investigate it. My life was somewhere else and I wanted to resume it.

When I got back to London I went to fetch Fara from Jam's flat. There was no one there. I went home and phoned them every half hour. I went back to the flat at night. No one. It was driving me crazy. I didn't sleep. The next day I went to all Jam's haunts and rang up everyone who knew them. I had been away a week from Fara now and I had to find her.

I told myself that it was a misunderstanding. I had said I was coming back earlier but had stayed a couple of days extra, maybe they'd gone to a friend's place. I stalked their flat every day. Nobody knew where they were. I waited for the milkman early on the third morning. He confirmed that Cressida had left instructions for no deliveries till further notice.

It was torture, I could do nothing but wait.

I had left the envelope under my bed and almost forgotten about it. I opened it, thinking it might, at least, distract me. Three pads of closely handwritten stuff in my grandad's final, creaky hand. With it a scrawled note in an even feebler, less legible hand. The note was addressed to me with great affection. It said this was his life's work which he had been secretly doing for years. It was the story of his life, a book to end all books. He knew that it was the one thing of value in his life, the wisdom he'd picked up by living it.

He knew it would be worth some money too. Of course he had left me deeds in the land for my children but for me, I could publish his story, 'all my best thoughts', and 'the West can pay you for the wisdom of the East'.

I began reading. The first few pages made some sense. It was written in the same sort of turgid prose as *Parsee Lustre On Indian Soil*: 'I hail from Surat, the land of my great great forebears and ancestors who claim, like Darius the great, that they are Parsees, Zoroastrians, followers of the great God Ahura Mazda' . . . and in this boring vein the first fifty pages were at least coherent, telling the story of his great grandfather.

Then something strange happened to the manuscript and continued happening. It became a stream of consciousness and then utter gibberish, words scrawled together, no punctuation, no sentences, just the longest concatenation of verbiage I had ever seen. Sample: 'EFG came from inside Gandhiji ate banana emergent Nehru the Motilal kerosene from inside emanates Vallabhai Patel bring one maternal uncle sings . . .'

Of course three national leaders are mentioned and from time to time that persistence of words from a context comes back. Oh God. So he died demented or deluded.

I didn't need more uncomfortable thoughts. I put the manuscript back under the bed.

Ten days after I returned there was a note from Jam to say 'She's fine'. Just that. No address, no explanation. Some days later a notice board went up outside their house saying 'Flat For Sale'. I accosted the estate agent. Yes, Mrs Cressida Jamal had put the flat up for sale. Did they have a forwarding address? They were not supposed to divulge any information, but if I was interested in viewing the flat I could pick up the key the next day.

I viewed the flat. They had cleaned it out. No furniture, not a mouse.

I went back to the estate agent and made up a story about having come from India and being Mrs Jamal's brother-in-law, and could I have their forwarding address or the phone number. They were snooty about it. No, I couldn't and if I wanted to leave my name and phone number, the next time Mrs Jamal got in touch they would ask her if she wanted to contact me. What would happen if I wanted to buy the flat? Oh well, it was obvious that I wasn't a serious buyer and they'd consider their position and take a view.

I set off the burglar alarm when I broke into the estate agents that night. Before I could get the filing cabinet open with the spanner and wrench I had brought, the police had arrived. I could make one phone call from the magistrates court the next day. I was charged with burglary. I couldn't tell them that I was looking for a stolen baby.

You want to know what it's like in Brixton? I spent three months on remand, working in the laundry and in the library. The estate agents came to see me and told me that they had been in touch with Cressida who had been very sympathetic to my plight and in view of the fact that their flat was now sold, they would not give evidence against me but would co-operate with my lawyer and give evidence to the court to say they were aware of motives other than theft for material gain.

I was found guilty of breaking and entering and given a suspended sentence. It was when I got out that I saw a poster of Jam's new play running at fringe venue. A 'modern version of the Brechtian classic *The Caucasian Chalk Circle*'.

I had asked the landlord to be patient with me when I phoned him from the police station. He had been partially patient. He hadn't thrown my things into the street, but he'd changed the locks on my door and was waiting for me to come out and pay the arrears in rent. There was a note saying I should get in touch with him and he had twenty clients waiting for my room. I smashed the door down. It made a noise and a mess, but there was nothing else I could do. I begged money off the Paraguayan and went to Jam's opening night.

The cheeky bastard. He comes to me and says he's very sorry I've been to jail, perhaps they owe me an explanation, but no, they haven't moved to Wales, they live in Clapham, they bought a house and yes, they did it partially to escape from me and partially because Cressida had luckily been given enough money to put a deposit down. Would I go and see Cressida and Fara after the show? Of course with a baby and that sort of responsibility she couldn't make the first night. Had I enjoyed the play?

My heart skips two beats when I see Fara. She's asleep. How fast her hair has grown and her head is hot and the wet strands of hair cluster together with sweat.

Cressida behaves as though she is guilty of nothing, owes me no explanations, as though I had stolen a baby just to give it to her. It is two in the morning now as we've stayed drinking at Jam's first night and then he's brought me here. He is more conscientious. Cressida is still awake and says she's been feeding Gazal. And who is Gazal? Oh yes, they've changed her name. Don't I see? Her stage name is Cressida Field, and she wouldn't want the child called Fara Field Jamal would she? So Gazal Field or Gazal Jamal is fine and the spelling can be left flexible so she has a choice when she grows up of whether to adopt the Gazelle Europeanisation or the Gazal Urdufication.

'I'm taking her home and she is going to be called Fara.'

'You don't have a home, be reasonable,' Jam says. Cressida picks the sleeping baby up and says, 'You just try. You think we don't know why you brought this child here? To this country, I mean?'

I have never seen such hatred dripping from a woman's eyes. She snatches my baby, gets me thrown in jail, gives me three months of sleepless nights, has me debarred and homeless, and she hates me? The baby wakes up. She smiles at Cressida who plays with her and rocks her up and down with google glug conversation.

'I'm sorry but I'm taking her,' I say.

I don't know where I'll take her and it's true as Jam points out that I haven't a place to take her or money to feed her with.

'I'll call the police and have you thrown out, Xerxes,' Cressida says.

I am amazed at myself. I have sworn murder in my heart and my every dream against these two. But the sight of the baby . . . she's happy. She looks as though she has everything to do with Cressida and nothing to do with me.

Jam clutches my arm and turns me away.

'Listen, leave her with us till you sort things out? Why don't you be her godfather? What are you going to do with a baby, you idiot? She'll kill you. She won't let her go now.'

Then, with an eerie inevitability he proposes it. The baby will not be happy with me, she won't even go to me. She cries when he tries to pick her up and she doesn't stop till Cressida's hands are below her. The Chalk Circle. Cressida puts the baby down. I go to pick her up. Cressida grabs my arm and stands in between me and the baby but Jam moves her gently, persuasively away. I pick up Fara.

She lets out a howl. I walk with her up and down. She cries and the tears roll down her dark cheeks. I give her to Cressida, she instantly shuts up.

Jam offers to let me stay the night, they have a spare room. The next morning Cressida asks me if I'd like to go for a walk with the child, the nanny and her. When we're out she says, 'I haven't forgotten my threat about the police. And if you think you've got documentary proof, my dad can also get a birth certificate and besides it's a country doctor's certificate, British, so who will they believe? She is the right colour and our parents are willing to lie to the death to keep her with us.'

She offers me uncle status.

What can I do? The world is full of starving children, homeless, parentless. What mad thing possessed me to become a baby thief?

Yet her name is still in my passport and I did it again. I transferred a child between continents. I passed off another girl as Fara Xavaxa. But that comes later.

TO CARTHAGE I CAME, BURNING
BURNING

I spent half my money on women and wine
Like a fool, I squandered the rest . . .

                                                    Benny Hill

If the Persians under Xerxes had not lost at Salamis, the history of the known world would have been different. There might not have been a Christian era, there might have been a domination of Europe by Zoroastrianism or Mithraism or one of the heresies springing from the ancient religion. There might never have been an explosion of Islam. Europe might have taught what it knew to its masters, the Persians. Of course for all this to have transpired the Persians would have had to have taken Greece and the Greeks more seriously than they did. By all accounts, except those of the Greeks, of course, the great kings of Persia treated the Greek wars as skirmishes with barbarians on the outskirts of empire. And beyond Greece there were only more barbarians.

When I left Cressida and Jam's house, they gave me a hundred pounds again. I felt too proud to take it but took it all the same saying I'd return it and as I turned the corner from their house to take a bus, I burst into tears. What kind of a man would leave his child in the house of strangers? A wretch. Hello, wretch!

'When my friends, actresses, are out of work or strapped for cash, they go and do supply teaching, darling. They take anyone.'

Cressida's words in my ears.

The Paraguayan offers me coffee.

'Your English so great, eh, you do the supply,' said the Paraguayan.

I presented myself at County Hall and walked through the corridors of municipaldom to earn my first honest crust. It was defeat, but it was regular.

As I underwent the torture of teaching, I told myself, repeated it a thousand times a day like a bead of reassuring prayer turned over and over, that I was really a writer, maybe a poet even. If I had the leisure I would get down to it seriously. Maybe find another group that had funding, but this time without the nationalistic politics.

I tell a lie, and am resolved to correct it. For years, through Cambridge and the stray years after, I have sent bits and pieces of the grand book, or descriptions thereof to publishers. And what is this grand book? I've told you about my grandfather's three manuscripts, remarkable in their sheer meaninglessness. Was I engaged in the same enterprise? Writing without having anything to write about? Convincing myself that my dynastic story was important, mixing it with some of the stuff I've put down here, random thoughts about Zoroastrianism and the paths not taken by history?

I have become a collector of shamelessness. I have rejection slips with not even polite interest from thirty-two publishing houses for my projected book. I have made a study of my own shades of shamelessness in salesmanship. I have begun, to publishing houses whose owners I knew were Jewish: 'The study I propose is of a race often called "The Jews of India", the story of a people destined never to found a new Israel.' Or words to that effect. 'Dear sir, fuck off.' Or words to that effect.

To other publishers I have written with shock tactics:

'The Parsees should have patented God,
We invented Him.'

And so on, but No!

I recall my last night in Bombay before the flight with the bambino. Tilak has bought the rum. He has been seeing Canadian and European delegations about seeds which yield crops twice a year and explaining to them how in his commune's experience they eat up the goodness of the soil. He has first-hand evidence. He carries samples of mud in little bundles of cloth. They may take it back to their countries and analyse it.

Fara is asleep. She is, was, I am now convinced, no more than a bundle belonging to me . . . but leave it! I ask Naomi if we can wander out, I shan't see Bombay for some years maybe.

We walk to Chowpaati beach. Tilak talks about my writings and about keeping children and gives me his blessing. -We meet a man of my acquaintance as we are getting ourselves massaged on the Chowpaati beach. Tilak is reluctant to have a massage but I persuade him and we lie down and the supple masseurs get to work. It is sunset and the dark gathers fast. As the massage progresses from the head down to the calves and toes, the masseurs make a suggestion. They have spotted the two of us together and made assumptions about interest in pressing pleasures, Tilak giggles like a fool and says 'No, no, no, no' to the guy. All manner of things are on offer. The massage is delicious but I am not tempted. As we finish and pay, a Parsee man of my acquaintance comes up with an umbrella. He is from my home town and has been watching the people being massaged though he is tightly buttoned himself and wouldn't dream of stripping on the sands and lying down on one of the mats. He recognises me and says, 'Xerxes, I thought you were in England, haven't you become a writer?'

'No.'

'All rumours circulate about you yaar. Someone told me you'd become an alternative psychiatrist.'

'What's that?'

'You're kidding. Don't you know? Like R. D. Laing.'

'Well, we must go,' I say wanting to hurry back and see what Fara's doing.

'You must be enjoying in UK, hunh? I'd love to talk to you.'

It begins to rain, suddenly, as it does in Bombay. The massage boys roll up their mats.

'If you want to talk to him you'd better open up your umbrella,' Tilak says.

'Surely,' says the Parsee whose name I forget and opens his umbrella. The rain falls heavily on the beach and sea and the three of us stand under his huge umbrella while he tells us all about R. D. Laing.

I sign myself Xerxes Xavaxa. The Parsee from Poona. Girls behind tills in banks look at me. They think the xignature is an affectaxion. Such is the power of the X. As Malcolm discovered and used. As the hustler Michael De Freitas, alias, Michael Abdul Malik, alias, Michael X used and was brought by the self same cross that he bore, somewhere else to grief.

I shall never, can never forget the newspaper accounts of his hunting down. Here was a guy who pushed his way through London, riding in the high saddle of hype, a Portuguese black man from Trinidad, impressing John Lennon, impressing the heirs of large business houses, impressing the lady journalists of the national newspapers with his talk of black armies. Finding footage, mileage and money in

178

the ways he could impress them, becoming something of a revolutionary leader because the press acclaimed his mystery, taking a girl, an
earl's daughter to Trinidad to some pretend commune he set up,
deserted there by the British newspapers, the John Lennons, the
everybody, lost incommunicado, killing by knife and spade this
wretched girl. X. The syllable haunts. X: he shaves his beard when the
crime is discovered. X: he is caught, plain old Mr Botany B in the
deserts of Guyana, hunted down by primitive police helicopters. Xed:
he was hanged and his mamma cried. But my XXX, its real, for real,
that's what I inherited, Xerxes Xavaxa. Good day to you too, sir!

Mr X, supply teacher extraordinaire. Gandoo and lund fakir. Useless
to the world of wealth making.

You may ask why I stayed on in London at all? At least schoolteach-
ing had stabilised me. The most casual acquaintance with Mr Khan and
Mr Dexter, attendants at the removal of the body of Wigasekaram, the
co-bed sit-person, had given me hope.

There was a brief period of starvation before the translations at the
Beeb began, when I had known what it was to throw myself on the
mercy of others. And for why? Why not phone my uncle or grandad
and reverse the charges and ask for a ticket back to India and make a start
teaching somewhere with a Cambridge degree. It still impressed some
departments of some universities there. Why not indeed? Random
thoughts as I painted the exteriors of houses in Earls Court because my
landlord, a stingy Scot, demanded three weeks rent for my bed-sitter
one day and I had not a penny in my pocket and only two potatoes left to
boil and eat and when I said to McCurbin that I was broke and threw
myself, tenant of room 11, on his mercy he proposed I did the
equivalent of what they do in the comics, the washing-up after the big
unpaid for meal.

Up the ladder I went, scraping with sand-paper till my knuckles bled,
at precarious heights on shaky ladders, the scales of Victorian peeling
paint. Green, he's bought tons of cheap dark green paint as army surplus
and we painted seven houses dark green, defacing the leafy groves of the
fashionable (not the Aussie) end of Earls Court. Monuments to bad
taste. My contribution to this city in which I studied, in which I picked
up the wisdom of great scholars about oriental religions, my speciality.
Slap, dash, my paint work, At first when I looked down from the
ladders my stomach churned. I was in the circus, I was dicing with
death, sand-paper in hand, a rough end, so to speak. I clung to the
ladder. These wooden spars were my friends, my saviours.

But McCurbin didn't pay. We painted his wretched green houses, myself and another unfortunate tenant who also lived beyond his means, and he was jailed in a paternity suit and no one paid for the labour.

It was my third school. Supply teaching takes you, maybe every day, to a new school. Sometimes they like you and need you and keep you. It was thus I came after pedagogic peregrinations to . . . well, let's call it Sonya's school.

I knew nothing about teaching, nothing about timetables, nothing about London children. But I learned. They danced on the desks, they locked me in the book cupboards, they played radios in class and paid not the least attention to my calling registers or opening my mouth in some mockery of instruction, or scribbling on the blackboard because there was little else at my wit's end that would suggest itself. My manhood and sense of self took a battering. It was better than painting Earls Court houses a dark and brooding green.

It was how I met Sonya. May Ahura Mazda, the God of all light, smile on her and the very mention of her name. She has done no wrong. She was in the senior sixth and this was my third school.

The deputy head was a kind woman and she asked me, one week into teaching there, whether I would take a group of children to the theatre to see *Romeo and Juliet*. I would get some help. There would be three sixth formers with me. They would help to look after the class. She said she knew that I was a man of literature.

The man of literature told the story of *Romeo and Juliet* to the thirty children in the hall. It was magic. They listened. There was Sonya and two others sixth formers deputed to assist me. We set out by tube to the theatre. All went well till the second act. A boy, no, not a boy, a demon, named Albert Trunk, the name is etched in my memory forever, began the assault.

We were seated in the balcony, two rows strong and around us a sea of faces from other schools, some in neat uniforms, some in the gruff attire of the London unwashed, and he, the man Trunk shouts 'PBM'.

The shame of it. The PBM was pre-planned. There I was, culturally pleased and proud on behalf of Shakespeare and every educative noble impulse that my rendition of the story had inspired this party of ragamuffins to do, for once, what good for them, to shut up and listen to something worthy. What self-deception. It was for the PBM that these wretches had accompanied me pliantly to the theatre. Perhaps schoolchildren entering theatres should be subject to the sort of security checks done on airline passengers. These bastards, girls and boys, took out tubes of brass and steel, one, one and half, some two feet long and bags of seeds of some sort, and began to pea-shoot them into the audience below and at the stage. I was in charge of them. Horror and realisation struck through twin barrels. It was the Pearl Barley Massacre. The PBM.

There was consternation below as the barley struck the innocent and began bouncing off the stage and the actors like hail. The play was stopped, the lights came on. I was hauled from my seat by three extremely irate men from the management. My children were delighted. They hung over the balcony and did for *Romeo and Juliet* what King Leonidas did for the Zoroastrians trapped in the pass.

I shouted, remonstrated and then I fled. On the phone I told the headmaster that it was a conspiracy and I'm never good against conspiracies.

It was Sonya who took the children back on the tube. I went home, reconciled to the fact that my week's salary was gone, that they'd probably come and take me away and try me for dereliction of duty. The end of supply teaching.

I spent my last pounds on sherry and cider and mixed the two and had a few glassfuls. The bell rang and I went downstairs to let them in – the police no doubt. It was a girl, eighteen years old maybe, short black hair, very startling eyes and a chin that seemed trim and small as though sculpted with fine attention. Her skin is dark enough to be Indian, but could easily be some European hue. She was wearing a salvaar khamiz and she smiled. Could she come in?

It was then I recognised her. Sonya, the sixth former. I was not sure whether I should invite her in – teachers – pupils – perverts – prosecution – blackmail.

'Yes?' I said, immediately ashamed of myself for my defensiveness.

'All the kids are OK. I just came to say you've got to come back to school. Can I come in?'

'I couldn't deal with it.'

'So what?' she said.

'How did you find where I lived?'

'The sixth form kids have keys to the school office. Sshhh!' She put her fingers to her lips.

I said she could come in if she'd excuse the room, I only had a bedsit.

She could see I was embarrassed and said she had only wanted to see me face to face. She had to go. She wouldn't come upstairs.

'You've got to come back to school tomorrow. We all got back safely. It's not all that bad. Please!'

'They'll sack me, how can I come back? And just as I was beginning to like the place.'

'Don't be silly, sir, these fifth years have behaved worse. We were even badder when we were fifth years, you shouldn't have run away. I'm sure the headmaster will understand. It was one or two instigators, I'll point them out, tomorrow. Please come back.'

Did I dream of her that night?

I presented myself in the staffroom at eight forty-five the next morning and read my *Guardian* as though nothing had happened. No other teachers paid any attention to me and I read the lead story about the Indo-Pakistani war six times without taking it in, waiting for the head or the deputy to summon me, or for the bell to ring.

The theatre had complained. The head had suspended four of the ring leaders. I was given a Geography timetable for the rest of the term.

The sixth formers brought out a newspaper every week, a xeroxed thing. The same day the latest edition circulated in the staffroom. The headlines accused the headmaster of racism. I was the paper's hero.

MR X VICTIMISED BECAUSE HE IS INDIAN

The article told the story of the Pearl Barley Massacre and took the line that actors had to perform Shakespeare in an engaging way to win the attention of the working-class child. If Shakespeare was presented in a boring way, the companies which presented it deserved more than the PBM. It was outrageous discrimination and racial bias for the deputy head to have used the service of Mr Xavaxa who was giving up his valuable time in the evening to take children to the theatre, and then victimised him for the failure of British class culture by putting him on a Geography timetable.

It wasn't signed but it was Sonya. I had a free period after break so I sought her out in the sixth form room. I called her out and we walked in the playground. I didn't care what the other teachers would think or say, they were already whispering about it being inexcusable and the headmaster being soft on supply teachers and allowing me back after my dereliction of duty. There was no way I could explain to them that I had been sick to my stomach with anxiety and had run from the theatre and the manager's office in blind panic, never expecting to be trusted in that school or any other, again. But I explained this to her. Thanked her for valiantly bringing the kids back on the tube. Not that they needed escorting, the louts, but someone had to put their official seal on ending the trip.

'I don't think you should have written that thing this morning.'

'The rest of the sixth form thought it was OK.'

'But it isn't racism, he's giving me a chance. Geography is not all bad.'

'You don't seem to understand your own experience,' she said.

'It just creates too much trouble. They want to forget the incident.'

'Well, they're not going to be allowed to. Suppose the blacks of South Africa said "let's forget about Sharpeville?"'

'It's an embarrassment in the staffroom.'

'There are two issues here. First they put you in an impossible situation by sending you with these hooligans to watch Shakespeare. What do these kids want to see Shakespeare for? It's not working-class culture. And then they get rowdy or have a little joke and the head victimises you because you're Indian. I hate him actually, he's cowardly. He's using you. They'll have you teaching R.E. next.'

'I'd love that, I was trained in languages and religions.'

'Yeah, I forgot,' she said.

'What do you mean you forgot?'

'I mean I knew you'd done a degree in oriental religions and Zoroastrianism and all that.'

'How did you know that?'

'I know all about you,' she said.

I hadn't paid much attention to her before she volunteered to come to the theatre with my group. I vaguely knew that she was half Indian. Green eyes, though.

I averted my eyes because she was staring at me intensely, her brow knit. Her sharp features never hid what she was thinking. She could be an actress, she'd be a natural.

'Surely not all about me,' I ventured.

'Yes, all, Xerxes Xavaxa. Everything. I know how old you are, where you live, where you were born, what you studied, when you came to Britain, that you live in Earls Court, that you wash your laundry in the place down Marloes Road, that you shop in the Diwana Continental, an Asian food shop, and usually take a bottle of white wine home, that you've worked for the BBC and written religious stuff for them and you spend time sitting in the British Museum library during half term and that you're not married.'

I was thinking, 'And you don't know I've been to jail and you have no idea that you are face to face with a notorious baby-snatcher and international flesh trader.'

It's not what I say.

'So you don't know about my girl friends?'

'What girl friends?' She jumped at that.

'Why do you know all this? And how? But *why* is more interesting.'

'Because one, you talk to my sister, Asha in the second year and she's a sharp little bitch.'

'I didn't know she was your sister.'

'Unfortunately, we are sib-bloody-lingams, and two, because I've followed you around and I'm on the school council so I look at cv's of teachers sometimes, secretly when I'm in the office after meetings and because – and you're right, why is most interesting – because, well, because I think you need looking after.'

'I need looking after?'

'Yes, you do, Xerxes, Mr X. And you can start by giving up this stupid job, doing some proper writing and not taking shit any more from these kids. Asha told me about the time they locked you in the maths cupboard and you were too embarrassed to knock on the door and weren't released till the school-keeper rescued you.'

'Yes, well, they tricked me into going in there.'

'But they're only twelve and thirteen years old. For God's sake. If I'd have got hold of them next day I'd have beaten the lot with a clump of wood or something. What's the matter with you?'

'Ah, you know my movements, but you don't know my psychology. I believe in silence, cunning and a regular pay packet. Who else would give me a job? I happen to think the head is one of the most enlightened people in the modern universe.'

She smiled. A row of small teeth with three gaps between the upper front ones.

'I volunteered to come to *Romeo and Juliet* because I thought I could get to know you.'

'Why me?'

'I read your stories in the black arts magazine. You lent them to someone, remember? They were good.'

'Penny gave them to you to read?'

'I didn't mention her, did I? She's a friend but she's not your type and besides she's got a girl friend, a regular, and you're wasting your time trying to impress her.'

Penelope was the drama teacher at the school. Yes, I had tried it on. I only felt vaguely betrayed, but magnificently introduced.

At that time I didn't know whether Sonya was telling the truth or lying. She seemed to have Penny's confidence, because that was the only way she could have got hold of my stories. I had been drinking with Penny and she kept her living arrangements, her other relationships, friendships, everything, quiet. I had taken her out and explained myself to her as one does when one wants to be in love and what shocked me was that she had related some of it to this girl.

'I'd like to talk to you, now that you've noticed me,' she said.

'I'd always noticed you, you stand out . . .'

'That's the bell, Mr Xavaxa. I believe you have a class to attend to. I want something from you.'

'What?'

'I want you to tell me lots of things. My mum doesn't. She's the Indian side and I don't have grandparents and my parents don't much mix with Indians and I feel deprived. So I've latched on to you. OK?'

'Very OK,' I said.

'I'm culturally deprived. Some of the girls in the sixth form think you're cute and the boys think you're a wally. I think you're both and lots more and I want to find out.'

'You talk very plainly, don't you?'

'Best way,' she says and flounces off.

I try to introduce the topic of Sonya to Penny that afternoon when we go for a drink after school.

'So she's finally got to you. Ambition and cunning.'

'Have you told her my age?'

'Come to think of it, X, I don't know how old you are, but I don't think Sonya will give a shit. If she wants lessons on Buddhism and Hinduism she'll take them from anyone. Tough kid, but she refuses to read anything. She can't get through one or two books to find something out, she wants to be told. Spoilt.'

Penny takes me that evening to a six-hour film in two parts. Dickens. Just to thank me for standing in for her on the trip to *Romeo and Juliet*. She's had a personal ruck with her 'flatmate' so she's been away and she feels terrible about the occurrences. It goes without saying between us that she wouldn't have had any PBM on her hands.

She is well respected by the kids. Short hair, short skirts, very shapely legs, big breasts, long nose, pink patchy skin and fed up with the rest of the bods in the staffroom. She has the reputation in school of being the animals' best friend.

We'd slept together twice and like a husband going back to his wife she had dressed herself and kissed me in bed and gone out into the night.

Sonya became a song in my heart. She was definitely flirting. We spent quite a lot of time after school sitting in the sixth form room and then we might go off to the pub together. I was too timid to ask if she wanted to carry the conversation on at home, my place. Once or twice we stayed in the pub round the corner from the school till closing time and she would go to the phone every hour and phone home to say where she was. I don't know what she said. But it was apparent her father and mother kept a close watch on the rebellious spirit. She was seventeen or eighteen then.

I didn't care that at the school I was just a bod. I never struck up, apart from Penny, any relationships or friendships. When the bell went for the end of day, a particular crowd of teachers would get into their cars and head home. Another crowd would stay behind to disappear into preparation rooms and departmental enclaves and come into the staffroom with books and xeroxed sheets and equipment. They never paid much attention to me. I didn't belong to any department, I was the floater and would get work and reports and prepared schemes from the others who spoke to me politely enough but with a tinge of patronisation which always told me that there was a gulf of suspicion between the career teachers and the long-term supply-wallas, the ones whom they knew had ambitions other than the welfare of children or their own careers.

There were others in a similar situation to mine in the staffroom, an Australian music teacher who really wanted a career as a serious baritone. He had a beard and long hair and the kids called him Jesus. His name was Jameson. There was a technical teacher who fancied himself as an inventor, who left the same term that Sonya and her class graduated because he'd succeeded in inventing some system whereby parking meters could not be jammed by foreign coins, the ring-pulls of coke and beer cans, pieces of wire and other gadgets that a generally inventive but crooked British public have used to deprive the parking authorities of thousands and thousands of pounds, not to mention the nuisance value of repairing the meter. For some reason he feels that I am natural audience for him and he has spent the term telling me about the progress of his invention, the amazing number of meters that had been reported jammed in central London in the previous year, the statistics of car-parking in large and small towns. Every time I walk into the staffroom he is there, wheezing and panting and coming up to me with what has become our little secret. I have thought of adopting a velvet mask to avoid him, of eating onions for lunch, of feigning Muslim prayers to turn him off; I have even gone to the trouble of collecting ring-pulls from the waste baskets of Earls Court in order to casually, as if by mistake, pull them out of my pocket by the handful in his presence in order to arouse his suspicion that I may just be one of THEM.

In a moment of extreme candour he confides that he feels personal about parking meters. He has studied them so closely, he has opened up so many of them and he has seen such damage inflicted upon them that they have, in a sense, become like pets, or at least like favourite trees that grow in one's garden.

He now leads a Dr Jekyll and Mr Hyde existence. A humble technical subjects teacher by day but by night a rapacious thief, stalking lonely streets with tools to break into parking meters and take their entrails home. If, of course, he is caught with these cogs and gismos, he has as good as had his chips. Thus flows our dirty little secret and in his eyes each time I see him there is that little beseeching softness which urges me to not betray his fat panting parking-meter thieving self.

I am happy to see him go. The possibilities of his life are endless. I'm sure people jam other machines with undreamt of devices, foreign coins and pulls of cans are self-evidently only the tip of a very bulky iceberg.

But before I get too lyrical about his narrowness, I should consider myself. I do. I go home to the one-room flat in a locality which is fast losing all one-room flats and becoming a haven of property speculators who convert the buildings in which life's refugees have found sanctuary in London, into houses for the very rich from the City. And what do I do as opposed in action and non-absurdity to the noble task of finding ways of unjamming meters? I write my thoughts down on the folly of Xenophon who treated the skirmishes at the edge of the great Persian empire as though they were wars.

After all I am named after Xerxes, King of Kings, son of Cyrus, grandson of Darius the great, the conqueror of Egypt, warriors who with their disciplined armies had spread the empire from Perseppolis through Assyria and into Africa. And who the fuck were the Greeks anyway? Pirates and bandits. Wasn't the reaction to Paris fucking Helen a rather obvious example of overkill?

(And half the time, but now only half the time, I think of the baby and yes, I go to see her on the quiet. I still can't get used to calling her Gazal.) That's what the Greeks were like. Exaggerators. The Zorastrians treated them as the Indian state treats the rebel tribes of Nagaland. I have six essays, carefully argued on the subject. No one wants them. The *Journal of Historical Research* sends me six rejection slips: 'The editors have considered your contribution and are sorry to say they cannot use it in a forthcoming issue. Thank you for considering us.'

I do not consider them. They are beneath my consideration. They publish crap about Hitler and the Dresden bombings and some American junk about Africans contributing the idea of democracy to Europe. Xerxes they don't want to know. One editor even scribbled a note at the bottom of the rejection slip asking whether I had tried to get the article published in Teheran University's journal, because he knew for a fact that they were interested in that sort of thing about their country and would translate it for me.

When Sonya comes to my room she looks through the papers. Penny says she doesn't read but she's quite willing to take my papers home and read them. What she wants to know about is Hinduism and I set out six lessons for her. Then Buddhism.

She can't grasp the idea that Buddhism is in love with death. The minimal popularised junk that masquerades as philosophy has soaked into her head. Her friends are Buddhists. They believe they can be successful actors by chanting gibberish. I tell her about the Buddha – Gautama, who was in love with perfect and ultimate oblivion. He wasn't looking for the answer to life, he was looking for the perfect and ultimate death. How to tell the lovely Sonya, brimming with life, that the kind of deaths we know and are terrified of in imperfection, are only states of being which bring us back through rebirth. So the ultimate is to seek a way of annihilation, complete, utter, never, never, never, never, never. And why? How can a religion expect to raise money amongst ambitious British actors if it declares itself in love with death?

Answer: it can't. Some bullshitter has to distort it into being a formula for success: chant this and you'll find peace and what's more, you'll soon be able to afford that mortgage on the house in Earls Court and then a little more chanting will pay for an *au pair* and even more, if your wife joins in, will pay the public school fees and Bob's your Nirvana.

She doesn't get it. No, my darling, you will never get it. And I will never get you.

Penny is curious.

'Make it?'

'Don't be dirty.'

'I thought a deep discussion on Hinduism should result in a bit of Kama Sutra.'

'I think she's a virgin.'

'Didn't you try to find out?'

'With Sonya that's not difficult, you just ask her.'

'She told me she loves you.'

'She told me you've got a girl friend, a Head of P.E. . . . . someone called Eileen?'

'Wondered when you'd ask, darling.'

'I'm not asking, you've been marvellous and a marvellous friend and I love you to bits and distraction. Now what about this woman lover?'

'My flat mate.'

'You never call me round to your place.'

'No, I don't because she'd be jealous as hell and throw me out. You see, we talk about our common hatred of macho men and the crippled bastards who want to get their leg over. But the moment she set eyes on you she'd know you were a kindred spirit and an intellectual and she wouldn't like it one bit. It would threaten her.'

'Thanks!'

'I don't mean it like that. I just don't want to be forced to decide. Not yet.'

'I'm not forcing you.'

'You are if you carry on with Sonya. She was my pupil. She's very headstrong and I resolved some years ago never to allow a man to put me into a race. No competition. Not from that little bitch and her search for her Indian roots anyway.'

'No competition. It's an old Indian tradition to be an elder brother.'

'And an older Indian tradition to be a bloody poor liar. I can see your tongue hanging out when you talk to her. And I know it's not bodies with you, it's flattery. Who flatters you the most. Understanding you and your stories and your confusion about not wanting to live in England and not knowing why you don't go back to India and become a real Parsee. With a prayer cap on your head and a vulture under each arm.'

'My, my! The little "bitch" – not very sisterly – has got you going.'

'Of course she has, I'm not a push-over and she knows what she's doing. She pretends we're still in a beautiful teacher-pupil scene and gives me a blow by blow account.'

'There haven't been any blows.'

'She kissed you.'

'Once.'

'Seventeen times.'

'Very good, real blow by blow.'

'And you shivered like a little boy and your heart beat as if it was going to burst. She said it was as clear as Big Ben from Westminster Bridge.'

I kissed her and we laughed and we drank the bottle of white wine and she stayed the whole night. She phoned Eileen in the morning and said she was at a friend's and had been too drunk to drive so she hadn't tried because the police had stopped her once already on Putney Bridge. It was Saturday so there was no school.

EENY MEENY MINEY MO,
EVERYBODY COME FROM ORIGINAL JOE

The Zoroastrians fled to India in AD 760. The Arab explosion in the Middle East following on the rise of Islam, forced them by sword and fire to abjure their religion in Iran. Small bands of guerillas took to the hills. When they were pressured by marauding troops of the sultanate, they fought a guerilla war which they lost. Then they fled along the Makran coast to Gujerat and some went by boat and got to the same place.

The story goes that when they landed the King of Gujerat asked them what they wanted and they made themselves understood saying they wanted to settle peacefully. The king sent for a pitcher of water and filled it to the top to signify that the land was full. The priest amongst the Parsees asked for a grain of sugar, or was it salt, and sprinkled it into the brimming pitcher. The water accepted the salt and didn't overflow. Thus was a tryst made. The Parsees were absorbed.

Bullshit. Of course. There is evidence to show that the first settlers had no women with them and must have intermarried with the natives, the Hindus, so the first claim of the Parsees to be racially pure is suspect.

We worship fire and claim to have brought the original flame of Zoroastrianism from Iran to the shores of India and kept it alight. And through the centuries, every fire-temple is blessed with a fragment of that continuous flame. A lovely idea, but obviously nonsense. Priests fall asleep on the job and fires die and tinder is replaced by safety matches.

Humata, Hukta, Huvereshta. Pure in thought word and deed. Only we didn't invent the three monkeys. Someone slipped up and the trade in monkey statuettes has gone to Taiwan. I picked up a plastic version in Oxford Street.

Penny is willing to see Sonya depart her life and doorstep.

She has taught Sonya for seven years and she says there's no more to teach. Sonya joins the Academy of Dance. She gets three 'A' Levels, she can go to university. Her daddy desperately wants her to go to university. But he is a very modern daddy. He sits and talks to her and when she tells him to fuck off he accepts it.

She returns to me. School is a little emptier without her. In the last months of her last year I would go into the sixth form room. Her classmates knew that something fishy but clean was going on. And Penny couldn't spend the night with me again.

There had been a terrific row. Eileen knew where she had been and tried to cut her wrists in the bath after twenty-four hours of sulk and alternate argument. She did cut her wrists, Penny told me the next week, but not the veins, just bits of the flesh and it bled a bit and then was plastered over.

I said, 'I could have predicted that.'

'You don't know her.'

'Not from any knowledge of her. Just from, let's call it Zarathustran sorcery.'

'How?'

'When I was born the good spirit Ahuramazd and the naughty spirit Ahreman had a brief discussion and decided I wasn't worth it. Nothing exciting would happen to me. No one would kill themselves through jealousy or any emotion I could provoke in anyone.'

'You're silly. You should take it more seriously.'

'Why should I?'

'Because it means I can't sleep with you again, except in the afternoons.'

'It cannot be. There was once a movie called *Love in The Afternoon* with Cary Grant and Audrey Hepburn or someone, and it all ended in tragedy. Around me there shall be no tragedy. Remember the pact made in – well, it wasn't heaven or hell, it was in the street, in a casual meeting between the two great spirits. Never on the agenda.'

'Do you feel sorry for yourself a lot?'

'Not a lot. Just four or five times an hour.'

'You don't really, you're an angel.'

Mr XX, angel *manque*!

'You'll have to get rid of Eileen.'

'You're still seeing Sonya, aren't you?'

'What's that got to do with it?'

'My theory of relationships.'

'I've got a class, bloody 3M, but I'll catch up with your theory of relationships over a pint at the Maple, OK?'

'Eileen bursts in and we die of stab wounds in a pub in the nethers of London: "Schoolteachers stabbed in lesbian triangle".'

'Never willing to take risks, Xerxes. Haven't you got a class?'

'First-year modular studies all afternoon. Maps of the Caribbean. Where are the Far Tortugas?'

'I never knew there were any close ones. Bye.'

She takes her bags of ropes and props and goes. Xerxes takes his xeroxed maps of the Caribbean. With the first years he affects a sternness which they will soon learn to see through. But it cows them for the present. It is a new year and they don't yet know he is not on permanent role at the school. Kids have a nose for hierarchy.

My simple and precious theory of relationships, as set out in the Maple to Ms Penelope, love of my (present) life:

Lesson one: 'Do not surrender the mystery of your organism.'

Lesson two, or one and half: 'Do not let on that you haven't quite discovered the mystery of your own organism but are working at it, through writing, seeing plays, reading books, earning a living and analysing your interactions.'

Lesson three or two: 'People love you only if you can help them grow in their own eyes. That's why pupils fall in love with teachers and inadequate teachers fall in love with pupils.'

Lesson three or four and a half (because this is a massive leap in the science): 'When lovers stop growing through each other, which might be the second instant after they meet, they won't admit defeat because human beings are hopeful and stubborn. They try and re-stimulate the feeling of growth through conceiving projects together. The project may be something as simple as writing an essay or as complicated as buying and furnishing a house together or making a few babies. These are all projects and they must be seen as substitutes for true love which need never die but usually does.'

Lesson six (we proceed in quantum leaps): 'Out of the project each draws the benefit of their own growth. When they stop doing that a terror of death begins to recur.'

Corollary to above hypothesis: 'Younger lovers are bastards and prone to run away. Even if Othello was wrong about Desdemona when he killed her, he would have been right sooner or later, had he let her live.'

Corollary two: 'Murder and suicide are not always the right solution to the impasse. You can call your solicitor and agree to split half the proceeds from the sale of house or other worldly goods with him. Bear no sentimental attachment to objects, however big and expensive, like houses, cars, estates, especially bits of tables and wardrobes and dressers.'

Conclusions: 'Live in a flat and let Sonya and Penny visit you and don't object to Eileen living with, kissing, fondling, playing role models, politics, advanced physics and consciousness with Penny. Only be wary that Sonya and Penny don't meet too often, they may run away with each other, leaving you to write further theses on aspects of Zoroastrian history, ancient and modern, and call it a quest for self.'

Penny isn't amused. She proposes we go to Brick Lane and eat a meal in a Bangladeshi café. She eats a prawn korma because it isn't hot and I eat goats' trotters with naan and lots of onions in vinegar. It's very cheap.

Penny drives me home.

'You won't come in?'

'Can't!' She always says that when she knows I won't need an explanation and she'd rather not give it. Eileen!

I get out and say goodbye and take my school satchel. I have to go down the side of the house to approach my door. I am turning the key when a voice says, 'Don't say hello, buster!'

Sonya is sitting at the end of the side-alley and her cigarette glows.

'Sonya.'

193

'Where the fuck have you been? It's two hours I've been waiting.
Well, between trips to the pub. But that shut half an hour ago.'
'I was out, with a friend, for a meal.'
'I know the sound of her car, you idiot.'
'OK, so it's not a crime. What's up? Haven't seen you for ages.'
'Trouble. I want to talk to you.' We climb the stairs.
She swigging a bottle of port.
'That can make you very sick.'
She pours me some. She rolls some marijuana and sits on the carpet
in my untidy room.
'What's the problem?'
'They're sacking this black guy, our tutor. The other kids don't
seem to care.'
'Why do you always care so much? What's wrong with him, why
are they sacking him?'
'Why do you think?'
'Because he takes advantage of his position? Corrupts the girls?
Boys?'
'Can't you ever think of anything else?'
'He can't do the fox trot? For God's sake, Sonya, how would I know
why they want to get rid of a teacher in a dance academy? Maybe he's
lost a leg by mistake in a National Health Service operation. I thought
you'd turned up for love or discussion of my latest work or just to tell
me that you're well and dancing your arse off . . .'
'I'll give you some love later,' she says. 'I just want to talk. The truth
is, Dudley's an alcoholic. But he's the best teacher we've got. He used
to be with the New York Dance ensemble, he's lived ten years in Paris
and danced with the Bolshoi and now he's a wino, so out!'
'Seems fair'
'Do all old people get as cynical as you?'
'Why don't you publish another newspaper and send a petition
round the students . . . that sort of thing, your speciality? Say it's
anti-racist, anti-sexist, pro-alcoholic, human bill of rights, against the
Vietnam War . . . Oh, no, that's over already, unless I haven't caught
the news . . .'
'Bastard! He's got greying hair and he colours it black at the
temples. He's afraid to get old. Are you afraid to get old?'
'Stop all this shit about old.'
'I've been bonking him.'
'That's your business, Sonya.'

'It's got me confused, so I thought I'd talk to you.'

'I don't want to be an anti-confusion device. I'm fed up of it. Everyone tries their confusions on me.'

'That's what friends are for.'

'I stopped being your teacher, I don't want to be your friend.'

'What do you want to be?'

'If you don't know by now, my magnetism must have dried up. No vibes. Start talking about old age again.'

She gets up and says she's sorry but she's wound up and what was I thinking of doing when I came in?

'I was going to read, maybe write.'

'Don't, then. Smoke this.'

She smiles. Then she takes her clothes off. All of them.

'I'm noisy,' she says huskily as I get into bed with her.

'Put a pillow on your mouth.'

She is noisy.

She screams, 'Fuck me, you horny bastard, you animal, there, there, there, you've got it, there, just there, oh God! There, there there!'

The Paraguayan starts banging on the wall.

'Ssshhh!'

'Shush yourself. Go on, please go on, it's there!'

Then the phone rings and it rings and it rings.

I give up, get off her and pick it up motioning her to be quiet. It's Penny.

'Why did you take so long to answer the phone?'

'I was just writing something and I'd gone out to the loo and I was in mid-piss when it rang.'

'Oh. I just wanted to say I really wanted to come in with you, but you understand, I don't want us to argue about Eileen any more.'

'Where's the wonderful Eileen?'

'She left a note saying she's gone to a disco.'

'Ravers never relent,' I say.

'We must talk it out properly. I'll see you at school tomorrow.'

'Yes, we must,' I am saying and something gets into Sonya so she gets up on her knees and screams down the phone, 'Get off, you've interrupted a beautiful moment.'

Click.

Can I go back to her after that? Yes, I can. X has his mind in three places at the same time.

I make her a cup of coffee in the morning in silence and leave for

school. She is sullen, gets dressed fast and says she's got to be at the
Academy later. Dudley cannot be saved. The big bottle man of dance
has to retire gracefully.

(Leslie, I'm writing this as you asked me to. You're part of the story so
I can't make out you're not. Isn't it fascinating to be treated
'objectively'. By the time it reaches print you can of course change the
name.)

She never told me what her dad did. And in eighteen months of
knowing her I never asked. A few days later he rang me at school.
  'Mr Xavaxa. Pleased to make your acquaintance. I'm De Freitas,
Leslie. Sonya and Asha's dad. We're having a few friends to dinner and
for the past year I've heard so much about you, Sonya thinks we
should invite you and since it's my party I want to do it, sort of
officially. My wife and I would be delighted if you come. Yes, of
course Sonya will be there. She tells me you are a bit of a writer. Me?
No, no, no. Hasn't she told you? Bloody typical. I work, for my sins,
in publishing.'
  He mentions one of the biggest publishing houses in Britain.
  Yes, I accept. How much has she told Daddy and Mummy? She still
lives there with the licence due a big college-going girl.
  My only jacket has a nasty biro-leak on the left patch pocket. I ask
the Paraguayan neighbour if I can borrow one of his very fancy
jackets. He owes me. I lent him my typewriter for three nights and
when he couldn't write his own cv in coherent English, I banged it out
for him.
  He's led an exciting life. He was in the Paraguayan Navy. I didn't
know it had a coastline, despite teaching geography to first years.
Now he wants to be a security guard in a good West End firm. He
looks like a 'fifties pop star or film actor.
  He has credentials. He was assistant chef at the Royal Garden Hotel,
he says. Then he fell in love with an Argentinian maiden and her dad
scoffed at the idea of his daughter going with a cook, so he gave it up.
Then the girl gave him up. He became a life-long hater of what he calls
Argentinian snobbery.

Mr De Freitas (the name itself is a topic of conversation at the party) is
a shock. He is young, so young. He looks like Sonya's older brother.
Theirs was an Oxford romance. Sonya was conceived while Mrs De F

was still doing her degree and they must be just a couple of years older than me. No wonder Sonya hasn't introduced the subject of them before. She is ashamed of their youth. Mrs De F wears a dress. Sonya wears a saree. On the walls are originals by Indian painters and some by expressionists of the English school whoever they may be. The house is so smart. Books everywhere. Antique furniture, original fireplace and Victorian fittings. Huge house.

Mr De F is very very nice to me.

'Heard so much about you. On the topic of her parents, Sonya is unusually silent. But I want to thank you and so does my wife, and I'll do it now to avoid saying it again later, that we appreciate all you've done at school for Asha and Sonya.'

'I never taught Sonya, really. We just became friends.'

'Yes, the Pearl Barley Massacre, and the head behaved disgracefully with you. I can't understand it, he's such a decent man . . .'

'Sonya exaggerates, but I needn't tell you that.'

'No, you needn't tell us that, we suffer from it every day,' Mrs De F says.

'But Asha,' she adds, 'you know she's learnt so much about India since you took over their Geography classes. And the stories, she repeats them.'

'Not all of them, I hope.'

Then the moment of disaster. Jam. He walks straight up to Mr De F and me. My glance goes to the door. Perhaps she's still in the corridor adjusting the baby's nappy?

'I came alone,' he says to Leslie. 'The baby's playing up a bit, flu or something. No, nothing serious. Cress thought she shouldn't make it. Yes, I know Mr Xavaxa.'

'Stupid of me,' Leslie says. 'I suppose there are only so many distinguished creative intellects in the Asian population of Britain. Of course you know each other.'

'Not through anything creative,' I say. 'We share a baby.'

Leslie looks puzzled but decides it isn't something he wants to pursue.

Sonya interrupts the moment of awkwardness, bursting in.

'Daddy wouldn't call Dudley and so I gave up. I thought if you were going to be here, the two of you might get antagonistic and Dudley might get drunk on free booze,' she says.

I get drunk on the free booze.

I haven't seen Jam for months. It becomes obvious that he has written some 'risky' novel for Leslie. It attacks Thatcher's Britain and Leslie invites Jam to tell the group a bit about it. There were people there from 'the frivolous worlds of acting and television and other pretentious self-deluding bullshit.

Jam was rolling out the story of his great novel. A humourless presentation – he suddenly became the great writer asked to disclose or display the treasure of his genius. I'd drunk a lot but I shall swear to this day that the son-of-a-bitch had the effrontery, to say in my presence that the novel he was writing was about the cruel trade in flesh, women and babies – Holy Mary Mother of God, enough to turn anyone Catholic! 'The country with nothing to sell, sells its people.' It was how slavery starts and how slavery continues, only over the century less and less force is used to enslave. The audience approves. A great theme. Our host, Leslie, is sort of proud to have a fellow there who actually seems to know about the trade in flesh. The kids call it street-cred and their parents fall for it. Tandoori quail.

The conversation unwinds around house prices. Everyone's house price has gone up but they protest they still need somewhere to live. Lebensraum.

Jam says that Labour is opportunist.

Mrs De F notes that I am standing alone and perhaps with some sympathy for the shy, asks me when I last went back to Bombay (myself, who am humble supply teacher and not in published bracket but still with aspirations).

'Last year,' says I.

'It's a fascist society,' Jam feels blithely entitled to join in, loses Mrs De F's sympathy. 'I met some of the most vicious people I've ever seen in my short and happy life.'

'I think "fascist" is an exaggeration. Of course the Shiv Sena and some parties are getting very nasty with Hindu fundamentalist philosophies and they stimulate riots and kill people,' I venture.

'Yes, it's nasty,' says Mr De F.

'It's a Cartesian puzzle,' says Jam – (give back my baby, you bastard!). 'I can't see what holds that country together. I went to Kerala and I went to Delhi. And I was interviewed all over. The journalists are a joke. They don't bring tape-recorders, they expect you to – speak – very – slowly – beg – your – pardon – please – again – like – that.'

'I think they write quite well though, compared to some of the stuff that gets published here,' I say. I don't know why I'm getting defensive but suddenly I feel nationalistic.

Sonya I can see is on my side.

'Why a Cartesian puzzle?' Mr De F prompts.

'Because their secularism exists by not existing. Everything is its opposite. Nehru and Gandhi started by raising great nationalistic feelings in the name of a nation that didn't yet exist.'

'I see what you mean,' says one of the other ladies in a saree, over weight, unabashed by her midriff that hangs over the saree's folds at her waist. If she could fall at Jamil Jamal's feet and lick his toes she would draw some sensual satisfaction from it.

'If that thing gets nasty,' says Jam, 'every minority will have to fight to stay out of gas ovens.'

'I grew up a Hindu. What do you feel, Mr Xavaxa, or Xerxes? As a Parsee.' Mrs De F asks.

'Parsees. We don't feel threatened, I don't think.'

'Sikhs do and Muslims certainly do and there's been slaughter these last forty years,' says an actress girl.

A feeling of being on automatic pilot overcomes me. I find myself talking like a US vice-presidential candidate, programmed, ready, unthoughtful: 'The only solution is for India to declare itself a non-secular Hindu state. Iran burns with fervour, Pakistan is going that way and Bangladesh and China have religions of their own. The paradox is that only by becoming an official Hindu state, with the damned thing enshrined in the constitution can the country get protection for its minorities.

'That's very interesting, Xerxes, I've never heard that before. Why?'

'Because Hinduism has never been codified and its political development has always been interrupted. In the time of Ashoka or Chandragupta, pre-Muslim, pre-Moghul and pre-British, centuries ago, Hinduism had something to do with politics, but it's been kept out since. The reaction now, under democracy is pretty devastating. Look at it.'

They are all listening to me intently and I feel, even to myself, that I am making sense: 'If you look at the countryside, the rural districts, the vote is delivered by the landlords. If you have a Congress landlord, you vote for the candidate. It's only in the cities that real democracy works, where the vote is not tied, is really free. And what do we find in Bombay, Calcutta, Delhi and Madras? Delhi goes for the chauvinistic narrow Hindu party the Jan Sangh. Bombay votes for Maharashtrian Hindu, if you like, fascists. Madras is ruled by a non-Brahmin, which means lower-caste party of Tamil nationalism with right-wing and capitalistic philosophy and Calcutta, it might seem the exception, but it is a Bengali revolutionary party of the lower orders. Communism in name.'

'That's very interesting, so what should be done? You think democracy should be abolished? Xerxes has studied religions.' Mr De F seems almost possessive and proud of me.

'If we could let Hinduism constitutionally into the framework of political recognition we could codify it. And in that codification the Hindu theologians would have to argue for everything that Gandhi stood for. Secularism is part of Hinduism, because it isn't a religion at all in the normal sense. Then the constitution would say that Muslims, Parsees, Sikhs, Buddhists, Christians, Jews all have to be free to practise their religions and have equal political rights. What we are doing now is disenfranchising everyone under some liberal nineteenth-century British notion of the state.'

'There are only 250,000 Parsees, aren't there?' says Jam.

'I haven't counted. Nobody has,' I say.

Sonya says I should have another brandy. The conversation breaks up into clusters and Mr De F says he'd dearly like to meet me officially, not here, and see my work if I would like to show it to him.

I go to sleep glowing, alone. The phone rings. Penny says she was wrong for banging the phone down the last time and avoiding seeing me in school and why didn't I invade the drama studio and see her and talk to her and ravish her. I say all is forgiven and I beg forgiveness too. She forgives.

IF YOU ASK THE TRUTHFUL ONE WHAT
THE LIAR WILL SAY AND THE LIAR
WHAT THE TRUTHFUL ONE WOULD
SAY, YOU GET THE SAME ANSWER;
UNLESS YOU ASK THEM ONE PARTICU-
LAR QUESTION. ONLY THE ANSWERS
TO THAT PARTICULAR QUESTION WILL
BE DIFFERENT.

With Sonya I've played the game of saying I'd take her to India, she'd see it through my eyes.

We'd eat kaleji masalla on Grant Road the first day and drink beer and declare a supreme immunity to all hepatitis and dysentery. Then we'd stroll by the seaside and go shopping in the dingy markets.

We'd shelter from the downpours in an Irani restaurant and sip hot tea and so to bed.

A fantasy which I know in my heart of hearts will never come true. What would a young girl like her be doing with . . .

So then Tilak. At the time I couldn't see it, but there was a momentum behind it. Tilak phoned me to say he was living at the YMCA and could he see me. He was in Britain doing an exhibition.

How was I to know that the brothers and sisters of the Left would rally and Sonya would be with them? Convinced for the moment and screaming against exploitation?

I go to the YMCA, a cement block with glass building off the Warren Street. The hall has portraits of Nehru and Gandhi and next to it an eating place where they dish out food from a counter into plates as you line up, as though it were the canteen of some Indian university.

Tilak hardly has the time to talk to me. But the first thing he asks is, 'How's the baby?'

He has to look after his people. He's brought a troupe of players or performers whose welfare in London he has to ensure. I indicate that he shouldn't speak about the baby. I say I'll tell him in good time. He hugs me effusively. I must bring friends to the exhibition.

Thereby hangs a tale. I ring up Sonya. Yes, she knows about the exhibition. I have news for her, I know someone in the exhibition and we can get in free. She says she's not interested in getting in, she's interested in keeping people out. There follows a lecture on the phone. She's working with a group of Asians, she says.

'What's wrong with calling them Indians?'

'Don't be nationalistic,' she says.

'What's the objection?'

'They, the Indian government if you want to know who "they" means, and the establishment here are treating street people, ordinary performers like cattle, herding them on to the British stage to be gaped at.'

'What do dancers do?' I enquire.

'They have a certain amount of free will.'

'You mean you choreograph yourself?'

'You're difficult and objectionable as usual.'

I tell her I'll meet her at her demonstration.

Thousands of people flood in. Her group is a paltry gathering of protest wallas. People with nothing to sell but their objecting power. I talk to Sonya briefly. She is holding placards. Then I go in.

Tilak is much more effusive than he was the day before. He hugs me in public and speaks rapidly in Hindi. I am his brother and long lost with it.

He recalls our nights in Bombay. I walk around the exhibition with him. It is a genuine attempt to bring the street ingenuity of the folk arts to the British public. The circus they represent is a natural appendage of poverty and these jugglers and petty magicians and balancers look lost in the great exhibition centre of London. I think about Sonya. She is infuriating. I ask Tilak to come with me and we step out to find her. She's still there. Her comrades have gone to the pub and she is packing up the placards. There is nowhere to put them. Tilak says the placards can go in the performers' bus. That way they can be brought back the next morning, conveniently for the demonstration to progress again. I introduce them. Sonya is fascinated that the man wants her to carry on her objecting under the auspices of the management. She wants to see the show. He takes her round, explaining the meaning of *Sanskriti*, the lives of the common people, the particularity of the acts and which region of India they come from. I can see she's going to be taken up by this for a time. I leave them. I must go back to my work I say. She is casual with her goodbyes.

Tilak says I must come again tomorrow or at least leave a message at the 'hostel', as he calls it.

Then he takes me aside. 'Your girl, the little one?'

'I gave her to a couple,' I say. For the first time it occurs to me that that's what I've done. I used to say to myself that she was loaned. That one day, when she grew up there'd be a scene, sixteen years on maybe, in which I, Uncle X, take her out and reveal that I'm her real daddy, not the profligate Jam. And she'd cry. Then we'd laugh and buy balloons at the fair.

'You gave her away?'

'Just to somebody who can look after her for a while. She has everything, rich people.'

Tilak nods his approval as though he is in some way a patron of all Indian babies moved from the sub-continent.

Sonya calls me six days later. She has been to the exhibition every day. Tilak is a lovely man.

Of course he is. But he knows so much about everything. He can teach her Indian dancing. They have an academy in Madhya Pradesh. He owns a model village, or at least he doesn't own it but he runs it and the agrarian problems of India! Wow, it would blow my mind, I have no idea.

They bring me the books I ask for from the public library in this detention centre. Don't forget, please, where this memoir . . .

> Lashed round and round to the fish's back; pinioned in the turns upon turns in which, during the past night, the whale had reeled the involutions of the lines around him, the half torn body of the Parsee was seen; his sable raiment frayed to shreds; his distended eyes turned full upon old Ahab.
>
> The harpoon dropped from his hand.
>
> 'Befooled, befooled!' – drawing in a long lean breath –
>
> 'Aye, Parsee! I see thee again – Aye and thou goest before; and this, this then is the hearse that thou didst promise. But I hold thee to the last letter of thy word. Where is the second hearse?'
>
> Herman Melville, *Moby Dick*

And then the commentary on Melville: 'In that "Parsee" lurks an "arse".'

In this Parsee an itchy one. Some guy, maybe Melville himself is pointing out that both 'hearse' and 'Parsee' have one thing in common: they both envelope and cupboard the precious outlet, the fundament of abuse the 'arse'. Big deal. Fedallah is dead. His sable garment torn like his body. The only mention of the Parsee in American classical literature. Torn and lashed to a whale, lashed to fate itself, in line with his own prediction, lashed to perdition, lashed to that which, rising from the boundless deep, turns home.

(Notes for a work in progress)

I have a story in a magazine and I cut it out. I could send the whole rag to Mr De F but I don't want him to read the cover or the illiterate editorial it contains or see what sort of work it is surrounded by. I am bashful of this cutting. I chose to be published by Roby and his black writers' magazine – what was it called again? Black Print! Now I was ashamed of being ashamed.

One story two articles. And so to his publishing house.

It's an impressive building, tastefully restored in a small square off central London with a brick church in a corner and the sort of peace, with three trees standing in the small green, that befits a publishing house.

Mr De F comes personally to pick me up from reception.

'Xerxes, so nice to see you. Shall we pop out and talk over a meal?'

'Sure, anything you want.'

'That'll be nice.'

It is nice, a very posh restaurant off the square where I go for guinea fowl and he eats a salad with cheese and hot asparagus. Am I being too greedy? Do writers choose particular sorts of things? He offers me the wine menu.

'What shall you have?'

I don't know anything about wines, except that Muscadet is dry and Chablis is more expensive. I go for the Muscadet and he asks for a bottle of water. I find I have the bottle to myself.

'You haven't decided whether you want to be a non-fiction writer or a narrative-walla?'

'Both, I suppose, whichever sells.'

'A clean mentality, none of this artistic crap!'

'You said it.'

I don't want to ask what he thought of the pieces. He should start and he does.

He has such an innocent face. He looks straight at me as he speaks. Sonya's eyes and eye sockets. Also the slightly protruding chin. But Sonya is heavier in jowl like Mummy.

'I enjoyed your poem and learnt a lot from the articles, but let's put the articles aside. That's special academic publishing and it needs the help of market research to see which texts in such a specialised subject are needed. But the story, lovely story.'

'Thank you.'

'I think we have something there. Congratulations.'

He is friendly.

'I can do some more stories like that, in prose or maybe try out verse, I've sketched about fifteen . . .'

He holds a hand up and wipes his mouth with a napkin while finishing his lettuce.

'Shouldn't the stories be about your experience in Britain or a cross between the two settings?'

'Why should they?'

'I never tell writers what to write, but it really depends on what kind of readership your imagination demands and commands.'

'Sure.'

'There are touches of the West in your story – the Associated Board of the Royal Schools of Music, the British examiner, but then you lose that thread and take up another with the honeymoon and the lover and very sort of unexplained, well, inaccessible customs and mentalities of Parsees. I love the ending, though, the Oxford Street and Marks or wherever it is.'

'Thanks but . . .'

'And the telling detail, the man Nouzer is wearing several sweaters, I can see him, bundled against the cold.'

'Yeah. But the point of story was the relationship and the song he writes.'

'That works marvellously, but I just wanted to know a bit more about the English examiner. Maybe it would unbalance it as a short story . . . Tell me, Xerxes, are you really a Hindu fundamentalist?'

'Me? The conversation at the party? That's not what I said.'

'I know you said something very careful. I was being careless. Sorry. You said the constitution needs to change to being a Hindu one so they can codify their laws and be compelled into tolerance.'

'Yep. That's what I said.'

'Do you think that'll work? God knows, something ought to. I don't know what a government of a place like India can do with the immense problems. You know, I've never been.'

I'm surprised and say so.

'Lyla is Indian born and bred and she's been back regularly, but somehow . . . I've been afraid it would steal her away from me. I've booked one or two trips these last twenty years . . . yes, we've been married that long, since university . . . and I've cancelled them. Maybe she'll never go back but I can't bring myself to see the land I think will claim her in the end. Am I talking nonsense?'

'Not at all, I know what you mean. It claims me.'

'I thought it did when I first met you, at our place. But Sonya talks so much about you and Asha, she rattles on, we felt we knew you very well.'

Does he want to ask me whether I've fucked his daughter?

Maybe he's not interested in my writing at all. If he's not interested in my writing I'm glad I've fucked his daughter. I stop myself thinking this before the sentence is formulated. It's not what I think at all. I'm not glad about anything. Slightly hurt.

'She talks about you too.'

'We love her very much.'

'You should forget all that and go to India.'

'Maybe this year. I know so much about it, but I'd rather think of it as a reality in print and drama and in the newspapers. But Sonya and Asha, they must go, they have no such problem.'

'It's funny Sonya hasn't been.'

'No. Lyla would never take her.'

'Very strange.'

'We've talked it over. The girls have begun their education here, they've met a cross-section of society. We kept them in state schools for that reason and they're very British but maybe it's the first generation that's really bi-national and they ought to go. I think I kept Sonya from going, but I've changed my mind.'

'I go back and return to earn my living. I don't think about it, I must admit.'

'That's remarkable. I thought you thought of nothing else, you exude that sort of preoccupation, Xerxes.'

'Sometimes I get fed up being just a supply teacher. If I was a writer or could do something useful, that haunted-by-India look would probably go away.'

'Yeah, maybe,' he says. 'You know, though he writes about it a lot, young Jamil has never been haunted by it, has he? Sorry, you don't like him, do you? I got the feeling that one of you had done something awful to the other. But it's none of my business.'

Jam.

'I don't mind talking about him.'

'I think he's very clever.'

'I think whites think he's very clever.'

'Let's face it, those are the only people who can think he's very clever, and educated Indians. That's what I mean by demanding a readership and constructing one. He's done it and is content with the middle classes. I don't suppose very many working-class Indians want to go to the theatre and I don't blame them. They've got a distinct culture and if you're writing in the English tradition it doesn't reach them.'

I don't want to offend him or to sound envious of Jam.

'I'm dying to read the novel he's written for you.'

'You should, because I did say educated Indians like his work, but if I think about it, they don't. Frankly I haven't heard a good word about him or any other Indian work we've published from middle-class Indians. Maybe that's why I never sent Sonya to Lyla's family in India. She'd mix only in those circles and it might destroy her idea of the Indian side of her self.'

'It makes some sense.'

'I believe you took her to an exhibition of Indian street art . . . she loved it. She brought Tilak home, she's made friends.'

'Yes, she's quick at that.'

'He was talking to us, me and Lyla. Nice man, your friend?'

'Yeah, we met in Bombay. He writes in Hindi, beautifully.'

'That's lovely. But he too was complaining about his other organiser in the venture, Binky, and he didn't like David Stream's *Ramayana* and he didn't like the paintings we've got. Baroda school painters. Strange.'

'We carp at each other. Maybe we're looking for perfection.'

'Tell you a joke, I learnt very early on. Dante goes to Hell and Virgil shows him around. The place is an exact replica of Earth, like a huge mapped globe, in darkness. They first wander, naturally, to America and Virgil points out the pit in the centre. A huge volcanic pit, the fumes of hell leaping up out of the craggy depthless sides and souls trying to scramble out, screaming in everlasting agony. Have you heard it?'

I shake my head and look encouraging. I mustn't patronise him.

'And on the borders the CIA and the FBI and the nasty marines shoving them down. Next they go to Germany. Same crater, same scramble to get out and the SS on the borders, in charge shoving the damned down – "down Sweinhundt". And so on and they eventually come to India. The same scenario, but this time there are no guards or police at the periphery shoving anyone down.

'Dante turns to Virgil – "No Indians in Hell? There don't seem to be any guards?" "Don't need them," says Virgil. "They're all there deep down. Each time one of them tries to scramble out the rest drag him down."'

OK, I laugh.

I must draft the other stories. He leaves me saying he's anxious to see them.

Tilak calls me from the exhibition. Have I seen Sonya? He hasn't seen her for a whole day. Wow! Is he distressed? Is it like finding you've lost your shadow and something has gone very funny with the universe?

I don't ask him these philosophical questions. I say I can't be bothered. I am rude. I am deliberately very rude. I have work I say, I don't see Sonya for months on end sometimes, she's like that. It doesn't reassure him. He goes silent at the other end. What the hell, I can be reassuring, he's obviously bewildered. She said she would turn up. He is my soul brother and he really wants to thank me for introducing him to such an 'angel person'. He talks of Sonya as a madonna (small 'm'), Sonya as Laxmi the goddess of wealth and Kali the goddess of darkness and death. Sonya is all these things. What am I thinking while he pours a little blood out of his heart? I am thinking that when we last fucked I wasn't thinking about Sonya at all. I was thinking about some article I had read in a newspaper in which some female sexologist, American of course, was studying the anatomy of the clitoris. Her researches had found, surprisingly at this late date in the anatomical calendar, that the clitoris was in fact a sort of penis which was connected by continuous muscle or whatever into the crotch and round towards the hips. There were illustrations. And the juice which lubricates and makes it fun, comes from deep inside, like an ejaculation. An appropriate thought when clutching her by the hips and moving inside Sonya's moist cunt. So that was where the wet came from. You can live years without knowing these things.

I assured Tilak that if she called me or one of our mutual friends, I would get her to call him, no matter what time of day or night it was.

And where was Sonya? She was with Dudley. He had been arrested for causing an affray in a betting shop. He had won five hundred and thirty-six pounds, before tax, on a two-pound bet. But they refused to pay up. The management of the betting shop said they had just dismissed a girl for colluding with the customers and she had punched his bet when they accepted it and all bets pertaining to those wins had been suspended by their rules. Dudley was, to say the least, disappointed. He thumped the counter.

'What could he do? He never mixes with rough people in betting shops or anything like that. He got the sack from college so he was trying to drown his sorrows with a bet. The rest of the people in the betting shop were black, but not like him, you know what I mean, the usual Brixton crowd. And they started thumping the counter and tore the place down. Smashed the board and threw things till the management vacated the staff inside the cage by the back door and called the police. Dudley was arrested for starting a riot.'

'So you got involved in that?'

'I went to try and give him bail, but they won't accept my bail because I don't earn any money.'

'So?'

'Don't worry, I don't think the police will accept your bail either. Your face doesn't fit. But a nice female schoolteacher . . . someone respectable . . .'

'You ask her yourself, Sonya.'

'She hung up on me. Because of you. You can tell her we're not . . . well . . . put it nicely, we're not intimate any more. Or maybe you've told her . . . about me and Tilak.'

'I don't know about you and Tilak. And what do I do? Call Penny to stand bail for some dead-beat alcoholic lecturer of yours and tell her you've got nothing to do with the lecturer, just with Tilak and not with me so she'll be pleased and immediately be willing to put herself in shtuck for five thousand pounds or whatever against . . . I can't see it.'

'Oh please.'

Who put the sucker in Xerxes? I phone and tell Penny she should meet me in a pub. Please.

She stands bail. Sonya can sweet talk anyone.

THE DRUNKEN DANCE TEACHER RE-
TURNS WITH AN INVERSION OF REALITY
IN HIS HEAD

Sonya's gone, the actress Anjali is dead, Ali has palled up with his husband-in-law to run guns and I'm eating in the prison dining hall. It's like a barracks, not really like a prison at all, and one doesn't have warders on one's neck like in London all the time. There's a black man brought in, obviously off his head, clutching a betting slip. It is encased in a plastic wallet. There can't be two of them. It's Dudley. The black guy is Dudley, Sonya's dance teacher.

I get to speak to him and tell him I know Sonya. He has been forcibly dried out in a prison hospital and is deemed sane now. He firmly believes that he has made a protest on behalf of all black people in the world. I tell him I know his story. How he broke up the betting shop after being framed. No, he insists, he was first framed, jailed, beaten, dismissed and then he took to smashing up the 'institutions of capitalism' as he calls them. He was a dance teacher. From some past of student activation he remembers propaganda phrases. No good telling him that he was cheated by the betting shop after patronising it. He believes that he entered it to bring fire and brimstone to the gambler and usurer. And his job? He had gone into the dance school stoned out his mind and fallen all over the pupils while someone else was taking a class, waving his betting slip and asking for his job back. The police, I gathered, from his meanderings, had been called and he had been handcuffed in front of his former pupils and dragged off still wearing his leotards.

Our headmaster was more compassionate. A certain teacher did cut up loose, have a breakdown and was sent away. A religious studies person. He used to wear a black velvet jacket and was going bald exactly where monks go bald, with strips of hair hanging around a clear moon.

He was sent for a rest and came back to school to convert his old flock to 'militant Buddhism'.

He marches up the length of the hall while we are holding a secular assembly and begins to preach his thing. The head is in the middle of some sports day announcement and says the equivalent of, 'Oh hello, Fred, nice to see you, would you like to wait in my office while we finish this assembly? Won't be long.'

He gets a punch in the mouth and Fred continues to proselytise with his arms aloft. The teachers are embarrassed on his behalf and start hustling the kids out of assembly and the head gently calls a few of the man's old and close colleagues on to the stage and has them surround him like friends surround an Indian bride and take him, entrapped and puzzled into the head's office where he is given a cup of tea and then taken home by the deputy head. No police and no rough stuff. The head even calls another assembly and tries to explain to the children the stress that their ex-R.E. teacher is suffering.

There is a revolt in the staffroom. A small brigade of young teachers seek me out to tell me that they think the head's speech is racist and terribly colonial because a boffin like him wouldn't be expected to be sensitive to the fact that Buddhism is a religion to be respected and so are people who want to evangelise it. The head has branded passion as madness because it doesn't fit his world view.

'The militancy was a bit strong. He shouldn't have smacked the head in the mouth,' I say. I can't help admiring the head.

'The kids thought that was fun.'

Factions, I didn't want to get into them. These people, including Penny wanted me to say that as a Parsee, or as a scholar of Buddhism, one of the three non-European teachers in school, I found the head's handling of the whole thing racist or offensive in some way. I who had run away from the Pearl Barley Massacre and been reinstated with no complaint to the Education Authority for dereliction of duty, I who had had a job as Geography teacher handed to me on a plate when my just dessert was a boot in the buttock. I was not going to bite the headmaster's hand, it had fed me too generously in my adversity.

This I said to Penny and she says, 'You don't see the wider implications. It's always you and miserable Parsee pound shillings and pence.'

By this time Sonya was gone or she would have kicked up a fuss. She hated the R.E. guy so it might have been fun.

Sonya comes around with Tilak. She wants to know how I got on with Dad and whether he had instantly spotted my genius. She wants

Tilak's stories to be translated into English. He has explained them to her in English and she thinks they are beautiful even in his English. 'But I've lived long enough with Dad to know that publishers want completely conventional grammar or some grammar that someone has made up. They are not willing to accept the kind of English that has really evolved in a place like India.'

'Doesn't it depend on whether it's good enough?'

'Yours is good enough and you don't write like Shakespeare or anyone.'

She had allowed her hair to grow and wore it in a tight plait with a few white flowers tied to the end. It was oiled and thick. He had done it for her. She was proud of that. They had gone down to some freak shop and bought Indian oils.

'Her hair is so beautiful, nuh, Xerxes,' Tilak says. 'Really proud hair.'

Sonya glows.

'I can only trust you and same with Tilak. There's no one else in the country who could do the job of taking down his English and just giving it a touch to make it acceptable to publishers, up-tights like Daddy.'

'Thanks. But really, Tilak, and Sonya, I'm not up to the task. I love Tilak's stories. He must have told you I compared him to D. H. Lawrence when I heard him read them in Hindi on Firdaus's balcony at nights. I can't hope to get that right. And I think telling you stories is one thing, translating his own stuff from Hindi is quite another. I'm willing to look at it once you've got it written out.'

'You're the only one who can type.'

'You're pushing it. A monkey can learn to type and I suggest you do. While Tilak is oiling your beautiful hair and making the right massaging and loving motions, you bang out his stories as he reads or recalls them.'

'That would be wonderful.' Tilak is beaming. He means it. Sonya doesn't know whether to be insulted by my tone or to enter Tilak's innocent vision of really doing it – massage behind, typewriter in front. She goes for the latter and beams at Tilak.

'Even if you don't know typing. I'm sure your fingers will find the words.'

Awwwww!

And Tilak will go away soon.

*

This is not one of Tilak's stories as corrected for only outrageous grammar by Xerxes Xavaxa.

Xerxes was the son of Cyrus who was the son of Darius the Great of Iran who conquered Egypt and left his tablets there. At least, I don't know if they were tablets, they might have been pillars or something altogether heftier. But on these tablets he says that he is Darius and that he believes in the faith of Zarathustra, and now he's done his conquering he's off home.

About Cyrus nothing much is known (by me).

About Xerxes, a great deal is known. He conquered a lot of places. He left his name to a great many Parsee boys. He got badly mauled at Thermopylae. According to Greek historians Leonidas inflicted heavy casualties on Xerxes's chaps before the pass was sold. The Parsees won by cunning and the use of the correct bribe to the correct person (a profound knowledge of who could be bought, of human nature even). Fuck Leonidas and his terrorist gang of Spartans. That bastard Xenophon talks of reading entrails and a fellow sneezing on parade and the whole Greek host taking it as a sign. What palpably utter moonshine. Greek civilisation? Kiss my cock and call me Charlie! (And a good day to you, Charles!)

This isn't the story that isn't Tilak's.

Here's the one I sent to Mr De F:

In our town there were many kinds of Hindus, many kinds of Muslims, some who believed in the Agha Khan, a colony of very Iranian Shi-ites, the butcher colony of Sunnis, the Bhoras, the Lucknowri, Hyderabadi Mughalai aristocrats, pathans with a reputation for money-lending and ruthless buggery; there were two types of Parsee, the rich and the poor, a few types of Sikhs – the military and the trading – a number of sorts of Christians, from Catholics with Goan padres as teachers to Anglican Anglo-Indians and the 'Indian Christians' who were insulted if you called them Goan to the Seventh Day Adventists led by Americans in the salubrious suburbs and there were two types of Jews: the white and the black.

The Moses boys went to school with me. Six of them. George, Michael, Ben, Iky, Sassoon and Moses Moses. Iky and Sassoon were in my class. On Saturdays they went to the red synagogue where the white Jews convened. The black Jews had a synagogue in the 'City', the denser area of our lovely plateau town.

The rest of the week they spent wasting their time in school and in the evenings walking up and down main street in Hawaiian bush-shirts and outrageously brief American-styled shorts. Their family owned the only ready-made garment store in the town. They used to sell pith helmets to the British and Malacca canes and hosiery from England. But now they sold ties with painted nudes, made in Singapore, shirts with pedigree labels, swim suits which they made a point of displaying in the shop-windows to allure the passer-by and provoke the old fashioned who didn't want to see mannequins with sunglasses and bikini tops held in their hands.

The family had come from Baghdad. They looked what we then thought was typically European, with blonde hair and red skin that burnt easily and left them in the hot season with blisters on their faces.

Iky, Sassoon and I were great friends, besides them being brothers and we would call for each other on our bicycles and whistle a code tune to fetch the others out.

When we were about eleven years old a change came over the Moses family. The other Jewish family in town, the Mordecais, joined the Poona Yacht Club. I would hang around their house playing Carom or swinging on their grandmother's huge Indian-style wooden swing with bolster cushions on the veranda. I would hear Mr and Mrs Moses, Mr Moses's brother, the two elder boys, the grandfather, the grandmother, all embroiled in conversation about the crisis. It was very clear to 'uncle', Mr Moses, that the Mordecais were making a break from Jewish society and joining clubs and would no doubt be going to dinner at the homes of Hindus and Muslims and the like and eating from their kitchens.

'Our boys already do,' says Mrs Moses.

Grandma agrees, she regrets it, she's spoken to them, but they are uncontrollable, they break bread with anybody. Grandad comes and shuts the glass door to the veranda so the sound won't carry. Maybe he is the only one who thinks that a Parsee, albeit twelve years old, may report this debate, or may be hurt by it.

The eldest says, 'We can join too.'

'We have to beg them to put us up for membership?'

'Come on, Dad, you have a lot of high-class friends who must be members.'

'Next they'll be joining the Freemasons,' says Grandad.

The mannequins are taken out of the shop window. Instead there are tables laid with lace from Europe and Indian-fabric bush-shirts. The counters are moved around so the Singapore ties are discreetly at the back of the shop.

Even Iky and Sassoon are made to wear long trousers in the evenings. And they are sent to Mr Beau.

This Mr Beau has been in Poona for the last year. He rides a threadbare-looking bicycle, only frame and wheels, seat, bar and chain. No brakes or mudguards or any extras on it. He carries a rucksack on his shoulders and he lives in a garage.

He arrived penniless in Poona. He is a craftsman and carves little statuettes of Beethoven and Mozart out of ivory, wood, stone, chalk, plasticine, mud, anything. He plays the violin consummately. He offers his service as teacher of the violin to several people, whom he has reason to believe have Western musical tastes.

At the time I was in the piano class of one Miss P. K. Sidhwa. It wasn't much of a piano class, though some girls and boys did learn to play to a very high standard. Mr Beau at first came and offered himself to Miss Sidhwa as a violin teacher. He offered a deal. He would teach the violin from her premises and she could advertise herself as having expanded her musical academy into a range of instrumentation and, what's more, she would have the services of a foreigner. She fell for it and began to invite rich Parsee families to invest in violin lessons.

With Mr Beau she made a paltry and shameless deal. He would live in the barely converted motor car garage which the absence of her grandfather's Model T had left empty these last thirty or forty years. He would teach in 'the parlour' and he would get paid a third of what his pupils paid for pocket money, the rest being kept back for rent and use of the 'academy' – a good word which promptly went up on Miss P. K. Sidhwa's board: Musical Academy for Piano and Violin and Musical Theory.

We were fascinated by Mr Beau. He became a friend. He rigged up the garage, literally with ropes and springs and a bed which could be hauled to the ceiling when he wanted to let the table down for a meal. He had contrived his own electric cooking range and was to us the master of practical and artistic detail and accomplishment. Neither Iky, nor Sassoon or I, or any of the other pupils had seen such a man before. He was magic. He carved Beethovens out of the monsoon mud. He invented pulley systems and built furniture the like of which we hadn't seen. He played the violin like Yehudi Menuhin. His fame spread.

The boys were sent to him to learn the classics as fast as was possible. Mr Moses paid good fees.

In the late evenings if we were out on bicycles, Mr Beau would join us. He had a wooden pipe. He would use his tennis shoes to stop the brakeless bicycle. He had tremendous control over it and his agile, old body didn't puff and pant as hard as we did when we rode the slopes up to Poona racecourse and waited for the stars to come out so he could point out to us which was Venus and how to recognise Ursa Major, the Pleiades, Orion's belt and Mars by its colour and size. He knew lots of things. He had no friends apart from us.

Iky commented on the absence of books in his 'home'.

Sassoon said he's read everything already maybe.

I said maybe he spoke English but didn't read it. His English wasn't all that good anyway. He had a thick accent. Like in the movies when Frenchmen or Germans came on, they spoke funny American English. We laughed at their inability to do American accents. Iky was good at cowboy accents. Every time the opportunity arose, he would say, 'When Portogee makes a deal, it's a deal!'

Anthony Quinn said that once when he was playing a Portuguese anti-villain in a cowboy movie.

They couldn't do much with the violin. Iky moved on to sight reading things but Sassoon had bad technique and Mr Beau said bad bone structure, but good 'stubbornness'.

Mr Moses would be sitting on a cane chair with Grandad and Grandmum Moses and other friends when he came to their house after violin lessons and Mr Moses would always remark on the violin cases: 'Don't shoot boys, I'm only the owner of the shop!'

Even the twentieth time, the company laughed.

Then Mr Beau was arrested by the police and his case was in the national newspapers. Reporters came down by the trainload from Bombay. There were photographs in the papers and lead stories and my aunts talked about it endlessly. There hadn't been that much national excitement about our town since some Bombay journalist had discovered that the people in a British government sex scandal, the Profumo Affair, had started their debauchery in Poona Military Hospital.

Now there were pictures of secret Israeli agents in town. The Indian government had made a deal for extradition to some country other than Israel so that he could be extradited from there to Israel to stand trial for war crimes under the name of Walter which was his real name and not Beau at all. Yes, he was German, but he had lived in France all his life and had helped some traitors or something to round up and imprison and liquidate Jews.

One of the other pupils of Miss Sidhwa saw Mr Beau being arrested. He went quietly, his jaw set in resolution. His eyes had no sense of recognition, she said, for Miss Sidhwa or any of the people to whom he would doff his beret. He had no reason now to recognise or acknowledge them or ask them for anything. He was taken, handcuffed and handled by heavy-looking policemen with guns.

The boys were kept in. I whistled for twenty minutes before Mrs Moses came out and said, 'Sorry, Xerxes, they can't come out today,' and I turned my bicycle alone to the racecourse and Ursa Major and Venus.

I had written more but that's the form into which Mr De F or his script reader cut my story. There were at least six paragraphs about what happened to the boys and me and how I heard from Iky from Israel and met Sassoon in London but he was an absolute stranger and pretended that he didn't even remember a Mr Beau and his violin lessons. Mr De F called me in and said, 'This is where we think you ought to end it,' and then, 'Lovely story, Xerxes.'

'You wanted something with a Western connection. I've kept Miss Sidhwa.'

'Yes, you have, a stump of the old story shows through, but it works.'

Dear dear Leslie, you did not know that in me there is a hidden Beau. Once, just once, you allowed yourself to say that you had seen Jam's baby, she was growing up, how obsessed Cressida was with it, how Jam was flirting with some woman in another publisher's and how he didn't return for weeks on end to his woman and child who had taken off to live in Wales. So that's where they'd gone. Whenever I phoned, the answering machine said Jam was not available and Cressida and Gazal were away but I could leave a message. I never left a message.

I got a lot of money and I signed a contract.

217

Penny came over and I told her I had and gave her the modified story to read.

She said, 'Sonya wants me to sponsor her for some Churchill scholarship.'

Penny is aware that since she got the Barclay's sponsorship and put her black and white youth musical on stage, she has become a person of value and a signatory worth having as a reference. She's been in the papers and magazines. The play has been reviewed even though it's a schools production for a studio theatre.

'She wants to go to India to study Indian dance.'

'Sign it,' I say. 'Write something nice, for God's sake. If she's dying to go to India and Daddy will now let her, she can catch up with her roots and she's in for a bit of a shock.'

'What are you going to do with your advance?'

'I'm going to leave pedagogy and the maps of the Caribbean for twelve-year-old rascals behind. I'm going to go to India and drink and write – stuff that's relevant to the West, mind you, we don't want to offend Mr De Freitas – but just freak around for a few months and then come back, I suppose.'

'Can't I come with you?'

'Can you?'

'I suppose I can't,' she says.

'When I was a kid,' I say, 'my grandfather, this is the other one, not the one I told you died, had a house in Bombay in the gullies of Byculla. A decrepit old place, falling apart but one could see that it was built with pretensions which had been stripped away. It was surrounded by undesirable houses and relegated to an alley when the main roads were built. And in the evenings, just after dark, when the children would be called in from play, the fires would be lit with incense in silver chalices, sandalwood and fumigating powder, and carried round by a servant or one of the aunts to each member of the family and to visitors when they were there, and they'd waft the smoke with their right palm as it came off the chalice and breathe it and join their hands in prayer. Cleanliness and holiness.

'In that particular twilight hour, a Goan fellow would come and sing with a guitar outside our balcony. Sometimes my grandfather would throw him a one-anna or two-anna coin. He wore a hat like an old discarded solar topee, shorts and he sang his heart out: 'Give me five minutes more, only five minutes more, let me stay, let me stay in your arms. Here am I begging for, only five minutes . . .' and so on.

'Or his other song, only heard on his way back when I and my cousins would be in bed with a single white cotton sheet to keep out the steam and heat of Bombay, the windows open to the sky and rain:

Irene Goodnight Irene, Irene Goodnight.
Goodnight Irene, Goodnight Irene, I'll see you in my dreams.

'Those last six words are masterful, just as the listener begins to suspect that the song has run out of vocabulary.

'And I tell you, the poignant thing about this singer, something that made us uneasy, something about him that didn't quite fit the way of the universe, was that he was an English-speaking beggar. Of course we were used to the lame and the halt who stretched out palms and stumps and dragged themselves along roads and waylaid you at streetcorners and begged for alms. But none of them ever spoke English. They asked in Hindi chants and Marathi entreaties and south Indian accents some of them.

Maybe my grandfather gave him coins because of that.'

'You are a stupid cynic, but a sweet boy,' says Penny.

'Not so sweet, Penny. I meant Eileen goodbye, Eileen. Eileen goodbye. Goodbye, Eileen, Goodbye Eileen, we'll see you in our dreams.'

'Bastard!'

I kiss her and yes, she'll stay. Till late. OK, very late, but not till the morning. Not even to celebrate my first commission.

She knew she was staying. She's brought her diaphragm and spermicidal jelly tube in her school bag.

Where do these juices really come from? I put my finger on her clitoris and massage it as subtly as I can while I'm inside and on top of her. She draws her knees up. I love her really. Cynic! As Kipling wrote:

Them that takes cakes
What the Parsee man bakes
Makes dreadful mistakes.

Oh Mr De F. My only begetter, haven't you read any Kipling – to your darling daughter?

A children's rhyme:

219

> Parsee, Parsee, kagra khao,
> Mhama bola biscuit lao
> Ek biscuit kachcha
> Mhamma ka peyt may buchcha!

Which being translated becomes:

> Parsee, Parsee, eater of crows
> 'Get a biscuit,' your mummy goes
> One biscuit's underdone
> Mummy's oven's got a bun.

They'd say it to us in school. Evidence of the disintegration of India? Parsee versus Muslim versus Hindu versus Sikh versus Christian versus Buddhist versus Jain versus animists versus Jews versus spirit worshippers versus dollar worshippers versus Harvard Business Management degree worshippers versus people who bought things because they were advertised on television versus come-hell-or-high water-I'm-going-to-survive-in-India wallas? Hardly! You wished, as the kids in school used to say. The bond was more enduring. Indians are used to each other's filth and cunning, that's why they stay together.

There isn't a servant in the country who doesn't know the corruption of the master and mistress or a master and mistress who don't know that the servants know! Not a landlord who isn't aware that the peasants are aware, that the landless agricultural labour are aware what money he makes and what ostentation, if any, he keeps.

Abuse. It would be cute if from one nursery rhyme I could elaborate a pattern of discrimination. Cute, cute, cute, I could probably apply to some soft idiot local council for funding for a revival of Zoroastrian culture. Never trust that which is given out of compassion. Unless you are a cousin of the compassion itself. Parsee's don't deserve sympathy except for the fact that you go to a Parsee wedding and outside the gates where hundreds of guests are being fed, there gathers a knot of Parsee beggars, the wretched of the city. My rich male relatives, and female, sorry, tell me that these people are lazy, that they ought to work harder. One eats, one analyses. Socrates never did less and there were slaves in Greece.

At the navjote – the investiture thread ceremony of a Parsee girl, a friend – six hundred guests were invited. We invest our girls early, before puberty, so that the priests don't feel up the young bodies as they dress them in vests – the sudras – and tie the holy string, the kusti, around their waists. Some of our priests would try on anything, the cheapest thrill. (One old girl got converted to Christianity and then reconverted to Zoroastrianism at the age of thirty-eight. She lived in Los Angeles and lost her head for a while till she came back to Bombay. She wanted to make a public scene again.

She'd met this Parsee fundamentalist in Bombay who had miraculously found the bunch of car keys she had lost under a bush in a public garden on Malabar Hill and she wanted to belong again. Her relatives looked for the oldest Parsee priest they could find, eighty-three he was, and had him do the navjote. The guests flocked to see a woman's breasts bared in public. The priest had her turn her back as she said the investiture prayers.)

The navjote of my friend with six hundred guests: everything was ready and then China went to war with India. The Chinese continent in spate came rumbling over the walls of the Himalayas and an emergency war regulation was passed. No party must have more than fifty guests and no party must serve rice even to those. Panic. They couldn't un-invite people. They would have to declare to five hundred and fifty people that they were not amongst the dearest fifty. Daddy's business couldn't afford that. His guest list was mainly people he wanted for commercial reasons to impress.

If they chose 'relatives only' and used that as an excuse Mummy'd have to call some she detested and rebuff her good friends. Baby didn't care. Grandma was most indignant. God only knew what these Chinese people wanted with a place like India. Not that there was much gold to be had. They could come to the navjote too and see for themselves. Nowadays Parsee women didn't wear their gold. If they really wanted Indian wealth they should attack Switzerland. That was Grandma's opinion.

However, unbeknown to Mummy, Daddy had plotted the huge celebration in order to turn money which he had not declared as earnings to the tax office into legitimate money he could use.

Gifts handed over on religious occasions are tax free. The day after a navjote takes place, the hosts can declare that thousands of rupees came in as a result of the affection in which their son and daughter are held in the community.

So China's war had put the cat firmly amongst the pigeons. Whatever happened they must hold a navjote. Again unbeknownst to Mummy, Daddy, pressured by Uncle and a business partner, contrived to follow the announcement with a whispering campaign that free booze would be available to all who came, even though Bombay was under prohibition and no booze without drinking 'permits' was allowed to be distributed. The day came and the grounds of the fire temple where the navjote was to be held were stormed by the largest crowd of revellers in recent Parsee history. The uncle was at the gates to see that all were allowed in. The more numbers he could show, the more names he could register as gift-bearers for the taxman.

Events began. The priests gathered. The ceremony got under way. The cry arose for free booze. Where was it?

It was nowhere. Daddy was by now sweating profusely. He wiped the sweat from under his silver-rimmed spectacles with a large blue silk handkerchief. He sat with his brothers on the black cane chairs provided and the band began to play as the ceremony ended. Uncle had done for him. All manner of men, known and unknown, had turned up to the ceremony and were now waiting around the tables at the side of the garden for the crates of booze to be unloaded. In its place came fizzy raspberry and bottled lemonade. They threw benches. The saree was riped off one of the fat women relatives who intervened. A priest was spontaneously defrocked. It was very unpleasant. Of course they announced that the dinner had to be cancelled.

That night Granny, who could do that sort of thing when extreme circumstances called for it, forgot the religion of her forefathers and using a satanic chant that an aunt from the last century had taught her, put a curse on the Chinese, on the Indian government that consented to go to war and on the government of the state that had made liquor illegal. One or two of the curses eventually worked.

Suddenly the world begins to extend promises again. My uncle writes to say he has managed to wangle some money out of the grandfather will. He wants to know if I've got a girl friend. He jests in the letter: I had better get legally married or they may contest the paternity and rights of my off-spring.

Sonya and Tilak come to see me in my room. They bring with them a Bangladeshi restaurant owner called Ullah. I don't quite know what's going on when Ullah starts offering me money and crying into a large checked handkerchief.

'His life's been ruined since his boy friend was sent home. His wife won't have sex with him.'

I didn't see how this was my business. Ullah had a cup of tea, said he was relying on me and was taken to the tube station by Sonya. Tilak remained behind.

'I would do it myself,' he says, 'but if he pays the fare, will you go to Calcutta and fetch their adopted daughter, it's really their niece, because that will console Ullah's wife? Your passport is fixed.'

The cheek of it. Was there a hint of blackmail in what Tilak said? His expression was innocent. We were fellow Indians trying to help one another.

'But he's Bangladeshi.'

'Sure, but his sister is married to a Hindu in Calcutta and they have a baby the right age, just the right age who you can bring in.'

Why do I do it? I don't know. To save Ullah's peace of mind. To improve his sex life. To play demi-God alongside Sonya who pretends to everyone that all is possible? These are not my motives. Some antic in my head tells me that I too can do a runner. Suppose they entrust their baby to me, this sister of Ullah's who is trying to have herself redeclared a Bangladeshi and has reconverted to Islam and wants to go back to Bangladesh and is stranded with Hindu children in Calcutta. Suppose they let me take the youngest – I could return to England and do a Cressida, take the commission money for the book, bring up the child, forget about Fara and the landlord McCurbin and Jam and maybe invite Penny over, somewhere in the country, see how she softens, or maybe even . . . no, I shouldn't even think of that. But I did.

A simple flight to Calcutta, three days there and Ullah's sister, who turns out to be young and speaks English fluently, sees me to the airport. I have to change planes in Delhi. Again no one cares that I take a baby out. It says on my passport that I may be accompanied by Fara, now two and half years old. I haven't informed anyone of my arrival. This time there are no questions asked at immigration. As I cross the barrier Ullah is waiting for me with two other men. They say they'll drive me to town. They take charge of the baby. I have no qualms this time. I have looked after it for fifteen hours and most of those with the assistance of air hostesses. No more than a courier.

'Tilak will do the needful,' Ullah informs me, smiling.

He hugs and kisses me. The needful, I suppose is the pay-off. I don't say I don't want it. They drop me in Earls Court. They've taken my baby back home.

Tilak goes with Sonya to Cardiff to check out a group which will host his peasant *Ramayana* and will house the funds he has procured from the funding bodies.

He mentions Ullah's needful. How much money did I want for the jaunt? Ullah's relatives can pay. The mischief enters my soul, I say two thousand pounds. There is silence at the other end.

'C'mon yaar, you can't ask him that much?'

'I risked my freedom, I could be in jail.'

'That's true,' Tilak says.

'I'm kidding, I don't want any money.'

Another silence. Then he says OK, thanks.

The next day Tilak comes round with two hundred pounds and tries to force them on me. They are not his, he protests as he tries to put the stack of five-pound notes in my shirt pocket. He doesn't believe that I mean what I say.

I use the final card.

'You are insulting my Indianness.'

He puts away the bundle of notes crudely tied with a rubber band. He apologises. For the first time with me he is uneasy.

Tilak phones two days later and then Sonya comes on the blower. They've gone to Cardiff. They've found an arts centre that wants to do the *Ramayana* Tilak's way. But that's not what they phoned about. Tilak's written this story. And he's taken these terrific pictures of England from the train . . . it gives you an Indian's vision of the countryside . . .

Sonya arrives the next day with the story. Yes, and the photographs which are nothing to do with the story. They're blurs and names of stations. The railway sidings of Crewe.

I take half an hour to read the story then invite Sonya to argue the toss.

'Shanta was the belle of the ball!'

I change it to: 'Shanta was the belle of the village!'

'That sounds like a bell on a church tower.'

'It's all in the spelling. They don't have balls in the village.'

'You want to bet?'

Saint Xerxes. I go on with the second sentence: 'She was buxom and full-bosomed and the men of the village respected her even though they had made love to her.'

Can't take exception to that.

I cut the next few sentences under protest from Sonya: 'You see, in

224

Indian villages life is not so innocent as you think. People have sex and use their power to get sex everywhere.'

'That's implicit in the story.'

'People are not familiar with Indian villages like you are.'

'In the interests of honesty, I shall never pose as an Indian villager.'

'That's very noble, Xerxes, now get on with the translation thing.'

The story itself is good. The landlord in the village encourages the government people to set up a birth control unit with the free medical centre. Yet he doesn't want his mistress, the buxom Shanta, to go in for birth control. She is his secret and an unmarried girl going to the clinic would blow the gaff. A young male doctor administers these pills and inserts intra-uterine devices and the like. He also offers abortions. The landlord makes Shanta pregnant while the other women attend classes on birth control sponsored by the landlord and the government. Shanta has an abortion. She is forced to by the landlord. The young doctor has to perform it and keep the secret of the landlord's doings. Shanta gets disillusioned with the landlord as a consequence and goes off with the doctor. Her ambition is to come back to the village to preach birth control. She goes to the city with him and trains as a helper in birth control projects. She and the doctor are assigned to another village and she is eight months pregnant when she begins her job as birth control adviser with the doctor who hasn't bothered to marry her and is fed up giving birth control lessons to village women. He lets her do it. The village has the best birth control record in the district.

Sonya is going to send my reformed version to an environmental magazine whose editor has become a friend of Tilak.

Penny says she had a real boy friend once. Of course I am insulted and ask her to explain. A fellow who used to work on a left-wing magazine. Not your group-collective-style magazine, a real one and now he's quite famous. Eats in all the flash restaurants, does industrial and social coverage. Meets people on telly.

'Why didn't you stick with him. Sounds just your type. I can see you Mr and Mrs Yuppie Journalist eating lunch at some Soho dive they think is a non-sexist gentleman's club and exchanging credit cards so the nanny can get paid on Thursdays as Friday is her day off.'

'You know, X, I think I understand Sonya as you never ever will.'

'You understand the thirst for identity? Very good, British lesbian seeks other girls to talk about. I was talking about your prospects with

Mr Credit Card. And I'm not jealous either, it's just a memory, but it means so much to me.'

'You're an arsehole, Xerxes, I was trying to be serious.'

'You can only try! What was wrong with the guy? He ran away?'

'Sure he did.'

'With whom?'

'With a woman who was interested in listening to union politics, and which director of his wretched magazine had right-wing Labour tendencies, and which directors of the board of the bloody magazine were going to be replaced because a conversation had taken place in some wretched club in Soho. Nothing to do with anything. He wanted wifey.'

'You aren't wifey, darling. That's why I love you.'

'They're all like that.'

'You mean younger men.'

'Yes. White younger men. That's why Sonya fell for that lunatic Dudley, because he was really really interested in her and she sensed it. He used to analyse her character and make a lot of every little quirk of her behaviour.'

'You mean your little boys don't want to be challenged?'

'No, no, that's rubbish, cliché. They don't mind being challenged. They're so busy making their way, they have no mental space for a woman or a life away from the wretched scramble of being a columnist on a left-wing magazine that's losing readership by the ten thousand every week.'

Sonya and Tilak ask if they can come over and just sit with me, talk to me one evening. He's going back to India to research his own *Ramayana* and the group in Cardiff are happy to play host to the players he brings back. Sonya has her Churchill scholarship. She is off to India too to study Indian dance as a theatrical device. I give them the news.

I am to India too. I have crossed the divide. I shall give up supply teaching. I shall abandon London but I'll keep my room on. I'll be away for six months researching what I want, stories, Zoroastrian backgrounds, Parsee lustre on Indian soil, etc. The Paraguayan has his mother coming. She has money. She'll live in my room for six months and pay the rent.

In Tilak's presence I feel uncertain about India. Maybe beneath all the fraud he knows something about the country I don't know.

When you ask him to speak about himself he refers to himself as a kulak. What he means is his family owns land.

'They are going to rot and ruin. My brother is a landlord and once a landlord always a landlord. He doesn't believe in my philosophy and I got a telegram that the government has cut off funds and I must come immediately. That's why I'm going.'

'I thought you were going to research your play.'

'Xerxes brother, which comes first? The land is parched. Drought. My brother can't handle the peasants. Nobody is coming to any cultural activity because of drought, cows are dying by the hundred. *Ramayana* is religion and culture. This is life.'

We talk through the night. His wife has written asking that he comes back. His son, aged twelve, has sold his tablas in the nearest town and donated the money to the drought relief. His brother is blaming him for having taken himself off abroad and neglected the village in this hour of need.

'Then you must go,' I say, feebly.

'What difference does one man make? The farmers know I can't fight the drought.'

'He's lying. In his village the farmers believe that Tilak is the one person apart from God who can fight it or deal with it,' says Sonya.

He is genuinely distressed. They haven't had a good time since all the telegrams and letters, I can see. He is good on the agricultural question and on the Sikh question. All these are questions and India has been seeking the answers for a long time. But once he gets going he is eloquent. I switch on the tape-recorder. Let him talk. I shall learn. Sonya asks if I have any contact with any left-wing magazines.

'Penny had a boy friend once on one of them.' I give her his name.

'I've read his stuff. He'll publish Tilak's articles?'

'Which articles?'

'You can take the taped stuff we've been talking about and turn them into articles, can't you?' Sonya says.

Disregard the presumption. Tilak is interesting. The next day Tilak is leaving for India's sunny clime. I transcribe his precious words.

I read what I've transcribed. Tilak can't be bottled and sold. The ideas seem flat, clichés, stuff we've heard before without a thesis, second-hand thinking. And yet when he tells it, there's something in his manner that makes it compelling. He's speaking with the passion of experience, he really cares about the land, the mud, the soil quality, the cattle, the colours that people wear, the fineness of their weaving

227

skills, the music, the drought. The burden of his song is that politicians and planners have not dented the surface of India's agrarian problem. They've created more problems with dams that silt up and canals that make the rich farmers richer and the poor farmers poorer and fertilisers that chemicalise the soil and pollute the earth.

For Sonya this is no intellectual green argument fellow. Not someone who has given up cigarettes to save the world. Here is a man who actually lives to change it. He is not even an intellectual from an international charity agency with the same vocabulary of top-soil erosion and forestry preservation and stuff you see endlessly on TV in Europe about why the Third World must be left pure and untouched and how native solutions, tested by time, are better than 'scientific' ones . . .

Dudley waves his betting slip in my dreams.

Sonya tells me she gets a letter every day. A blue air-mail letter, stuck down on itself on three sides. She carries them with her in her Indian shoulder bag. She has taken to wearing tikkis, the red and black and green spots on her forehead and long Indian skirts and tight blouses with her midriff showing. And slippers. Winter is here but her pose is more important than warmth. She shows me the bundle of air letters. They are in shreds.

'Can't figure out how to open the damn things. Can you read bits of Hindi?'

It's just her excuse for showing me that he has written to her in a particular tone. The English is punctuated with Hindi words in devanagari script.

'My dearest flower and stem, my Sonya.

'Such a pretty name I can never keep it from my mind.

'The drought is awful and has taken a toll. The land is full of shrouds and persons are digging with their bare hands in the beds of the streams where water used to flow in hope of getting wet mud to squeeze down below. The fields are crying and split, like the skin of man with scabs. Our well is still barely trickling with water. The villages surrounding us are completely dry and a useless military truck comes once in few days and allows one bucket to everybody. And then too, they are taking bribes. They are filthy 'chooth key pissoo' (this in Hindi. Which means the lice of the pubic hairs which hide themselves in private places away from the sun).

228

'When we built our well I had the right things done to leave the bottom porous and in fact with water divining which is an art in our village we found the best place which might be fed by soils which are fed by underground streams. Government relief is non-existent here. Our government pays more attention to people who are killing than to people who are dying.

'I showed my wife the photographs you sent in the Indian dancing costume and if I have pretty friends like this in England why did I want to come back to the drought and dry earth and crying babies? She doesn't say anything to me severely, just as a nice woman.

'We can't wait for relief work so I have organised all our shakas into light industry. The weavers in the craft centre are doubling and trebling production with the help of lay-peasants who are just learning from them the simpler skills and we've built more looms and we must set up a relay to sell all this co-operatively in the market in Delhi. I talked to Binky from the district commissioner's phone. I went on an elephant, such a beautiful ride, and phoned him and he will help with sales in Delhi because we have made a compromise. He had sent patterns and he thinks we can sell to foreigners and tourists if we make a special kind of quilt with mirror work which the people are doing, men and ladies together. We normally make only for the market in our town, a small place, and the village markets, but not for Delhi. If the damned thing is too successful some of these greedy fellows in my shakas in the village will never want to go and till land again, they'll think they can sell to foreigners or something. I will be careful of this and am asking God how in this kind of emergency, just because of Binky's designs to copy and his market we might get corrupt by riches which are more than we get by sweat in the fields.

'But Sonya, the "haalat" of the other villages makes me feel ashamed. I devote lot of time to going around for whatever little relief we can share with them. They are moving away with bundles and few things and going to outskirts of towns to beg and try and find something to do as honest labour perhaps, maybe lifting mud for buildings being built. At least my population hasn't started bleeding, but a lot of stock is lost. Maybe the other villages which have resisted all methods from us for last twelve years will now realise some things about our organisation.

'Some of their craftsmen are better off than our ones but that richness is destroying the fabrics of the society of the village.

'They think those who live near the river don't need to dig a well. They have let their wells be poisoned because their minds are poisoned with superstitions.'

The same letter flows from one air letter to the other and Sonya sorts out which follows which from the bits she has torn, still puzzled by the construction of the Indian air-mail form.

'And what does your dad think of one or two, or three, is it, letters a day?'

'They love Tilak.'

'He's got a wife and three kids or something, hasn't he?'

'He was honest about it, he never kept it a secret. He loves his wife and kids.'

'So he should.'

'He can adore me, but he can't love me till I know completely who I am and where I belong.'

'Bit of a dodge, isn't it? Your Tilak lacks a sense of the corny.'

'I've never met a man so sincere. Daddy thinks so too.'

'And Mummy rolls on the carpet and purrs every time he approaches.'

'They're not patronising him, they genuinely like him and see that he has ambitions for other people, for the good of a community rather than his own ego.'

'I suppose he does.'

'Daddy says it's surprising that he is such a good writer in Hindi and we can find him a translator and he'll think about it. But shall I tell you really, Xerxes? I don't want him to publish those stories about his wife and his sex life and his awakening to his own body. People here don't understand. They'll treat it as the kind of soft porn that amuses the caring trendies.'

'How long will the drought go on?'

'Daddy is going to get some money together through people he knows, because Tilak is beginning to start on the other villages, apply some of the methods to them and they need capital.'

'So it's got round to that?'

'He didn't ask. In fact he doesn't even know. I'll take the money and give it to him.'

'What? Carry it in a bundle? Wrapped in the end of your saree?'

We drink two bottles of wine and she says she doesn't want to go home. 'Can I sleep here?'

'I thought that was all over.'

'It is, but I just want to sleep tonight in the same room with someone. I'll sleep on the floor. I've started sleeping on the floor anyway. It's good for your posture. And I feel stupid asking to sleep in Mum and Dad's room. Anyway I just want to stay if that's all right.'

'Of course it's all right.'

She phones her mum and says she's staying the night with a friend.

I can't sleep for a while and she on the floor seems still. Then she speaks to me in the dark.

'X, are you awake?'

'Yep.'

'Do you believe in genes putting a cast of mind or primitive thoughts into your mind that you didn't know existed.'

'I don't know what you mean.'

'I'm an English child, yeah?'

'Granted.'

'But I can carry in my head, in my blood memory, if you like, some images that I didn't know existed.'

'You can't.'

Silence. Then she sits up on the floor and I lean on my elbow and listen.

'I was brought up with Wee Willie Winkie and the bogey man and Santa Claus and Peter Pan and the fairies who take teeth away. So was my mum. Even in India. But Tilak told me that what they use to scare the children there, in his village, are old stories of churails. Do you know what they are?'

'Yeah.'

'Women with their feet turned backwards, demons. And around his village when he was a child there was the Hakmaribai.'

'This one I don't know.'

'A voice in the dark, outside your hut, or when you're walking in the countryside after nightfall alone. It calls to you in a familiar voice, your name or whatever, and you think it's your mother or sister or a close friend or someone whose voice is familiar and when you fall for it and get up and go outside the house or deviate from the path you see the torchlit face of horror itself and it glows like a million diamonds in its mouth and it laughs at you and eats your guts.'

'I know the "eat your guts" story. There was a crow man on the rampage when I was a kid, or so the servants said, and the word had spread through the ayah sorority, so my friends had heard it from their own servants. The head of a crow and the body of a man, as big as a large dog. It would perch on your window and pass through walls and come and sit by your bedside.'

'Not only in Poona. The crow man visited Tilak's village too. And that's what I'm getting at. When he told me, you know, X, I'd seen those things somewhere in the back of my mind. He didn't have to describe them to me, I can see churail and crow man and the Hakmaribai and I remember being afraid of them when it got dark but I wasn't able to identify what I was scared of. I didn't give a toss for Wee Willie Winkie. What do you call that when you feel you've been there before or get a snapshot of having being there in your head?'

'Déjà vu.'

'And I feel I can see his village and the well and the kids playing Carom under the peepal tree which is where they meet. Can I come and snuggle up to you? Just snuggle, OK?'

MOB KILLS ACTRESS IN BRITISH PRODUCTION

DAVID STREAM'S RAMAYANA HIT BY RIOTS

HINDU MOB MURDER OF BRIT THEATRE

DEATH OF AN ACTRESS

RIOTS SWEEP DELHI IN THEATRE PROTEST

That girl in the Ramayana, Anjali, with whom that son-a-bitching Jamil was having it away. Dead. I phone De Freitas. He to a publishing fair in Europe has gone.

A Parsee prayer:

> Ashem vahu, vhesta musti, oosta asti,
> oosta mai, yehedashai, vehastayi Ashem.

Don't ask me what it means. Or anyone else for that matter. There are translations, but no one knows for sure. Such is the power of the obscure.

CURFEW IN DELHI AS STREAM RETURNS

David Stream refuses to give any interviews.

The Guardian and The Times pontificate. They get actors to speak. Ali tells the newspapers his version of what happened.

Then there is the set of headlines I collected at the time, horrified by events.

FINCHLEY TEMPLE BURNS

ARSON RETALIATION FOR ACTRESS DEATH

The most bizarre was:

ACTORS BEATEN BY ASIAN MOB

Some actors doing a Noel Coward play in the Leicester Playhouse were set upon by a Hindu fundamentalist mob after a matinee and severely assaulted. The arrival of the police prevented them from being killed. Eleven Hindu men were arrested for the assault. There was no connection between the actors, the play, the burning of the Hindu temple, (probably by some neo-fascist white group – three organisations claimed the attack and released warnings to the press against Asians behaving badly) David Stream's troupe, the *Ramayana*, Anjali, nothing, nothing, nothing connected with anything and yet the connections had been made.

It was reported that David Stream was being protected by the Special Branch since his return to Britain after the burning of the Hindu temple and the demonstrations by Hindus in Leicester, Balham, Leamington Spa and Glasgow against all theatrical endeavour including in Bradford a call for an end to Shakespeare.

Here's the article that Jam wrote for a Lefty paper:

'To say that Anjali Patnaik was a great actress who died in the cause of her art would be insulting, but it would have made her laugh. I write as a friend of hers. I made no secret of the fact that I didn't like David Stream's production of the *Ramayana* (I wrote a review for this magazine in August).

There have been umpteen talk shows and editorials on the death of Anjali, her murder by mobs in New Delhi, the subsequent heart searching within the liberal establishment and within the liberal canons of discourse from which, of course, the entire idea of an international theatrical event arose.

'Anjali was the first to be killed. Since then there have been four deaths in India and riots in British towns. -In the history of immigration to this country we have seen nothing like it before. Let there be no mistake either. It, the tragedy, the folly, is part of the story of immigration to these islands and nothing else. It fits no other

233

scenario. If David had dreamt it up without there being a brown presence in Britain and taken a troupe of white actors to play in India, things may have turned out different. If a white actress had been killed, the incident would have been seen as an extension of nationalist war. The supreme irony is that those who launched the arson attack on the temple in Finchley did it on behalf of a "British" actress which Anjali was not. She held an Indian passport. Through martyrdom she was adopted by those she despised, the British fascists.

'In a sense they were right. She did have an Indian passport and her family live in India, but she was, by historical accident, education and choice, a mind and talent moulded in the Western intellectual tradition. She knew as much about Joyce as the educated Irish person and as much about Proust as the educated French man or woman. About English theatre from Shakespeare to David Stream, she knew and cared a great deal. And she came here to work.

'Others came here to work too. They worked in the mills in the factories in the clean-up industries, in anything humble and alienating. They drew very little power or satisfaction from the understanding of anything such as Shakespeare. To popular television and to the popular newspapers they had an ambiguous attitude. They could see that it was amusing and it passed the time, but it lacked a centre of clean values. For that they looked back to their religion, to the old gods, to the old book, to the certainty of a country, or a vast section of a country which was headed in a direction very different from that of modern Britain. It is all very well to say as the Archbishop of York says and several journalists and commentators say from the heart of liberal Britain that in the end all religions are the same, the goals of Christianity are those of Islam and of Hinduism. Alas, it's not true. For the fundamentalists, be they Khalistanis, Hindus or Khomeinites, the world is headed a different way.

'The different trajectories for the world could be traversed in parallel except that economic reality has brought people from one world into the heart of another. My people shall be your people, and before it is done, blood shall be spilt . . .'

It's signed Jamil Jamal.

Then the matter dies out, fizzles.

PUNJAB KILLING ON THE INCREASE

TERRORISTS SLAUGHTER 14 IN INDIAN BUS MASSACRE

The focus of the Indian stories shifts away from Anjali, from Stream and to the killing of a crowd of bus passengers in the Punjab. Hapless peasants going their way on a bus. Lined up and machine-gunned. A journalist reports the claim of some British Khalistani organisation that the murders are being perpetrated by the Indian government's secret service the Research and Analysis Wing (RAW) in order to justify further repression of Sikh militants by the police and the army.

Month after month the killing goes on. Penny introduces me to a girl who calls herself an Indian communist. She is here to research lesbian theatre. We sit in a pub in Lambeth. It is inevitable that when two Indians meet we talk about what has happened in India. The death of the actress. Yes, she was in Delhi at the time. No emotion. The Sikh question? I say it is the most important insurrection against the Indian state since the Indian mutiny. She says the Khalistanis pay no attention to the struggle of women.

I laugh. She gives Penny a dirty look and walks out of the pub.

Mr De F calls me. He and Sonya and I should meet. He'd really appreciate a little help with where Sonya is going, what the conditions are like. Mind you he is not anxious exactly, but it would be nice to talk it over with a friend . . .

Sonya and Mr De F are lying on their bellies on the floor of his office over a big map of India and they are marking things. She's going to a south Indian dance academy for the first month. When will I be in India, do I still plan to go?

He shows me an article from the morning's papers on the Third World page. It carries Tilak's by-line. The English is not his and the subs on a paper are never that good. The blurb introducing him says he is going to write one a week so that the situation in India, the story behind the headlines, becomes clear to our readers:

'Our two countries share the saying, though you probably learnt it from us, that he who rides a tiger can never get off. Much has been made in all the reports that appear about the Punjab in the West of the fact that Indira Gandhi herself set loose the terror that was to claim her life and create the seemingly unanswerable demand for an autonomous Sikh state. It was she, say the pundits, who with money and political alliances and secret pacts, encouraged Sant Jarnail Singh Bhindranwale, the young man who went on to hoist the standard of separatism. She did it to divide the Sikh opposition to her own party. She got on the back of the tiger and spurred it into motion.

'Did the pussycat turn into a tiger? Or the tiger change his spots? Can' we understand the Punjab in terms of one man, his charisma and the simple generalisation that all over the world people are turning to fundamentalism so why not the Sikhs?

'Indira created the crisis, not by inventing Bhindranwale's faction but by making Punjab rich. It is the state that first converted through a green revolution to large-scale farming, to capitalist methods, to ownership of the few and the labour of many. Hand in hand with this governmental support went the repatriated money of Sikh immigrants to Canada and Britain, savings from Southall, treasure from Toronto to buy land outside Chandighar or Amritsar, to buy the second tractor, to bolster the family's new fortunes.

'Earlier this decade the miracle of the green revolution began to slow down. It left Punjab with a set of new classes. The agro-capitalists – you see them in the hotel lounges of Delhi and the new agricultural landless labourers whom one doesn't see at all.

'As one generation dies another takes its place and the land must be decimated again, unless the elder son inherits it intact.

'Enter the problem of the second son. The young Sikh entrepreneur goes to Bombay. He finds he is in a land of sharks richer than himself. No contest. There they stand loaded with bonds and debentures, raw in tooth, claw and government contacts and bribery, versed in the law, in dodging taxation, in setting up family networks and partnerships as a safety net and banking device. Poor second son in both senses. He's seen off. He takes himself off, back to the Punjab to make an alliance through religion with the other angry and dispossessed, those who have been thrown off the land and have not adjusted to being nothing but seasonal labour. Second sons and seasonal labour plus scooters and Kalashnikovs. There you have it . . .'

'You have it indeed.'

Mr De F is visibly moved. 'He writes such crystal-clear stuff. You know, I've never understood this Punjab business before.'

Sonya doesn't refer to it in front of Daddy but when we leave the office and go for a drink she shows me Tilak's latest letter. The letter says Sara Fraser Stuart sought refuge from the storm in his village after the play-murder (as he calls it) and helped him with the fight against the drought. He says he is going to write a few more articles in a series, about the drought, about fundamentalisms, about the technology that the Third World needs. He writes that Sara seems stunned by the David Stream affair. Ali was injured and stayed in India for a few

236

weeks. David Stream and the rest of the cast came back immediately. Sara stayed on. She doesn't talk about the murdered actress but she asks Tilak about fundamentalism, how it operates, what makes it work.

The Hakmaribai, the crowman, the Wee Willie Winkie, the Churail, the woman with her feet turned backwards, the cry in the wilderness, the suffering in the sands of a parched desert, the death by Hindu fundamentalist fervour of Anjali Patnaik.

'That was the girl I met at your house.'

'Tilak says thousands of people die of drought and of malnutrition, but the newspapers pick up on the one actress who dies in some riot about some wretched production.'

'Because art is dearer than life.'

'They should be priced the same.'

'They should be the same,' I say. 'So it shall be written, so it shall be done.'

'Don't know what you mean.'

'Forget it. It was a movie with Charlton Heston and that fellow we used to call "carom board", the one with the smooth head – Yul Brynner.'

But there was no forgetting it. Sonya was due to leave for India and the weeklies had caught up with David Stream's reluctance to talk about the experience of real riot, of real death, that subsumed his fake (as all drama is fake) replica of estrangement, war, and the triumph of life. Nothing in Anjali's death was remotely noble. Some men who didn't know her had clubbed her to death and slashed the throat of the negro man who played a god. Nothing. They cremated the body, smashed from face to foot. A hatred of devils is the devil itself and the devil had been unleashed by this devilish scum on Anjali and the black man and a Chinese actor who was also clubbed senseless.

Ahriman! The hand of Ahriman, the counter-balance to Ahuramazd in the Parsee pantheon. Not Beelzebub, not Azazel, not Mammon or all the devils named by Aquinas and Milton, nothing. Only the Zoroastrian explanation holds. For the Christian, evil comes in mysterious ways to tempt and to waylay and take the spirit of the malfeasant. For us, and this is so much more true, the rapist lurks around the corner sweetshop, the mob pours its curse behind police lines in Hampstead and Islington. Evil is the collective will of fundamentalists who kill an innocent girl trying to earn her credentials and her sense of self in this fucking world by acting in one of David Stream's well-meaning, insight-lending plays.

Ahriman, all evil, son of Zurvan, twin of Ahuramazd, born of the same father: Time. Zurvan! Time itself gives birth to Siamese twins, not good and evil, but God and evil. Good is what we construe as good. God is!

Evil is! the killing for no reason of an actress who was born rich, was sent to France to study, got involved with a Frenchman because of the snobbery in her blood, because of the million things that make women behave in the way they do, ending up with a David Stream production and a death in the avenues of Delhi. No blame, no blame. Step forward Ahriman, child of time itself, and answer the jury's additional query: will it ever stop? Yes, members of the jury, your verdict will no doubt be guilty: evil, guilty of murder, but no sentence can be passed because the judge is my ally, and saloon bars do not a sentence make nor wooden boards a stage.

Leave me alone. I Ahriman have erected no tablets in Egypt like that vainglorious time-bound tyrant Darius, godfather of your silly long lost, god-forsaken religion. My etchings are dark deaths by bludgeon in alley-ways, the rape of children, dragged from cars in remote fields, the hurt that poisons the unloved.

'He has buried the bodies of seventy-three people who died of the drought,' says Sonya.

Two men hold a sunshade over the head of a man who digs graves throughout the day. They can't wait till the cool of evening to dig. The bodies begin to stink in the heat.

The hand of evil doesn't seem to extend to drought. It is just the negligence of God. Perhaps the revenge of God for unforeseen offences. As in Kafka. The victims of drought are condemned to be a newspaper statistic.

I get the urge to visit Fara, my daughter, my kidnapped baby. I make contact with Jam who gives me the address. He doesn't tell me that he doesn't live there any more. It is awkward. Cressida is now alone with the baby, but sure that Jam will return. She shows me a letter he wrote to her after Anjali's death. I haven't a copy, but will try and reproduce it the way it approximately was.

Cress honey,
            The Anjali business has fucked up my head. You might have seen me on telly last night yapping about it. What you accused me of was wrong, baby, it wasn't like that with her and

238

me. I just picked her up during her infatuation with the Stream business.

I feel emotional about it, because the bastard Stream killed her, sacrificed her under the searchlight, honey.

What you saw on TV was what I have to say publicly. The guys from the tabs were lying. I thought it was a bargain with us that we'd be honest with each other mostly about our motives rather than about our actions. And in mind I haven't sinned. If my motives and my deep down affections for you and for Gazal are the witness . . .

Jam

Cress puts the letter away. We are sitting in her back garden and the baby is playing in a rubber-dinghy-like sandpit.

'You know what the bastard did? He rang up the rag newspapers and asked them if they'd be interested in an intimate story of his love and sex with Anjali, God rest her soul. Honestly, Xerxes, I have no malice against that poor sweet woman and I know he fucks everything that moves, but this is vile. They phoned me up and asked me whether I could be part of the story and started making up stuff about how her parents disapproved of a married man being their daughter's boy friend, all sorts of bullshit. He denied it and it was only afterwards that he wrote that piece for the Third World page. Good piece, but he's definitely hungry for attention. I can see it in his eyes and his jowls, the whipped dog.'

Cress had kept a last cutting.

PRIVATE FUNERAL FOR ACTRESS

The remains of Anjali Patnaik, the actress murdered in the riots following the production of the *Ramayana* in Delhi, were cremated in a private ceremony by her family and a few friends . . .

Terror stalks the streets. An actress is murdered in a riot, no one is questioned and the police say nothing. Buses are set on fire, there's drought, so what do the Indian authorities do? An article from the same newspaper which Cress has cut out:

MASS IMPERSONATOR ARRESTED

Mr Ram Sundram of 72 Dinbhar Bagh, New Delhi was yesterday arrested for writing six hundred letters in different hands and scripts to the Prime Minister's office. Mr Sundram, posing as six hundred different people, had sent, from various addresses and locations throughout the country, in differing typewritten as well as handwritten scripts, letters of protest to PM's office about the PM's holiday in the Andaman Islands with his family and Italian in-laws, the immediate family of his wife Sonya Gandhi.

Mr Sundram had taken the trouble of making some of the letters very polite and couched in critical but decent language. The others were extremely abusive, pornographic and obscene in content. Suspicion was first aroused when all the letters adopted the phrase 'anti-national activities'. Mr Sundram admitted after questioning by the special branch of the security service, the Research and Analysis Wing, that he had fabricated all the correspondence accruing in this case from patriotic motives. Mr Sundram has been charged with attempting to embarrass the Prime Minister and has been remanded in custody without bail. In a statement to reporters Mr Sundram said people must judge him after taking into account the fact that he had spent months of his time and quit his regular employment and moreover deployed a small fortune in postage to carry out this operation. He will appear before Delhi Sessions Court 2 within twenty-four hours.

CHOP SUEY

There's a black man, maybe thirty-six years old, who wears his hat on the back of his head and has gold inlays in his teeth shining through an eternal, predatory grin.

Two white guys pass by.

The man says, 'Yes, bwoys! Me know yuh, me know yuh.'

The boys are flattered and part with thirty pounds for a wad of marijuana extract, known to them as 'hash'. They go home and find they've bought, in the dark of the street lamp, some artfully flavoured rubber tyre off an old car, cut and burnt. Someone must have spent time on that rubber tyre.

A Chinese diplomat gets lost in Hampshire. He stops in a small town to ask directions. He feels uncomfortable. The people are hurrying by and they don't want to stop and answer a Chinaman's question: 'Which way to London, please?'

He's driving round the one-way system and he sees a sign that gladdens his heart. It is the sign of a Chinese restaurant called the Red Dragon. It's not open but he parks his car and knocks and is let in by the Chinese proprietor. The diplomat explains himself, his need for geographical direction. They both speak Cantonese. They get on well. They've sorted out the way to London and the restaurant owner is honoured by a visit from a true and in-the-flesh representative of Deng Xiaoping whom he admires a great deal. He asks the traveller if he's hungry.

The traveller politely says he will have something to eat. He's starving. He grasps a menu off a table, not wanting to accept a free meal on the diplomatic ticket, as it were. The proprietor snatches the menu from his hand.

'I'm offering you food,' he says. 'Don't look at that, it's all chop suey.'

There's no such thing as 'onion bajẹe'. What they hand out under that name is onion pakodas, or onion bhajias as they are known in Bombay.

Popadom is a corruption of the south Indian word. In the rest of India, the crisp, brittle biscuit is called 'paapudd'.

Bombay Duck is not a duck at all. In fact it should be spelt Bombay Dak. What it is, is dried fish (known in Bombay as Bombil) and when the British introduced the railway system to western India under their Raj, it started going in waggonloads to the interior from Bombay. The crates stank of dried fish, like stale penises. They were marked 'Bombay Dak' literally 'Bombay Mail'. At the time the railway was run by whiteys. The English may call a spade a spade, but they don't call 'stinking fish' by that name. They referred to it euphemistically as 'Bombay Dak', the Bombay Mail.

Some short stories were sent by a literary agent to two publishing houses, both of whom pride themselves on having feminist lists. They only publish that kind of thing, a political act and a viable business. The stories were purportedly by an Asian girl who'd grown up in Britain. The authentic voice of the young Asian female. The stories were praised by the editors of both publishing houses. They both wanted such an author to add to their list, or they wanted to help the Asian author gain recognition for her writing. The writer asked that she remain unknown to them, that the merit of the work should speak for itself. Also, she had family reasons for staying out of view and they must understand that Asian families and traditions require that she use a fake name to avoid being identified with some of the revelations she had been compelled, in all literary honesty, to make in the stories. An auction was held by her agent. One publishing house won, the other lost. Perhaps one bid higher than the other. Perhaps the literary agent used criteria other than money to decide. The book was published with a long title and the Asian woman author's name on the paperback jacket. It was issued in the normal way with publicity blurbs praising the authenticity of its voice, experience, struggle, whatever.

The literary agent it was who blew the gaff. The author of the book was not an Asian woman, young or old, but a white, male Church of England priest.

The publishing house was stung into denunciation, recalled the book and pulped it. The author and agent reminded them that George Eliot was a woman and people wrote under pen names for very politic reasons.

A famous food store begins to sell a packet mixture labelled 'Onion Bajee'. The spelling of Dak changes to Duck, the vicar reverts to being himself, never again will he try to publish under an Asian woman's name. The point is proved. The whites may not buy birdseed or flavoured soft-rubber solution from the 'frontline' of black British ghettos, once bitten, twice a sucker for the next con.

An ammunition dump goes off in Rawalpindi, Pakistan, perhaps a thousand people are killed by the rain of missiles and anti-tank weapons that go off in all directions. The explosion demolishes houses, streets, kills randomly. The population begins to run. They didn't know the dump was there. Panic opinion spreads – the Israelis are making a pre-emptive strike on Pakistan's nuclear installations and neutralising the 'Islamic bomb' which Pakistan is supposed to be developing. Others say the Afghan refugees have blown up the CIA armaments dump. The government says American arms protect Pakistan. They call it an 'umbrella'. Pure Zen: the umbrella *is* the rain! In Bhopal a chemical factory owned by Union Carbide emits a cloud of smoke that becomes a fog. The poisonous gas kills thousands. The Indian government says American investment provides jobs.

Chop Suey is when you've bought something to whose authenticity you cannot attest. Usually because you're ignorant. Usually because the vendor has contrived to culturally mug you!

Penny rings up.

'Eileen wants to meet you.'

'What for?'

'The both of us want to talk something over with you.'

'God, I knew this would happen. I don't want to discuss triangular relationships. I don't have a soul to bare and have got plenty to think about without more personal confessions.'

'Nothing like that, Xerxes. Isn't it time you met her anyway? She knows about you, you know about her and there's something we want to ask your advice about. Well, it has something to do with all of us but not what you think.'

I meet them in a pub.

Eileen is tall and thin. Very short blonde hair, jeans with a brown belt and thick yellow cotton shirt, extra large. Still her bosom shows through. There's a brown shadow under her eyes. And clear spread of crow's feet.

She has the most alluring smile and all her conversation sparkles. Not at all as I expected.

'We should go back and talk in the flat,' she says. 'I'm sure you're dying to see it.'

They say there's a topic they want to discuss.

The tape-recorder plays reggae all day in their flat to scare off the burglars except when they're in. They switch it off.

'You're off to India in a few days?' Eileen asks.

'Yeah. Away from telegrams and anger.'

'But we can write to you?' Penny asks.

'I'll leave three addresses.'

'Do you know the man Tilak?' Eileen asks.

'Sonya makes out he's an influential kind of fellow.'

'I suppose he is in his own way.'

'Why don't you ask him straight?' Penny says.

'All right. Penny and I want to adopt an Indian child and bring it up. Can Tilak help us? Is he the sort of person we should be contacting? You see, we don't know whether Indian adoption agencies would object to a child being adopted by two women. We both want an official claim on it, like a straight couple has.'

'I don't know anything about it? I don't even know if they allow Indian kids to be adopted.'

'They do. I read an article about it by Tilak.'

'Yeah, written probably with Sara Fraser Stuart. She's another fan of his and chased him to his drought-torn village.'

243

'He wasn't against adoption,' Penny says. 'He was saying that your home is where your heart is and your heart is where it blossoms, in India or Indiana. So adoption has to be early.'

'You don't know how long you're going for, Xerxes, and if you can find out something about this for us, we could use next summer holidays to come out to India and meet you and see if it is possible.'

'I'd love to see you in India, both of you.'

'Do you think I'd be able to deal with it? I don't mean India and hepatitis. I mean you and Penny and then me. Are you sure you'd be able to deal with it? If you were helping us with a kid and moving to some state of permanence, a commitment.'

'Why should it bother me?'

'Don't be so defensive,' Penny says. 'I knew you'd think about it and maybe think it was cheeky of me to ask you to find us a child. There's a reason.'

'An offer, really,' Eileen says.

'What offer.'

Mr XX is all ears.

'We've talked it over for weeks and some of the talk hasn't been easy. We've had rows. Over you. That's why an Indian baby. And if you ever came back to Britain, or stayed in India, Penny says you're the only man she'd have as a godfather.'

'Great. What about as a real father, sperm to ovum?'

Silence. Eileen looks at the wall and speaks.

'That would cut me out. And Penny is reluctant to say it, but I have a feeling that the plan wouldn't survive the pregnancy. Not that Penny is feeble or . . .'

'Who's talking about Penny, woman. I meant you.'

'If I didn't know you well enough, Xerxes, I'd kick you all the way to Bombay. I know it's just your deranged sense of humour. A Parsee laugh. The man who put the arse back in "Parsee".'

Eileen is very nice. I have dinner with them the next day and she cooks. Starter, vegetarian meal in French style and a lavish alcoholic pudding.

Penny says if my writing fails and my work for the BBC and all my essays of self-discovery into born again Parseeism, then I should write a book on British–Indian etymology called *Bombay Dak*. I say I'd kick her all the way to New Zealand. Penny drops me home after and just to show that Eileen understands she comes upstairs, stays for an hour and makes frantic love.

Penny dearest, stealing moments of passion. She masturbates while she fucks, fingering herself – an attempt to be uninhibited and bold and assertive and pleasure-seeking and then, every time, when I'm in her and holding her very close, she clings and shuts her eyes and fixes her lips on to mine like a vice, wet and sucking. She doesn't open her eyes till it's over and she always asks, 'You came?' in a whisper. Nearest thing to the love of my life at the moment, why, why, why do you want to carry on with me? Are you in the remotest way challenging me to offer you something better, different? So you ask Ali Baba to give you just one jewel (or to lend you one of the forty thieves?), you ask Ahab for only a chunk of blubber . . .

I meet Ullah purely by chance. I suppose I am in the vicinity of his wretched restaurant. I haven't been in touch with him or my second 'daughter' (such are they to me, these twilight's children). He is very slowly walking a dog with its rib-cage in plaster. The dog is weighed down by plaster, one of its legs doesn't touch the ground. Ullah hails me.

'What's this dog?'

'A fellow who eat in my restaurant sell it me. Say plenty fierce, most biter, all these things, fight every racists. I pay good money for it. I was on walk and two racist beat up the dog. Some other people start to interfere and beat shit out of the racist fellows for touching the dog.'

I don't ask him how the kid is or whether it has sorted out his marital problems. I am tempted to ask if he has any contacts with babies to give away, but no. Sleeping dogs, or dogs in plaster, rather, must be left to lie.

I call on Mr and Mrs De F before I leave. Leslie has sent the money he's collected for the drought relief to Tilak who is using it for a special kind of well. He's got all the children of the village to sign a thank you village painting to the donors and sent it to Leslie, who is most gratified. If he read about it in a newspaper or a book he'd think it was sick and sycophantic.

I ask about Sonya. She too has written and apart from one paragraph to say what she's doing, it's all about wells and pumps and pebbles for the floor of the well and won't Daddy get some more money to send an engineer and a pump?

Yes, says Mrs De F, they've already started a small collection amongst concerned people.

She tells me that Binky, who is Tilak's Delhi friend and was his manager and artistic mentor with the exhibition, has sent a whole horde of foreign drought observers down and Tilak is proud to show them around while protesting that they are development vultures.

On the way home I think it curious that neither Sonya nor Tilak in their letters have mentioned Sara. My brain's befuddled with good wine from the De F's cellar, but I can see Tilak in the midst of the drought, while his own little girl is elsewhere in India and Sara has come burdened to him or freaked out after the Stream affair, taking just that bit of advantage. Trying to screw her, not because he wants her but because he tells her stories and is stimulated by the sound of his own hardships – his own aphro.

Shakespeare makes Othello tell Desdemona stories she would not have heard elsewhere.

> She lov'd me for the dangers I had passed;
> And I lov'd her that she did pity them.

I've never told my uncle what the solicitor's parcel contained. My grandad hasn't swindled me of an inheritance after all. He has stipulated that my uncle be executor and that on my getting married to a Parsee girl of whom the family (my uncle and aunt) approve, I am to have the shares he has left, investments in various Tata Ltd companies. On the birth of a first boy I am to have more and when each of my first three children are eighteen they are to have measured amounts of the rest from a trust. I suspect my uncle wants to get hold of the lot. He hints that he has already started some sort of legal proceedings to extend his own rights in his father's money and assures me that we have to work together. Of course he and my aunt dearly love me and always have. And to that end they want to even suggest a nice Parsee girl whose parents it seems have approached them for talks about talks on my hand in matrimony. Now what the hell is this? A way to get my back up and make me confess that I am secretly married to an English woman and surrender my claim? I have only his word to say that my grandfather stipulated a Parsee girl. Maybe he specified a Zoroastrian? He may not have envisaged converts applying for the job.

I spend a month in Bombay in Firdaus's flat most of the time and in my uncle's house, my aunt's house, the houses of second cousins, far-flung denizens of the Xavaxa clan.

I don't tell Firdaus or Naomi the object of my curiosity about myself, because I want to see, measure for myself, after years of denouncing this way of doing things, how fast my heart beats when I am ushered into the presence of someone who, if I say so, can be my wife.

I tell Naomi I'm checking the intrigues of my clan.

'Don't get involved in all this Parsee in-fighting.'

You know what's happened to them? The Sikhs seem to have set them loose. All sorts of demagogues arise in every religious sect.

'Everybody is out-fundamentalising each other.'

She has a going argument with Firdaus about his creeping interest in things Zoroastrian.

I tell my uncle to leave the specific cause alone for a while, I must get used to Bombay. I tell my aunt, his good wife, that I want to research the modern Parsee. She is in favour of my researching this girl that she and her family, her great aunt, if the truth be told, has found 'for me'. My God, it has happened to me! I have wandered into an arranged marriage story.

I am directed by Firdaus to a lecture entitled, 'Anyone Can Be a zoroastrian'. It's by a brave and radical dastur, a priest who has the reputation of having converted people to the faith in America. The hall, a traditional venue for weddings and navjotes, is packed out. The sareed ladies and suited gentlemen who park their ambassadors and indeed their Mercedes in the street in the front rows and the 'handamasters', the wide-boys of all ages, in the back.

The dastur's speech is measured, erudite about the gathas, the holy books and their message, erudite about the annexation to Zoroastrianism of other peoples on the fringes of the Persian empire in the time of Achamenian dynasty and other dynasties of Persia. His simple thesis is that the Parsee reluctance to allow converts to our religion is a product of bigotry and racism brought about by a self-protective instinct. The immigrants keep to themselves. They have to mystify the natives. They revel in their distinction from the natives while borrowing customs and prayers and even gods from them. So much of the original religion as we practise it today is tainted, tinged with absorbed Hinduism. He doesn't mention Islam. The hall is restless.

Then he gets to the point. We don't know our religion. It preaches tolerance as a department of good. Human beings have a monopoly on belief and that is something we should share with all human beings. Anyone can be a Zoroastrian because it is a matter of belief. If we want to stop them being Parsees, well, we'll have to separate Zoroastrianism from race and claim the purity of the race on some club basis. For his part he would divorce the fire temples, the religious practice, the Towers of Silence and all restricted places from the racial question. All would be welcome. If those who think their blood is pure want to form blood-purity cabals, he wouldn't join them but he wouldn't oppose them and under the constitution of India it may even be legal.

All hell broke loose. The men in the back had come armed for arguments. Their champions in the audience stood up to challenge the speaker. When the good doctor tried to reply he was abused. Now no one could hear him.

'You are out to fuck everybody's mother. You are out to kill the religion's mother! You are a traitor and an American lover and a Muslim agent and an antichrist (the actual word, though it should of course have been an anti-Jarthost).'

The dissidents started bursting fire crackers and the reports blasted through the hall. Women and children began to scream and some men gathered round the good doctor to prevent him being assaulted. The dissidents, protectors of the faith, all pulled out their staves. They donned huge saucepans on their heads, the sort used in wedding celebrations to make dal and rice, and charged forward like some ragged Quasimodian army.

Chairs were flung from one side of the hall to the other and portraits of venerable ladies and gents of the nineteenth-century, philanthropists who had laid the foundations of that hall and meeting place, were smashed. There were scuffles next to the speaker's table. The public address system was turned on full and the sound of the dastur praying, saying his satan-exorcising prayer, dominated the hall and infuriated the strong-arm dissidents even more. The front rows poured into the street but I held on to Firdaus and Naomi and said we must see it to the end. He was afraid one of the rowdies would assault him or Naomi for thinning out the blood. They were certainly the sort who wouldn't approve of inter-marriage. We put a bag over Naomi's head and led her out through the ruck.

There were other meetings that month of the fakes and fakirs. Articles in the newly sprung Zoroastrian English newspapers.

One advocated the re-siting of the Towers of Silence outside the city as at present their situation on Malabar Hill allowed the tenants of the higher floors in this fashionable district to look down into the Towers and see the vultures eating the bodies. In neighbouring gardens and streets little bones, fingers and bits of bodies had been deposited by vultures with bad table manners. Snoopy and spooky.

Another reformer was for the abolition of the system of disposing of the dead. He warned against the growing necrophilia amongst the small community of virtually outcast Parsees whom the community used as body-carriers, the nasresaals. They would wear their white cotton garments, from cap to shoes and carry the bodies on biers up to the Tower. They would fortify themselves, with little flasks of raw spirit against the sights they encountered beyond the iron and wood door at the top of the Tower, past which no other uninitiated human may go. Yesterday's bodies would still be there, half eaten.

Necrophilia and other bad habits amongst nasresaals. Hardly a best seller but some value to recommend it, I suppose.

In a very small way I am famous here. One story which some people have discussed. A reporter comes to see me at Firdaus's flat. She is a young Parsee girl who wears, for the occasion I feel, a saree.

Her name is Roshan. She writes for the English Zoroastrian paper. She has heard that I am working on the Parsees, fact and fiction. Would I do an interview?

Yes, Roshan, I would. She has a shorthand pad in her bag and takes out a pen. I squat on the balcony and carry an ashtray to place next to me, a bronze-carved thing, black with being stubbed into.

'Do you really need that?' says Roshan.

'What?'

'That thing you've got there.'

'Oh this, no, no, it's not any lingam yoni symbol, just an ashtray.'

She's taking notes.

'Mr Xavaxa, that's what I mean. You're not going to smoke?'

'Why on earth not? Have you lived in America?'

'No. Because it's against our religion. To touch fire to your spit. Disrespect.'

I could see she meant it. I was about to say I wouldn't smoke while we talked but petulance got the better of my judgement.

'Do you know what, Roshan,' I said.

She looked up straight at me.

'When I don't have an ashtray and I'm smoking, I often go to the loo and put the fag out in my piss-stream.'

I demonstrated, in mime.

'Just one pica-second in the parabola of piss and the fag's out. So

249

touching fags to spittle is as nothing to me who have sinned with ur-ine.'

No interview. She left. She told Firdaus at the door that she'd write an article instead.

Now the long story gets cut short.

My uncle phones me at Firdaus's and asks if I can go over urgently. I have to leave the evening free. They will take me to a wedding, not because I know the bride or the groom, but the family happen to be relatives of the girl who has been chosen for me, an educated girl, very intelligent and absolutely compatible.

My curiosity gets me. I go. The wedding is in the gardens of a fire temple. There are cars arriving like limousines at an Oscar ceremony.

There is a band of people with bow ties and dinner jackets playing Lara's tune on electronic instruments, disco fashion. We greet the bride and groom and we sit down. My aunt takes me over, grabbing me by the wrist to a group of young men and women and introduces me. There's Roshan. We say we know each other. My aunt's jaw is slightly out of joint. She takes me aside as the group begins to chatter and says, 'You're not supposed to know her, that's the girl we've found for you.'

'Does it matter that I know her? She came to interview me.'

'I suppose it doesn't matter. Do you like her?'

'I need to talk to her some more.'

My aunt leaves us. Roshan is very interested in the fact that I am at this wedding at all. She stands up and isolates me from the group.

'So how did you get here?'

'Shall I tell you the truth and then we can talk about something else?'

'Of course,' she says.

'They brought me here, my uncle and aunt, who know your uncle and aunt, to check you out. Yes, you. To marry, you know. Absurd, isn't it?'

Give it to her. Only a vague flicker of disappointment showed in her face. She had been told, no doubt, over the months or weeks that her relatives were, according to custom, looking for a husband to introduce her to, a man from the West. And brass monkey, John! It turned out to be me!

'They dream up a hundred plots these relatives, Mr Xavaxa, you mustn't take them all seriously.'

Wonderful! Marvellous, what a fucking put-down, one in a hundred, jokes/mistakes, one a day, no skin lost from a pretty, bent nose.
'But there's no mileage in it, is there, Miss . . . Ribbonwalla?'
'You really are so rude, Mr Xavaxa, but it doesn't matter. No, there isn't any, whatever you call it, mileage in it.'
She turned and walked away. I told my aunt precisely what had happened, word for word when we got home. She didn't understand or sympathise.

I think to myself I shall probably never hear from or see Ms Roshan Rib again. Firdaus thinks I am getting restless, drinking and not thinking and he suggests I go to their country house in Mahabaleshwar, a long-distance coach ride away. They are going to be there for a few days, but they're soon going to Darjeeling and they'll gladly leave the place to me.
I book the coach and attend to unfinished business, pretending to relatives that I've returned to London. I make several mendacious phone calls. Ms Roshan bugs me.
I take my typewriter and two suitcases full of books packed in with a few shirts and trousers. Four of us have formed a chumminess across the aisle of the bus.
The fellow next to me approaches the question carefully. May he ask a few things? He has always been intrigued by what he hears of England. I have lived there, indeed do live there, can I answer some of his queries perhaps without being offended?
'Yes.'
'They say, now don't be offended, sir, but you are Indian you'll understand my question . . .'
The others are paying close attention now. This man sells perfume. He has come from the north-east of India and spends a few months in Bombay selling the stuff he's accumulated from tribespeople whom he has on contract. He has a panoply of bottles and invites me and the rest of the passengers sitting in front, behind and to the side of us to sniff his wrist, then his elbow and then his bicep, nearly upto his armpit and see if we can make out the different scents. He continues, 'They tell me that in England you can get money without working. Just go to a place and get it.'
'Yes, if you're unemployed.'
They mull this information over.
'Then why does anyone work?'
'It's not much money, barely enough to keep you in the rice and dal.'

Next question, 'Now, saving the deep respect I have for you as a travelled man and a man of education and obvious good social class, they tell me, and it's a bit bad to say, thank God no ladies are listening . . .'

'Come on, what?'

'That ladies are sleeping together in England.'

'Some,' I said. 'Some, yes, you've heard a correct thing there.'

I pretend to meditate on it, on the difficulty of the question.

'I can't believe this.'

'You're not alone. I believe Queen Victoria was a bit sceptical too.'

'Pardon me what is sceptical?'

'Glasses,' a fellow says. 'That is scepticle.'

'That's right. She didn't believe it.'

'She's right. How can you believe it?'

'There are Asian girls who do that too. In Britain.'

'They are not ashamed, these ladies?'

'They start by being, but then they start writing articles in newspapers to explain why they are different from white women who do the same things.'

He looks totally incredulously at me then breaks into a grin.

'If that is UK, what must be happening in USA?'

'I can't really say,' I confess.

Later on he asks me the question he says that has bothered him the most.

This time he whispers so the others can't hear, 'Someone, perhaps it's wrong, perhaps mischievous fellow tell me that people are paying other peoples to beat them with whips as a kind of *shauk*?'

'This too is true. Miss Whiplash of the Bayswater Road. Fifty pounds a go – thousand rupees.'

'Buy why?'

'English school system,' I say.

After a while he asks, 'If I go, will they pay me to beat them? What do you think, Mr Xerxes?'

I look him up and down to signal that it's not a straightforward beating that's wanted. Looks count.

'Mmm. I think some might. They call it "kinky".'

'Kinky?'

He is satisfied. I feel he is sitting back and thinking about the sterling exchange. Britain, a magical place where he doesn't have to, but can earn a living by whipping Englishmen.

I have left a forwarding address for Penny if she writes. I have enquired casually about adoption laws. Fairly strict. An Indian magistrate would not give a declared lesbian couple custody and the right to bear away an infant to an alien land. People say there are ways.

Firdaus and Naomi are going to the real hills. They've booked a hotel in Darjeeling and are flying the next day from Bombay. They are there for a few hours to see me in and hand over charge of the house. They will be back in a few weeks.

I expect a shack in which I can type and read and cook some rice and make myself tea.

It's an establishment. The place has four bedrooms and a glass bay in the drawing room with a fireplace. The glass overhangs a precipice and the view of successive valleys is good. There is a cook and a man to fetch and shop for him because he is old and was their family cook but has retired here and has bad arthritis which allows him to get about the house but not to negotiate the few miles it is to town to buy groceries and fresh meat. There is a freezer.

Then there is Kamla. She's – can't resist it – comely. She's the maid, the housekeeper, the light laundry woman, the waiter at table, brusher of Naomi's dog Mowgli which has come back from Europe, was with us in the Bombay flat and is now travelling to Darjeeling by plane.

Naomi hasn't lost her accent. She understands Hindi and Marathi and she shakes her head in understanding like a native.

The interior surprises me. Their flat in Bombay is in modest taste, Indian middle class all over. The house in Mahabaleshwar has a touch of Hollywood. Panelling, a built-in bar, an American oil painting. It's Naomi's fantasy, one she wouldn't want discussed because she is straightforward enough. It's a house, the servants are bare necessities. She earns her money and Firdaus does and why shouldn't they live as they can and must to stay sane? Fine.

The cook lives in the outhouse. I am given the keys and told to work hard and that I will be looked after and Kamla will tell me where everything is. They leave in their car, waving as it goes round the bend. I go and unpack.

The house has been built by gutting the previous one on the site. The veranda and wooden balustrades of the former house remain. So does part of its pyramidal tiled roof. It is surrounded by trees and is at least two miles remote from the next clump of houses and three miles from the town proper. They haven't changed its name, Oak Dene.

I should take a walk into town. I go in the early evening. There is a lake and a clubhouse on the lake and a high street, but the town is basically set around two long streets and the houses come off them dotting the hillside and built along the various winding paths up and down the ridge.

Darkness falls fast. I've forgotten and I regret the fact that I didn't bring a torch. The last miles are in total darkness. I take it easy and am back at twelve.

I go into the front room. I can hear animals stirring in the jungle below me. The place has electricity so I'm well lit. I find a book from my suitcase, a history of Persepolis. There is a knock on the door.

Kamla asks when dinner should be served.

I speak to her in Bombay Hindi. 'Have you stayed awake for dinner?'

'I made you very good one. Please say where and when?'

'You stayed awake to make me dinner? Are you crazy? I could have been out all night.'

'I would have stayed awake all night.'

'You need the job that bad?'

She begins to giggle and holds her saree in front of her mouth.

One of the books I've brought with me is a libretto of Handel's *Xerxes*. I'd scoured the music shops of London for it. To no avail. I found it in a music shop in Bombay. They had to go to the godown to get it, but they found it for me, dusted it off and charged me the price on the cover, converting the shillings to rupees. No antique value added.

I skipped through it. It was called *Serse* – these Germans couldn't get our names right.

I had imagined an opera about the war of the Zoroastrians with the known world, the Emperor lashing the waves, a cast of millions. It was some bullshit drawing-room comedy of obvious Germanic errors. Fie! Thus do we go looking for our heritage in the wrong places much as a dog digs for bones in the very garden where he will be buried (Confucius say).

Balls. No good. I have seventy-five tomes in my bag and begin to unpack them the afternoon I get there. Nietzsche. The big book *Thus Spake Zarathustra*. This I am resolved to reread. I read it once when I was in Poona, a college boy trying to show his colleagues the covers of the important and obscure books he read. The practice was to carry it with you and to ask each other. 'What you reading, yar?'

Some carried Perry Mason 'mysteries' as we called them. Some, to show they were really smart, Mickey Spillane, the forerunner of all that's cop-and-robbery on telly, some to show they had a disdain which must be respected carried *The Brothers Karamazov* or Nietzsche. The comment from friends was: 'Wow, yar, can't even pronounce this bastard's name, what is it all about?'

Yes. I would re-read it and compare it now to what I knew of Zoroastrian ethics. All this superman and will to power doctrine didn't seem like 'asli' stuff to me – distinctly 'nakli' – Nichy's own invention. I can see him with his moustache poring over some Zoroastrian text, professorial and mad. He must have imagined himself pitted against the folly of a whole religion, a whole past, a few worlds. One man against history, the rest and all comers! Wow! I know a couple of idiots in London who try and write like that. Their efforts await psychiatric care. The Maudsley! It doesn't have the ring of, 'He's gone Doolally', or, 'Doolally Tap!' The unfairness of history, never can we ex-colonials annexe to our tongue the joy of 'Maudsleyfication'. Never mind. Xerxes boy, you ramble. This is hardly the stuff Mr De F or the Bombay journals will buy from you. Has your prose died? Has India soaked your abilities? Does jet lag last a month? One thing plays on my mind? Every time I see an urchin in the street, I think of grabbing him or her for Penny and Eileen.

I eat the dinner that Kamla puts before me. She heats chapattis while I eat.

'I'm dying for a drink. Look, three chapattis is enough.'

'Sahib eats seven. Memsahib even eats four sometimes. Some guests eat twenty.' She giggles.

'I don't want to know about belching Indians,' I say. 'Is there a beer?'

There are twenty-five beers. She has chucked them in the fridge because Naomi has told her I like my drink and varied. She fetches it. She fights with the bottle opener. I ask her to give it me. The dining room where I sit overlooks the back garden. I suggest we drink the beer in the front room and let the dark of the valley grace the occasion, draw back the curtains, turn down the lights. I sit on the carpet. She stands in front of me with a tray and a glass and a bottle of beer.

'Aren't you drinking any?' She looks at me as though I'm a half wit and then her expression changes. She maybe sees that I'm sincere. I'm a creature she hasn't quite ideologically sussed.

'No, no, no,' she says. 'You drink!'

'Not alone. Get a glass.'

'No, sahib. What are you saying? Me drink with you? I don't drink.'

'Don't act up,' I say talking in Hindi. 'Get another bloody glass. For me.'

'Oh well, if it's for you . . .'

She goes and gets a glass. I pour the beer and hold it out to her.

'I don't drink,' she says.

'You don't drink and I'm Hanuman's son.'

She laughs. I'm still holding the glass out and she is shrinking with embarrassment and her smile tries to cover her averted glances. She holds her hands out in front of her breast, as if in prayer, 'No, sahib.'

'Go on, I won't tell.'

She takes the glass. 'Memsahib will kill me.'

'We'll die together,' I say.

I ask her to sit down. This is an even larger outrage.

'You're sitting on the floor,' she says.

'So?'

'If you sit on the couch then I could sit on the floor.'

'For a young girl you talk a lot of shit.'

She laughs. I use the word for cow-dung, no other translation seeming apposite.

'Well, I order you to sit down,' I say.

Of course I know what I'm playing at. All my early life there have been servants in the house. I know India like frogs know water. I know she'll sit down. I know she'll talk. There's nobody around for miles except the arthritic cook and I don't know how much I'll see of him. She tells me she cooked this lot and let him get off to bed.

I tell her about myself. She listens and sips the beer and I fill her up again and we get through seven bottles.

She is marginally curious. It is not her place to ask guests questions.

The next night the ritual is shorter. I spend the day researching Nietzsche and trying to find parallels. I pace the wooded paths. Kamla is nowhere during the day. She wakes me up with a cup of tea and asks me what sort of egg I'd like for breakfast. I clutch the covers and say I won't eat any. She looks disappointed but she goes.

I see no more of her and wonder whether to lock the doors or to wander out. There's nobody around so I wander. A mile down the road I hear a stream and a swish of cloth. I turn from the road down a smaller path. There's a mountain stream and waterfall. Kamla is washing sarees in the waterfall.

'Why don't you chuck them in the washing machine?'

'I do when memsahib is here.'

She looks like a little girl, her saree tucked in for hard labour, with no leggings and loose ends. Her hair is wet.

'Did you bathe in the waterfall?'

'I stood under it. I bathe in the bathtub. I have become very American,' she says.

I say I'll see her back at home. Nietzsche takes over. The closest he gets is in his concept of time. In the ancient books time is called Zurvan and the sons of time are Ahuramazd and Ahriman, the good and the evil. Born of one father they must dispute the inheritance of the estate of time itself. Nice one.

It suggests a story. I set up my typewriter and begin.

It is all about a dialogue between the spirit of good and evil fighting over the soul of one man, a Parsee umbrella seller, who has umbrellas in the blood as his father and grandfather before him were umbrella sellers and the expansion of their empire from street corner stall to multi-city umbrella shops. Good story. The evil Ahriman turns himself into a bat and spreads himself into all umbrella fabric. Not one for Mr De F.

I'm half-way through and Kamla knocks at the door. It's meal time again. We go through the beer routine of the previous night. Easier but still a bit of role playing. We drink and I ask her about herself.

I have gained her confidence. She wants my assurance that sahib and memsahib will now know that we have talked. At all. Her job is not to talk. I tell her I don't believe in jobs. She relaxes and tells me that her husband died and his family was not nice to her. She came to the city looking for a job and Naomi picked her up and after a few months asked her if she would be caretaker and maid to this remote house. She doesn't regret her decision. What else can a poor girl do?

'It's nice here. But it must get lonely.'

'Are you married?' she asks.

'No.'

'You should be. There must be lots of pretty girls in England.'

'Sure. Is there any whisky?'

'There's everything.'

I finish the story the next day and send it to Roshan the interviewer.

Three days later I get a telegram saying they are happy to print the story. What's more they have sold it to a national magazine. Would I object if I was sent two hundred and fifty rupees?

I take a walk to the telegraph office in town. It takes me half a day but I wire my acceptance of the proposal. Fame at last.

I want some champagne when I get back. The dark is coming up from the valleys and Kamla brings ten bottles because she doesn't know which one is champagne. I choose and try to explain to her why champagne is for celebration and how one has to have a ceremony of clinking glasses. She has seen it done. No, she'll tell the truth, they do it in her village and she has been at sessions with women and other servants where they've done it too. If the truth were told the cook raids the master's bottles and mixes it all up in a glass and drinks it. Arthritis is only half his trouble. The rest of the time he gets stuff from the villagers, potato liquor, cashew-nut liquor.

I have not seen hide nor hair of him. Late at night, after Kamla and I go to our own beds, me in the spare room, she on her blankets on the veranda, I sometimes hear a guitar plunking. A Goan song goes softly out into the night air. Frederick, the cook.

I spend the days reading, the nights talking to Kamla and drinking.

'What do you do with your day?'

'Work.'

'Don't you like doing anything else?'

'I've seen the videos that sahib has a hundred times. Sometimes I watch them.'

I know the videos. Humphrey Bogart films, W. C. Fields. Some Buñuel films, Antonioni, the sort of thing Naomi and Firdaus watched at university in the States.

'Do you understand them?'

'Little bit.'

'What do you like to see?'

'Real films. I love real films.'

The next day we set out to town to get videos of real films. Kamla doesn't want to walk by my side. She knows it's absurd to walk down wooded paths a step behind me and walk into town two steps behind. It would be presumptuous besides. Like a wife. She nervously walks by my side.

We get seventeen Hindi movie videos. The man in the shop is impressed.

258

We walk back as it is getting dark and the night is spent drinking whisky and watching Hindi movies on the video. Kamla falls asleep on the carpet. I put a pillow under her head and then I shift in order to move her head on to my lap. The hero of the movie is clambering precariously across a rope between two skyscrapers with a cast of millions anticipating his fall as a baddie tries to set fire to one end of the rope and a gang of policeman who misunderstand his goodness tries to get a helicopter to haul him in from space with a net.

She wakes up, sits up and rubs her eyes. Was she sleeping on me? She's sorry. Oh God, if Frederick came in?

'So what's with Frederick? He's got some claim on you?'

'He's tried, but I haven't given him anything.'

'How will you decide when you want, as you say to "give anything"?'

'I've been married,' she says. She's stopped calling me 'sahib' but I can't get her to call me Xerxes. 'Now it's a matter of love.'

'And you'll know when it comes?'

'One knows one's own feelings.'

'But here in this place, year in and year out. Who do you meet?'

She looks at the floor, casts just one quick glance in my direction. 'Who could I meet?'

Yes, I know, I am now supposed to say she could meet the likes of me, but what the fuck am I doing here? I've come to write something, to meditate on myself. Why have I fed this poor girl alcohol and my stupid ugly insisting presence? She looked as though she belonged to the waterfall, washing clothes, bathing, descending to the village below.

'It's dawn, I think we should sleep.'

'It's sleep you want?'

'Yes, Kamla, it's sleep I want,' I say.

I get to the spare room and she to her bed and then I hear her come back to the front room to retrieve the rest of the bottle of whisky. She listens at my door.

I go to town the next day to fetch the newspapers. My short story arrives in the mail. There are floods following the drought and pictures. The news is two days old.

I read the clippings I've brought in a file from Bombay. An article tells me about Parsee landlords in the fifteenth- and sixteenth-centuries in Gujerat growing toddy trees and fucking their women labourers.

Kamla doesn't know how to kiss. She is shy of kissing, she moves her mouth away and her eyes get moist.

I sleep naked and she seeks me out in the dark without a knock at the 'sahib's' door, without a word.

She sees I'm awake.

'Do you want to lie next to me?'

She makes no reply. I have never felt anyone tremble like that.

In the morning she makes breakfast while I am asleep. A man beats his path to our door and she is back to the game.

'Sahib, a gentleman.'

I dress in a T-shirt and jeans and step out. There is a man on the veranda. I address him in Hindi. He is carrying a garland and he insists on putting it round my neck after asking me in English if I am Mr Xerxes.

'Who are you?'

'Just one insignificant fellow, but I am your town-mate. I have come from Poona all the way to see you.'

He is Mr Rao. He has seen my dissertation on good and evil and the sons of time. He thinks it very good and timely as the earth is descending into terrible evil.

I ask him to come in and have a cup of tea or a drink.

'Tea,' he says and Kamla fetches it. We sit in the room with a view.

'Why do you believe the earth is descending into evil.'

'I have made a study, Mr Xerxes. Of cities. Call Hong Kong, call London, call New York. What is the greatest evil? Including Bombay?'

'Corruption?' He is obviously dismissive of the very suggestion.

'Drugs? Crime? Fundamentalism?' I hesitate.

'No, no, sir. You know the true answer if you look in your heart. Traffic problems. Science has outstripped space. Just as you say time has given rise to evil, so I say space has given rise to motor transport and that is a manifestation of evil.'

I sip my tea. I don't really want him to say more but I find myself asking him to do exactly that.

'You can help me. You are from England. I have tried my utmost here but Indians are stupid. They will appreciate my theories abroad.'

I ask him what these theories are and out of a cotton shoulder bag he pulls three typed tomes. He hands them to me. One is called *The Walking Incentive Traffic Scheme Explained*. The other is called *Literature and the Walking Incentive Traffic Scheme*. The third bears the title *Walking Incentive Traffic Scheme and the Religions of the World*.

He talks of the WITS.

I say it will take me time to absorb all this. Can't he leave his address?

'I have time,' he says, 'now that I have found a man who is willing to listen, a writer of great vision and understanding. I have stationed myself in guest house only five miles from here, the other side of Mahabaleshwar and I will give you seventy-two hours to read and absorb and then I will be back. To begin, Xerxes sahib, our great partnership of good works.' He stands and lets out a little, hesitant, stuttering laugh, 'Ehe, ehe, ehe!'

I wish him farewell, holding the three tomes. He goes.

The Walking Incentive Traffic Scheme is easy. What you have to do, I discover after a hundred pages of reading, is walk out of your door and as far towards your destination as you can. On every street corner the government stations a man or woman with tickets marked with the name of the corner you have passed. You gather these tickets as you pass and when you have earned enough tickets you buy yourself a bus ride to work or back home. It's a game. You can walk all the way to work one day and save up the tickets and when you've walked long enough you can use them on buses which go to other towns. All travel has to be earned by walking. At a stroke it will diminish traffic on the streets, introduce free public transport, stimulate camaraderie in buses through comparative conversation of how far you've walked, and reduce pollution in the cities.

The second typed manuscript has an introduction which claims that thinkers from Gandhi to Arthur Conan Doyle and John Keats have supported the Walking Incentive Traffic Scheme. All adherents of WITS to a man. Chapters follow. I read the first one. It starts with a long quote from a Sherlock Holmes story in which Holmes and Watson get called to Soho from Baker Street. Holmes chooses to walk and tells Watson that his coach will encounter traffic. Watson haplessly takes up the challenge and reaches Soho when Holmes has been on the spot for hours and is half-way to solving the mystery. The conclusion to the chapter is that Mr Arthur Conan Doyle had obviously had the Walking Incentive Traffic Scheme in mind when he wrote those words.

So also with John Keats who describes in a letter the splendours of observation while walking in London, architectural curiosities, points of interest and atmosphere. He too is obviously to Mr Rao a devotee of the WITS.

There is D. H. Lawrence. There is a quote from the Hong Kong traffic authority.

He is coming back in seventy-two hours. This is the reader I have attracted with his garland of stale flowers. But there are people I know in London with a passion for cycles and a passion against the pollution of petrol fumes. Must I laugh? Shall I not rather examine my own ignorance and prejudice? Maybe there should be inspectors at every street corner handing out tickets to testify how far you've walked. People jog on the commons of London. Mr Rao claims health, wealth and social prosperity for the millions are obvious corollaries to his reasoning.

He comes back as promised. I have made a decision. He folds his hands in greeting and I encounter him on the veranda.

This time I don't invite him in.

'You've read my humble work, Mr Xerxes?'

'Yes, and I think you're mad. Barking mad. Take it and go away.'

In some strange way I sense that he is prepared for this most insulting of responses. He has had this before.

'Can't I have a cup of tea and discuss with you?' he pleads. He turns to Kamla who is hovering in the door. He speaks to her in Marathi and asks her to get two cups of tea, maybe it will cool me down.

'No,' I say. 'Don't order my . . . er . . . servants to do anything. Just take your madness and go. I have read every corrupt deluded word you've written and I think we should never meet again.'

'The United Nations has read my work and sent me an acknowledgement,' he says. He is nearly in tears and pulls a grubby letter from his pocket and unfolds it, 'Look, look here! United Nations. Additional Officer in the Administrative Secretariat of the World Health Organisation.'

'They are completely mad too.'

'I think you are not feeling well today,' Mr Rao ventures.

'You should walk all the way back to Poona,' I suggest calmly.

'Has something swerved his brain?' he asks Kamla.

She retreats into the front room. Mr Rao goes. He mutters something about thinking I was a great author with an understanding of his purposes. I hesitate for a good ten minutes and then I run down the path after him. I can't explain why.

He is wiping his eyes with a handkerchief when I run up behind him crying, 'Mr Rao.'

He stops. 'It'll never work in London. Maybe a movement will enforce it in Bombay and Delhi and maybe some Ayatollah will adopt it in Teheran, but you haven't got a chance in New York or Paris or Berlin or London. I am afraid Hong Kong too is lost.'

'I understand you, Mr Xerxes,' he says and he weeps. 'You have insulted me. What's more you have insulted WITS. You are now sorry. It is too late.'

I accompany him to the bus stop where he'll have to wait at least half an hour. His manuscripts are in his cloth bag. We are not friends again, but I feel I've explained myself.

Kamla is of the opinion that he is mad.

From Kamla I learn fascinating things about Firdaus and Naomi.

I had no idea they played bridge but she tells me I should go on Saturdays to the club where Parsees play bridge. I say I don't know how to play bridge. Also that Naomi memsahib wants to buy land the other side of the house, right down to the waterfall and grow things. She has learnt some things about growing and wants to call in farmers from some distant land. Kamla doesn't know the name of the land but Frederick does if I care to ask him. I don't care to ask Frederick much.

Something about my writing worries me. The figure of Mr Rao and the traffic scheme keeps coming back to me as I am at the typewriter. Am I banging away to no avail? Mr Rao has taken twenty-five years to evolve the scheme. There is something about isolation that makes you cranky. He makes me evaluate the quality of my aloneness. Are my imaginative articles on Parseeana as ludicrous as the WITS? Maybe it wasn't Mr Rao at all. It was the manifestation of the spirit of Ahuramazd arriving to give me a warning about vanity, about screwing the ayahs. God help me, it's not what I'm doing. Am I? No, no, it's a 'relationship'. Oh really? Not just isolation and boredom and the sort of attraction that springs from a master-servant relationship as flies spring, though convolutedly, from maggots?

I get a letter from Penny. She misses me. Brief mention of Eileen. 'If you can see what's available' is her code. Idiot. If she's trying to keep a secret from Interpol, they'll think she's talking about heroin.

The floods have hit central India and Tilak's problem is probably reversed. Water galore.

Kamla leaves me alone to type and to wander about the house and look at the moon from the side of the veranda. She seems to respect a man thinking. If I call her, abandon work for the evening, eat and drink and watch videos till sleep-time, she assumes we shall make a night of it. In the early morning she creeps out and sleeps on the veranda in case Laxman the bicyclist, the fetcher of groceries and carrier of dhobi bundles, should pass by very early on his errands for other large houses.

She tells me he gossips. He has been responsible for the dismissal, indirectly, of several servants. If bottles of gin go missing and turn up at some shack in a neighbour's servants' quarters, Laxman will be there to enjoy the pickings, oh sure he will, the dog, he is the main fence of the countryside, the disposer of what the servants can purloin. But once he has knowledge over you you fall into his power. If you quarrel with him he slips the word, perhaps to the local barber who comes round on a bike or the soda water man who has a little van, to the master and mistress. Out. And no finger on Laxman. His sins give him power and power gives him alibis. A bad one.

I meet him every second day when he dutifully enquires if I have any shirts for the dhobi or hankies or sudras or anything at all. Memsahib has enjoined him to enquire even if I tell him there is no need. He must wonder what I do with my dirty clothes. Kamla washes them in the waterfall because I think it's romantic, sexist and no one's looking.

'Actually,' she says, 'he knows I wash the clothes, he's just coming to see if anything has happened.'

'How do you mean happened? How would he know?'

'He reads people's eyes. He's good at that.'

'Have there been other guests here – of memsahib or sahib?'

'Of course. There are always guests, even in the rain when the place has to be shut down.'

'Men alone?'

'Once or twice some sahibs have come.'

'And does anything happen?'

Kamla looks up coyly, a Hindi film look of mischievous shame. She's not going to say but she wants me to believe nothing like that ever happened. That's what she means by slapping herself lightly on both cheeks. But really she enjoys my hint of jealousy, possessiveness.

'They are fat seths and some white people from memsahib's side. The whiteys play golf with sahib. Laxman takes the trolley, real leather and very silvery iron sticks.'

'I know what golf is.'

'You must be playing all this in England? Squash?'

'Nothing at all.'

'Then how do you get so strong and don't fall ill?'

'My constitution. Nature.'

Nazar! My God, I forget to touch wood or to avert the evil eye. The word has been spoken. The next day I fall ill. Frederick comes, Laxman comes. They want to know if they should wire the sahib and the memsahib, they will surely come and take me away. I remind them Darjeeling is a very long way off.

'But they will come if it's a telegram. Not letter, I am saying telegram.'

Another charm. I have very high fever. Kamla sits by the bed and soaks handkerchiefs in iced water and eau de cologne for my forehead. Laxman calls a doctor. I vomit, I have diarrhoea and my legs can't hold my weight. The doctor takes away an injection tube full of blood. It will have to be sent away for analysis. He leaves pills.

Kamla sits by me all day and moves her bistra into my room to look after me at night. The explosion in my centre has blown away my stomach, windpipe, oesophagus, and pushes painfully upwards.

Later they tell me the doctor came twice and gave me injections. Kamla says she thought I was going to die. For three days I've been delirious and not eaten, just had water which Kamla has raised to my lips every few hours.

'Did I go to the toilet? Did I get up?'

'Don't worry about that. Your fever seems to have gone.'

'Where are Frederick and Laxman?'

'They saw you sick and they know there's nothing to be done, so they've gone off.'

'Off where?'

'Never know where men go to indulge their filthy ways. On a bus to the valley town maybe. Get what they want. Memsahib calls it "shopping" when Frederick asks permission to go.'

'Even the arthritic must get their kicks.'

I get back to reading and then to the typewriter. My nightmares of delirium are still with me in flashes. Literary nightmares. One of *Dombey and Son*, in which Kamla plays the part of the girl servant, Tattykoram, and is pursued, ravaged and abandoned.

I don't have the book and it's not on their bookshelves either so I can't look it up. But in my dream Tattykoram/Kamla is from India and is carried to England as a little baby and forced into slavery.

She politely presumes I am too weak as I convalesce to think of sex. She sits next to me when she has nothing to do and combs out her hair or just stares. She says she can't read and if the memsahib knew (through Laxman) that she was watching videos on her own, she'd be angry.

'Does she get angry with you often?'

'Nothing like that. Sahib and memsahib are best. They are educated people, you see, if servants just do the work, they don't think of them as servants and they give Laxman too much money for just riding his bicycle about, bastard.'

I remember talking to Firdaus and Naomi in my room in Earls Court. They were passing through London on their way back from America. Maybe fifteen years ago? We'd have laughed if we thought there would ever be a Kamla, Laxman, Frederick and the four other servants who chauffeured and dusted and cooked and washed, albeit on a part-time basis as had become the custom with the shortage of domestic labour in Bombay.

All those years ago Firdaus knew his Maoist texts backwards: *On the Correct Way to Run a Revolution, Seven Theses on Literature*. Buff-coloured covers and spines. Red star on the paperback cover of the American editions. How can a man write seven theses on literature without referring to one book? Firdaus would probably concede that there is no correct way to run a revolution. Would the Walking Incentive Traffic Scheme count as a small urban revolution?

The flowers on the garland that Mr Rao gave me have turned from white to yellow and still the garland lies in the kitchen and Kamla sprinkles it with water every day.

'Why didn't you throw it away?'

'Only the person who is garlanded can throw it away. And anyway, if it's been round your neck I want to keep it.'

'The flowers will begin to stink.'

'Laxman knows that we have something.'

'How do you know?'

'He could see it my eyes.'

'What did he say?'

'Just . . .'

'Just what?'

'He said that human beings have fun and that very fun turns into deepest pain.'

'Maybe he was talking about his own shopping trip. Maybe he's in love or sick or something.'

'He was talking about me!'

Before I have time to gather my thoughts and broach the subject in the way I have been meaning to for all the days since we began this affair, she is gone.

I follow her out. But she has run off. I put on my shoes and go to the waterfall. The sound of the torrent but no one there. I turn back. I see a woman's figure in the distance, but not in the sort of saree that Kamla wears. A woman wearing a long skirt and a tight blouse and carrying a huge cloth bag like a dhobun.

She shouts, 'Xerxes,' and waves.

Sonya. Hoarse but unmistakable. Sonya De Freitas a serving Indian, enlisted and proven.

We hug in the path. No need to ask what she is doing here. She has tracked me down. She is going to stay a few days. India is fantastic, but sad and she wished people didn't have emotions and she's come to look for traditions but she wishes people didn't have traditions, but then they wouldn't be people, would they?

I agree with everything. She throws her bundle on the veranda. What a sumptuous house? My rich friends? Sure.

Kamla, without bidding, brings in two glasses and two opened beers on a salver. Sonya has thrown herself down on the floor and says thank you to Kamla.

'Dying for a beer. Sister, you are a mind reader.'

She speaks only English, except for the thank you. She has picked that up. She has travelled by bus, on foot, hitched rides in trucks, by train, and she has been through seven states of India. Wow fantastic.

I am about to tell Kamla that she should get a glass and I think better of it. Instead I stroll into the kitchen and fetch her a glass. I pour some beer as she watches. She pretends she doesn't know it could be intended for her to drink with us so she turns and goes to the kitchen. I follow her.

'You come back and have a drink with us.'

'You think you can make a fool of me,' she says and she jerks away her wrist which I am trying to hold tenderly.

She goes out of the back door. I go back to Sonya.

'It's like that, is it?'

'Don't be a bitch. You shouldn't be eavesdropping on people's conversations.'

'Only a couple of words were said. I can read her eyes.'

'There's a fellow called Laxman who can read eyes.'

'You won't have to read mine, I've come to tell you all.'

267

We talk into the night. Kamla gets Frederick to cook dinner for two and keeps coming in ostensibly to see if we are ready to eat. I markedly tell her to make the next bedroom ready for 'Sonya'.

'Which room would memsahib like? Big memsahib and sahib's or the other guest room?'

'I'll sleep on the floor,' Sonya says when I translate.

Sonya is trying to radiate sisterliness and the message that we are just good friends. I am an idiot. I should have told Sonya to play my younger sister.

Maybe not, I think I told Kamla what family I had and there weren't any younger sisters. Cousin, then.

After dinner Sonya opens her bundles. She has bought new clothes from Kerala, from Madhya Pradesh, from Tamilnadu and she's left piles of the stuff in Bombay. She was with Tilak three weeks and then the floods came. Poor man, he's working himself to death. There's devastation. The well from the Well-Well project was barely complete when the floods came and it filled up to the top and overflowed. The villagers hadn't seen that before.

Then the rains came and the streams flooded. The villagers said the well was a thermometer of drought and flood, it was built by white men and by Tilak with the arts learnt from abroad. It had warned of impending flood but they had not know it was an omen.

'Tilak says it's simple, they must have hit a layer near some more powerful artesian pressure well or some stream which flooded through the hole they had made before the overground streams broke their banks. I tried to work it out but I can't. You know they still rely on land survey maps from the time of the Raj. Tilak's brother is a swine. He's taking Tilak to court. Tilak doesn't want to fight over land, he's quite saintly.'

Of course I am dying to ask how she got on with Tilak's family. Save it for later.

Sonya says the whole of India is haunted. Not grand ladies in white lace, but screaming disfigured monsters that howl their pain. Curious things. Yes, she was looked after by Binky as she passed through New Delhi. The chattering classes of New Delhi are much exercised by some startlingly critical articles written by an anonymous person who calls herself Adela Questless. They come to the attention of India via the diplomatic corps and now they have been reprinted from London's *Sunday Telegraph* in a magazine called the *Circuit*, an Indian pretence at *Playboy*.

I reproduce most of one article here:

Environmentalism is the latest fad in India. It has caught on like a cure for boredom, the mah-jong of the post-Raj in the salons of Delhi and Bombay. The participants are of course awfully rich and awfully idle, some of them educated abroad at Oxbridge or Harvard or the LSE (none from Lumumba University Moscow in these salons, NB).

My hostess starts a conversation on land preservation with me. I know nothing about it, I admit. I am the worst kind of ignoramus. The buzz words are 'north and south' and 'the periphery'. The horrendous poverty of their nation is reduced to a post-structuralist game.

It is a pleasant Delhi evening and we are sitting on cane chairs on the lawn. Set designer of *Jewel in the Crown*, eat your heart out! A pakora and whisky gathering – and of course profiteroles and canapés. The clothes this set affect are not ostentatious, they are the intellectuals. They wear cotton bush-shirts in imitation of the clerical staff. The women wear cotton sarees and sometimes Western clothes. No gold-bordered sarees while discussing the environment.

The hostess and two journalists are discussing the drought. The fundamental problem lies in the misuse of land and overgrazing. One of the group is on a project which is trying to shut off the routes from the state of Rajasthan to the state of Gujerat. Why? So that the Gujerati herdsmen, to whom the holy project is dedicated, can rebuild the grass lands under the instructions of his project.

'We have to be ruthless. The Rajasthanis come down when there's drought and eat us dry.'

The conversation moves to cities. These people approve of the slum-clearance programmes of Delhi, approve of the police keeping beggars off the streets. The same people tell me that Bombay is run by the Shiv Sena, a fascist sect of Maharashtrians, whose politicians have, horror of horrors, made noises about expelling the south Indians who live on the pavements of the city.

'What's the difference between keeping Rajasthanis off grazing land and the south Indians off pavements?'

Awkward question.

'Why is one set of plans fascist and the other set not?'

'Because one is trying to get a solution, the other is only

269

fermenting religious and regional trouble. They'll start by saying south Indians, then non-Maharashtrians and soon it will be Muslims, Sikh, anyone else.'

'And what about the Rajasthani herdsmen? Won't they be annoyed? Aren't they free as Indian citizens to travel about?'

'They can have their own development project,' says mein hostess.

Indian double-think pervades most arguments. There will probably never be an Indian Lenin. Phew! . . .

So it continues. The next article is more virulently anti-Indian. It's about Indians pretending to be secular and modern and practising in their lives and attitudes the most severe backwardness, pandering to tradition, superstition and a pseudo-religious framework within which the murder of fundamentalist cults becomes possible and passable.

Interesting. But Sonya's looking at me as though it's more than interesting.

'You had something to do with the Sara woman, David Stream's Sara?'

'Sure,' I say, 'I did. I've got her flat in London. I've left it to her friend Ali while I'm here. He's feeding her cats.'

'More than having her flat, I mean. You didn't just move in there. You were screwing her.'

'So?'

'You know she stayed in Tilak's village?'

'Your dad told me.'

'Well, I think it's her. Writing all this shit.'

'It's not her style, is it? So you came to tell me because we're both aggrieved lovers?'

Of course it is Sara's style.

'Don't be ridiculous, Xerxes. I don't own Tilak. I didn't even ask him. His wife owns him, anyway.'

When Sonya goes to bed I hover about in my room and then go out to the veranda. Kamla is wrapped up in her blanket and has covered her head in it like a corpse. There's moonlight and I kneel down by her.

'She's just my friend.'

Silence from under the blanket.

'In fact I used to teach her at school.'

270

'She's learnt fast, has she?'

'Kamla, don't be silly. Very soon I'll have to go back to Bombay and then go back to England. My work is there.'

'I know that,' says the voice from under the blanket.

'I didn't know she was coming. We should have spoken about it before.'

'It's not important.' She pulls the blanket from her face to uncover just her eyes. 'I've seen one man out.'

'I won't be dead, though. I could come back.'

'What will you do with an ignorant girl like me? I can't read.'

'You must learn to read. I'm sure Naomi will teach you, English if you want, and Laxman or Firdaus could teach you Hindi.'

'What's she want to dress like that for? Why doesn't she wear frocks? She's some kind of memsahib, isn't she?'

'She's half Indian and she has an Indian man somewhere in Madhya Pradesh. She came to tell me about it.'

'Yes, but you go back to England and she goes back to England and then you're alone there, aren't you?'

'There are six crores of people there, Kamla.'

She replies in Urdu. 'When there can be no veil from any god, then what purpose is there in hiding love from mere humans?'

'You've been memorising the videos.'

'I could be your servant in England.'

'Don't talk rubbish and stop being annoyed.' I smile.

'I am thinking,' she says.

'Tell me what you've thought tomorrow morning.'

'Eggs for breakfast for memsahib and sahib, scrambled, fried or "haap-bwoil" and garam garam toast?'

I touch her forehead and go back to bed.

Tilak meets her at the station of the nearest town. They travel by bus to the village.

She says he looks drawn and tired and she cares to describe what he is wearing and what she is wearing when she gets off the train, a little girl playing a game. He is delighted with her Indian clothes and the gestures she has picked up at the dancing school in Kerala. They were so welcoming. It was incredible. The humanity of the people!

He has been writing to her about the drought, about the well, about Sara coming to stay, about his wife. He has written that theirs was an arranged marriage. Later he fell in love with her but he was never sure she fell in love with him. She did her duty.

He explained the concept of love, what devotion meant in the scriptures; how even the Hindu scriptures differentiated between passion and wifely obedience. She had always been such a good wife to him. The children were lovely. Sonya confirms that his children are absolutely gorgeous. The boy, thirteen, was shy but the little girl, who called her 'aunty' was always with her, always teaching her rhymes and jingles. Tilak had set up a school and he had insisted they learn English as a second language there. It would be a school that would take the best from middle-class city practice and it would teach in a mixture of the traditional rote-learning way and the new Western modes that were coming in with painting and sculpture and typewriters. But they wouldn't teach the children to be typists. They were from the land and would learn respect for the land.

'Even Tilak, really,' Sonya says. 'He has stuck by his principles, even though he's a beautiful writer and a photographer and if he'd gone to a big city could have done anything. He could have been a politician and if the system had not been so corrupt he'd have been something big in politics now. But he doesn't care for all that. He's stayed with his village and with the district and really, Xerxes, he's seen as a kind of god there. When I told him they love him, he just said that he loved them too and love was like the chicken and the egg, love and answering love.'

'Great. So get to the point. His wife.'

'I think she understood, you know. Tilak put me in the barn which was cleaned up for the English engineer and crew with khats, string beds and straw mattresses and everything. He said I should set up a little temporary home there. He said he loved having me in his village. He was bursting with pride, never mind about the drought, there was so much else. He was busy with the government people and the well and the rest of the district and he used to come home exhausted.

'I went about with him all day. He wasn't ashamed of me at all. He would just hold both my hands, because we'd be sitting outside and he'd wait till I went inside the barn and then he'd go into the house. Jayant, his son, came with us, most days. He used to watch us holding hands and he told Tilak that he'd not seen him hold hands with his mum.'

'Did you talk to the wife?'

272

'Of course I talked to the wife, but Tilak had to interpret. She would cook and offered to do my washing, even though there was no water to drink let alone for washing. She said she'd find the water if that was what I was used to. Tilak never spent a day without pointing out her good points to me. And I understand them. Then one night he came to my barn. We were lying in the dark, talking in whispers, when she came in. Their house is completely isolated, about fifty yards from another cluster of huts and then the main village, and the night has all kinds of sounds, even though Tilak said in the drought the insects die or run away. The countryside is alive.

'She came with a hurricane lantern because she wanted to be absolutely sure. There's no lock on the door, they are honest in their village and she burst in and held the lamp up. Tilak just said, 'Jayant's mother, go back to your bed.' He calls her Jayant's mother and not by her name but he said I should call her by her name, because sisters do.

'She was no different to me the next day. He had left a few minutes after she had and she gave him no sign of anything having changed. She had always known, Tilak said, because when they were together sometimes he had kind of told her that this girl existed and was coming.'

'He had only kind of told her?'

'I didn't want to pry into every little piece of his relationship. What he wanted was to love me too. I just began to feel extremely uncomfortable. I think I grew up ten years in two days.'

'About time,' I say.

'It's funny. I've come half-way across India to tell you all this, but I don't want your opinion really.'

'Fine. I won't give it.'

'No, you must give it, but I won't take it. I'm going to sort out my feelings by myself. Anyway I'm not going back there. I've got to go to Lucknow and then stay in Calcutta and Gujerat for a month and then six days and then two months. I'll get right into a million things.'

'Don't you miss London?'

'Not yet.'

I sit while Sonya packs her bundles again. I offer her a suitcase but she says she likes the experience. She has bought old silver ornaments and an old gold chain in Bombay.

'Are they easy to get?'

'They're not all that expensive and look, it's beautiful.'

273

'Can I buy it off you?'

'You can have it,' Sonya says.

'Not if I can't pay for it.'

'You've listened to me. I needed your head the last few days. I wanted somebody from London. I'm not going crazy, am I?'

'No. How much did it cost?'

'To you? Two thousand rupees.'

I put the money in her shoulder bag.

I see Sonya off at the bus station and go back to the house. A telegram has arrived for me and there is some excitement from Frederick who is sitting on the steps of the veranda with Kamla. They hand me the khaki envelope and I tear it open. Firdaus and Naomi are following the telegram in a day.

Kamla and Frederick start chattering about the things they must do before they return. Frederick goes off to leave messages for Laxman at the next house he is to visit. He must fetch chickens and yoghurt and all the things they'll want. Naomi likes the place stocked.

'When they come back I can't talk to you,' Kamla says.

'We'll talk.'

'Do you know what happens to servants who get dismissed here. How do you get back to Bombay? How do you get another job? All the foreigners know each other in Bombay and they don't give jobs to servants who've been "kick-out".'

'You won't get kick-out.'

'You should know, you're the sahib.'

'Kamla!'

'Kamla who? I've got beds to do. I haven't even dusted or cleaned the copper things.'

She leaves.

She busies herself furiously scrubbing brass ornaments, vases and Natarajs and stuff I hadn't noticed in the house. Then she disappears. I've spread my papers in every room and I gather them up. I catch a glimpse of Kamla on the cross bar of Laxman's bicycle, her two legs raised up almost horizontal, going for a bumpy ride.

In the afternoon Firdaus and Naomi return.

I am welcome to stay as long as I want. They'll be there just for a few days because there's a new lift being put into their house as both lifts broke down and they're not going to flog up to the twenty-third floor. They'd starve in Bombay so they came up here. The workmen say four days – but they'll take twenty.

274

I say I'm going back via Poona. I want to stop by and see if there's anyone I know, indulging my nostalgia a bit.

I try to see Kamla on her own but she is avoiding me. They ask about work; I ask about Darjeeling.

The chauffeur is taking the car down to Poona anyway. That's why I leave hurriedly. The family lines up to say goodbye. The custom is to tip the servants who line up, almost on parade, at the edge of the veranda. I have fifty rupees each for Frederick and for Laxman and as I carry my books out to the boot I ask Naomi to give me three envelopes. 'They don't expect envelopes, for Christ's sake.'

'I have turned English to that extent, I'm afraid.'

She gives me three envelopes. I slip the gold chain in one.

Kamla lines up. The others take the envelopes protesting that it isn't really necessary, sahib, thank you very much, sahib.

Kamla stares at the floor. There's a knot in my throat.

'Write to me, give me your news,' I say and press the envelope into her hand which she holds limply by her hip.

She must know I'm not just handing her money. I press my hand around her fingers to make her take it. She says thank you with her joined hands raised, clutching the envelope, a servant on guest-departure parade.

I spend a few days with Firdaus and Naomi when I pass through Bombay. I don't talk of Kamla but they mention Mahabaleshwar and again ask if I was treated well. Everything was perfect, theek thaak.

One evening, sitting among the plants on the veranda overlooking the harbour, Naomi says casually, 'You know the girl Kamla.'

Yipes!

'Yeah.'

'Got on well with her? I mean did you find her strange?'

'Not in the least.'

'Naomi salvaged her,' Firdaus says.

'From what?'

'Well,' Naomi says, 'village girl. Her husband died and soon after, her infant died. In-laws accused her of killing the child.'

'Preposterous.'

'Sure. They'd made her life a misery from the day the husband died. Drove her crazy. The cops were called and she was locked up. In fact that's how I got to know her. Jill, a friend of mine, does social work among women prisoners. Jails, remand homes.'

275

'How did you get her out?'

'There was no evidence. Jill got a solicitor friend to convince the police that there was no circumstantial evidence. The child had been ill. Kamla had cremated it, she claimed. She had to be released, but she would have gotten killed if she'd gone back to her village.'

'And you were convinced, Jill and you, that she was innocent?'

No answer from Naomi. She looks hard at me.

Firdaus says, 'She lies. I've caught her at it.'

I have gone so far as to get typed and cyclostyled copies of handbooks on adoption from the authorities.

The Brits invented bureaucracy and we perfected it. Doing things illegally should always be made harder than doing them legally. Rely on human laziness to keep us straight.

The image remains with me of Kamla – I can't take it! What did she do? Did she go crazy and smash the infant's brains out on a rock by a river. The woman, pliant as the stem of a young tree, twisting with determination, bashing the mangle of sarees against the rock at the waterfall, the foam of the soap rising from the twisted yards of colour. The dye runs, the water is coloured for a brief moment by the fabric and then goes. Dilution is the essence of purity, the water of the fall sweeps all. She squats by the waterfall next to the rock and turns to look over her shoulder, twisting her head to what seems uncannily close to 180°. The woman with turned back feet, the shining figure of Sonya's dreams, the churail . . . which muscle of the churail is pliant as a fracture, does she turn from the thighs or the ankles? The horror is only in the visualisation, only in the mind's eye. Someone with really turned back feet is a disabled person with a handicap. In Britain, the crow man or the churail or the hakmaribai could apply for social security and a disablement allowance and they would have Sonya and people of conscience clamouring for their rights against the wickedness of the state.

My country is a chamber of horrors and I'm only a tourist. I know Kamla better than Naomi. I don't go back to the flat after our conversation. I walk the streets of Bombay.

I say nothing to Firdaus or Naomi about Kamla. What desperation caused her to lose the child? Did it die of natural causes, dwindling away in the misery that enveloped her mother or did she kill it? Couldn't it have been adopted by foreigners? Can't people take the view that nothing is 'The End', that nothing is as bad as it seems? I

276

don't know Kamla. A flirtation with a gold necklace to pay for it, borrowed from someone I understand better.

Sonya said she came to see me because she needed to see someone she knew from England. We are both tourists. A shitty conclusion for those who set their hearts and minds on the discovery of their roots. The root has turned to slime in the mud. Dust in the air suspended marks the place where a story ended.

I had contemplated asking Naomi for a baby, or Firdaus, if he could get me one legitimately, or whether they could sneak a baby for me to take back to Penny and Eileen. They knew about Fara and how she'd been adopted by Cressida. I told them about Ullah's baby and again how I had been the surrogate carrier. I hadn't mentioned Penny or Eileen. Kamla had ruined the sketch, stolen the punch-line.

The wretched girl Roshan has been phoning me. She suggests we meet again.

In her voice I can hear the rehearsed sentiments. She has thought out the sentences carefully. After all I am the monster who rejected her (or she me, it was never clear). Can we be friends though, she still finds me interesting?

'What it is, Mr Xavaxa,' she says, 'is that I have read your essays on Zoroastrianism, which my editor accepted, and you've really stirred it up amongst our readers. We've had hundreds of letters.'

Journalists are excited by letters and by reactions, the rest of their life is dross.

'I'm going back to Britain,' I tell her. I haven't told anyone else. No one else wants to know. 'I'll write some Zoroastrian history. I have sources, untapped ones in the museums there.'

'What about the questions that bother us here? Don't you think we Parsees lack intellectuals?'

'I don't know about that.' (I do actually, the answer is no, we don't!) 'History is safe, till it touches a nerve. When it touches a nerve, I'll be back.'

'Mr Xavaxa, you are very mischievous, aren't you?'

'Yes. I got some big mischief planned. Tell me, is there a Parsee adoption society for unwanted children?'

'Which unwanted children?'

'Any children. Some charity or something. I just want to get my hands on a Parsee child and smuggle it away to Britain.'

'Why?'

'If you must know, because some lesbian friends of mine want a baby and have offered to have me as well if I can get them one.'

She looks at me as though I'm mad.

'Forget it. I knew you wouldn't understand.'

'I am sure you say these things to shock people.'

'My darling Roshan,' I say, 'I don't.'

She stares, shakes her head and there's a flicker of wonder in her face. She is quite attractive in a scrawny sort of way, I find myself thinking, but maybe I've got the whole thing wrong. Maybe she thinks I'm a revolting egoist, too old for her anyway and perhaps already she has had twenty-eight proposals from Parsee atomic scientists and doctors with flourishing practices in Boston or Toronto or wherever.

Firdaus takes me to the orphanage attached to his teaching hospital. There are thirty-five unclaimed children that week. They range from the age dot to seven years old. Two of the six- and seven-year-olds have been smoking. They are not street kids, used to wandering about and begging on trains or sleeping rough or in groups on the railway stations, they are family kids who have suddenly been abandoned. Not lost. They are not property that awaits tracking down, they are children who await at best a change of heart on the part of those who left them. Some of them should be able to tell the police who they are and their parents could be brought to book, but these things, Firdaus says, are never done. They move from there to a home, to state or charitable orphanages. No, one can't just walk in and take one of them away. There are papers to fill, the state appoints guardians and visitors, there are reports and magistrates' procedures to go through. Can't he cut through the red tape? No, that's not possible – now that he's been seen with me. The young women who look after the babies in shifts, not nurses really, they are trained as baby-minders, have turned it into a racket. Of course they sell babies, but they have to be careful too. If they can be sure it's for the foreign market and the baby-buyers won't blackmail them or do the kid to death in some superstition or perversion, then a transaction is possible. But he can't be associated with it, they would definitely blackmail him. He would lose his position. Three of them sleep in shifts through the night in the abandoned babies ward which is an annexe to the hospital, in the same grounds but a full fifty yards from the main wards in a sort of stone barracks with a kachcha roof.

*

The rest is simple but spectacular. I've never told a soul how it was done. Firdaus read it in the papers the next day and he and Naomi knew, but I didn't say a word. Sonya was going to pass through Bombay, just one night she'd spend there.

Fate. Sonya was the only one I could trust. Put it together – she had been to Kerala to do Kathakali and had learnt something of the make-up.

She was carrying several wigs. We spent the afternoon in the theatre gully and found the right mask on to which we could put dough and paint. She fitted coloured torches into the dress and carried her Walkman, with Little Richard tapes.

At one in the morning we drove to the hospital gates. There was a guard sleeping there. We went round to the wall by the side. Sonya climbed it and I carried her false head in my hands.

She looked through the window and flashed the torches. Both the women on duty were asleep, but they set up the most piercing screams when they heard the sound of the dance bells and Little Richard's voice screaming 'Good Golly, Miss Molly' and saw the lights and the face at the window. The women ran to get help. Sonya screeched like an eagle on heat (if that's how they get) or maybe a vulture at the sight of young flesh. It took me twenty seconds to get through the door and pick up the lightest skinned baby I could see. Then we were over the wall.

They told the papers that a churail had attacked the ward. How they explained the one empty cot was their problem. None of the reports spoke of a missing baby, only of the coming of the ghost.

I had to have new pages stitched into my passport. It's the most beautiful baby you've ever seen. She has light green eyes flecked with brown. I remember from Fara at what age they learn to smile. She also has defective toes, three on one foot, five on the other, but one toe on each foot is tiny, just a wart without a nail. Naomi says it's because of the drugs that are dumped on the Third World.

Firdaus and Naomi don't want this baby in their house. Understandable. If the women we terrorised stopped for a moment's reflection they might put the ghost and the machine together and end up with Firdaus. I can't take her to my uncle's. I beg Sonya to stay a day longer till I can book a ticket and we move into a hotel on Marine Drive. It's a dive for arabs who bring boys to fuck. Procurers sit in the hall night and day. They don't seem to mind a crying baby. They want their money in advance. With all our baggage we look very much like an international family on the move. I've told Sonya for whom the baby is intended. She helped. She says nothing, but smiles. India has matured her – anything that's taught her not to express her opinion must have matured her.

I speak too soon. That night she says she wants to tell me something, a story. The room overlooks one of Bombay's big cricket stadiums. The baby sleeps. I get a bottle of Indian ·whisky from the corner and we sit on the balcony.

Sonya: I've been riding trains. Somewhere, I've done it before. A dream maybe, or someone's description, but the moment I got into a railway carriage, Xerxes, I felt I'd been in one in India. You know the peculiar smell of the upholstery, the disinfectant they use, the stink of the stations and sidings, it was in my nostril memory.

It's not a good story, it's puzzling me but I have to tell you. You know Dad always says he's never been to India and that we, me and my sister, haven't either. Well, it's shit. I think it was when I was two or something like that – I can see myself and Dad on one of these very busy railway stations and we get the coolie to carry our baggage into a compartment where there's just two bunks. First class, I suppose, with barred windows and the huge heavy door that opens inwards and has those funny locks top and bottom for safety. It's night and I remember the basin that folds out of the wooden panels. I don't know where we're going but it's a journey that takes days and nights with hundreds of miles between stations. Daddy's clearly English, with shorts and a cotton long-sleeved shirt rolled up. Yeah, I remember it in that much detail. Don't know where Mum is. In the night, with the blue night light, someone starts banging on the window shutter and my dad calls out. It's strange. Someone must have gone from foot-rest to foot-rest along the train on the outside. We're chugging along, I don't know how fast. Dad opens the shutter ever so slightly and the voice says let me in. At first it begs. It's a man in rags. Dad tells him he can't come in, there have been murders on the trains. He tells me to close my eyes and put the pillow on my head and he tells the man he'll have to wait another hundred miles. The man begs, pleads for the door to be opened because he's hanging on, won't last much longer. He'll fall off the moving train and die. Dad says no, he has a child, he can't risk letting anyone in. The man begins to shout and swear. I think Dad bangs the shutter on to the arms that come through the window and with a scream the man lets go and falls to his fate.

Dad says he's never been to India. But this scene keeps coming back to me now. Maybe he's responsible for killing a man, a beggar.

Me: Bullshit. You made it up. He wouldn't lie.

Sonya: I'll see you very soon in London.

Snow and a taxi back from Heathrow to my room in Earls Court. I've handed Sara's flat over to Ali and having still kept a kind of lien on my room, I go back to see if the Paraguayan will relent and let me have it straight away. That's the arrangement – back when I need it.

He says he's not expecting me. The room is legally mine but he's got a girl staying in it. He gives me coffee with my bags on the landing. I have nowhere to go, can't she move in with me? He explains. It was on his last trip back home. The girl has landed up here. He is trying to persuade her to have an abortion. She wants to have the baby and hand it over for adoption. Only she's not a British citizen and it's all very expensive. Besides, he can't really have her sleeping with him while all this is going on. Can I give him some advice?

Is he a fucking idiot or what? Can't he see what I'm carrying, it's not a doll, it's my baby. Oh yes, he says, he knows about me and babies – like a pimp with prostitutes, eh, I really care for them. Oh God, will he shoot his mouth now. I ask him to calm down. How can he? Same way I can. Let's not quarrel. OK.

So can I loan him the room for a few weeks more. Why have I come back? I said I'd give him three months notice.

No, I won't settle for that, fuck the room, I've got a place to go. If he wants he can keep it forever. I'm sick of the room. Can I take my remaining belongings from it this week or the next?

I phone Penny. I hadn't intended to. Like a parcel I hand the baby over. Both Eileen and Penny are dreadfully nervous, like accomplices in some murder. They know nothing about babies, and I show Eileen how to hold her.

'What's her name?' Penny asks.

'It's up to you, I called her Gazal on the passport.'

'What does it mean?' Penny doesn't know about the first Gazal.

'It means love song, lyric, poem.'

'Beautiful,' Eileen says.

It hasn't sunk in yet that this baby will stay, that this rock thrown in the pool is going to cause tidal waves not ripples. I suppose when people come by a baby through the adventure of giving birth to it, seeing through a pregnancy, living out the expectancy, or even when

281

they adopt and the ritual takes over, or when they steal and something of the personal will aligns itself to a plan, one expects the mixed joys and sufferings of parenthood. But standing in this room in east London, a perfectly good home for the couple, it was clear that no space and no time had been made for the baby. Yes, I could have phoned from India but I didn't want to say anything.

They sat down immediately and began to plan what they would have to buy.

Eileen had at least thought it through.

'Penny, we'll have to move, we can't stay here. As it is the neighbours talk about us.'

I'd stay the night. After all I'd brought them their baby.

I'm tired. I sleep on the couch. In the night I hear the baby scream. Penny darling, it's your problem.

Ridiculous that I have become an authority on babies. I go to the chemist and to Mothercare. I have never seen Penny so animated and Eileen looks instantly ten years younger. I know it sounds mad but both of them are suddenly into surrogate motherhood. In one afternoon the house is equipped. A cot, a shelf of foods, phone calls to friends which bring forward teddy bears, mobiles to hang, decorations and tons of baby clothes which arrive with the congratulations. What are these girls doing? Do they want us all jailed? I've come through immigration where I fancy they're getting to know my ways. No, Penny says, these friends are safe, they don't want to know.

'All we have to say is that we have a baby now, she's called Gazal and we think her birthday was yesterday, even though she's nine months old or so . . .'

She's right. The people who come are mangy old hippies and care-nothing libertines; maybe they are care-something libertines, friends of the earth, good to animals and against wars and hanging. I will see Penny later. I have sealed our fates. Something in Penny's eyes as I leave with my bags says that I'm a fool, this could have been our baby, for real.

DOES THE IMAGINATION DWELL THE
MOST UPON THE BABY WON OR THE
BABY LOST

I have a few hundred pounds in my pocket and some in the bank which Leslie De Freitas has paid. When I call him he asks about Sonya. I spend the evening with him and don't tell him I am homeless. He says he needs stories for an anthology.

I move into the Hilton Hotel.

The room does not overlook Hyde Park. The reception desk treats me as it would any other mad person. The man carries my bags to a room overlooking the back streets of Mayfair.

I unpack and pace the room. Exile at last. I type a few sentences. Science fiction, incorporating Zoroastrian history. Some lunatic Americans land in Britain and declare that the second coming is imminent.

The media rush to the spot, to ask the leader of the movement what this is all about. He has already issued a statement that the second coming of Christ will be a man and the man will be from the Asian community of the East End of London.

The man will not know he's Christ till the cult choose him and contact him. Then the newspapers will come and advertisers may move in. Someone will want to sell microwave ovens on the back of any new Christ.

But transform the story. A handful of people in Britain need a new religion. The best starting point is that which gives hope, the myth of being born again. So Zoroaster must come again . . . the last time for redemption, this time for profit. The world has forgotten God. Painfully, he reconstructs Him/Her – whatever gender people will buy.

Again she tracks me down. Reception calls.

She comes up and I meet her at the lift. Sonya! Older, sunken. Wearing jeans and a shirt and a blue cardigan. Brown, dull moons in semi-circles under her still star-like eyes.

'Sonya!'

'Xerxes. Your room?'

'This way.'

We send·for room service.

'Tilak is coming. If I talk to Daddy about it, he listens to me as though I'm telling him travel anecdotes. He doesn't see these are real people. He knows they starve, he donates wells to their villages, but he doesn't believe in their meanness and their absolute bastardly behaviour.'

I listen, I want to say nothing. The second coming of a great prophet is on my lips. She should go.

'The good news is that the *Ramayana* is happening in Cardiff. I'm going tomorrow to negotiate the space and money and all this.'

The room at the Hilton is not the ideal escape I thought it might be. What was my anxiety? That I couldn't take on England again? London, Earls Court, the room, the Paraguayan and I banging away across the thin partitions, he in his bed, I at my typewriter, and each wishing it was the other way round – or so he said.

'A writer! Xerxes, you speak so nice, like a bird, eh? In natural air in Englaiz! My Englaiz, is Shaftesbury Avenue, foreign language school, is for outsiders. You want me choose, I would have literature creativity and Shirley Bassey . . . just like . . . we exchange, eh?'

It used to puzzle me till I figured out he didn't mean my taste in music, he meant 'celibacy'.

I thought a transition should be marked by extravagance, but I'm not one who can wear it nonchalantly. I worry about the pennies dwindling, the pounds going to perdition in room service. I count the three weeks that the remainder of my advance from Mr De F buys me, in hours. I wander in and out of the hotel and search the sky for a sign. I buy myself ties in the concourse shops. I wander through the back entrance during the daytime into Curzon Street and up the small staircases in the alleyways. I gaze at the prostitutes without a tinge of longing, at the buns in the patisseries with more; I resolve not to buy newspapers, not to buy shaving blades or cream, to grow my hair till some inspiration comes. The room service waiters get used to my orders, tomato juice, glasses of ice. I know that they know my type, one who will buy his own vodka and pretend he is a juice-drinker. But I adopt a tone which is meant to tell them that I don't care, I am a man who can wear his meanness even on his sleeve.

*   *   *

The trial, I am suddenly told, has been postponed for three more weeks. Nothing to do with the case itself, but with the trial of six others, a cartel who made it their life's work to sell babies to Canada via Britain. There has been some delay in the extradition of one of them from Canada and it has had a knock-on effect on my own miserable trial.

Some mornings I lie in bed (they don't have an exercise or slopping-out routine here as they did in Brixton) and think of Sidney Carton walking in to rescue me – we change clothes, we clutch each other as we say farewell, mindful of the greatest sacrifice a man can make and I walk out free, pretending to have hayfever, covering my face as I'm escorted out. Then I take the bus to the nearest tube and find I don't have the tube fare. I get on the Central Line train anyway and a burly West Indian inspector stops me at Hainault and asks for my ticket. He happens not to like 'cheeky Indians. The police take me away. I can't pay the fine, I am sent to jail . . . no, I'm not much good as Charles Darney. No Sidney Carton would sacrifice a fucking bean for me. Except Robin. He comes again. (He looks nothing like me.)

I don't know why he's come.

He asks after my health etc. He has heard from my solicitor, he says he keeps in touch with her, that my trial has been moved forward.

That's not why he came. We are sitting at tables in the lawyer consultation rooms. They bend the rules here.

Robin looks anxious to look unanxious.

'Aren't you an expert on fundamentalism, Xerxes?'

'I wouldn't say that. I studied religions.'

And you've written some political articles on religion.'

'I don't know how political.'

'Who, for instance, do you think would want to kill fundamental leaders? I've asked my Indian correspondents and other India hands in the business, but they can't tell me. Nothing satisfactory.'

'Which fundamentalists. The Sikhs are fighting the Hindus and the Muslims are fighting the Hindus and God knows what else. Why?'

'I'll tell you why,' he says. 'A little bit of fear in my enquiring journalist soul. What do you make of these?'

He holds out a sheaf of paper, computer paper with perforations at the side. 'I get all this stuff on my desk, reams of it, agency material, we subscribe but very rarely use any of it, but these few clippings . . . well, have a look, they caught my attention.'

I strain to read the stuff. Three small separate stories.

An intruder entered the office of Satya newspaper in Worli, Bombay and attempted to fire a pistol upon the person of the editor Mr B. N. Kamte. Mr Kamte was alone working late in the offices of the paper which represents the Shiv Sena official point of view. He sustained injuries of two bullets to his body. Mr Kamte is recovering from bullet wounds occasioned by the attack. The attacker was absconding. Police at Worli Naaka Chowki issued a statement that they were looking for a man with a very thick beard and a Nepalese-style hat who was seen at the time of the shootings by neighbours entering the building.

The report was from a Bombay city paper.

'Read the next one.'

The next one was a longer report with diagrams and arrows. Like the shooting of John F. Kennedy from the book depository. It was the story of an attempt on the life of the mayor of Bombay, a big boy in the same fundamentalist party, the Shiv Sena. He was arriving to support a candidate in the ward election of south Bombay and he stepped out of his car at the Gateway of India and was making his way to the bamboo podium to make a speech. A crowd had gathered or been gathered to listen to his address. He was shot in the hip and other bullets went wide and broke a pitcher of water but no one else was hurt. The police were working on the thoery that the shot which injured the mayor was 'discharged from a rifle which could have been fired from the windows of adjoining buildings'. Superfluously, the report added that the police were treating the attack as attempted murder.

'You of course know the Gateway of India?'

'Yes. They can't mean that the shots came from the Taj Hotel? There are other buildings, but that's sort of in line, if he was coming down the sea front.'

'A gunman in the Taj Hotel? The rich don't shoot people, they get other people to do it.'

The third report was not from Bombay, it was from Delhi. The empty office of the Hindu Culture Preservation Society had been sprayed one night with Kalashnikov bullets. The police were puzzled. Spokesmen for the organisation were not.

There were some more clippings. No more incidents. The first shooting of the editor had resulted in the retaliatory killing of two south Indian pavement dwellers by Shiv Sena goondas.

'So what about these?'

'Does anything strike you about them?'

'You must get hundreds of these things from India, or from Pakistan . . . who knows what . . .'

'Yeah, Pakistan. The police in that Kalashnikov spraying incident said that it was the kind of automatic rifle that had been introduced into Afghanistan by Chinese suppliers only the previous week. So the gun must have come from Afghanistan or from Pakistan where these Afghan arms are sold and bartered.

'So what?'

'The editor of *Satya*, the mayor of Bombay and the office of the Preservation Society. Did you know Anjali? Patnaik, the actress.'

'A bit.'

'Did Sara tell you that goons from the Hindu Culture thing called on her and on Anjali just before the performance?'

'No, I haven't spoken to her since she left. She's written to me, and I had the flat . . .'

'Well, she used to call me,' Robin says, 'and one of the dates of her phone calls remains fixed in my memory – she called me from the Taj Hotel in Bombay. I just wondered if she's ever called you from one of these places.'

'No, but why?'

'I was going to ask whether she uses her real name with you. The phone call to the Taj broke off. I had to get back through the operator and I forgot the number. I asked the hotel for Sara Fraser Stuart. They said there was no such person registered. No one of that name.'

'I'll play Watson,' I say,

'Just the date. Same day as the mayor gets shot from the Taj.'

'Well checked, Holmes . . .'

'And she went to Pakistan . . . you know Indians can't travel about between India and Pakistan without forms in triplicate. Neither can they buy Chinese arms. But perhaps foreigners can.'

'So what?'

'So someone is shooting fundamentalists. A sort of avenging angel . . . and since she writes to you, maybe you have a clue or . . . maybe more.'

'I have nothing,' I say.

I search his face. Sure, he's convinced that his girl of words is the woman of action and, sure, he doesn't like it, but the respect and wonder are written large. And something else is going on here. He's virtually saying to me, OK, I recognise that you had a relationship with this woman too, we are partners in this girl and she's proved herself big enough to accommodate both of us. Can I take this? Now that he suspects she's a terrorist, Sara is allowed to have other lovers, the boy Robin will countenance the thought.

You know what I do? I stand up, go across the plastic and steel table that divides us and embrace him. An urge to undermine his reserve, to force embarrassment on him if nothing else, making me go straight for his lips, but he turns away, and I get him on his cheek. He's startled and I feel a faint shudder at the outrageousness of my attempt. But he started it.

He clears his throat and mutters.

He'll, ahem, keep me posted.

Back to my last night at the Hilton. I am dozing off in front of the telly when some programme brings on a clip from the film *Bitter Rice*, starring Silvana Mangano. It wakes me up. When I was a kid in Poona, the film caused a sensation, sub-titled though it was. It was one of the first sexy films to be allowed on our screens and Silvana was famous amongst my circle of acquaintance for dancing in the fields with arms up, showing her under-arm hair. The cry from the five-anna seats was:

> Showcase mey itna,
> Tho godown mey kitna?

'If there's so much in the shop-window, how much is there in the godown?'

(Nah, it doesn't work in English. Who said English isn't long-winded???)

From the Hilton, my bags packed, I try to phone Ali at Sara's flat. The phone's been cut off. I go round and knock, bang. A very distraught Ali emerges with two other black men and seven or eight suitcases.

'Thank God you've come. I didn't know what to do with the cats. I gotta evacuate, boss, split, you know? You see it, Jerksi, bwoy, hard times, man must live.'

He gives me the keys and he's gone.

The flat is filthy. Not one fucking electric bulb works. At first I think it's the electricity. It is. I pay the bill, they assure me they've turned the supply on and I'm doggone puzzled till I scratches mah head and makes mah analysis of human character. If it ain't the supply, it's the wiring and fuses and if it ain't those, it's the laziness of man and crimes of Ali, he with the suitcases who is into the big time, who hasn't the gumption or need to change the flippin light bulbs.

The light bulbs. Mazda. The lord of light. The older the religion the easier it is to plunder its myths, the less like blasphemy it sounds. I mean, you can have Mazda light bulbs, because the guy was the god of fire, or Mercury sports shoes, but Jesus crackers would be in distinct bad taste.

We can't charge for the use of the Mazda label, but as I said, if we'd patented God, we could collect royalties at every church door in the Christian world, at every mosque in Muslim belt. No Parsee need ever work, if ideas are capable of retrospective copyright and descendants can inherit the patent. A bigger discovery than the North America was in real estate. More valuable idle money than the oils of the Middle East . . . dream dream, dream, a collective dream of the whole race, Parsee race i.e.

Cardiff

My Dear Friend Xerxes,

        The great Mr X, I feel speaking to you on the phone that you were not heartfelt with me. What can be wrong between us?

Sonya feels your strangeness too.

This is why I put my heart on paper. I know you are a busy man and in the jungle of England, with everybody exploiting everybody you have to look for your own ways to exploit, like, and please don't take offence, it is just a metaphor for other people not you – dogs who are not relaxed and spend all time sniffing each other's arse and other's urine on posts and pillars. I sincerely wanted to invite you to come and see the humble work we are doing. I hope you are not insulted when I say just come and we shall pay.

While I had been away my brother was up to no good. He has invited chemical firms to contribute their name to our projects, in chemicals, fertilisers, patented dyes which we can make ourselves. They want to undermine our independence by giving gifts and then publicise on the back of my philosophy and hard work and that of the people in my village. Now my brother wants to let them in. I have sat so many hours to reason with him but he has followers too and they are goading him. It seems to be all for money. Share, yield, turnover, all these terms. But I know it is a disturbance in our brotherliness.

This is one reason I wanted to come to England again and bring with me some of the people who are so dedicated. All the skills and crafts which remain with us we have brought. This is not the only reason I call you to Cardiff. Some other things which only friends can talk about. I couldn't talk anything on the phone, I felt like I was making a call to outer space and the person I had known as Xerxes, in Delhi and in London, was like some remote voice from another planet.

I hope I have melted the ice around your heart.

Your soul friend,

Tilak

I make no reply to Tilak.

I'm frustrated at first by the flat. It takes me two weeks to get the services put on again. The bastard Ali has left a massive phone bill unpaid. He's called Abu Dhabi, Senegal, America, Iran. The detailed trunk call bill is presented. What has he been doing? I day-dream of him playing a black Shylock in Zambia or applying for an audition for a cowboy movie, *Buffalo Soldier, Dread Locks Rasta*. It was he, I think, who said that the first buffalo soldiers were Rastafarians. By candlelight in the first few days I write. I let Firdaus know where I am, send out cards to other people. Then this:

Dear Mr Xavaxa,

I suppose you remember me. I want to take up one thing with you. I want to tell you that you were, when we spoke some time ago in Bombay, correctly in favour of the conversion of all people to Zoroastrianism. My conversion to this point of view has come about by two circumstances. Firstly, I was at a meeting of the Charity Commissioners of the Parsee Foundation. A delegation of people with dark skins came from Gujerat. They are peasant people and were quite lost in Bombay but had been told by some instigators that they could get large sums of money from the Parsee community's officials if they presented themselves and their case.

Frankly, Mr Xavaxa, these are the bastard children of Parsee fathers who have bred them by contact with servant classes. They were petitioning to be recognised as Parsees under the rule that our community has, that the children of Parsee fathers shall be Parsees. I witnessed at this meeting the most blatant rudeness and cruelty from people whom I have looked up to all these years. They would listen to no arguments at all. One gentleman, a lawyer who has a reputation for being very radical in his dealings with the Supreme Court was most offensive to these poor bewildered people.

It was unanimously decided that they weren't to be deemed Parsees and when they tried to stage a sit-in in order to demand to be heard, the police were called.

They were evicted. I personally had to see that they got to the railway station and buy their tickets back to their villages.

May I say, Mr Xavaxa, that I hope you don't remember or hold against me if you do, the episode at the baug – I'm talking about the wedding and all that nonsense between our relatives. I still think of you as a friend. The other circumstance for which I write is also personal. I have been invited by Dastur Antia to Dallas in Texas where he has set up the Zoroastrian American People's Association (ZAPA).

I have been invited to be the editor of this newsletter in the USA.

I am writing to you as I respect your ability to write for a Western audience and I will be passing through London on my way to USA. If it is possible for you, can you please meet me and discuss the kind of articles or pamphlets you could write for us? On the 24th of July for two days I shall be at the Cosmopolitan Hotel in Kilburn. So please get in touch and let me know. Otherwise I have your address and as soon as I come I shall make a pilgrimage to your very house!

Yours as sincere as I can be under the circumstances,

Roshni

I have known her as Roshan. 'Roshni' is probably what her family call her. At the top of the lavender-coloured paper is the gold emboss-ment: Roshan Ribbonwalla.

Zoros believe in duality, in the co-existence of good and evil, of the two sides of a universe, as though, for all the world the universe were a coin. No, that's bad. It's two pans of a balance. Evil weighs as much as good, and every time one does a bit of one, one adds that little aluminium weight to the other. So Sara and Adela, one and the same person? XX – baby-trader and religious guru.

Zoroastrianism has to make itself more commercial and it strikes me that religions reform in order to make themselves have a larger appeal.

These gurus who reform Hinduism in their minds and melt it together with trendy psychology, the modish objection-politics of the Western young (anti-this-ist, anti-that-ist) are diluting to expand. They want a larger audience. If Zoros would only reform and take converts, we would expand – and now I know that the process is the reverse – you don't expand because you have spontaneously liberalised, you reform because you want to make money from an expansion. Good luck, Ms Ribbonwalla. Did your great grand forebears sell ribbons to ladies in grand carriages, stopping by a hot Bombay evening at the bandstand or the beach?

Penny calls and says she'll pay for a meal at an expensive Indian restaurant. She has two thoughts on her mind. One, she wants to finish the meal and go home with me and two she wants to talk about Gazal, and about Eileen and Gazal, and her and Gazal and the neighbours and Gazal and King Kong and Gazal, anybody and Gazal. And why had I been such a bastard and allowed them to continue calling the girl by the name of Gazal when I knew that Jam and Cressida's child was also called Gazal? I had of course plagiarised the name from Jam, hadn't I? And they met Jam and Cress (yes, they were back together) and Eileen and she had to make up some bullshit story about why their daughter was called Gazal. Jam knew. Cressida didn't. They had turned up to the same party and found their half-Indian kids called the same thing and the hostess asked if it was a common Indian name and both pairs had to say it was extremely uncommon, but a coincidence nevertheless.

What was I to say? We walked home and she started the argument again, the same question, why had I not been 'more sensitive'? Penny didn't want an answer, she wanted something else. To say she wanted to make love would not be the truth. She wanted to assert something – her own attractiveness? Was Eileen too absorbed with the kid?

She only stayed in bed for as long as it took me to come. When I paused in my mechanical, distracted rhythm on top of her I could see she was crying. I wiped the tears and the silent cry became a sob. Her skinny body shook with it. I was saying 'don't cry' or something feeble, indicating that I'd roll off her and discuss the problem. She wrapped her arms tighter around me.

'Don't stop, nothing's wrong,' she said and her hips moved so that her thumb of a clitoris scraped the base of my prick, the line where hair stops.

*

292

Robin sends me an article from *The Indian Abroad*. It says that a fundamentalist member of parliament who had the previous week denounced the import of an English film into India on the grounds that it was anti-Hindu, was shot at and his car riddled with bullets as he was going to a cricket match in Delhi. The bullets were again identified as from a Kalashnikov of the type used in the raid on the offices of the Culture Preservation Society.

This time it was fatal. So to murder.

And I don't know whether Robin and I are the only people doing sums. They say the Indian special branch or FBI-equivalent are pretty sharp, shrewd, crude, ruthless.

The sums add up. The report says the police have interviewed witnesses to the shooting. One witness said that the gunman was a person disguised as a woman, wearing a burkha. He had seen this woman step out from a car which was about a hundred yards ahead of the victim's car. The burkha-clad figure stepped out, aimed, shot and got into his car again and drove on. The curious thing, said the report, was that the burkha-clad person clutching the gun wore black silk gloves.

The report said that a government notice had forbidden publication of this fact but the magazine was taking the risk and publishing the truth.

In their own words: 'We choose to publish because we believe that open discussion rather than rumour-generating censorship is in the interests of communal harmony. If Mr Paranjpe was shot by a Muslim, or even seen to be shot by a Muslim, there would be the seeds of a major communal incident in the capital. However, we feel that the assailant wearing gloves is significant. It is the hand of foreign intervention that masks itself in black gloves. Why would an Indian, male or female, need to wear black gloves to disguise their hands? It means only that the hands have either a distinctive deformity, *or are of a different colour from that of recognisable Indians, who come in all* shades except very pinkish European.'

Roshan passes through London. I pick her up at Heathrow and we take the tube back into town. She wears jeans and three sweaters and she confesses that she has on some long johns that her grandmother had saved up. Moth-eaten but warm. She smells of camphor, despite the air-freshener of the Air India flight that clings to her and her baggage. The Cosmopolitan Hotel it is.

She can't bring herself to call me Xerxes, always Mr Xavaxa and 'thummay' and 'ji', the respectful forms. She wants research, she wants history. The American will pay. She would like a collection of Parsee legends. I am not aware that there are any substantiated ones, my standards of proof are scrupulous. I am to relax them. Americans like a good yarn. There are stories associated with Zoroaster which I could dig up, with the miracles of the kings and the great Dasturs.

I spend two days of chaste discussion with her. I make her try Guinness, I take her to see the Crown Jewels in the Tower of London. She is impressed by the riverside walks from Putney to Hammersmith.

She leaves and I begin my work for her. She thrusts seven hundred dollars in an envelope and says that the Dastur is quite willing to pay me a commission to send the typescripts. He is too busy himself with navjotes, ceremonies and lectures to read or research anything any more. He may use my stuff in his lectures. He would love me to join the organisation, to be a full member of ZAPA, but I must visit the States to do that. The books are all here in the British Library and in the oriental studies departments of the great universities.

A missive from Michigan:

Dear Xerxes,

Your pamphlet on the doings of the prophet was a great success. Very many respectable people have joined the movement and we have as our co-religionists now professors of zoology and accountants and stockbrokers. Your essay on the Gathas and the atomic theory being predicted by Zoroastrian texts has been sent by the Dastur to a friend of his in the American Academy of Arts and Sciences. Would you mind if the Dastur put his own name to this article? It will help the movement. We thought we should seek your permission. Any payment for the article would accrue to you without delay.

So much only for money matters. I am here at the university town of Ann Arbour and we have had three packed meetings already. I met a lady who teaches dance as therapy to the mentally handicapped. She has come to all the Dastur's lectures and our discussions. She is so interested in everything you write also because she thinks that through Zoroastrianism there may be a new breakthrough in her therapy of dancing to mental health.

Personally I am enjoying the States a lot because it is very eye-opening for me. You must really come here and spend some time. Dastur Antia asks about you all the time and jokes with me about you. I told him I still call you 'Mr Xavaxa' and he was a bit shocked. He didn't know I was such a good girl!

Enclosed is the cheque for next month.

Tandarosti to you,

Yours,
Roshan

Yes, my dear Ms Ribbonwalla (it's Roshan again and not 'Roshni', so the Dastur's probably got his hook in there), but I don't believe a fucking word of it.

Finally, Ali (good name for a play) comes to visit me at the flat a few days before I get jagged. He forgot something. I am to say nothing to anyone. There are two guys with him, one Asian and one black.

I broach the subject of the unpaid phone bill.

'I can't get into that just now, Jerks, gotta go clear.'

He goes into Sara's room and opens a wardrobe that I haven't touched. In it there are three briefcases. He pulls them out and opens one with a key from a bunch in his pocket. I look on.

The briefcases are packed with plastic bags full of stuff. I don't care to ask what it is. I've been living on top of this. So that's why Ali doesn't have a flat or house of his own and keeps moving? The lads carry it out and Ali hesitates. He needs to square me. He can't just bribe me. If this is his dealing, surely he's loaded, surely he can afford to pay the fucking phone bill.

If it was cocaine, the proceeds would buy the whole telephone company.

Ali squeezes my hand.

'Jerksy, I'll just deposit things and come back feh check yuh. Is time a maan had a drink like brothers.'

He goes. True to his word he comes back less than an hour later. I offer him a beer. He stares at me as though he wants to explain about the drugs but I don't really want to talk about that. The less I know the better.

I want to talk about the *Ramayana* experience. He doesn't. Instead he gives me a lecture on his dread locks.

'See this, Jerksy, is a mistake, you know. Not my mistake, a mistake of the founding fathers, but I still wear it. Out of mistake come hit-take, dig it?'

He touches his locks affectionately.

A badge of courage.

He says he had read somewhere that it came about, the hairstyle, because Jamaicans had seen photographs of propaganda that the Italians were putting out in the 'thirties in Abyssinia to counteract growing world feeling for an end to their colonial adventures in Africa. The pictures portrayed blacks as savages and one of the peculiarities of their 'savagery' was propaganda pictures of men with plaited hair, and wild 'locksed' bushes. The Jamaicans loved it. They adopted it because it was the badge of the people who scared the white man. Such, says Ali, was the solidarity of the internationally scattered blacks who would with his assistance and that of his friend, who had a business which dealt in highly confidential goods with highly confidential governments, reassert the power that whites had denied them.

I say interesting and he says he can't finish the beer but I seem to be 'all right'.

'Sure. But what about the phone bill?' I ask.

'Man, I tell you about international salvation and you want to fuck my head with some petty money matters?'

Dear Roshan,

Here's the pamphlet on the monotheism. If you'd given me more time, I think I could have proved to anyone's satisfaction that the Egyptians got their religion from the Zoroastrians. I also want to prove next time round that Mithraism, far from being the loser in the battle with Christianity, is in fact the root of Christianity. That will be the most important piece as far as Americans are concerned. They pay a lot of heed to ancestry etc.

You said that you are now enrolling a lot of Parsees from Bombay, Poona and Aden who have settled in the States. One personal request. Can you trace, through the grapevine that all Parsees seem to be able to generate wherever they go, an old friend of mine from my neighbourhood in Poona. He is called Bomon Virji. He disappeared into darkest US under circumstances which I have always found intriguing. I haven't thought of him for years but a remark in your last letter triggered the thought. He was a bit anti-religion when I knew him, but time may have changed some things. He should be about forty years old now.

Give my respects to the Dastur and send me the copy of article as soon as it comes.

Of course I want to come over.

Love,
Xerxes

Dear Xerxes,

      You're right. US Parsees live in a small world. I have found your wonderful Bomon Virji. He is married to an American dentist and he lives with his mother who also knows you very well and with his sister who I think is older than him, in Atlanta, Georgia.

He is not called Bomon Virji any more. He is a most obnoxious character and tried to disrupt one of the Dastur's lectures when we were in Georgia. First I thought he was an American, a white guy, but his accent still has something of your Poona in him.

Something in his voice reminded me of you. Anyway I am sick of him.

The New York mission now has seventy-two members and the Californian mission has six hundred adherents. The Dastur has been offered a house in Las Vegas. What a joke, no?

I'll write soon again. Your pamphlet on the Zoroastrian ethic which we've issued in gold lettering is selling brilliantly.

Ya Atha, thhari madad.

Yours with love,
Roshan

I visit Penny. Am I really going to see Gazal II? And what do I expect of Penny? It's all exciting again, I feel that in some ways she is still trying to manipulate me round. I am reassured.

Gazal's not in, gone for walkies. Eileen is being difficult. She doesn't understand the baby. She treats it as she would treat any other adult. Penny is worried. Their emotional life together hasn't been very good since the baby came. Eileen thinks of it as my baby. She is constantly provoking Penny.

'But she's very good. She's given up her job and gone part-time to look after Gazal.'

Boston, Mass.
USA

Dear Xerxes,

      Your Bomon Virji is really a pain where the Americans say hunh? He came with twenty-five thugs and broke up the

297

Boston meeting of our association. He is now a born again Christian and against everyone else.

The Dastur sends his heartfelt regards. There was one matter in England which we would like you to send us cuttings on. It was reported in the *Herald Tribune* that a Liberal member of the House of Lords wanted to leave his body after his death to some place called Battersea Dogs Home to be made into meals for the orphan dogs they keep there. He says it is an ecologically sound method of disposing of dead bodies to pass through the guts of the living because it doesn't leave any smoke or other pollution behind. The Dastur and I were very impressed. It seems to us that our ancient practice of feeding bodies to the vultures was done on the same basis of ecological purity. After all Zarathustra said that we mustn't pollute the fire with death and we mustn't pollute the earth that gives us bread with dead bodies.

Can you find out more about this lord and the thinking?

I hope you can come over soon and see the work we are doing.

Yours ever,
Roshan

London
UK

Dear Roshan,

Several salaams to the Dastur. Thank you for the info on Bomon. You've started me thinking.

About the Liberal dog meat: the Battersea Dogs Home has turned down the request to take in Liberal peers' bodies for cutting up into food for their clients. The Tory peers decline to do this as it would undercut the manufacturers of dog food which is a very powerful lobby in Britain and donates money to the party. The Labour peers considered the same gesture but they are sure it will not pass at their party conference because of the block vote of the crematorium operators and grave-diggers' union (they were amalgamated six months ago and now have massive influence on the general council). So I am afraid the dogs will have to rely on less savoury snacks than peermeat. Now there's a good name, and I'm sure someone in America would be willing to market human flesh to dogs in cans under the name if each can could carry the crest of the relevant lord.

Yours as always,

love,
Xerxes

BOMBER VIRGIN

Across the road from where I lived, though I was not born at the time, a woman gave birth to a baby. Her husband and two children were admitted to the chamber when the other, older women of the household turned their backs on the new baby in a gesture of disapproval. There was great wailing and crying of old ladies and young cousins in the household.

The husband took one look at the baby and the woman in the bed and, grabbing his other children by the wrists, marched out of the house. The baby had blond hair and blue eyes.

It was a Parsee household, the Virjis of Poona, well known in the 'thirties and 'forties as Mr Virji had built, with his sweat and ingenuity, the European bookshop at the end of Main Street. It was just before and during the war and Poona was a garrison town for Tommies.

There had been a Raj community in the town for hundreds of years but suddenly there was an influx of troops. The military hospital for the whole of the southern command was in our town and the one thing the troops, the magistrates and their ladies, the boxwallas and all the other ranks of empire shared, was a need to read English periodicals, comics, paperbacks, Shakespeare, Marie Corelli, Everyman editions, the poems of Kahlil Gibran, Penguins, ladies' periodicals, everything except Gandhian literature or nationalist propaganda.

The bookshop succeeded. Homai Virji was particularly proud of the way she could pass the time of day and allude to the weather just like an English lady. And she took to having little tea parties in the back room of the bookshop because the Tommies were lonely and wanted more than a good read to take back to the barracks in Kirkee. They missed home, they were let out on furlough into the town perhaps once a fortnight and the more rakish amongst them braved the cordon of military police to get into Poona's red light district or spent their time in the forbidden taverns of the city where some sharks knew how to give the sahibs a good time. The more timid came to the bookshop.

Her friendship with sergeants and NCOs gave Homai Virji some status in the neighbourhood. The other women who lived around, my grandmother and her friends who were much older and my mother and aunts who were much younger, all gossiped about Homai. The wags of

299

theneighbourhood dubbedher 'Juliet'. She was flattered. She was small and snub nosed and wore her embroidered sarees in Parsee fashion.

When Bomon was born, she was denounced by her husband's family and though she left home to take up a room, seven or eight doors away from her in-law's traditional ancestral home, she would not admit that anything untoward had taken place. It was her husband's baby. Many an argument overflowed into the street. People came from other neighbourhoods to see her walking her baby in the pram that kind neighbours, braving the contagion of scandal, had secretly offered her. They would stare into the pram and remark on the child's blue eyes. Homai, spurned by her husband, her two children turned against her, even forced by their grandparents to cross the street when they saw her coming, kept her snub nose as high as she could.

How she kept body and soul together no one knew. Some said her husband gave her money on the quiet. Some said her sister-in-law who hated the tyranny of living in the ancestral home brought her food and clothes and whatever little money she could.

I knew Bomon from when I was a boy. He was eight or ten years older than I or my friends and he would stand behind the wall of his three foot square garden and gaze at passers-by each evening till it grew dark, a book from the public library constantly in his hand. The only people who stopped to talk to him were us young ones who played in the street, riding bicycles up and down and when we were older, dressing up with folded sleeves of our cotton shirts and crisply ironed trousers to walk on Main Street and watch the girls or sit in a café all evening over one or two cups of tea and talk of Rock Hudson or Elvis, discuss the plot of the latest western.

Bomon couldn't join us. He had no money to buy a round of tea and he had a lot of shame. He only had a few sweaters with holes in them and a few shirts and one or two ragged pairs of shorts, acquired from the army surplus store.

He would talk to us. He would read from the books he held in his hand. Thomas Hardy, Moscow Publications texts of the speeches of Lenin, the Communist Manifesto, complicated and abstruse treatises by Russians on agricultural reform. We understood not a word but admired the fervour of his readings and knew that something far outside our world was going on in his head and in the print.

It was Bomon who first proselytised our gang against the empty customs, the shameful barbarism of our religion.

We knew the story. When he was seven his mother taught him the

300

Zoroastrian prayers and paid a priest from a remote fire temple to come to the house and perform his navjote. She insisted to the neighbourhood that he was a Parsee. She had toted him along as an infant to the fire-temple and only for shame had the priests allowed this boy in. They were shunned.

The navjote was a fiasco. Her husband, who hadn't bothered to get a divorce but had taken to drink and women and let the bookshop go to seed, came with a mob of supporters and waved black flags outside the house as the ceremony was in progress. When the lonely investiture was over Homai, aware of the protest outside, brought her boy in his sudra (the white muslin vest of the faith) out to the door of their one-room house for the public to see. A cry went up. Onlookers and supporters restrained her husband who was drunk, from doing her violence. After all, seven years had passed.

As he grew up, Bomon cast off the symbols of the faith. He didn't want to be a Zoroastrian. He told us he was a 'deist' and explained that this meant worshipping God without religion. Overnight several of us became 'deists' and were beaten for insolence when we declared our new faith. Then we became, as the years passed, Leninists and communists. Bomon was going through college and studying economics. He had befriended the Jesuits of the order of St Vincent who have a seminary in our town and his discussions with them led him to great academic sharpness. He still had no money. His mother, whose daughter, Katayun, had broken with the father and the eldest brother, now earned her living as a secretary and came and gave her mother her wages.

Bomon also taught us, obsessed as we were with his talk and his magnetism, the first rudiments of sex. He it was who told us that masturbation was not medically harmful but was morally debilitating and if we could control it we would control the world.

He it was also, who awoke in us a social conscience that should beset every middle-class Indian with one eye to see, one ear to hear and even a mildly uncluttered mind. From my grandfather he would take the newspapers each evening after he my grandad had finished with them. From Bomon too we learned to read about the world. We heard of Khruschev and of the death of Kennedy and of how it was possible to be fooled as the rest of the world was into believing that Kennedy was a good man and to be propagandised in our schools and in college to believe in his goodness, but also know that it was this same Kennedy who had indulged in the fiasco of the Bay of Pigs and had threatened to overthrow the great peasant revolution of Cuba. China was in spate.

The Chinese invaded India. Bomon told us to take China's side. Again we were slapped at home. Our fathers, grandfathers and uncles denounced the local messiah as mad. And bad. They had seen him using his mother's money to take street women into the house. We knew it was true, but we sprang to his defence.

Bomon came first in the university. He sat an exam to join the Indian Administration Service, which takes likely lads and lasses and projects them to giddy heights of civil management. He came first in those exams too and was chosen. He went away to the Academy to be trained and came home in six months' time with money in his pocket and wearing, for the first time, clothes that were tailored for him. He had a new air of confidence.

We went through college while he was training and when he became deputy collector for a district outside our town, now newly equipped as an Urdu and Marathi speaker, he strutted about our streets like a peacock.

Juliet was over the moon and made herself the laughing stock of the neighbourhood by sending out three tentative proposals to the richest and most beautiful girls of the families that had spurned her and her son. They spurned her again. They laughed and were polite but showed her out. Give their daughters to Lenin? No, thank you, absurd!

Bomon, or Deputy Collector Virji, was enraged. One of the families his mother had approached ran a huge provision store in town. They were the doyens of the Parsee community, contributors to fire temple funds, commissioners of charities, owners of several businesses. Their store sold everything. Canned food from abroad, a liquor section, umbrellas, watches, foreign cheeses, what they called fancy goods – anything. It was common knowledge that their shop had on its shelves imported whiskys and smuggled lipsticks, powders and aftershaves. They were sold openly, despite prohibition in the state because the family paid the police and had through the years, by bribery and through municipal influence virtually made the police force into their own private guardians. The cars of their daughters would be saluted as they passed through traffic junctions.

Bomon would fix them. One of the duties a deputy collector has is being in charge of the police. He had their shop raided. So perfect was the family's police network that they were tipped off about the raid a few hours before warrants were put into effect and the smuggled goods disappeared from the shelves. The raid, led by the deputy collector himself, was abortive. Nothing was found.

The DC was mortified. The neighbourhood laughed. Boys who joined the IAS should not get ideas above their station. India didn't function in that way. He was bitter but resolved. He was on holiday to see his mother. He gathered old friends together that night and denounced the bourgeoisie. The young men of the family were not generous in victory. They rubbed it in. During the raid he had made some remark about lipsticks and they began to call him 'Lipstick' when he passed in the street. Others, hearing of his humiliation and always ready to take a dig at authority, followed suit. They called him 'baked beans', 'Wincarnis', 'Old Spice' everything that was known to be sold as smuggled contraband in the shop.

He sought a transfer from his superiors and was given one. He was moved from the district's collectorate to a civil service job involving intermediate technology. I saw him once. He had come home to say goodbye to his mother because he was off to America. The government had sponsored a trip for him to the States to lecture on aspects of village technology and to be part of a delegation with two cabinet ministers asking the US for aid.

The night before he left he conferred with his two last remaining disciples. I was defiant enough, interested enough to ignore the injunctions and the ridicule of the neighbourhood and spend the day and most of the night sitting on the doorstep of his mother's one-room house with another friend and listen to Bomon.

'You boys better think of what you're going to do. They (the population, the suffering masses) will demand bloodshed and the revolution will turn ugly. They will murder us in our beds. Yes, me too, as an agent of the state, because in the hour of revolution, ideology is tested by the blade.'

He never came back from America. He absconded from the delegation. It was in the local papers. His mother refused to be interviewed or even tell his close friends where he had gone and what happened to him.

Soon she left for America. She came round to each and every neighbour, the community that had pitied her and treated her like traditional Hindu villages treated untouchables, and gave each household a bunch of flowers and to some a packet of biscuits.

Her daughter, Katayun, left a year later.

My own life took me to England. I would often think of Bomon Virji and what became of him. Especially when I began to take political writing, Marxism and other literature of which I had first heard from him, seriously. But there was no news.

Years later a letter came from America. I had enquired about him and a friend wrote back, simply, without any indication of the process by which they had got there, that Bomon, his old mum and his sister were living happily. He worked for a firm of international investigators, private detectives really. The family had all converted to fundamental Christianity. They were popular in their neighbourhood his friends who found his name difficult now called him Bomber Virgin. His mother was called Homer and his sister Kitty. Bomber, Homer and Kitty Virgin! Lenin laughs.

I call Leslie De F.

'Thank God you called. Lyla and I want to talk to you, would you do us a great favour and come round?'

To the De F household. Good white wine.

Of course it's about Sonya. Mrs De F is dressed in a saree as though my turning up is special.

Leslie begins.

'I am afraid it's not the best of news. It has broken our hearts. That's why it was urgent. I was going to come to your place, perhaps even in the hour you phoned me.'

If I look carefully I can see that Lyla's been crying.

'There's drought again in India.'

'So the well must have come in handy,' I say.

They look at each other.

'Xerxes, we look upon you as a friend. Sonya has wandered off.'

'How do you mean wandered off? Where to?'

'We don't know,' says Lyla. 'But we know she left the country. We think she's gone to India. She'll probably try and get in touch with your friend Sara.'

'To Tilak's?'

Again they look at each other. Lyla's eyes moisten and she wipes them with the end of her saree. Her mouth curls down at the corners. She is endeavouring to control herself.

Leslie looks at her and continues to address me.

'We went down for the Cardiff *Ramayana*. It was ramshackle, it didn't work. Both she and Tilak had put so much into it, but it didn't get any attention and finally there was poverty written all over the production. Poverty of all sorts. But it was a try. No one came, it was nearly empty night after night. Perhaps Cardiff is not the place to launch such a venture.'

'Happens to all black theatre, audience is outnumbered by cast, nothing to get . . . er . . . just the way it is.'

'No. I mean, yes. I think you know they were very much in love.'

'Yes.'

'And we didn't mind. She is old enough to know what she is doing.'

'Is one ever?'

'Maybe not. But one has to behave after a point as though one is. She was pregnant.'

'Was?'

'Yes. Telegrams. They started coming thick and fast. You know how Indians would rather send telegrams than phone or write or travel.'

'So?'

'From his brother. Abusive telegrams. At first about his abandoning them. Sonya came back to London to talk it through with us. She wanted to see you but you were in some hotel and then left without saying where you were going. We assumed you'd gone back to India and we wrote there and tried to phone your friend.'

'I was here.'

'Poor child couldn't take it. Tilak was also very disturbed, full of guilt. They said filthy things to him about abandoning his children and never being able to get a divorce. But that wasn't what either of them wanted. I finally spoke to Tilak and he's such a brave man. He said he was attempting to confront his own weakness, if his love for Sonya could be called a weakness. He had nothing in Cardiff; a room, a project, very little money. But for a few weeks they were happy.

'When she found out she was pregnant, Sonya was worried but really radiant.

'Tilak wrote home telling his wife and son what he felt and that he would return to them. He said that Sonya was pregnant and that he had to be honest with them. He told me all this with Sonya present. It was quite touching, they held hands. He hadn't kept a copy of the letter. She said he spent three weeks writing it. It was the most painful piece of writing he had ever done, but he poured his heart out. He recalled their relationship, his own and his wife's in Hindi of course, and the sad times and the happy times and tried to say how much and how little would change. Sonya also wrote saying she was happy to have the child and she didn't want Tilak permanently, that she had him for a few months more and they had agreed to his leaving for that long and that was all. He would return to them and his duty lay with them.

305

'We undersood what she was saying. She said she would visit them and take her child with her but it would be an English child, or if she settled somewhere else in India, it would be an Indian child but she had the wherewithal to bring it up. She wrote to the wife and the son in English and asked that the letters be translated by the son who reads English, just.

'The last telegram came. The son had . . . has . . . drowned himself in the well we sent the money for. The brother's telegram. The wife is half crazy. Tilak is here, in England, with his evil mistress. Dead, there was no hope. The well still had water. Very very deep. They presume he threw himself into it, they weren't even sure. Tilak took the next plane out. I've never seen a man so broken, so cursed.'

Leslie is reading my face.

'Sonya followed?'

'No. We said she should live here and we'd do everything we could to help her recover from the shock. We'd bring up the baby. That was our agreement. She didn't talk. She went and got . . . she got rid of it. We knew she was headed that way. Lyla sat up all night with her, night after night and talked, tried to persuade her. It was another life, there could be a beginning without a past. She wouldn't say anything after the first few days when it all came out of her.'

'She didn't cry,' says Lyla. 'Just went and did it. She came back and lay on her bed and dressed up, not in Indian clothes. Then she made herself up, horrendous make-up, and went to discos. She'd come back at three in the morning with the same expression. It was as though we were guilty of something. She wouldn't speak. Are we guilty?'

'Of what?' I ask.

'Who knows? How can you recover from that kind of thing?' Lyla asks.

'Then she left without telling us. We were careful not to keep too close an eye on her. I went to work. I don't think she was suicidal, just going through something very deep. I didn't even have the courage to interfere though nothing else crossed my mind. The little one knew what was going on. Very bad for her too. And now she's gone.'

'Do you think she'll try and see Tilak?'

'I don't think so.'

'You know where Sara is and we think she could help. We tried Robin – he said she's not in communication, she seems to have disappeared. He can't reach her in the ashram. That was her last address.'

'I am staying in her flat but I've lost touch too.'

'I know you'd do anything to help Sonya, Xerxes, but this is probably not helping her, it's helping us. Just to know what she's doing. Not even to know that she's all right. That's beyond our control.'

'I don't know what I can do? Can't we leave a message at the ashram with whoever's there? If she turns up to ring London?'

'We've done that.'

'The only thing is for one of us to go, today, tomorrow.'

'Maybe that's right,' I say.

'But where would I start? I've never been to India and Lyla can't go looking for her on her own.'

Penny comes home and finds the baby howling, alone, Eileen has gone. It has only been a few months of joint motherhood. She comes round with Gazal II in the small hours of morning. Eileen hasn't returned. She's worried. We go back to her flat together. The baby stays asleep in its cot. Penny is worried. Sometimes Eileen doesn't speak for a day. Like Gandhi, she takes mini-vows of silence – 'too much noise pollution'. (Even though the baby is just about mobile on its tummy and can crawl, their flat suffers from toy pollution.)

We stay awake talking philosophy. At six in the morning the police turn up. They ring the bell. Penny talks to them at the door. Eileen has been apprehended for snatching a baby outside the local supermarket. She ran with it to the tube and got as far as Heathrow. She has hardly any money on her and certainly no passport. Can Penny come down to the station? The police believe that she is 'very disturbed' and before questioning her further they would like someone close to be there, because, they say, to be frank, the police get a lot of stick for ill-treating people nowadays and they are going to play it even straighter than the book.

I say I'll see to the baby. I'll stay. Penny leaves with the police.

Robin comes again to the detention centre. He can't publish of course, but yes he's got stringers in India who have assembled the available facts.

'No sleuths.'

Do I understand?

He shows me the summary of the article which the investigative stringers of India have turned up.

a) There is a thread of violence. There have been seven or eight unsuccessful attempts at killing fundamentalists of the Hindu sort.

One fatality. So far no assaults have been made on Muslims, Sikhs, Zoroastrian or other sorts of fundamentalist.

b) Perhaps the intention always was to wound and not to kill. That, or we are dealing with a very bad shot who has access to at least one revolver, a twelve bore, and the latest manufactured Kalashnikov.

c) The victims have all somehow been associated with cultural fundamentalism. The first four were associated with the Anjali Patnaik or David Stream affair.

d) Two or three clues point to the fact that the terrorist is white and female.

e) It appears that the terrorist acts mainly alone, although sometimes in association with Indian men.

f) There are rumours that the avenger of anti-fundamentalism is a skull with long hair, wears the dress of English memsahib and rides a Japanese jeep with its top open.

g) The police have no theories apart from foreign subversion of some indescribable sort.

'What shall I do with it?'

'Destroy it, hope it goes away. Hope she does nothing more.'

He nods.

'Have you seen articles in the right-wing press by one Adela Questless?' he asks.

I tell him I have.

'Women have very distinctive prose styles, you know. More so than men.'

His brow is knit, with a double K.

I go with Penny to see Eileen. She's in the women's psychiatric prison ward of the King's Hospital. Penny thinks we should leave Gazal with the other girls who have moved into the flat since Eileen was taken ill. It is Penny's idea to take me to see Eileen. She has gone silent. She scowls, sees Penny and doesn't want to talk. Penny tries taking her hand. She has given the nurses trouble and frolicked with some lunatice men when she was let out for recreation. They are free to roam the grounds, not convicted prisoners yet. The nurses, two burly women, talk to Penny. They tell her that Eileen has probably been 'having it away' with one of the older men who hangs around her and talks to her. The last time Penny visited her she asked her about this and Eileen went all sulky. When she asked her who she should bring, whom she'd like to see, she said 'Xerxes, our man.'

So as Xerxes, our man, I go. We meet Eileen in a corridor with tables and chairs with nurses lining the walls, one between every two desks. The door is locked behind us. Eileen is wearing her own clothes, as are most of the patients. She sees me and beats a hasty retreat from the visiting area, trying to bolt back to her room or whatever. The woman attending her grabs her arm and says, 'Your visitors, look, your visitors.'

Eileen struggles free of her grip and starts to run. I can't be sure, but I think she throws a punch at the nurse's face. The nurse shouts for assistance and four women appear and grab Eileen. She screams. I hold Penny back and as I grapple with her, a warder moves between us and the door. Eileen is dragged away.

After ten minutes of hanging about, Penny arguing with the warders, we leave. Eileen has been taken 'down below'. It sounds ominous.

I go home with Penny. She goes straight to the baby. Does she feel that it has lost a parent? There's a message for Penny. She reads it. It's from Jam. She has been rehearsing a play of his about the Third World and gun-running and Pakistani immigrants and he wants to see her in order to stop the rehearsals. He has been there three times and the actors and the stage manager are complaining that Penny is not coping. Penny changes the baby's nappy and weeps. She asks if I'll stay the night. Please. Or can she come to my house with the baby?

An ornithologist from Harvard has been hired by the Parsee Anjuman to write a report on why the vultures aren't performing efficiently. There are reports from the attendants that half-eaten bodies lie about and the vulture population is dwindling. The ornithologist has been to Bombay and finished his secret research. His report says in short that the vultures don't have enough take-off room, not enough runway from the Tower of Silence to the sky. They crash and an unacceptable number smash themselves, kamikaze-like, just off the Tower. When unburdened with a huge and easy meal, their weight-to-wing ratio is OK, but with Parsee on board – smack! Death! He recommends building platforms for them to run along.

Penny and the baby are staying till Eileen is better. Penny says I probably understand the pressure under which Eileen has lived. I don't.

They have questioned Penny at her own flat for six hours. Eileen has made a statement to the psychiatrist who has passed it on to the officer in charge of her case. Patient confidentiality doesn't quite work in prison. They've questioned Eileen who has clearly told them something to the effect that I procure children for lesbian couples. The two officers who come to question me, from their demeanour, believe some such thing about me. Penny has also confessed after they tell her that they will take the baby away immediately for blood tests and send it back to India for the Bombay police to carry out their investigations unless she co-operates. They give me time to get a few things and to ring Leslie who gets me a solicitor.

My solicitor Mira turns up. I am free to see her or she me any time. They've set the trial date and she says there's not much hope of keeping me in the UK without the police prosecuting me for twenty-five breaches of the law. Still, she feels I'd be better off facing an immigration-avoidance charge in an English court than deportation and trial for 'abduction' in India. I could get life imprisonment there.

She brings me the weekly magazines and the previous Sunday's tabloid which runs the trial of another baby smuggler.

The same tabloid contains this:

MEMSAHIB SKELETON TERRORISES INDIA

In fifteen incidents over the past year the skeleton of a white woman has attempted the murder of two hundred Indian religious mumbo-jumbo men. She strikes always at night and rides in a jeep, standing tall in the front seat, like Clint Eastwood in the saddle.

Indian police are baffled but afraid. A chief superintendent told the *Sunday Sport* that it is the revenge of a white woman who worked in Gandhi's national agitation team and feels that the Indians have betrayed the cause for which Gandhi stood. Hindu kills Muslim and Christian, the Sikhs are against everyone. The Raj Memsahib, whom some say is the ghost of Annie Besant, fires upon the evil-doers with a machine-gun. She has injured at least seventeen men associated with campaigns of hatred and killed one . . .

Two puzzles.

How does one get on and off a penny-farthing? Say at the traffic lights?

Second, why, if this creature whose real story Robin won't print and whose legend, bent and balderdashed, has been picked up by the Sunday junks, is a real avenger, does she not send a note to the newspapers claiming revenge for Anjali's death, or retribution in the name of free speech? Why not claim responsibility instead of allowing the press to speculate on the identity of one perpetrator of violence among the ten or fifty that hit the news that week? What was the old bullshit that they sold us in school? 'Justice is only done when it is seen to be done'; and I suppose that's true even if the instrument is violence.

Ali turns up at the detention centre. Primarily he wants to know if I've said anything to anyone about the substances he was moving. The police have searched the flat once but only taken possession of some of my letters which they've returned to me. The bombshell he drops is that he knows where Sara is. He is cautious, though he doesn't know exactly what it may be Sara has been doing. He hints that she may have been in touch with his partner, his husband-in-law, the arms dealer who now lives with his ex-wife.

He says he wants to go back to acting.

'Man, I must locate myself in art, not in race relations. Not because art is better than race relations or anything, boss, but because race relations has lost and the fate of art is at least uncertain.'

I say I didn't know he was in race relations.

'Yeah maan, we deal spare parts and ting to Africa and improve international co-operation, because if Africa don't free, black maan can't free!'

Smiles.

Penny comes. My solicitor has said that it would be advisable for her to stay away as she'll be a witness in my case and however lackadaisical this detention centre is, they may bug our conversation or overhear it or simply make it up.

The prosecution want her to bring Gazal II to court. They assure her that the social services will leave the baby with her pending investigations in India. If they can't find the missing parents, and where will the Indian police start? she can start adoption procedures – one happy ending. Of course she'll need to be married. So she proposes. I say it wouldn't look good if the application form said, 'Adoptive father's profession: convicted child-thief.'

She gets the point, but the fact that my extradition and the supporting evidence are taking months means people don't really give a toss about babies and how they move about the planet. Maybe that's how it should be.

Penny has had a short letter from Sonya. She's well and in Bombay and has seen her father who has caught up with her in India. She has a six-month visa and has decided to work in India. She doesn't want to be a dancer any more. She wants to be an 'activist' – a good Indian word. She has joined a street clinic movement.

'When you write back, tell her I'll be in India soon and she should visit me. Bring me a hack-saw in a naan or something.'

The Times of India, 10 July
Bombay

In the Bombay High Court today, Doctor Steinmann and Doctor Fontaine of the Street Clinic Movement of India were accused under the IPC 420 for trespass and nuisance. The case has caused protest from the US government, as Dr Steinmann, a citizen of the United States of America, has jumped bail and is seeking asylum in the buildings of the United States Consulate accompanied by two assistants, Miss Sonya De Freitas, a British citizen, and Miss Kalpana Krishan, an Indian.

Dr Steinmann is accused of using the property of Bombay Municipal Corporation, viz. the pavements of Bombay city, to set up illegal temporary building structures and using them for the purpose of hospitals for the infirm and the dying.

A police spokesman said they will not enter the Consulate and the library building but will wait till the three fugitives surrender themselves.

The Times of India, 17 July
Bombay

The police siege of the US Consulate building behind Marine Lines took a nasty turn yesterday when a crowd supporting the three sanctuarists, Dr Steinmann, Miss Sonya De Freitas and Miss Kalpana Krishan of the Street Clinic Movement, gathered and had to be dispersed by police.

Two hundred students and others from locations which have been assisted medically by the SCM, chanted slogans and abused the police.

Dr Steinmann and Miss De Freitas were convicted in absentia by the High Court of trespass on Bombay municipal property and are wanted for deportation.

The Times of India, 22 July
Bombay

A mob of students unable to get into the United States Information

Services (USIS) library in the American Consulate because of the ten-day-old siege of the building by Bombay police, today staged a protest which broke into a riot at three-thirty in the morning. The rioters stormed police lines and threw brickbats. The police protection to the building has been supplied at the request of the government of the United States of America as trouble was anticipated when three members of the Street Clinic Movement sought refuge in the embassy.

The protesting students say that they now have no place to study particular medical texts only available in the USIS building. Dr R. Steinmann, Ms De Freitas and Ms K. Krishan who are holding out for the second week in the Consulate building said they will not move until all sick and dying are eliminated from India's streets. The mayor of Bombay said this was an unreasonable deadline.

Dearest Xerx,
                    Thanks for putting us in touch with Leslie. He was great. We couldn't meet your Sonya again.

Leslie returns so I'm asking him to post this to you in London.

You've never seen anything like it. Sonya and her Schweizer locked up, holed up in there and the Indian press has never seen anything like it in their lives. ABC, CBC, NBC, BBC, the Canadians, ITN for Channel 4, the Australians, the Russians, the lot, interviewing her from the fifth-floor balcony across a cordon of police with long-distance microphones and telescopic lenses. Hot shot stuff. And then Leslie, they got hold of him and got wind he was her dad from London. They even thought I was her boy friend from abroad.

The police won't violate American diplomatic immunity, but neither will they relent on the charges they've placed against Steinmann. Accusations of CIA floating about.

Indian embassies have been flooded with money donations for the street clinics after Sonya appealed on world TV for succour for the street people, her people, Steinmann's people – word of life supplying, comfort to the dying. It was an embarrassment because the money came in by hand and by post and by courier and they didn't know where to return it to. As far as the government of India is concerned there is no Street Clinic Movement.

Leslie spent most of his time with us. He savours the drama. We went with him and he stood in front of the cameras, the publisher from London, carrying a police loud hailer.

'Dad, it's not really you?'

'Yes, Sonya darling, it is. Mum and I support what you are doing a hundred per cent. And your sister, a big kiss. She's raising money in her school.'

'The pig! No, tell her I love her, Dad, and we'll win this in the end. Can't you come in?'

'They said no, sweetheart, but I won't say anything to upset anybody!'

All this at full volume from the street to a balcony on the fifth floor with an audience of a few thousand on neighbouring buildings and walls, on the streets and in front of the TV crews who are treated as VIPS by the villains of the piece, the Bombay police.

'Give my love, give my love, say I love her, say I'm well, OK, all right, love, regards, salaams, we shall win, bound to win . . .'

Naomi sends her love.

Firdaus

Tilak finds me.

He of course remarks on the fact that I am awaiting deportation to India and Sonya to Britain and both of us want to be in the other place. That's the only irony that makes him smile. Otherwise, he is quiet. He stares at me. No, he hasn't seen Sonya but he heard of the siege, in Delhi, no, not in his village. His village doesn't hear of such things.

I want to make conversation, a deadly earnest business – he answers questions – the land is going OK, the brother has begged forgiveness, the wife is . . . well, the wife will never recover . . .

'Why are you in England?'

'Oh never mind.'

'Yes, tell me.'

'It's nothing, yaar. The farmer's co-operative. Last time just for fun I bought some seeds of European vegetables – brussel sprouts, asparagus, turnips, artichokes and they came up beautifully in our soil. But the people, our stupid people wouldn't eat them so the co-op, my brother, he sold them to the big hotels in Rajasthan and Delhi and now they want more. Big contracts from the tourist trade. I am little bit ashamed.'

'Nothing to be ashamed of.'

An awkwardness sets it. For a few seconds he's mute and the corners of his lips quiver. 'Her father.' The words come very hard: 'The grandfather of the baby . . . Xerxes sahib, you understand.'

'Whose sahib? I understand nothing of what you've done or what you intend.'.

'Shall I see her father? He said he wanted to see me? Though I'll never see her again, eh, Xerxes. Intentionally I won't see her.'

'I think Leslie and maybe Lyla even would be glad to see you. They look at all your affair and tragedy their own way.'

He meets Leslie on his own at the office. He says he won't intrude in Sonya's life again. Leslie describes the scene. A man with a garland and the look of a beaten animal. He carries the garland in a plastic carrier bag. The secretary announces him and he goes into Leslie's panelled room. Tilak walks in and as Leslie moves to greet him, Tilak bends and touches his feet. Then they embrace, Tilak cries.

Roshni writes, signs herself Roshni again. She is sure, she says, we should meet, that I should come to the US and stay with her. 'We have a bad history, but a good future,' she writes. The Dastur is convinced. Has he stopped screwing her? This is an offer of marriage. Penny and Roshni. Only Roshni doesn't know that I am in a detention centre awaiting deportation proceedings and Penny doesn't know that I have smuggled kids before and it's bound to all come out. Not that anybody will squeal. Still.

Some nights I can't sleep. I lie awake and allow the old movies of life to flash by. The ayah in my grandfather's house forgets to bring in the clothes she's washed and it's the monsoon. It begins to rain. I'm maybe five years old and it's the first time I don't have pyjamas to wear. She says I should get under the sheet, it'll be OK but somehow it seems evil, sleeping without clothes on. Thus do we carry unspoken guilt.

Funny thing is that since the baby cases were reported in the tabloids, the man Roby, who used to edit the new black writers' efforts, has become sort of black-satirical-magazine editor. He's conned someone into giving him some finance and he writes a vicious article against me saying he knows me. It denounces me as a 'racist rat' for having brought Indian children into the heart of corruption and given them to whites to adopt. His great brain doesn't mind the money he thinks I'm taking. He minds the fact of brown children being brought up by whites. We are dying, Egypt, dying.

A dream:

I see Sara on a horse with a scythe riding above all the eclipses of the city, of life, the blindness, the bloodthirstiness, the pure and sharp indifference, and below the city goes on.

The urchins have come out on the waterfront and are tumbling over each others' backs in invented toad-lift formations, three and four at a time. The tourists are occasionally impressed and donate a coin.

There isn't much of a crowd at the Consulate this night. Bombay seems still, the smell of the sea never far. The buildings rise in imitation of some other city, some phantom Babylon, by day a tumid ocean of people, by night clear salt air and echoing streets. This is the city Sonya wants to reclaim as her own. This city is the stepmother of the millions who come into her labyrinth; pushed by hunger, lured by a dream, they come seeking her tit, the whore on the shore of the Arabian sea. Sonya's town. I see her in forty years' time, a scarf on her head, a new century, the hutments of Bombay, the sick, the dying and Sonya De Freitas, grand dragon of the street clinics, six hundred public prosecutors devoured, twenty American consuls at least, ten generations of judges, and a few generations of 'helpers' and devotees from Europe, from the United States, from Africa. The lady with lots of drugs, injections, no lamp.

In my dream I wander the city in handcuffs.

The tumbrils roll, I am walking and riding a tumbril and the mob cheers as they put the rope around my neck. Then the cry (as seen in *The Flame and the Arrow*), 'Dado!'

And the avenging angel Sara swings from the rooftops, masked and in long black boots and, at the same time, in a burkha and Sheherezadian veil and a burning arrow cuts the rope and a horse carries me through the crowd at a gallop, to the challenge of music. A machine-gun staccatoes – the typewriting of death.

I'm walking home to Firdaus's, late at night and Bombay's hushed under a crescent moon. As I get to the porch of the house the chokidar, the night watchman, mistaking me for a flat-owner or an important person, wakes up and stands to salute, still half asleep and falling over.

Out there, away from the road lights and apartment blocks, there is the swishing Arabian sea, part of the Indian Ocean, another chunk of planet that's lost its terror. The breezes float in from Africa, but there isn't the scent of a great continent upon them, or the lonely odour of the sly sea; there's only the corrupt smell of Bombay Duck drying on the sands, just a few hundred yards away.